Seanan McGuire is a California-based author with a strong penchant for travel and can regularly be found just about any place capable of supporting human life (as well as a few places that probably aren't). The Toby Daye novels are her first urban fantasy series, and the InCryptid novels are her second series, both have put her in the *New York Times* bestseller list. Seanan was the winner of the 2010 John W. Campbell Award for Best New Writer. She also writes under the name Mira Grant. She is the first person to be nominated for five Hugo Awards in a single year. You can visit her at www.seananmcguire.com.

Also by Seanan McGuire

Toby Daye novels

Rosemary and Rue

A Local Habitation

An Artificial Night

Late Eclipses

One Salt Sea

Ashes of Honor

Chimes at Midnight

The Winter Long

A Red-Rose Chain

Once Broken Faith

SEANAN McGUIRE

A LOCAL HABITATION

A TOBY DAYE NOVEL

First published in 2010 in the United States of America by DAW Books
First published in Great Britain in 2015 by Corsair

1 3 5 7 9 10 8 6 4 2

Interior dingbat created by Tara O'Shea.

All characters and events in this publication, other than those clearly in the public domain, are fictitious and any resemblance to real persons, living or dead, is purely coincidental.

A CIP catalogue record for this book is available from the British Library.

ISBN: 978-1-4721-1627-7 (ebook)
ISBN: 978-1-4721-2008-3 (paperback)

Printed and bound in Great Britain by
CPI Group (UK) Ltd., Croydon, CR0 4YY

Papers used by Corsair are from well-managed forests and other responsible sources

MIX
Paper from responsible sources
FSC® C104740

Corsair
An imprint of
Little, Brown Book Group
Carmelite House
50 Victoria Embankment
London EC4Y 0DZ

An Hachette UK Company
www.hachette.co.uk

www.littlebrown.co.uk

For Amanda and Merav, who helped me find the map when it was missing.

ACKNOWLEDGMENTS:

Writing a book is a solitary exercise; actually finishing a book is not. Large portions of this book were written while traveling abroad, and my thanks go to Rika Koerte, Mike and Anne Whitacker, Talis Kimberley, and Simon Fairborne, for providing me with space while I was working in their kitchens and spare rooms (and who failed to complain about the crazy American who came to England to work on her novel). Forensic help, medical advice, and some serious logic discussion were provided by Melissa Glasser, Meredith Schwartz, and Amanda Weinstein, while my entire crack team of machete-wielding proofreaders provided merciless feedback and a lot of textual baby-sitting. This wouldn't be the book it is without them, or without Chris Mangum, who listened patiently as I complained about plot during multi-hour telephone calls.

My agent, Diana Fox, was tolerant of my endless need to whine about punctuation, and provided many excellent suggestions that helped to make the staff of ALH Computing come alive, at least for me, and my fabulous editor, Sheila Gilbert, once again cut straight to the heart of what needed to be done. Finally, thanks are due to Kate Secor, Michelle Dockrey, Rebecca Newman, and Brooke Lunderville, who put up with sharing my time with fictional people while still hitting this book with as many sticks as they could swing. (In Kate's case, thanks also for letting me use the TiVo. It did a lot to preserve my sanity.)

My personal soundtrack while writing *A Local Habitation* consisted mostly of *August and Everything After*, by the Counting Crows, *Engine*, by We're About 9, and *Tanglewood Tree*, by Dave Carter and Tracy Grammer. Any errors in this book are entirely my own. The errors that aren't here are the ones that all these people helped me fix.

Thank you for reading.

PRONUNCIATION GUIDE:

Bannick: *ban-nick*. Plural is Bannicks.
Banshee: *ban-shee*. Plural is Banshees.
Barrow Wight: *bar-row white*. Plural is Barrow Wights.
Cait Sidhe: *kay-th shee*. Plural is Cait Sidhe.
Candela: *can-dee-la*. Plural is Candela.
Coblynau: *cob-lee-now*. Plural is Coblynau.
Cornish Pixie: *Corn-ish pix-ee*. Plural is Cornish Pixies.
Daoine Sidhe: *doon-ya shee*. Plural is Daoine Sidhe, diminutive is Daoine.
Djinn: *jin*. Plural is Djinn.
Ellyllon: *el-lee-lawn*. Plural is Ellyllons.
Gean-Cannah: *gee-ann can-na*. Plural is Gean-Cannah.
Glastig: *glass-tig*. Plural is Glastigs.
Gwragen: *guh-war-a-gen*. Plural is Gwragen.
Hippocampus: *hip-po-cam-pus*. Plural is Hippocampi.
Kelpie: *kel-pee*. Plural is Kelpies.
Kitsune: *kit-soo-nay*. Plural is Kitsune.
Lamia: *lay-me-a*. Plural is Lamia.
The Luidaeg: *the lou-sha-k*. No plural exists.
Manticore: *man-tee-core*. Plural is Manticores.
Nixie: *nix-ee*. Plural is Nixen.
Peri: *pear-ee*. Plural is Peri.

Piskie: *piss-key*. Plural is Piskies.
Pixie: *pix-ee*. Plural is Pixies.
Puca: *puh-ca*. Plural is Pucas.
Roane: *ro-an*. Plural is Roane.
Selkie: *sell-key*. Plural is Selkies.
Silene: *sigh-lean*. Plural is Silene.
Tuatha de Dannan: *tootha day danan,* Plural is Tuatha de Dannan, short form is Tuatha.
Tylwyth Teg: *till-with teeg*. Plural is Tylwyth Teg, short form is Tylwyth.
Undine: *un-deen*. Plural is Undine.
Will o' Wisps: *will-oh wisps*. Plural is Will o' Wisps.

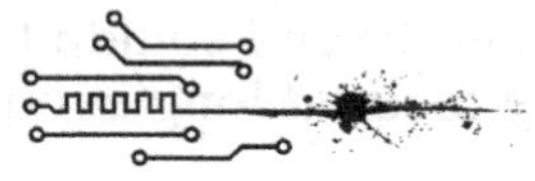

ONE

June 13th, 2010

And as imagination bodies forth
The forms of things unknown, the poet's pen
Turns them to shapes, and gives to airy nothing
A local habitation and a name.
—William Shakespeare, *A Midsummer Night's Dream.*

THE LAST TRAIN OUT of San Francisco leaves at midnight; miss it and you're stuck until morning. That's why I was herding Stacy and Kerry down Market Street at fifteen to the witching hour, trying unsuccessfully to avoid wobbling out of my kitten-heeled shoes. After the number of drinks I'd had, my footwear had become my new arch nemesis. None of us were in any condition to drive, and only Kerry was still walking straight. I blamed her stability on her fae heritage—pureblood Hob mother, Hob changeling father—giving her the alcohol tolerance of a man three times her size. No one keeps a house cleaner than a Hob, and there's never any dust on the liquor cabinet.

Stacy stumbled against me. Being little more than a quarter-Barrow Wight, she didn't have Kerry's alcohol tolerance to help her cope with the number of drinks she'd had. I grinned down at her. "Did you tell Mitch you'd be coming home smashed?"

"He'll have worked it out," she said. "I told him we were going out for girl-time." She burst out laughing, taking Kerry with her. Even I couldn't help giggling, and I was trying to stay focused long enough to get them to the train.

The lights of the station entrance beckoned, promising freedom from my drunken charges. "Come on," I urged, trying to nudge Stacy into taking longer steps. "We're almost there."

"Almost where?" asked Kerry, setting Stacy giggling again.

"The train."

Stacy blinked. "Where are we going?"

"Home," I said, as firmly as I could with my heel caught in yet another crack in the sidewalk. I would have taken them off, but my fingers didn't seem to be working well enough to undo the straps. "Hurry, or you'll miss the train."

Getting down the stairs was an adventure. I nearly twisted my ankle, while Kerry skipped blithely on ahead to the ticket machines, returning with two one-way passes to Colma. I live in San Francisco; they don't.

"I've got it from here, Toby," she said, taking Stacy's arm.

"You'll be okay?"

Kerry nodded. "I'll get a taxi on the other side."

"Great," I said, and hugged them both before waving them through the gates. I love my friends, but seeing them safely on their way was a relief. I have enough trouble taking care of myself when I'm drunk. I don't need to be taking care of other people.

Market Street was buzzing with club hoppers and people stepping outside to sneak a cigarette—California banned all smoking in bars while I was still busy being a fish. That's one of the few positive changes made during those fourteen missed years. No one gave me a second glance.

Catching a cab in San Francisco is practically an Olympic sport. I spared a thought for calling Danny, a local cabbie who's more than happy to give me a free ride whenever I need one. We met six months ago, about five minutes after I got shot in the leg with an iron bullet. That's never an auspicious way to start a relationship. Fortunately, it turned out that Danny knew me a long time before we actually met; I worked a case for his sister about sixteen years ago, and that's left him inclined to help me out. He's a nice guy. Bridge Trolls usually are. When you're effectively denser than lead, you don't have much to prove.

Calling Danny would mean finding a phone. Despite Stacy's hints, I've been refusing to get a cellular phone; none of my experiences with the things have been positive. Besides, Danny probably needed to make a living more than I needed to spare myself the walk. Heels clacking staccato against the pavement, I teetered around a corner and started for home.

It only took a few blocks for me to exit the commercial district and move into the residential neighborhoods, leaving the sounds of human celebration behind. There were fewer streetlights here, but that wasn't an issue; good night vision is a standard benefit of fae heritage. My lack of coat, now—that was more of a problem.

Several pixies had congregated around a corner store's front-porch bug zapper, using toothpicks as skewers for roasting a variety of insects. I stopped to watch them, taking the pause as an opportunity to get my balance back. One of them saw me looking and flitted over to hover in front of my nose, scowling.

"S'okay," I informed it, with drunken solemnity. "I can see you." It continued to hang there, expression turning even angrier. "No, really, it's okay. I'm Dao . . . Dao . . .

I'm a changeling." Whoever was responsible for naming the fae races should really have put more thought into making them pronounceable when drunk.

It jabbed the toothpick in my direction. I blinked, perplexed.

"No, it's okay. I don't want any of your moth."

"He's offering to stab you, not feed you. I suppose the difference is trivial, but still, one assumes you'd want to avoid finding that out firsthand." The voice behind me was smooth as cream and aristocratically amused. The pixie backpedaled in midair, nearly dropping his toothpick as he went racing back to the flock. They were gone in seconds, leaving nothing but faint trails of shimmering dust in the air.

"Hey!" I turned, crossing my arms and glaring. "I was talking to him!"

Tybalt eyed me with amusement, which just made me glare harder. "No, you were inciting him to stab you with a toothpick. Again, the difference is small, but I think it matters."

My glare faded into bewilderment. "Why was he gonna stab me? I was just saying hi. And he came over here first. I wasn't saying *anything* before he came over."

"Finally, a sensible question." Tybalt reached out to brush my hair back behind one ear, tapping it with the side of his thumb. "Round ears, blue eyes, smell of magic buried under the smell of alcohol . . . it's the perfect disguise. Well done. Although it doesn't suit you." My confusion didn't fade. Tybalt sighed. "You look human, October. He was protecting his flock."

"I said I was a changeling!"

"And he, quite sensibly, didn't believe you."

"Oh!" I blinked, reddening. "Oops." Then I frowned. "What do you mean, it doesn't suit me? I like this skirt!"

Tybalt pulled his hand away, stepping back to study me. I returned the favor, looking him up and down.

As the local King of Cats and the most powerful Cait Sidhe in San Francisco, Tybalt rarely bothers to go anywhere that requires him to wear a human disguise. As far as I can tell, it's not that he feels it's beneath him; it's just that he doesn't care enough about the human side of the city to bother interacting with them. This was one of the few times I'd seen him passing for human, and he wore it well. Tall, lean, and angular, he held himself with a predatory air that would translate into feline grace when he moved. His dark brown hair was short, curly, and banded with streaks of black that mimicked the stripes on a tabby's coat. The human illusion he wore concealed his sharpened incisors, pointed ears, and cat-slit pupils, but left his simple masculinity a little more noticeable than I liked. I tore my eyes away.

Saying that Tybalt and I have a complex relationship would be understating things just a tad. I endure his taunting because it's easier than having my intestines removed by an angry Cait Sidhe. On top of all that, I owe him for services rendered following the murder of Evening Winterrose. Sadly, my being in debt to him encourages him to prod at me even more frequently. It's getting to be a habit.

"The skirt passes muster," said Tybalt, finishing his survey. "I might have called it a 'belt' rather than a 'skirt,' but I suppose you have the right to name your own clothing. While we're on the subject of apparel, tell me, were you intending to walk all the way home in those shoes?"

"Maybe," I hedged. The straps were starting to chafe my ankles, making walking even less comfortable than it had been to begin with, but *he* didn't need to know that.

"You're drunk, October."

"And you're wearing really tight pants." I paused. That hadn't come out right. "I mean, those are really nice pants. I mean . . ."

Crud.

Tybalt snorted. I glanced up to see him looking decidedly amused, shaking his head slowly from side to side. "Indeed. I don't suppose you'd consider taking a taxi?"

"There aren't any," I said, feeling as if I'd won a battle with that stunning point of logic.

"Did you consider phoning for one? I understand they can be summoned."

"Didn't have a phone."

"I see," said Tybalt. "Well, as there are no taxis, and you have splendid reasons not to summon a taxi, and you are, in fact, drunk enough to be making comments about the tightness of my trousers, I believe it would be a good idea for me to escort you home."

"I don't need you to."

"That's nice," said Tybalt, shrugging out of his jacket and draping it around my shoulders. "You look cold."

"I'm not cold." That was a lie—it was a nice night, but even the nicest night gets chilly after midnight in San Francisco. I pulled the jacket tight, trying to preserve the illusion of dignity. The leather smelled of Tybalt's magic, all pennyroyal and musk. "I can get home just fine."

"Of course you can," Tybalt agreed, planting a hand on the small of my back and urging me to begin walking. "You are, after all, a perfectly reasonable, competent woman. It's just that at the moment, you're so drunk you can't remember whether or not you're wearing your own face, and I would really rather not scrape you off the sidewalk."

His hand was a firm, insistent pressure. I began to walk, steadier now that I had something to lean against. "Nah, no sidewalk-scraping. You'd find me in an alley somewhere."

"Probably true."

We walked for a few blocks, with me wobbling along on clattering heels and him pacing silently by my side, only correcting my path when it seemed like I was going to fall off the sidewalk altogether. Finally, I said, "I don't understand why you're doing this."

"I'm a cat. We aren't required to make sense."

No matter how hard I tried, I couldn't find any logical failings in that statement. It didn't help that my head was starting to spin. I yawned.

"This is too slow," Tybalt said, and, with that simple pronouncement, scooped me off the sidewalk and into his arms. I squawked. Amused, he said, "Oh, don't bother. We both know how this ends, and it'll be more pleasant for both of us if you just don't struggle. I trust you haven't moved?" I nodded. "Good. Now hold your breath; I know a shortcut."

That was code for "I'm going to take you into the Shadows." The Cait Sidhe have a lot of powers that my line—the Daoine Sidhe—don't share. That includes access to the Shadow Roads, a gift that is, as far as I know, unique to the Cait Sidhe. Frankly, they can keep it. The Shadow Roads are dark and bitterly cold. It's impossible to breathe there; your lungs would freeze. Tybalt seemed to take a perverse delight in hauling me through the Shadows, a convenient process neatly balanced out by the discomfort that it caused.

I took a deep breath, scrunching my eyes tightly shut. Tybalt chuckled, and I felt the muscles of his chest and arms bunch as he took two long steps and broke into a run.

The world flashed cold around us, all the heat ripped away in a few seconds. I nestled down against him without thinking about it as I started counting down in my head from ten, measuring the distance by the feel of Tybalt running. Drunk as I was, the experience was less disconcerting than it had been the first time Tybalt pulled me through the Shadows. It would have been almost pleasant, if it hadn't been for the cold.

My silent countdown had just reached three when we plunged back out of the cold and into the comparative warmth of the June night. I opened my eyes, squinting through the ice crystals on my lashes. We were at my own front door. To fae eyes, the edges were marked with the glowing red tracery of the wards I'd set before heading out for the night.

"Much simpler," said Tybalt. He walked up to the porch, noting, "I can't go any further than this, I'm afraid. Wards."

"Mmm." The cold had made me drowsy, and I was comfortable where I was. Waving a hand, I mumbled, "Hey-diddle-diddle, the cat and the fiddle, the cow jumped over the moon." The wards flared and disappeared, leaving the coppery scent of my magic hanging heavy in the air. I closed my eyes again. "There."

"Nursery rhymes?" He sounded amused.

I shrugged. "They work."

"Even so. The key?"

"Oh." I freed a hand to dig into my tiny purse, finding my house key by feel. Tybalt plucked it from my fingers, juggling me effortlessly as he unlocked the door and carried me inside.

I fell asleep somewhere between the living room and the hall.

TWO

WAKING UP WAS COMPLICATED by the fact that I had absolutely no idea where I was. I opened my eyes, blinking at the ceiling. The air tasted like ashes. It wasn't long past dawn; that was probably what woke me.

The ceiling looked familiar. There was a water stain roughly the shape of Iowa in one corner, and that was enough to convince me that I was at home, in my own bedroom and—I glanced down at myself—still dressed for clubbing, in skimpy lace-trimmed tank top and mini-skirt. Only the battered brown leather jacket seemed out of place. Maybe if I'd been trying out as the ingenue in an Indiana Jones movie . . .

I groaned, dropping my head back onto the pillow with a thump. "Oh, oak and *ash.*" My memories of the previous night were fuzzy, but not fuzzy enough. As drunken mistakes go, letting Tybalt carry me home ranked high on the list. And he was never, ever going to let me forget it.

Pushing myself into a sitting position, I swung my feet around to the floor, kicking one of the shoes I'd been wearing the night before in the process. The remaining shoe was sitting atop my purse with my house key tucked into the heel.

"At least he's a considerate source of aggravation," I muttered, and stood, walking gingerly toward the kitchen.

Three heads of roughly the same size and shape poked over the back of the couch as I approached. Two were brown and cream, belonging to my half-Siamese cats, Cagney and Lacey. The third was gray-green and thorny, and belonged to Spike, the resident rose goblin.

"Morning," I said. The cats withdrew while Spike scrabbled fully into view, rattling its thorns in enthusiastic greeting. Adorable, if weird.

The concept of "name it and it's yours" has always been part of Faerie. Unfortunately, I didn't think about that until after I gave Spike a name, effectively binding it to me. Luna was too busy being glad I wasn't dead to mind my taking her rose goblin—she has more—and the cats stopped sulking as soon as they realized it didn't eat cat food. I don't mind having it around. It's pretty easy to take care of; all it really needs is mulch, potting soil, and sunlight.

My illusions had faded when the sun rose, leaving me looking like nothing but my half-Daoine Sidhe, half-human self, pointy ears and all. I'm no more suited to the human world than Spike is, thanks to some genetic gifts from my darling, clinically insane mother. At least I can fake it when I need to, which makes grocery shopping a lot easier.

Most breeds of fae are nocturnal, and that includes the Daoine Sidhe. Circumstance arranges for me to be awake in the morning more often than I like, and that's why coffee has always been an important part of my balanced breakfast. After three cups, I wasn't feeling quite ready to face Tybalt again, but it was enough of a start to leave me willing to face the day. Mug in hand, I walked out of the kitchen and back toward my room. The first order of business: getting out of my club clothes, which smelled like alcohol and sweat. The second order of business: shower. After that, the day could start.

There was a note taped to the bedroom door.

I stopped, blinking. It didn't surprise me that I'd missed it in my pre-coffee stagger toward the kitchen; it surprised me that it existed at all. Wary of further surprises, I tugged it loose of the masking tape and unfolded it.

October—

You were sleeping so peacefully that I was loath to wake you. Duke Torquill, after demanding to know what I was doing in your apartment, has requested that I inform you of his intent to visit after "tending to some business at the Queen's Court." I recommend wearing something clingy, as that may distract him from whatever he wishes to lecture you about this time. Hopefully, it's your manners.

You are truly endearing when you sleep. I attribute this to the exotic nature of seeing you in a state of silence.

—Tybalt

The thought of Sylvester calling my apartment only to find himself talking to Tybalt was strangely fascinating. I stood there for a moment, contemplating its sheer unlikelihood. The idea that Tybalt stayed in my apartment long enough to take a message was more worrisome, but since I didn't think he'd want to steal my silver—if I had any silver worth stealing—I decided to let it go.

Letting go of the thought didn't do anything to resolve my more immediate problem: Sylvester was coming to visit. I scanned the front of the apartment, taking note of the dishes on the table, the unfolded laundry piled on the couch and the heaps of junk mail threatening to cascade off the coffee table and conquer the floor. I'm not the world's best housekeeper. Combine that with the fact that I'd been regularly pulling eighteen-hour days since getting my PI license reinstated, and it was no wonder my apartment was a disaster zone. I just wasn't sure I wanted my liege to see it that way.

Unfortunately, I couldn't say "sorry, come back later." For all that my fourteen-year absence means I'm currently somewhat outside the social order at Shadowed Hills, I'm still a knight errant in Sylvester's service. If he wants to drop by my apartment, he has every right to do so. Of course, his impending visit almost certainly meant he had a job for me. Swell. Nothing says "hangover recovery" like being called to active duty.

Spike was twining around my ankles. I knelt to pick it up, wincing as it settled to the serious business of kneading my forearms with needle-sharp claws.

"Come on, Spike. Let's get dressed." It kept purring as I carried it to the bedroom, calling over my shoulder, "Cagney, Lacey, watch the door." The cats ignored me. Cats are like that.

One advantage to being a changeling: my hangovers are a lot milder than they should be. Thanks to the coffee, my head was almost clear by the time I finished my dramatically shortened shower. I got dressed at double-speed, choosing practical clothing for what was bound to be a long day. I had just finished tying my shoelaces when someone knocked on the front door, the sound punctuated by the rattle of Spike's thorns.

"At least I'm not naked," I muttered, and rose.

Sylvester had his hand raised to knock again when I swept the door open in front of him. He stood there for a moment, looking almost comically startled. Then he smiled, offering me his hands. "October. Did Tybalt give you my message?"

"Hey, Your Grace," I said, taking his hands for a second before allowing him to pull me into a hug. A human disguise covered his true features with the dogwood flower and daffodil smell of his magic. I've learned to find that particular combination of scents soothing. It means safety. "Yeah, he did. I'm sorry I missed your call."

"Oh, don't be. You don't sleep enough," he said, letting go and stepping past me into the apartment. "I had no idea you and the King of Cats were getting on so well."

I reddened. "We're not. He followed me home."

Sylvester raised an eyebrow, saying more with a gesture than words could have expressed. I shut the door, resisting the urge to hunch my shoulders like a scolded teenager. There are some conversations I never wanted to have with my liege. "Why was the King of Cats answering your phone?" was the start of one of them.

Clearing his throat, he said, "I would have called sooner, but I only recently learned that I was needed at the Queen's Court."

"Do I even want to ask why?"

A shadow crossed his face, there and gone in an instant. "No."

"Right." We fell quiet, with me looking at him and him looking at my apartment. There was an aura of bewildered disapproval from his side of things, like he couldn't understand why I'd choose to live in a place like this when I had all the Summerlands to choose from. For all that Sylvester's one of the most tolerant nobles I've ever known, I knew that confusion was sincere. He really *didn't* understand, and there was no way I could possibly explain.

Sylvester's one of the Daoine Sidhe, the first nobility of Faerie. His hair is signal-flare red, and his eyes are a warm gold that would look more natural on one of the Cait Sidhe. There's nothing conventionally pretty about him, but when he smiles, he's breathtaking. Even dressed in a human disguise that blunted the points of his ears and layered a veneer of humanity over his otherwise too-perfect features, his essential nature came shining through.

All the Daoine Sidhe are like that. I swear, if they hadn't raised me, I'd hate them all on general principle.

"October, about your living conditions—"

I clapped my hands together. "Who wants coffee?"

"Please. But really, October, you know you're always welcome at—"

"Cream and sugar?"

"Both. But . . ." He paused, eyeing me. "We're still not having this conversation, are we?"

"Nope," I replied cheerfully, turning to step back into the apartment's tiny kitchen. "When I'm ready to come home for keeps, I'll let you know. For right now? It's hard to run a business when your mailing address is 'third oak tree at the top of the big hill.'"

"You wouldn't have to run a business if you lived in Shadowed Hills," he pointed out.

"No, but I *like* running a business, Your Grace. It makes me feel useful. And it's helping me get reconnected with everything I missed. I'm not ready to give that up yet." I leaned out of the kitchen, passing him a mug of coffee. "Careful, it's hot. And besides, Raysel would kill me in my sleep."

He took the mug with a small moue of distaste, agreeing mournfully, "There is that, yes."

Rayseline Torquill is Sylvester's only daughter and currently, his only heir. There's just one problem. Thanks to Sylvester's brother, Simon—an evil bastard if there ever was one—she grew up in a magical prison, and the experience drove her largely insane. No one knows for sure what happened to her there, but from the look on her mother's face when I've asked about it, Simon was actually merciful when he turned me into a fish. There's something I never thought I'd say . . . but whatever happened to Raysel and her mother, it was worse.

Unfortunately, feeling sorry for Raysel doesn't change the fact that she's a sadistic nutcase. I would have been happy to keep my distance, but in addition to being the daughter of my liege, Raysel is convinced that her husband Connor—my sort-of-ex, and her spouse for purely diplomatic reasons—still has the hots for me. Even more unfortunately, she isn't wrong. It wasn't that we had an untrusting relationship; I simply trusted her to kill me if she got the chance.

I leaned up against the wall next to the kitchen doorway. "So what brings you here today? Beyond the urge to critique my housekeeping, I mean."

"I have a job for you."

"Figured on that part," I said, sipping my coffee. "What's the deal?"

"I need you to go to Fremont."

"What?" That wasn't what I'd been expecting him to say. I wasn't entirely sure what I'd expected, but it wasn't Fremont.

Sylvester raised an eyebrow. "Fremont. It's a city, near San Jose."

"I know." In addition to being a city near San Jose, Fremont was at the leading edge of the tech industry and one of the most boring places in California. Last time I'd checked, it had a fae population that could be counted on both hands, because boring or not, it wasn't safe. It was sandwiched between two Duchies—Shadowed Hills and Dreamer's Glass—and had been declared an independent County three years after I vanished, partially on its own merits, but partially to delay the inevitable supernatural turf war.

The fae are territorial by nature. We like to fight, especially when we know we'll win. One of those Duchies was eventually going to decide it needed a new sunroom, and that little "independent County" was going to find itself right in the middle. The formation of Tamed Lightning may have been a good political move, but in the short term, it guaranteed that living in Fremont wasn't for the faint of heart.

I couldn't think of many reasons to go to Fremont. Most of them involved diplomatic duty. I hate diplomatic duty. I'm not very good at it, largely because I'm not very diplomatic.

"Good. That makes this easier."

Diplomatic duty. It had to be. "Easier?"

"It's about my niece."

"Your niece?" Talking to Sylvester is sometimes an adventure in and of itself. "I didn't know you had a niece."

"Yes." He at least had the grace to look sheepish as he continued, saying, "Her name's January. She's my sister's daughter. We . . . weren't advertising the relationship until recently, for political reasons. She's a lovely girl—a bit strange, but sweet—and I need you to go check on her." Sylvester was calling someone "a bit strange?" That didn't bode well. It was like the Luidaeg calling someone "a bit temperamental."

"So what's going on?"

"She can't visit often—political reasons, again—but she calls weekly to keep me updated. She hasn't called or answered her phone for three weeks. Before that, she seemed . . . distracted. I'm afraid there may be something wrong."

"You're sending me instead of going yourself or sending Etienne because . . . ?" Etienne became the head of Sylvester's guards before I was born. Better yet, he's purebred Tuatha de Dannan. He would have been a much better choice.

"If I go myself, Duchess Riordan could view it as an act of war." He sipped his coffee. "Etienne is known to be fully in my service, while you, my dear, currently possess a small amount of potential objectivity."

"That's what I get for not living at home," I grumbled. Dear, sweet Duchess Riordan, ruler of Dreamer's Glass and living proof that scum rises to the top. "So that's my assignment? Baby-sitting your niece?"

"Not baby-sitting. She's a grown woman. I just want you to check in and make sure she's all right. It shouldn't take more than two or three days."

That got my attention. *"Days?"*

"Just long enough to make sure that everything's all right. We're sending Quentin along to assist you, and Luna's made your hotel reservations."

Now it was my turn to raise an eyebrow. "You think I'm going to need assistance?"

"To be quite honest, I haven't the faintest idea." He looked down into his coffee cup, shoulders slumping. "Something's going on down there. I just don't know what it is, and I'm worried about her. She's always been one to bite off more than she can chew."

"Hey. Don't worry. I'll find out."

"Things may not be as . . . simple as they sound at first. There are other complications."

"Like what?"

"January is my niece, yes. She's also the Countess of Tamed Lightning."

My eyes widened. That put a whole new spin on the situation. January being Countess explained why Tamed Lightning had been able to become a full County in the first place; Dreamer's Glass might be willing to challenge one small County, but they wouldn't want to challenge the neighboring Duchy at the same time. Even if the relationship had been kept quiet, the people at or above the Ducal level would have known. Gossip spreads too fast in Faerie for something that juicy to be kept quiet. "I see."

"Then you must see how it makes this politically awkward."

"Dreamer's Glass could view it as the start of something bigger than family concern." I may not like politics, but I have a rudimentary understanding of the way they work.

"Exactly." He looked up. "No matter what's going on, Toby, I can't guarantee that I'll be able to send help."

"But you're sure this is an easy job."

"I wouldn't send Quentin if I didn't think you'd both be safe."

I sighed. "Right. I'll call regularly to keep you posted."

"And you'll be careful?"

"I'll take every precaution." How many precautions did I need? Political issues aside, it was a baby-sitting assignment. Those don't usually rank too high on the "danger" scale.

"Good. January's the only blood family I have left in this country, except for Rayseline. Now, January's an adult, but I've considered her my responsibility since her mother passed away. Please, take care of her."

"What about—"

"I have no brother." His expression was grim.

"I understand, Your Grace." The last time Sylvester asked me to take care of his family, my failure cost us both: he lost Luna, and I lost fourteen years. His twin brother, Simon, was the cause of both those losses. "I'm going to try."

"I appreciate it." He put his cup down on a clear patch of coffee table, pulling a folder out of his coat. "This contains directions, a copy of your hotel reservations, a parking pass, and a map of the local fiefdoms. I'll reimburse any expenses, of course."

"Of course." I took the folder, flipping through it. "I can't think of anything else I'm likely to need." I looked up. "Why are you sending Quentin with me, exactly?"

"We're responsible for his education." A smile ghosted across his face. "Seeing how you handle things will be nothing if not educational."

I sighed. "Great. Where am I picking him up?"

"He's waiting by your car."

"He's what?" I groaned. "Oh, oak and *ash,* Sylvester, it's too damn early in the morning for this."

"Is it?" he asked, feigning innocence. Sylvester's wife, Luna, is one of the few truly diurnal fae I've ever met. After a few hundred years of marriage, he's learned to adjust. The rest of us are just expected to cope.

"I hate you."

"Of course you do." He chuckled as he stood. "I'll get out of your way and let you prepare. I'd appreciate it if you could leave immediately."

"Certainly, Your Grace," I said, and moved to hug him before showing him to the door.

"Open roads and kind fires, Toby," he said, returning the hug.

"Open roads," I replied, and closed the door behind him before downing the rest of my coffee in one convulsive gulp.

Sending Quentin with me? What the hell were they thinking? This was already going to be half baby-sitting assignment, half diplomatic mission—the fact that I was coming from one of the Duchies flanking Tamed Lightning made the politics unavoidable. Now they were adding *literal* baby-sitting to the job. That didn't make me happy. After all, if Sylvester thought I was the best one to handle things, it was probably also going to be at least half natural disaster.

How nice.

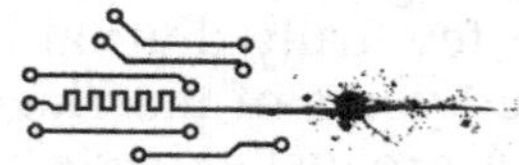

THREE

MINDFUL OF SYLVESTER'S REQUEST for an immediate departure, I shoved clothes into a duffel bag, tossed my bag of toiletries on top, and called it good. The cats had migrated into the bedroom, curling up atop Tybalt's jacket. I dislodged them and shrugged the jacket on, ignoring their protests. I didn't want to leave it in the apartment for him to casually come back for.

Stacy didn't answer when I called the house. I left a quick message asking her to come by and feed Spike and the cats until I got back. I glossed over how long my absence was likely to be. The last thing I needed was for her to start calling Sylvester, demanding to know whether he was trying to get me killed. I couldn't blame her for reacting that way. After all, the last time I went on a job for him, I got turned into a fish and spent fourteen years swimming around a pond in Golden Gate Park. Still. That sort of thing doesn't happen twice, and I didn't want her to worry.

My liege knew where I was going, and my cats were taken care of. That just left one more call that needed to be made before I could leave. It wasn't to a local area code, even though the apartment I was calling was only a few miles away. Strictly speaking, I wasn't sure I was even calling a phone.

Balancing the receiver on my shoulder, I pressed the keys in rapid reverse order. There was a click, followed by the hum of an expectant silence as I chanted, "Mares eat oats and does eat oats, but little lambs eat ivy. A kid'll eat ivy, too. Wouldn't you?" It wasn't much of a spell. It didn't need to be. All it had to do was remind an existing connection of where it was supposed to lead me.

There was a pause as lines that had no reason to cross crossed themselves and wires were rerouted to lead to an apartment that had never signed any agreements with the phone company. The receiver clicked twice and began making a deep, murky buzzing noise. I waited. The Luidaeg likes special effects: if you can't handle them, don't call her. You could always just drop by—assuming you aren't particularly fond of having legs. "Just dropping by" on a water-hag older than modern civilization isn't the sort of hobby meant to ensure a long life span.

The buzzing stopped with a final click, and a husky, aggravated voice said, "Hello?"

"Hello, Luidaeg."

"Toby, is that you?" Her irritation was fading.

"Yeah, it's me."

"What the hell do you want?"

"I'm going to Tamed Lightning."

She paused. "Tamed Lightning? Why would you go there? It's nothing but dirt and morons as far as the eye can see."

"Sylvester's sending me."

"Right. The head moron." She paused again. "Why are you telling me this?"

"I may not make it over this week, depending on how long things take. I thought I'd warn you."

"Oh." Her disappointment was briefly audible before she covered it with briskness, saying, "Well, good. I can get some things done without needing to worry about your happy ass showing up."

"Glad you don't mind."

"Mind? Why should I mind?"

"No reason."

"Good. Be careful out there. Don't go into the dark alone; don't let their eyes fool you. Remember what you're looking for. Don't trust what the blood tells you. Always look back."

"What?"

"Nothing, Toby—it's nothing," she said, sounding slightly disgusted. "Get the hell off my phone."

"See you when I get back."

"Oh—Toby?" Her tone was almost hesitant. That was a first.

"Yeah."

"I owe you an answer. Come back alive."

"I will, don't worry."

"I get to be the one that kills you." The connection cut off with a snap. I grinned, replacing the receiver in its cradle.

The Luidaeg and I met six months ago, when she provided me with an essential clue to the identity of Evening's killer. That meeting left her in my debt, owing me an answer to any question I wanted to ask. She couldn't kill me while she owed me, and I have to admit that it was kind of nice to know that she couldn't follow through on her threats. Unpaid debts weigh on the purebloods; I have no doubt they weigh on the Firstborn even more. She started calling after our first meeting—unlisted numbers don't mean much to someone who thinks the telephone is a cute idea that won't last—demanding to know when I'd clear her debts so she could kill me. They weren't the best conversations I've ever had, but they were reliable, and before long they were even welcome. It was good to have somebody I could talk to.

It took a long time for me to realize how lonely she

was. It's hard to think of the Luidaeg as lonely—she's older than nations, and she's watched empires die—but she was. People are afraid of her; they avoid her haunts, warn their children about her, and whisper her name when the lights are low. How could she not be lonely? Personally, I'm amazed she's still so close to being sane.

I started visiting when I realized why she kept calling. We'd play chess, or wander the docks feeding the seagulls and talking. She had a lot to talk about; it'd been a long time since anybody stopped to listen. So I listened, and every visit ended with the same exchange: "Will you ask me now?" "No." "I'll kill you when you do." "I know." Then I'd go home and so would she, and for a little while, neither of us would be lonely. I take my friends where I can find them.

With my calls taken care of, I just needed to gather my weapons. I pulled my new aluminum baseball bat from under the bed, peeling the price tag off the handle before I dropped it next to the duffle bag. Then I turned to my dresser, opening the top drawer and digging through the rolled socks and crumpled nightshirts to pull out a black velvet box tied with a golden ribbon. I tucked it into the duffel bag. It was the last thing I needed. It was everything I had.

Once upon a time there was a girl who thought I was a hero—or maybe she just thought I was *her* hero. There wasn't much difference, in the long run; I couldn't protect her, and she died. Maybe the knife she left me could do something to protect me. Dare was a good kid. I didn't mean to let her down. And maybe, if I carried her with me, I could still be somebody's hero.

I slung the duffel over my shoulder and grabbed the baseball bat as I headed for the door. Maybe I let Dare down. Maybe I didn't. One thing was for sure: I wasn't going to let Quentin down, and I sure as hell wasn't going to fail Sylvester. Not this time, and not ever again. I paused at the door, winding my fingers through the air and humming as I pulled together a quick but passable human disguise. The cut grass and copper smell of my magic rose around me, eclipsing the smell of pennyroyal that clung to Tybalt's jacket like herbal perfume. Spike sneezed, leaping up onto the back of the couch and rattling its thorns.

"Are we allergic today?" I asked. It rattled its thorns again, and I laughed. "Right. You guys be good. No wild parties. Stacy will be over to feed you, and I'll be back as soon as I can." I closed the door quickly, shutting out the reproachful looks from my pets, and started down the path toward the parking garage.

My apartment is what's considered "a lucky find" in the San Francisco housing market: not only is it rent-controlled and relatively spacious, but it comes with parking—an unheard-of luxury in a city where fistfights have been known to break out for a decent spot. According to my lease, covered parking is a deterrent to theft and vandalism, and justifies my increased rent. Given the kind of cars I tend to drive, I view it as a deterrent to public mockery.

My last car was the victim of a one-person car chase through downtown San Francisco that left the shocks destroyed and the brakes beyond repair. After I managed to find it—which wasn't easy, since I'd abandoned it on the street with the keys still inside—it was clear that the only decent thing to do was put it out of its misery. I sold the parts that still worked, scrapped the rest, and bought myself a lemon yellow 1974 VW Bug. I like Bugs.

As I let myself into the garage, it became apparent that my car had acquired a new hood ornament, since last time I checked it hadn't come with a blond teenage boy. He was sitting cross-legged on the hood with a pair of headphones on, leaning back on his hands and studying the cracks in the ceiling.

"Quentin, get off there! You're going to scratch the paint."

"With what?" he asked, pulling off the headphones as he turned toward me. "I didn't bring any sandpaper."

"Jerk," I said, and grinned.

Quentin and I didn't exactly get off to a good start: Sylvester sent him to bring me back to Shadowed Hills, and I slammed a door in his face. We've managed to smooth things out since then, and he's one of my favorite people these days. He's pureblooded Daoine Sidhe and too arrogant by half, but he's got a lot of potential. He just needs to figure out what to do with it.

I've never met his parents, although I'd bet good money that they're a long way from California. The nobles have an elaborate system of blind fostering, shuttling their kids from place to place to keep anyone from noticing that things around them tend to be a little odd, or that some of them don't age at the normal rate. Quentin was fostered at Shadowed Hills about a year before I officially came back to Sylvester's service. He spends his days at one of the local high schools, learning how the humans live, and spends his nights serving as a page, learning how to be a Faerie noble. One day he'll be a squire, then a knight, and finally, his parents' heir. A pretty tall order for a kid his age, but I think he can handle it.

He slid off the hood, slinging his backpack over one shoulder and giving me an expectant look. "So where are we going?"

"Tamed Lightning," I said, peering into the backseat before opening the car doors. "You all packed?"

"His Grace had me pack before we left home."

"Of course he did. Get in."

One thing I had to give him; he was definitely eager to get started. He was in his seat and buckled in before I had my door closed. I gave him a sidelong look, raising a brow.

"Little anxious, aren't you?"

Quentin squirmed. "It's summer break. I had plans."

"Right." I started the engine. "And what's her name?"

"Katie." A slight lilt on the word betrayed the depth of his infatuation.

"Katie?" I frowned, reviewing my internal list of the fosters at Shadowed Hills. "What Court is she with?"

"She's not. I go to high school with her."

"So she's . . . ?"

"Uh-huh." He paused before adding, with a besotted grin, "And she's *beautiful.*"

I didn't bother hiding my answering smile. "Well, that's cool. Are you being careful?" The question would have had a sexual meaning for a human teenager. For a fae kid, it meant exactly what it sounded like. We always have to be careful when we let the humans get close to us. The burning times are in the past, and mankind has almost forgotten, but we never will. Not forgetting is what's going to keep us alive through the years ahead.

Quentin nodded, utterly self-assured. I remember being that confident—when did I stop? Oh, yeah. When I grew up. "She has no idea what I am."

"Good. Keep it that way. I don't want to have to rescue you from the conspiracy nuts."

"Oh, yeah, because they really stress about the existence of elves."

"Do the words 'alien autopsy' mean anything to you?"

"Ew."

"Exactly." I pulled out of the parking garage and onto the street, heading for the freeway. It was a beautiful day, I had an easy—if unwanted—job to do, and I had decent company to do it with. Maybe things were going to work out after all.

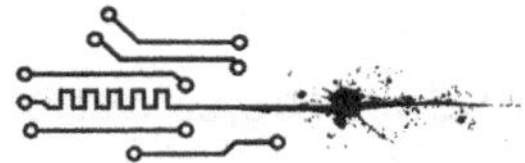

FOUR

"SO WHERE ARE WE GOING?" asked Quentin, for the fifth time.

We'd been driving in circles through the Fremont business district for the better part of an hour and had finally stopped in front of a park so that I could review the directions. A group of joggers made its way dutifully past on the sidewalk. I grimaced, eyeing them. I've always thought of joggers as being sort of like Blind Michael and his crew: deserving of respect, but slightly psychotic. Who in their right minds would want to get out of bed and run around in their underwear before noon?

"Place called ALH Computing." Finding Fremont hadn't been the problem. It's hard to misplace an entire city, no matter how bad your directions are. Unfortunately, Sylvester's directions were a lot more interested in defining fae territories than, say, providing me with street names. I knew exactly whose fiefdom we were in, when we'd entered it, and how far we could go before we left. I just didn't know where we *were*.

"We're going to ALH?" Quentin perked up. "They do Summerlands-compatible computer and wiring systems. I'm pretty sure they did the phones at Shadowed Hills. I have one of their MP3 players." He held up a little white box about the size of a pack of cards, adding proudly, "It works no matter how deep you go."

"Works to do what?"

"Play music."

I eyed it. "Where does the cassette go?"

"Toby." He rolled his eyes. "You really are a Luddite."

"I spent fourteen years as a fish, remember? I'm allowed to be clueless about your crazy modern technotoys." I waved a hand. "Anyway, I think the company's somewhere in the business district."

"You think?"

I thrust the folder of instructions at him and restarted the car. "Here. See if you can figure out where we're supposed to be going."

"Okay . . . hey." He flipped through the papers, frowning. "Where are the directions?"

"And thus you put your finger on the problem." I shrugged. "We go left."

"Left?"

"We've got to start somewhere."

"Left it is." He sighed. "I have got to show you how to use the on-line map services."

"Maybe later."

The two of us working together were able to make something like sense from Sylvester's twisted notion of "giving directions," and twenty minutes later we pulled up in front of a gate with a number that matched the one in the file. The fence stretched a full block in either direction, protecting a tangle of undergrowth Sleeping Beauty's groundskeeper would have envied. The plants I could identify were fast-growing varieties probably chosen for the ability to cover ground in a hurry, while the trees were all eucalyptus, the tallest weed known to man. They grow fast enough to create thick cover years before almost anything else, and here in California where they have no native predators, they grow taller than they were ever meant to.

A stone arch spanned the driveway, supporting a portcullis that looked like it was stolen from the set of *Camelot.* Something flashed in the darkness behind the gate; I doubted it was a deer.

"Are you sure this is the right place?"

I pointed to the wooden sign reading ALH COMPUTING and said, "Looks like it."

"How do we get in?"

"Good question. Hang on." There was an intercom set into the fence: high-security or not, they needed a way to know when they had guests. I got out of the car, moving to study it more closely. "Hey, Quentin, bring me the folder."

"So I'm your servant now?"

"Very funny. Give me the damn folder." I held out my hand. Laughing, he passed the folder over.

There was no security code in Sylvester's directions; there wasn't even mention of a security system. Lovely. I leaned forward, pressing what I assumed was the "talk" button. "Hello? Anyone there?" There was no reply. I shook my head, looking back at Quentin. "Ideas?"

He shrugged. "We could go home."

"Unfortunately, no." Sighing, I turned back to the intercom and hit the button again. "Hello? This is October Daye—I'm here to see January Torquill. Can someone let me in?" I waited several minutes, frowning. It was a nice day, but I didn't want to spend it outside.

Finally, annoyed, I blew the intercom a kiss and said, "Speak 'Friend' and enter," while projecting the firm belief that I'd entered the correct code. The smell of copper rose in the air as a sharp, stabbing pain hit me behind the eyes, making it clear that even if the spell didn't work, my body's limited magical resources had noticed it and debited me accordingly.

All fae have a limit to what they can do, and mine is

lower than most. Just maintaining my human disguise can be a strain; when you add the rest of my daily magical wear-and-tear . . . let's just say that I have more than my share of magical migraines.

At least the pain wasn't for nothing. The intercom crackled, displaying the word "welcome" on the reader screen as the portcullis began cranking upward. I straightened. "Right. Let's go."

Quentin frowned. "What did you just do?"

"I picked the lock." Seeing his disapproving expression, I sighed. "Look, we're here because Sylvester's worried. That justifies a little breaking and entering. Now get in the car."

He rolled his eyes but did as he was told. The security system was more impressive than practical; it took almost five minutes for the portcullis to open, and that's too long to wait for a door. With the purebloods, style almost always triumphs over substance. Once the opening was wide enough, we drove through, following the winding driveway down a short hill to the parking lot. The undergrowth dropped away, replaced by a well-manicured lawn that surrounded the two buildings at the blacktop's far side. Trees rose in a forebidding tangle around us, the illusion of wilderness only leavened by glimpses of the city skyline. They'd done an excellent job with it, especially when you considered that they were in the middle of Silicon Valley, where very few people can afford their own private forests.

The buildings were red brick, connected by concrete paths that wound in seemingly random curves across the lawn. The taller building was five stories high; the smaller one was only two. It looked more like a private school than a computer company. There was a distinct lack of steel and chrome.

The strangest thing about the landscape was all the cats. There were about two dozen scattered around the almost empty parking lot, strolling lazily along, bathing themselves, or just dozing in the sun. Even more were on the grass, lounging, watching us come.

"Toby . . ."

"I see them." The cats in our path didn't even bother to run as we drove down the hill; they just sauntered away, tails in the air. I pulled into a spot near the front of the lot, stopping the engine, and they promptly surrounded the car. One bold calico leaped onto the hood, staring at us through the windshield.

"That's just not right," Quentin said.

"Uh-huh," I agreed, unbuckling my seat belt. I got out of the car, tucking the folder under my arm. Giving the cats a confused, speculative look, I glanced back toward the gate.

There was someone—a little girl—standing by the trees. She was wearing denim overalls, and the wind was rippling her long blonde hair in a wave. The light winked off her glasses as she turned her head, looking at me. I raised a hand . . . and she was gone.

"Okay, that was creepy," I said. "Did you see that?"

"See what?" Quentin asked, stepping up next to me.

"That's a 'no.'" I squinted at the place where she'd been. There are several races in Faerie who can disappear like that. I couldn't for the life of me guess which one she'd been.

Quentin was giving me a funny look. "What're you staring at?"

"Nothing," I said, shaking my head. "Come on." I locked the car and turned, heading for the smaller building with Quentin close behind. Half a dozen cats followed us, stopping to spread out in a wide semicircle on the grass when we had almost reached the door. They didn't move any closer to the building, and their eyes never left us.

A brass plaque was bolted to the wall, out of place in its simplicity. "'And gives to airy nothing a local habitation and a name—William Shakespeare.' Huh." I reached out to touch the lettering, and a jolt of static stung my hand. "Ow!"

"What was that?" Quentin demanded, sounding alarmed.

"Low-level warding spell. It's not supposed to hurt people . . . at least, not the ones who don't mean any harm." I stuck my finger into my mouth, studying the plaque.

"How does it know?"

"See this line, here?" I indicated one of the streaks of silver, careful not to touch the metal a second time. "This is Coblynau work. It's probably the real security system."

"How so?"

"Even if someone manages to break through the gate, they won't be able to get in with this on the door. It's only a low-level ward for us because we're supposed to be here. If we were here to hurt things, it'd be a lot worse." And that "little spark" would have been enough to do some serious damage.

"Oh," said Quentin. "Is it safe to go in?"

"Let's find out." There was a piece of cardboard taped to the door, the words "please take deliveries to the back" scrawled across it in black marker. An arrow under the words pointed toward the corner of the building. I ignored it, pushing the door open only to be hit by the dual indignities of arctic air-conditioning and a truly tasteless pea-green carpet.

Most reception areas are meant to make people feel at home; this one combined the worst features of a seventies color scheme with plastic art-deco furniture. It seemed to be designed to make people leave as quickly as possible. The plants were also plastic, and the magazines on the glass end tables were all at least three years old.

"Ew," said Quentin, looking at the carpet.

"Agreed." I frowned. No one used this room for business; they didn't maintain it because they didn't have to. There was a door at the back. I started toward it. "Come on."

"Shouldn't we try to call someone or something?"

"The sign said deliveries go to the back, and this looks like the back to me." I shrugged. "We've just become a delivery." What we lacked in postage, I was sure we'd make up for in destructive potential. The knob was unlocked. That was all the invitation I needed.

"I'm not comfortable just barging in," said Quentin.

"And I'm not comfortable just standing around. Follow me or don't; it's up to you." I pushed the door open and walked through. I was halfway down the hall before I heard the door close, and Quentin came running to catch up. I smiled and kept going.

ALH Computing obviously started life as a warehouse: there were no interior walls, just a labyrinthine succession of shoulder-high cubicles stretching into the distance. The floors were concrete softened by industrial-sized throw rugs. A ladder on one wall led up to the catwalks crisscrossing the ceiling. They extended far higher than the room's evident ceiling, going up at least three tiers, maybe more, and only the bottom two were lit. It was impossible to tell what might be up there—and after a moment's thought, I decided I probably didn't want to know.

This was the smaller building, and it was huge. How were we supposed to find Sylvester's niece?

"Toby . . ."

"Shhh. Listen." Someone was shouting near the center of the room, dimly audible through the twisting maze of cubicles. It was the only sound breaking the buzz of the lights—as large as the space was, it was practically deserted.

"Whoever that is sounds pissed."

"Right. So we go that way."

"Is that a good idea?"

"Probably not," I said, starting into the shoulder-high labyrinth. The cubicle walls looked like they were made from loosely connected panels, like a series of giant corkboards. If I got lost, I could just knock things down until I found the way out.

The path ended at a wide spot that seemed to be the meeting point for all the trails through the maze. Several people were gathered there, staring down one of the narrow pathways with obvious interest. All of them were fae, but only one was cloaked in the flicker of a human disguise. Interesting. The shouting was coming from somewhere down that path; the voice was female without being feminine, and swearing a blue streak in at least four different languages. Whoever it was, she seemed to have been designated as the afternoon's entertainment.

"How many is that so far?" asked one of them, a tall blond man who could probably have made the cover of *Surf Weekly* without really trying. Though you don't see many surfers with poppy-orange eyes and pointed ears.

The woman next to him frowned, looking at her clipboard. "Six, if you count Klingon. Are we counting Klingon?" Her hair was brown with streaks of red, making her look like the victim of a bad dye job. The combination of that hair with her china-pale skin tagged her as Daoine Sidhe; she had the right sort of artful gracelessness, like she wore the world instead of letting it wear her.

"No," said another man. "Nothing fictional." He was the one wearing the human disguise; if I squinted, I could almost see the outline of his wings.

"Peter, that's not fair," protested the first man. "We allowed Elvish."

"Elvish is a language!"

"Only if you're living in a Tolkien novel," said the brunette, shoving her glasses back up her nose. I'd never seen a Daoine Sidhe wearing glasses before.

"Oh, come on," protested Peter. "Hey, Colin?"

The man next to the water cooler looked up. "Yeah?" His hair was shaggy and green, and henna tattoos covered most of his visible skin. A sealskin was looped around his waist, the ends tied in a granny knot. A Selkie? That was unusual this far inland.

"Is Elvish a language?"

Colin considered this, and then said, "Well, Gordan speaks it."

"Is that a yes or no on the Elvish?" demanded the brunette. She looked annoyed. I understood how she felt.

"It's not a language; Klingon is, and she just switched to Italian, which makes six." A new man stepped out of one of the walkways, hands tucked into the pockets of his impeccably tailored suit. His hair and goatee were clipped close, not a strand out of place. "That work?"

"Hey, Elliot. Yeah, that works," said the brunette.

This was worse than trying to watch opera without a program book. I cleared my throat. Quentin gave me a stricken look, but the crowd didn't miss a beat, continuing to debate foreign swear words. I cleared my throat again; either they couldn't hear me, or I was being ignored.

"Excuse me?" I said, finally.

Elliot looked up and smiled, taking his hands out of his suit pockets. Quentin shrank back. I'm sure the expression was meant to be reassuring, but few things are less reassuring than a smiling Bannick: their teeth are sharp and mossy, and they look perfectly equipped for a nice dinner of young Daoine Sidhe. The teeth are misleading—the Bannick are actually very friendly people. They like to live in bathhouses and on coasts, and unlike the Kelpies, they don't kill travelers. Well, not often. "I'm sorry; are you lost?" he asked.

"No, I'm not," I said. "I'm looking for Countess Torquill. Is she here?"

"Sorry, no," said the brunette, eyes still on her clipboard. "Can we help you?"

I bit back a sigh, saying, "I really need to talk to January. Will she be back soon?" Inwardly, I was fuming. It wasn't her fault Sylvester hadn't told her we were coming, but I'd still expected her to be there when we arrived. No one ever accused me of being logical.

She glanced up, smiling. "Probably not."

"Damn." The multilingual cursing was still going on. I looked toward it. "What *is* that?"

"That would be Gordan," said Colin.

"Why is she screaming like that?" asked Quentin.

"Because she found a flaw, an error, nay, a veritable bug in her code," said the blond, with obvious relish. "I think her poor obsessive heart may break."

I blinked. "Does she do this often?"

"Every time," he said, winking. For some reason, I felt my cheeks redden. Quentin scowled.

"You can set your clock by it," Colin added.

"If you bother to set a clock at all," said the brunette. The shouting stopped and she looked at her watch. "Twenty-one minutes, eight languages. She's right on schedule."

Talking to the entire group at once was making my headache worse. "Is there somewhere we can go to wait for the Countess?"

"Sure—have you eaten? You're welcome to wait in the cafeteria." Elliot glanced to the brunette, who shrugged and offered another brilliant smile. "You can get something in your stomachs while you wait for January to come talk to you."

"Great," I said, and realized I meant it. Headaches make me hungry. Next to me, Quentin perked up. Teenage boys are almost always ready for another meal. "Food would be wonderful."

"All right, then. Follow me." Elliot started down one of the paths into the maze, waving for us to follow. I shrugged and did as I was bid, nodding to the others as I passed. I had nothing else to do, and Quentin was looking almost pleasant for the first time since we'd arrived. Maybe after he ate something he'd stop glaring all the time.

"Later, Elliot," called the blond, joining Colin at the water cooler. The brunette had gone back to her notes, and Peter was wandering calmly down one of the aisles. It seemed this really was just "business as usual."

"See you," Elliot said, waving again. "Keep walking," he advised, more quietly. "They can smell fear; they'll be on you like hawks if they know they make you nervous."

"You're pulling my leg . . . right?" Quentin glanced to me, anxious.

"He's kidding," I said. People who stand around taking notes while their friends scream usually aren't dangerous to anyone but themselves.

"Yes, I'm pulling your leg," Elliot said. "You both look so serious."

"I'm on official business," said Quentin, tone going stiff and formal.

I shrugged. "I just have a headache."

"Some food and a nice cup of coffee will clear that right up." Elliot stopped at a blue steel door and pushed it open, letting sunshine flood into the area. From behind the wall, the woman that had been swearing earlier shouted, "Turn off that damn sun!"

"Sorry, Gordan!" Elliot called back, leading us outside. The door slammed behind Quentin, vanishing into the brick wall like it had never existed. If I squinted, I could just make out the handle. Elliot caught my expression, and smiled. "We like things tidy."

"Right," I said. Quentin was standing as close as he could manage, nearly touching my elbow. Shaking my head, I turned to consider the grounds—and froze.

The landscaping was better than the interior decoration, possibly because it didn't exist in the real world. The sky was a nonoffensive shade of blue, and the lush green grass was studded with a froth of tiny white flowers that I recognized from my mother's estate. Only the cats were the same. They were everywhere, watching us from picnic tables and the crooks of the carefully trimmed trees. At some point between entering and leaving the building, we'd crossed into the Summerlands. That did explain at least part of why the place seemed to be so deserted—someone inside the knowe would be invisible to someone outside of it, and vice versa. I doubled my estimation of the local feline population. If half of them were inside the knowe and half of them were outside ... that was a lot of cats. They probably avoided the buildings because they didn't want to transition between worlds again.

Why would a computer company have an unannounced gate between their mortal and fae locations and a cat population the SPCA would envy? I glanced at Elliot. He was continuing blithely, not seeming to see anything strange. Right. If he wanted to play things that way, that was how we'd play them, for now. Keeping my voice level, I asked, "Is everyone here so ..."

"Weird?" Elliot asked. "Oh, professionally so. If you don't mind my asking, when was your last shower?" I stared at him.

Quentin's mouth dropped open, and he sputtered, "How ... how can you ..."

"Relax, relax!" Elliot laughed, holding up his hands. "You just look a bit frayed around the edges. May I clean you?"

"What ... oh," I said, catching on. The Bannick are bath-spirits; they're obsessed with cleanliness, and Faerie being what it is, they can sometimes enforce their own ideas about hygiene. Nothing cleans a person like a Bannick. "Sure."

"Toby . . ."

"Go along with it. This is interesting."

"So I have your consent?" Elliot asked, looking between us. We both nodded. "Excellent. If you would close your eyes and hold your breath?"

Right. Closing my eyes, I took a deep breath and held it. Heat and moisture broke over me in a lye-scented wave. I understood why Elliot asked: it was like being scrubbed by hundreds of swift, impartial hands, and I might've taken it the wrong way if I hadn't been prepared. The feeling of damp heat abated after about thirty seconds, and I opened my eyes, looking first at Quentin, then myself. We looked like we'd just received the deluxe treatment at an upscale spa; my tennis shoes were white and clean, and even a small hole in the hem of my jeans had been patched with tiny, near-invisible darns. I pointed at it, glancing curiously toward Elliot.

He shrugged, looking embarrassed. "I can't fix clothes on purpose, but if you're wearing them when you have your 'bath,' they end up mended. All part of being clean."

"Cool," I said.

"So that's what your hair looks like when it's been brushed." Quentin grinned.

"Stuff it," I said.

"Now that you're presentable, if you'll come with me, Ms. Daye, Mister, well, Quentin?" Elliot said, opening the door into the next building. We followed him. This one looked more like a dorm, with long halls equipped with dozens of doors. "I hope you like donuts. Our cafeteria staff is out this week, so we're having to make do."

He continued to chatter as he led us through a series of increasingly mismatched halls. Some stuck with the dormitory model; others looked like they'd been stolen from hospitals, high schools, or government buildings.

I dropped back a bit, drawing even with Quentin, and murmured, "Keep an eye open."

"What's going on?"

"I'll explain when we're alone." Elliot looked back and waved, urging us on. I flashed a false smile, calling, "We're coming!"

"Just don't get lost!" he called, and turned a corner. I exchanged a glance with Quentin, and we hurried to catch up, meeting him just in front of the cafeteria door.

He held the door open for us, offering a shark-toothed grin as he said, "After you."

"Great," I replied, and slipped into the cafeteria. It was a vast, echoing cavern of a room, studded with oddly-shaped white tables. Vending machines lined the walls. Quentin and I wound up seated with Elliot pressing coffee and donuts into our hands. That kept us distracted for several crucial minutes, giving him time to murmur vague reassurances and dart out the door.

He'd been gone for several minutes before I put down my coffee, saying, "All right: did you notice anything odd about the landscaping?"

"You mean the part where it's in the Summerlands?"

"That would be it, yeah. We're in a Shallowing." I shook my head. "I think the bawn is at the front door of the other building. We didn't cross back while we were on the lawn, either." The bawn of a knowe, any knowe, represented the point where you crossed between worlds. Usually it's pretty well marked, at least to fae eyes. This one hadn't been.

"What does that mean?"

"I don't know. But I think we should be careful. They didn't tell us we'd entered their knowe, and that's a little bit suspicious." I looked at my freshly cleaned hand. "They're being too friendly without actually telling us anything."

"Right." He poked in the box until he found a powdered donut. "Toby?"

"Yeah?"

"You gave your name at the gate. When did we tell him mine?"

I lowered my coffee a second time. "We didn't."

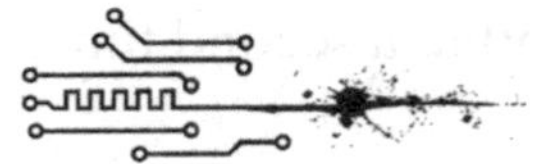

FIVE

"HOW LONG HAVE WE been sitting here?"

"Fifteen minutes."

"It feels like hours."

"The clock says fifteen minutes."

"Maybe the clock isn't running on normal time?"

"Possible, but unlikely." I stood, leaving my half-eaten donut on the table.

Quentin frowned. "Where are you going?"

"Out. This is unacceptable. They shouldn't be leaving us here."

"He said to wait—"

"And we waited. And now I'm leaving." I grabbed the door handle and pulled. It didn't budge. "Oh, great. Did they lock us in?"

"Try pushing." Quentin rose, coming to stand next to me.

Eyeing him, I pushed the door. It swung open a few inches before swinging closed again. Quentin was trying not to smirk. He wasn't doing a very good job.

"Very funny," I said, and shoved the door open as hard as I could. There was a startled yelp, accompanied by the flat smack of wood hitting flesh. The door swung back, and there was a loud thumping noise—whoever it was, I'd knocked them down.

What a great way to meet people. I rushed into the hall, already apologizing. "I am *so* sorry! I didn't know you were there! I—"

"It's okay," said the man on the floor, flashing a grin that made my stomach do a lazy flip. I recognized him as the blond surfer-type from the first building. I just didn't have a name to go with his undeniably appealing face. "That door should probably be labeled an unmarked traffic hazard—only then I guess it'd be a marked traffic hazard, so what's the point?"

"You're probably right about that," I said, grinning back. "I'm—" I paused as Quentin came skidding out of the cafeteria. "Hey. I appear to have found the locals."

Rather than offering the expected greeting, Quentin frowned, saying, "Oh. It's *you*."

"Quentin!" I stared. "Don't be rude." Rude, and out of character.

"It's okay, let him be," said the man, laughing as he held up his hands. "I'm used to it. I've got the sort of face that just pisses some people off."

"It's not pissing *me* off," I said, giving Quentin another sidelong look before turning to the man on the floor. "Quite the opposite, actually. Do you need help getting up?"

"That would be good of you, since you're the reason I'm down here." He reached up, and I grabbed his hands. He had a good grip; not too light, but not crushing. This was a man who didn't feel the need to prove much of anything.

Smiling despite myself, I said, "I didn't do it on purpose!"

Quentin rolled his eyes. "Oh, whatever." Turning, he stalked back into the cafeteria.

I stared after him, confused, only to be distracted by the sound of the man next to me laughing. It was an unreservedly happy sound, and it warmed me to the toes.

"Wait—you mean it *wasn't* calculated? I was just a victim of circumstance? I'm hurt." He pressed a hand to his chest, trying to look wounded. "There I was, walking down the hall, minding my own business, when a madwoman tries to kill me with a door."

"Cut that out," I said. It's hard to stay grumpy when there's a nameless six-foot-something surfer boy mugging for your amusement, even if your erstwhile assistant has just stalked off in an unexplained sulk. Besides, he was a cute surfer boy—not exactly handsome, but cute, with an angular face and freckles scattered across his nose. The cut of his sun-bleached hair was casual enough to look accidental, falling across his eyes in a rakish fringe. A small scar marred one cheek. It was the sort of face you don't see in the movies, but you'd take home to mother without a second thought. Definitely *not* the sort of thing I thought of when I heard the phrase "computer programmer."

"Why?" he asked, smile broadening. He had a nice smile. I upgraded my estimation from "cute" to "damn cute." "Anyway, I'm Alex. Alex Olsen." He held his hand out for me to shake, the other hand smoothing his bangs away from his eyes. His hands never seemed to stop moving. It was like they might get tired of our conversation and start performing sign language arias at any moment. "It's nice to finally meet you."

"Finally?" I arched an eyebrow, shaking his hand. "I've been sitting in the cafeteria." He was almost a foot taller than me, with the comfortable sort of solidity that only comes from too many years spent playing sports and doing a certain amount of heavy lifting. He was dressed casually, in jeans and a T-shirt that read "Nobody Does It Like Sara Lee" in bright red letters.

Alex laughed again. "Not quite that short term. When I start hearing stories about changelings coming back from the dead and tearing San Francisco apart, I start thinking, 'Now there's a lady I'd like to meet.'"

"That shows an interesting way of picking your friends."

"At least you know it's not going to be boring."

"That's true." I reclaimed my hand, using it to tuck my own hair back behind my ears. "Still, I'm surprised you heard about all that."

"News spreads fast these days. There's this amazing invention called 'the Internet'—have you heard of it? We use it to tell each other things." I wrinkled my nose at him, and he shook his head. "Oh, come on. We're sandwiched between two major Duchies. You really think we wouldn't have the best rumor mill in the Kingdom?"

He had a point. Dreamer's Glass was gaining a reputation for strangeness when I vanished in '95. Being considered weird by a race of people who don't see anything wrong with turning their enemies into deer and hunting them through downtown Oakland is an achievement. From what I understood, the Duchy just got stranger as Duchess Riordan, the local regent, became more paranoid about insurrection. Eventually, it got to be too much, and one of the larger fiefdoms declared its autonomy and split off, forming the County of Tamed Lightning.

The politics almost make sense. The technological advances behind them, not so much. Faerie was just starting to dip its toes into computer science and the Internet, and Tamed Lightning wanted autonomy partially so they'd be free to push those borders even further. I don't get it. The world I'm used to is simpler than the one I'm living in. There's too much steel and silicon these days, and I'm still not sure whether that's better than iron; I can barely handle my answering machine, much less all these strange new methods of keeping in touch. The technology that was in its infancy when I left had grown into a spoiled teenager by the time I returned, complicating everyone's lives and making a nuisance of itself down at the mall.

"Not that anyone bothered to tell us you were coming," Alex continued. "If we didn't have a picture of you in the database, we still wouldn't know who you were." Pausing, he asked, "Where are you?"

"What?" I snapped back into the present. "I'm right here."

"You weren't a moment ago."

"Oh. Sorry." Now that I was paying attention, I really was sorry; I hadn't meant to zone out. "I guess I didn't expect anyone to know who I was."

"You can't go around pissing off half the nobles in the Kingdom and expect to go unnoticed," he replied, cheering up again. "I swear Jannie was more excited by the trouble you caused with that Goldengreen affair than she was by the concept of fiber-optic Internet connections. And that's saying a lot."

"Hang on—Jannie?"

"Yeah, Jannie. The lady whose company you're standing in?"

"You mean Countess Torquill?" Maybe this orange-eyed Ken doll could point me toward Sylvester's niece.

"Who?"

Or maybe not. "Aren't you talking about Countess January Torquill?"

"What?" he said, eyes widening. Then he laughed, the rich, delighted laugh of a man confronted with something genuinely funny. "Oh, man. Oh, wow. Can I tell her you called her that? She'll have an aneurysm." I don't like being laughed at under the best of circumstances. This *wasn't* the best of circumstances. I glared. He stopped laughing. "What's wrong?"

"Will you *please* tell me who you're talking about?" I asked, plaintively. "We're here on official business from the Duke of Shadowed Hills, and I'd really like to know what's going on."

Alex cocked his head to the side. "Sylvester sent you?"

"He's worried about January, so he asked me to check in."

"Please don't get pissed at me for asking this, but . . . do you have any proof?"

"What?" I blinked at him.

Looking sheepish, Alex shrugged. "Proof. Do you have anything to prove that Sylvester sent you?"

"Just this." I offered him the folder I was still carrying. "Really crappy directions to Fremont, our hotel reservations, and some stuff telling me whose fences I shouldn't climb over."

Alex flipped it open, scanning the contents before offering a quick nod. "Okay, good enough for me; if you're dumb enough to be faking all this, I figure that's your lookout, and the real Toby Daye'll show up soon to beat your face in. Come on, I'll take you to January."

"Let me tell Quentin." I reclaimed my folder and turned, moving to stick my head back into the cafeteria. Quentin was at the table we'd been sharing, shredding a napkin into long, narrow strips. "Hey."

"What?" he said, not looking up.

"I'm going to go meet Sylvester's niece. You want to come?"

"Is *he* going?"

"You mean Alex?" He nodded, continuing to shred his napkin. "Yes."

"Then I'm staying here."

I paused. "Are you okay?"

"I'm fine." Quentin raised his head, meeting my eyes for a moment before looking down again. "I just don't like him, that's all."

"Already?"

A shrug.

"You sure you want to stay here all by yourself?"

"I'm a big boy," he said. "I think I'll be okay in the big, well-lit cafeteria."

"Suit yourself," I said, stepping back and letting the

door swing shut. If he wanted to be that way, I wasn't going to stop him.

Alex was waiting where I'd left him. "Well?"

"He's not coming."

"His loss. Come on." Flicking his hair out of his eyes, Alex turned to head down the hall. His legs were long enough to cover ground at a dismaying rate, and I hurried to catch up. At least we seemed to be staying in the same building.

"People come and go so quickly here," I muttered. I'm not used to walking with people who treat it as some sort of unspoken race.

"We drew straws to see who'd get to deal with you," he said, as he walked. "Gordan lost, but I owed her a favor, so she swapped with me. Something about wanting to actually get some work done today. Sucker. I would've paid *her* to let me check on you, instead of the other way around."

"Is that so?" I glanced at his ears as I caught up to him, trying to be casual. You can usually get a hint about fae heritage from the shape of their ears, and I like to know what I'm dealing with. Maybe if my mother weren't Daoine Sidhe—the blood-workers of a blood-obsessed culture—I wouldn't be as entranced by bloodlines. But she is, and in a lot of ways, I am my mother's daughter.

He was half-blooded, I could tell that much; the human in him was too strong to miss, and most fae don't freckle. Still, the curve of his ears was unfamiliar. They were too sharp for Daoine Sidhe, too delicate for Tylwyth Teg, and not long enough for Tuatha de Dannan. I let my lips part, "tasting" the air. Sometimes I can catch the balance of someone's blood on my tongue and sound out their heritage that way. It's not a common gift, even among the Daoine Sidhe, and a lot of folks don't recognize it at all.

That's why I was surprised when Alex turned, shaking his finger. "Uh-uh. If you figure it out on your own, fine, but no tricks."

I shut my mouth, blinking. It's not considered rude to taste the balance of the blood, but that's because so few of us can do it that it's never had the chance to become socially unacceptable. "You could always just tell me, you know."

"Now where would be the fun in that?" Alex stopped walking. His hair had fallen back over one eye, making him look slightly off-balance. "I bet we could find more entertaining ways for you to try working it out."

"Could we, now? Got any suggestions?"

He smirked. "How do you feel about breakfast?"

"Most men start with dinner."

"I can dare to be different."

"So far, I'm not seeing much difference."

"Is that a challenge?"

"Maybe."

Still smirking, Alex leaned down and kissed me.

His lips tasted like coffee and clover. I blinked, startled, before leaning in and kissing him back. He put a hand on my shoulder, pulling me into a slightly better angle, and deepened the kiss, drawing it out until my head started to spin. Then he let me go, stepping backward, and asked, "Different?"

"Different," I agreed. I could feel a blush running all the way to the tips of my ears.

"See you at breakfast." He winked, turning to open the door behind him. "Ladies first."

Laughing as I tried to sort through the spin of my emotions, I brushed past him into the most architecturally impossible hallway I'd ever seen. Real angles don't bend that way. I looked back to Alex, who was barely managing to contain his look of anticipatory amusement.

So we were going to play it that way, were we? Putting on my best innocent expression, I asked, "So when were you going to tell us that we were inside the knowe?"

Alex's amusement faded into surprise. "You knew?"

"Newsflash: you don't usually find lace-o'-dreams flowers growing on mortal lawns. Plus? The sky was the wrong kind of blue." I shrugged. "I'm guessing we crossed worlds when we came through the front door."

He stopped, folding his arms. "Okay, how did you figure *that* out?"

"Air-conditioning's turned too high. The first thing you notice is the cold, and that keeps you from noticing the shift. Estate?"

"Shallowing."

"Thought so. I'm assuming the mortal buildings overlay the knowe?"

"Pretty much."

There are two types of knowe. Some, like Shadowed Hills, are literally Summerlands estates connected to the mortal world by doors punched through the walls of reality. Nothing forces them to conform to mortal geography, and for the most part, they don't bother. The Summerlands-side of the Torquill estate is all virgin forest and cultivated farmland, and it looks nothing at all like the land surrounding the city of Pleasant Hill. Shallowings, on the other hand, are little pockets carved from the space between worlds, not entirely existing in either one. Because they aren't anchored entirely in Faerie, they rely a lot more on the actual geography of both realities. We've been banned from all the lands of Faerie but the Summerlands since Oberon disappeared, and Shallowings are getting more common as real estate gets scarcer.

"So what happens when you have human visitors?" In a way, it was a slightly more adult version of the question I'd asked Quentin earlier. *Are you being careful?*

"Well, we keep them to a minimum, but when we have to let them in, we buzz them through the gate under a different code and someone meets them at the parking lot. They're led to the human-side cafeteria or server rooms. That's why the buildings aren't connected; as long as you don't come in through the front door, you don't get into the knowe, and you can't see anyone or anything that's inside it."

There was a certain twisted logic to that idea. It was certainly no worse than the game of "ring around the poison oak" you had to play to get into the knowe at Shadowed Hills. "And there've never been any slipups?"

"One or two." He opened another door. The hall beyond was carpeted in a bilious green, and the walls were studded with corkboards covered in comic strips and memos. The windows indicated that we'd somehow managed to reach the second floor without taking the stairs—cute. "Nothing major, and they've all been taken care of with no lasting harm done."

"Meaning . . . ?"

"We had a Kitsune on staff until fairly recently." Alex's smile faltered, replaced by an expression I didn't have a name for. "She made sure they didn't remember anything."

Not all Kitsune can manipulate memories, but the ones that can tend to be damn good. I nodded, almost grudgingly. "Good approach."

"We thought so." The expression I couldn't name vanished as quickly as it came. "You don't have a phone, do you?"

"What?"

"A cellular telephone?" He mimed talking into a receiver as he continued, "If you do, it's going to be useless inside the knowe. If you want, I can have it modified."

"Modified?"

"Gordan replaces the battery with one of her special ones, works a little voodoo, and gets the circuits realigned. She's our hardware whiz." He shrugged. "I just use the toys she makes."

"Interesting."

"Believe me, so are you, but this is where the bus

stops." He gestured toward a door. "That's Jan's office. Try to be nice? She's usually easygoing, but it's been a hard few weeks, and she's a little cranky. I'd hate to see that pretty head of yours get bitten off."

"I'll be as nice as she lets me," I said, turning toward the door.

My hand was raised to knock when he said, "Toby?"

"Yes?"

"Nice meeting you."

That earned him a smile. "Same here," I said, and knocked.

The sound of my knuckles meeting the wood was sharp and slightly hollow, indicating that the room on the other side probably wasn't actually connected to the doorframe. Physical reference points don't matter as much in Faerie; Jan's office could have been almost anywhere in the knowe and still have been connected to the same door.

A voice called, "Come in!" Shaking my head, I turned the knob and did as I was told. There's a first time for everything.

SIX

THE OFFICE WAS THE SIZE of my living room, but was packed with enough stuff to fill my apartment. Shelves and filing cabinets rose out of a sea of papers, providing landmarks in the universally messy landscape. Computers lined the walls, linked together by a feverish tangle of wiring, and the glow from their screens added a green undertone to the light, making the room seem slightly unreal. A coffeemaker surrounded by an invasion force of green plastic army men rested on a shelf by the door; the toaster oven next to it had its own problems, since it looked like it was about to be gutted by a herd of brightly-colored plastic dinosaurs.

"It's the place where paper goes to die," I muttered.

A narrow path through the mess led to a desk in front of the room's single green-curtained window. The brunette from downstairs was perched cross-legged on the desk's edge, surrounded by towers of paper, attention focused on the portable computer balanced on her knees. Her glasses were sliding down her nose; they'd already made it more than halfway.

She raised her head and smiled, almost sincerely enough to hide the flash of wariness in her eyes. "Yes, it is. Can I help you with something?" Her tone was pure Valley Girl, implying a level of intelligence closely akin to that of granite.

I wasn't buying it. "I'm looking for Countess January Torquill. Is this her office?"

"Sorry, no. It's mine." The smile didn't waver.

"Well, I need to find her. I'm here at the request of her uncle."

The wariness returned, barely kept in check by her frozen-glass smile. "Really? That's fascinating. Because, see, normally people call before they send guests."

"He sent me because his niece hasn't called in a few weeks." There was something about her smile that bothered me. Not the obvious falseness—she was clearly on edge—but the way it was shaped. "I don't suppose you know anything about that?"

Her eyes widened, and she shoved her glasses back up her nose, smile abandoned. "What? Hasn't called? What's *that* supposed to mean? He's the one who stopped calling!"

Moving her glasses made them frame her eyes rather than blocking them and brought the goldenrod yellow of her irises into sharp relief. I only know one family line with eyes that color. Ignore the hair, take away the glasses, and she looked more like Sylvester than Rayseline did.

"That's not what he thinks," I said. "January Torquill, I presume?"

Her eyes narrowed, and for a brief moment, I thought she was going to argue. Then she deflated, shoulders slumping, and said, "Not really. I mean, I'm January. I'm just not January Torquill. I never have been." She shrugged, a flicker of humor creeping into her voice. "As far as I know, no one's January Torquill. Which is probably a good thing—that'd be a terrible name to stick on a child. It sounds like something out of a bad romance novel."

"So if you're not January Torquill, that makes you . . . ?"

"January O'Leary. I'm not full Daoine Sidhe—my father was half-Tylwyth Teg, and his last name was 'ap Learianth.' That doesn't exactly work on a business card. We settled on 'O'Leary' as the abbreviation when we incorporated." She smiled again. This time, the expression had an edge I recognized all too well. Sylvester smiled that way when he was trying to figure out whether something was a threat. "It's interesting that Uncle Sylvester didn't tell you that. Considering the part where he sent you here, and everything."

"You have a phone," I said. "You could call him."

"I already tried that while Elliot was stowing you and the kid in the cafeteria."

"And?"

"No one answered."

"I have directions in your uncle's handwriting." I held up the folder.

"Handwriting can be faked."

I bit back an expletive. Half the Kingdom knew me on sight and expected me to start breaking things the second I walked into the room, while the other half wanted three forms of photo ID and a character witness. "Alex and Elliot knew who I was."

"They know who you look like. There's a difference."

Sad to say, she had a point. I nearly got killed last December by a Doppelganger who impersonated my daughter. In Faerie, faces aren't always what they appear to be.

"Okay. If you know who I look like, you presumably know what . . . that person . . . can or can't do. Right?" January nodded. "It's sort of hard to prove that I *can't* cast a spell, so that won't work. If you want to give me some blood, I can tell you what you did for your fifth birthday . . ."

"That's okay."

"Didn't think so." I sighed. "I don't suppose dropping my illusions and letting you poke me with sticks would do it? I'd really like to get this sorted out."

She frowned. "It's a start," she said.

"Got it," I said, and let my human disguise dissolve, wafting away in a wash of copper and cut grass.

Jan watched intently, nostrils flaring as she sniffed at the air. Then she grinned. If her smile was bright before, it was nothing compared to the way she lit up now. It was like looking at the sun. "Copper and grass! You *are* you!"

"No one's ever been that happy about the smell of my magic before," I muttered. "How do you . . .?"

"I have files on my uncle's knights, in case someone tries to sneak in." There was a brutal matter-of-factness to her tone. She was the Countess of a County balanced on the edge of disaster, and this was just the way things worked. "We've had people who could fake faces and pass quizzes, but nobody's been able to fake somebody else's magic." The word "yet" hung between us, unspoken.

"Well, your uncle's worried, and he asked me to come see how you were doing. Why didn't you tell me who you were when I got here? We could've taken care of all this an hour ago."

"Do you know where you are?" she asked.

I frowned. "I don't see what that has to do with . . ."

"Humor me."

"I'm in the County of Tamed Lightning."

"Do you know where the County is?"

"Fremont?"

"Fremont, where we're sandwiched between two Duchies that don't get along. We're a shiny little independent County right where it's not a good idea to have an independent County."

"I was under the impression that things were stable." That could change at any time, of course, and there's always a risk of small-scale civil war in Faerie—it's something to do when you're bored and immortal—but the modern world has reduced that risk substantially. The fae are poster children for Attention Deficit Disorder: give them something shiny to play with and they'll forget they were about to chop your head off.

January sighed. "Uncle Sylvester is respected around here. Something about him having a really big army he could use for squashing people like bugs."

"So that makes you even safer. Dreamer's Glass would never bother you with Shadowed Hills standing right there."

"That's the problem."

"Okay, now you've lost me."

"People think that because Sylvester's my uncle, Tamed Lightning is an extension of his Duchy here to make him look 'egalitarian and modern,' and one day he's going to pull us back in." She slid off the desk, starting to pace. "They treat us like we don't matter, or they assume we can get them favors and come around sniffing for political leverage. It got old, fast. So we stopped helping."

"You thought I was here to ask for a favor?"

"The thought crossed my mind."

"Well, believe me, I'm not. I'm here because you stopped calling your uncle."

January shook her head. "That's not true. I've left about eighteen messages. He just hasn't been calling me back." A wry expression crossed her face. "I know his phones work. I installed them."

"Why haven't you just gone to Shadowed Hills?"

"Same reason he hasn't come here: if I leave, there's a good chance Dreamer's Glass will see it as an opportunity and invade." She looked suddenly tired. "Welcome to my life. I just have to keep calling."

"What's so important that you need to keep trying to reach him? Why didn't you send a messenger?"

She straightened, another smile blooming across her face. "Where are my manners? You can call me Jan. We're not big on formalities here. Do you prefer October, Sir Daye . . . ?"

"Toby's fine," I said, blinking at the change of subject. "Look, Jan, your uncle wanted—"

"It's funny that he didn't tell you I wasn't a Torquill. My mother was his sister, but she was just a Baroness. Dad was a Count, so I got his name."

Oh, root and branch, of course. When fae marry, the family name of the person with the higher title takes precedence under almost any circumstances. Faerie isn't sexist. It's just snobby. "Sorry. I missed that memo."

"Well, did he at least tell you about Mom?"

"He mentioned her, yes." The existence of a sister was an odd fact about an already odd family. The fae aren't very fertile, and most fae twins are too weak to see adulthood; the fact that both Simon and Sylvester lived was strange enough. Adding a sister to the equation made it almost unreal. "Look—"

"She was older by about a century. She died when I was little."

"Oh," I said. That seemed inadequate. "I'm sorry."

"It's okay." She shrugged. "It was a long time ago."

"Oh." What was I supposed to say? People don't usually sidetrack conversations to tell you how their parents died.

"Anyway, I run this place." Jan smiled. "I'm a Capricorn, a computer programmer, and a vegetarian. And I bake a mean chocolate chip cookie."

I've seen the "silly me" routine countless times from Sylvester, usually just before he goes for someone's throat. It's an effective camouflage when used on people who don't know it. I put up with it from Sylvester; he's earned my tolerance. Jan, on the other hand, hadn't earned a thing.

"Look," I said, trying not to sound as frustrated as I

felt, "are we going to have an intelligent conversation today, or should my assistant and I go and check into our hotel? I'm not leaving until I can reassure your uncle that you're all right."

"It's sweet that he's worried, but I promise, we're fine." Her face was calm as she moved to the coffee-maker, picking up the pot and waving it in my direction. "You want some?"

"He's afraid you might be having some sort of trouble." Was it my imagination, or did she jump when I said that? Her hands were shaking. Interesting. Maybe her flippancy was even more of an act than I'd thought. I looked at her face, noting the new guardedness in her eyes.

"There's no trouble here."

"Are you sure?" I asked. The trembling in her hands was getting worse. She put the coffeepot down, shooting me a defiant look. "He'd want me to help if there was."

"I'm totally sure. If there were trouble, I'd know—we have an excellent reporting system in place."

In English that probably meant the building was on fire and I was the only one who hadn't noticed. Shifting topics, I said, "I've never seen a Daoine Sidhe with glasses before."

"Consequence of the modern era," she replied, relaxing. "I stared into too many bright lights as a kid."

"And they couldn't heal you magically? I'd think an Ellyllon . . ."

"I did the damage to myself. I figure I should live with it."

"I see. So you figure you have to live with whatever's broken here, too?"

"Nothing's broken," she said calmly. "Everything is going great."

I shook my head. "You're a terrible liar."

Jan's mouth dropped open. I took a step back. Blood

means power, and this scrawny, bespectacled girl could probably fling me halfway around the world before I had time to ask for the truck's license number.

"I am not lying," she snarled. I flinched, and she took a deep breath, adding more calmly, "It's just been a little busy lately. That's all." She picked up the coffeepot again, finally pouring herself a cup.

I thought Sylvester was being overly concerned when he sent me to Fremont: thanks to Jan's reactions, I was rethinking my opinion. Even I don't normally cause panic attacks just by asking a few questions. She'd lied to me twice already. If nothing was wrong, why had she left so many messages for her uncle? "Well, do you mind if we stay a few days, just to be sure? Sylvester asked me to show Quentin the ropes, and I hate to disappoint my liege."

Her eyes widened as she realized she couldn't say no without risking her uncle sending an entire diplomatic detachment. I was her one shot at subtle. Then the moment of panic was gone, replaced by another glossy smile. "Of course. Do you have somewhere to stay?"

"Yes, we do," I said, letting her think that she was fooling me. If she wanted to lie to herself, I was glad to help: it might keep her from realizing how much she was giving away. "Luna arranged hotel rooms for us."

"Why am I not surprised?" Her smile became a little more honest, affording me another brief look at the fear lurking underneath. "How's she doing?"

"Luna's doing well; she's planning a new garden."

"Oh? What kind?"

"Wildflowers." It was going to be a mourning garden, dedicated to the memory of those who died while I was searching for Evening's killer. There was even a plot for Devin. Luna sent Quentin to show me the plans, and I cried until I was almost sick. But I didn't want to tell Jan any of that.

"It's good that she's keeping busy." The lightness of

her tone was obviously intended to divert me, and it didn't win her any points.

"Jan?"

"Yes?"

"Can we finish this later? I need to check in with Sylvester, and Quentin has studying to do." That last bit was a lie, but there was no way I was going to go off and leave the kid in this loony bin. I have too much respect for him.

"Of course." Jan glanced toward the window. "Wow, is it sunset already? How about you come back in the morning? That'll give me time to check on a few things."

Like whether or not we'd really come from her uncle. "That'll be fine."

"Great." She walked back to her desk, setting her mug on an already dangerously cluttered corner. "Do you need someone to walk you out?"

"We can manage." I wanted time to consider my options before I approached her again. If that meant finding my own way back to the cafeteria and out to the car, fine. I was a big girl. I could handle it.

"Great." With that, I was dismissed. She sat down on the desk next to her mug and retrieved the computer she'd been using when I arrived, attention already focusing on something else.

It's always fun when your allies are the ones you want to slap. I left the office without another word, somehow managing not to slam the door, and walked back the way I was pretty sure Alex and I had come. I almost regretted refusing Jan's offer of an escort; maybe I could have convinced her to send for Alex. Of the people I'd met so far, he seemed the closest to normal. Besides, I wanted to figure out what he was—a little mystery can go a long way, and he had just enough to be interesting.

After half an hour of wandering the halls, I was ready to admit that I was lost. Every window showed a different view of the grounds, giving me absolutely no help with my navigation. I considered climbing out one of the ground-floor windows, but dismissed the idea; with my luck, exiting that way would make it impossible to find the cafeteria again, and I needed to take Quentin with me.

I finally spotted the familiar sky-blue door at the end of a series of sterile white halls that looked like something out of a soap opera hospital. The cafeteria. "About time," I muttered, hurrying to reach it before it could find a way to disappear. If the hallways in the knowe were actually capable of movement, I wouldn't put it past them to change just to spite me.

The cafeteria was still almost deserted, save for a single addition: the woman sitting across from Quentin, her chin resting on the balled knuckles of her left hand. He had a wide-eyed, almost stunned look of infatuation on his face, like he'd just figured out what the female gender was for. I'd never seen him look that much like a stereotypical teenager.

I let the door swing shut, clearing my throat. Neither one turned. "Hello?"

Now the woman looked around and smiled. She had a pale, pointed face, framed by straight black hair in a pageboy cut. Her eyes were orange—the same poppy-bright shade as Alex's—and a scar marred one cheekbone, almost invisible against her pallor. If she'd seen the sun in the last three years, I'd be surprised.

"Hi!" she said, still smiling. "We were starting to wonder if you'd show up."

Quentin shook himself out of his daze and gave me a small wave, half-smiling. "Hey, Toby. Did you find Countess Torquill?"

"It's Countess O'Leary, actually, and yes, I did. Who's your friend?"

"Oh—sorry. I didn't mean to be rude." The woman stood, offering me her hand. The top of her head only came up to my shoulder. "I'm Terrie Olsen. Nice to meet you."

"October Daye." I took her hand and shook, once. "I see you've met my assistant."

"Quentin? Yeah. He's a peach. Where did you find him? He wouldn't say; he's such a man of mystery." She grinned. I didn't.

Quentin reddened, giving Terrie another adoring look. I frowned. "Shadowed Hills; he's one of Duke Torquill's fosters. He's here to help me check in on the Countess."

"Really? That's sweet." She glanced over her shoulder, smiling. "He's great company."

"I'm sure," I said, frown deepening. "Did you say your last name was Olsen?"

"Uh-huh. Just like my big, dumb brother." Terrie flicked her hair back, adding, "You've probably met him. Tall blond dude, goes by 'Alex'?"

"Ah," I said, nodding. "That explains the eyes."

"Got them from Mom." Terrie's grin broadened until a dimple appeared in one cheek. "There's a family resemblance."

"I . . . guess that's true, yes," I agreed. Dare and Manuel—the last brother-sister team I'd encountered—also had matching eyes.

"Terrie was telling me about computer programming," said Quentin, in a dopey, adoring voice. I looked back as he added, "She's really good."

"I'm not that good," Terrie said, with a laugh.

"Right," I said. "Quentin, get your things and come on. We're getting out of here."

"But, Toby—"

"Don't argue. Terrie, it was nice meeting you. Quentin, we're leaving." I started to turn.

Behind me, Terrie said, "I bet you got lost in the knowe."

"What?" I stopped, looking back.

"I bet you got lost in the knowe. Everyone does, at first."

"I got a little turned around, yes," I admitted.

"It happens to everyone, honest. Want me to show the two of you out?"

This woman had set me on edge faster and more skillfully than anyone I'd met in years, Jan included; I was afraid that if we spent too much time with her, Quentin was going to propose, just before I decked her. At the same time, my migraine was back with reinforcements, and I just wanted to get out and find the hotel before I killed someone.

"I would love to be shown out of the building," I said.

"No problem. Terrie to the rescue!" She winked at Quentin and stepped into the hallway with no further fanfare, motioning for us to follow. Quentin started after her, and I followed, watching them speculatively.

Quentin can be a lot of things, but I'd never seen him be fickle. Not that long ago he'd been blushing over his mortal girlfriend, and now he was panting after some strange changeling like a puppy in heat. It didn't make sense, and it was irritating me. I was sure I was overreacting—Terrie was probably a perfectly nice person who wasn't trying to toy with my underage assistant—but it was weird. Really weird.

After about ten minutes, Terrie pushed open an unmarked door, exposing the lawn outside. "Ta-da!"

The outside lights were on, and cats lounged in the lit areas, watching us with detached interest. The only flowers in sight were normal, mortal clover. We had left the knowe. I stepped past Terrie and Quentin, taking a deep breath of the cool air and relaxing as I felt my headache loosen. "This is wonderful." It was dangerously close to saying "thank you," but I was too absorbed in my speculations to care.

"Don't mention it," Terrie said, shrugging off my

near-slip. "Are you guys sure you've got to get going so soon? The night shift has hours to go."

"Well—" Quentin began.

"We're sure," I said. "Quentin, come on."

He started to protest, but stopped, catching my expression. Sighing, he turned to face Terrie and executed a deep, formal bow. "Open roads and kind fires to you."

That was the last straw. Whatever this was, it was moving a bit too fast for me to be even remotely happy about it. "Right. Good night, Miss Olsen."

I grabbed Quentin's shoulder and hauled him off. Terrie watched, hiding a smile behind her hand. I did my best to ignore her. Quentin craned his neck for one last look, protesting only when we were out of earshot. "What did you do that for?"

"'What did you do that for?'" I mimicked. "Did you see yourself back there?"

"I was being nice!"

"You were being a creepy little ball of hormones! She's twice your age!"

"You're like four times my age."

"But I, at least, am not hitting on you." I let go of his shoulder, letting him try to smooth his wounded dignity as I stalked toward the car. "We're here to work, remember?"

"You left me alone. I was gathering information."

"Yeah, right."

"Yeah! Did you know that ALH only employs faeries? They hire changelings and purebloods, and that's it—no humans of any kind. Not even in service capacities."

"Since most of the company is in the Summerlands, that makes sense. What else?"

"Most of the management staff has been with the company since the beginning. January and her daughter basically run the place, only Elliot does all the staffing. And—"

"Hang on. Daughter?" Sylvester hadn't mentioned a daughter.

"That's what Terrie said." I motioned for him to keep going, and he said, "The daughter's name is April."

"Interesting. Any mention of a father?"

"No."

"Huh. Did you notice how empty the place was? I wonder where everyone is."

"Maybe it's just a small company?" Quentin suggested, brow furrowing. We had reached the car, and I dug in my pocket for my keys, shooing cats off the hood and roof.

"Or maybe something's going on," I said, and unlocked the driver's side door. "Those weren't unused cubicles, just empty ones. There were papers on the desks, and most of them had computers. There were more people working here not all that long ago. Go check your door."

"So something changed," he said, as he circled the car to peer through the windows. I did the same on my side. Last time I got into a car without checking whether I was alone, there was a man with a gun waiting for me. There are some lessons you only have to learn once.

"Exactly," I replied. "Did you find anything else?"

"Not that you'd want to hear."

So the rest was flirting: got it. "Well, maybe you weren't just screwing around," I said, sliding into the car and leaning over to open the passenger door. Once Quentin was in the car and buckled up I handed him the folder with the directions. "Here. See if you can get us to the hotel."

He sighed. "Yes, O Great One."

"O Great One? I like that. You can stick with that." I started the car and drove back up the path from the parking lot to the entrance. The gate was apparently equipped with motion sensors on the inside, because it creaked upward as we approached.

Something flashed gold in the underbrush. I hit the brakes, peering into the darkness. Whatever it was, it was gone; there were no further signs of motion or light.

"Did you see that?"

"Huh?" He looked up from the directions. "See what?"

"Nothing." I shook my head, restarting the car. "It was probably just a raccoon."

We drove through the gate and out onto the street with no further delays. The business parks on either side were dark—the sensible people had gone home, leaving the night shift for the lunatics and the fae. That's how the world has always worked. The night is ours.

"Head for the freeway," Quentin said.

"Got it." I turned toward the nearest onramp.

"So did you meet her?" Quentin asked.

"Meet who?"

"January."

"Yes, I did. So did you; she was the brunette with the clipboard when we first got here."

"That was her?" His nose wrinkled. Quentin was young enough to be very aware of his own dignity, and his dignity wasn't the sort of thing that allowed for judging swearing contests.

"Uh-huh."

"What was she like?"

"Distracted. But a little bitchy at the same time—I don't think she wants us here."

"How old is she?"

"Not very. She seems pretty comfy with all this tech, so she was probably born no later than the eighteen eighties." For a pureblood, anything less than two hundred years is basically adolescence. One of the more ironic things about immortality; the immature period lasts a lot longer. "Tamed Lightning is probably her first 'real' regency."

Quentin frowned. "Do you think something's really wrong?"

"I think it's too early to say, but it's possible," I said. "Which exit?"

"Next one."

"Got it."

Fact: Sylvester was worried about something "going wrong" at ALH. Whatever it was, it was real enough to spook Jan. She wasn't happy to have us there. So what was she trying to hide? Fact: ALH Computing wasn't anything I was used to. It's not that I don't approve of modern technology; I just don't understand it, and that makes it hard to appreciate it. What were Jan and her associates hoping to achieve?

Quentin was saying something. I glanced toward him. "What?"

"So are we staying for a while?" he repeated.

"It looks like we may be, yes."

"Oh," he said. He didn't sound disappointed; in fact, he sounded pleased. Not a good sign.

The hotel was coming into view up ahead, and I turned toward it, angling toward the promise of material comfort. The idea of a bed—any bed—was suddenly compelling.

"I am *so* ready for bed," I muttered.

Quentin glanced at me. "The Duchess asked me to pass you a message."

"Oh? What's that?"

"She says, 'try to get some sleep, and have anything you want off the room service menu if it means you'll actually eat.'"

That was Luna, all right. I grinned. Sometimes having a collection of surrogate mothers can come in handy—between Luna, Lily, and Stacy, I was almost starting to eat regularly.

"Cool," I said. "You need anything before bed?"

"No. Wait—what time is it? I promised Katie I'd call."

"Almost nine. Calling Katie, huh? You sure you're not going to call Terrie instead?"

Even in the dim light of the car, I saw him redden. "Katie's my girlfriend."

"So you were flirting with Terrie, why?"

"I . . . I don't know. She was cute, and I was bored." His blush got worse. "It didn't mean anything."

"Uh-huh." I busied myself with pulling into the hotel parking lot and looking for a space.

Unbidden, another fact rose to my mind: Alex was definitely cute. I paused. That wasn't a thought I needed to have, especially not when I'd just been scolding Quentin for thinking the same about Alex's sister. But it was also a thought that didn't involve Connor, or Cliff, and I needed to move on to someone who was neither married nor mortal. Really, who was it hurting? I scolded Quentin because of the age difference. Alex and I didn't have that problem, unless he was a lot older than he looked.

I don't usually move that fast. Devin was my first lover, and I was with him for years before I left him for Cliff. The only person I'd so much as looked at since then was Connor, and he and I started flirting when I was still living under Amandine's roof. I don't get crushes. It's not my style. Still, it could be time for a change—and something was telling me Alex would be the perfect change of pace. So what if it was unexpected? That made it more appropriate. Out with the old, in with the new.

Quentin was silent, lost in his own thoughts. Probably thinking about how he was going to explain his sudden absence to Katie. Maybe we'd get lucky, and the only thing wrong at ALH would turn out to be some sort of computer error . . . but somehow, I didn't think so.

Whatever it was, I had to hope it was something we could handle on our own. Sylvester would never have sent me with nothing but a half-grown fosterling for reinforcements if he thought we'd be in any real danger. Right?

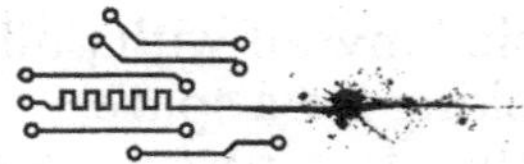

SEVEN

MELLY ANSWERED ON THE THIRD RING. "Shadowed Hills, how can I help you?" Her voice was broad, accented with the sort of jolly American drawl that thrived in the middle of the country about two hundred years ago. I've known Melly since I was a kid—she's Kerry's mother, and she used to sneak us sweets from the kitchen at Shadowed Hills—and just the sound of her was enough to relax me.

"Hey, Melly. Sylvester around?"

"Toby! How are you, darling? Did Himself really ship you off to Tamed Lightning with naught but a foster to keep you company?"

"Quentin's not so bad." Quentin was presently being "not so bad" in his own room, where he was hopefully going to get some sleep. ALH seemed to operate on a diurnal schedule, and we were going to be clocking a lot of daylight hours before we went home. "Put the boss on? I've got an update for him."

"You'll visit soon?"

"I will."

"All right, then. Hold on a second."

Sylvester must have been waiting for my call, because

I was on hold less than a minute before he picked up, breathless. "Toby?"

"Here," I confirmed. There were a few cold fries left on my room service tray. I picked one up, swirling it in a puddle of ketchup. "We've arrived safely, and I met your niece. You should've told me she was twitchy and paranoid."

"I would have, if she normally were. Did she say why she stopped calling?"

"That's the funny thing. She says she's *been* calling, and that you haven't been answering her messages."

"Wait . . . what? But that's ridiculous. Why would she say something like that?"

"You say she's not paranoid. She says she's been calling. You say she hasn't been. This sounds to me like something's up." I popped the fry into my mouth, chewing quickly. "Is there any chance you can send reinforcements without causing some sort of diplomatic incident?"

"Not without more to go on, no. Did you talk to her?"

"Yeah. It was about as productive as talking to Spike. Maybe less. I mean, at least Spike makes an effort. It could be because she's not sure I am who I say I am, and she's trying to be careful. Has she been having a lot of issues with Dreamer's Glass recently?"

"Not that I'm aware of." Sylvester hesitated. "Are you comfortable continuing?"

"To be honest, no, but if she's not getting messages somehow, I don't think swapping me for somebody else is really going to make her less twitchy." I sighed. "I'll go back tomorrow and see what I can find. If you need to pull me out of here, we'll reassess the situation from there. All right?"

"All right. Just keep me informed."

"Of course."

We chatted for a few minutes about inconsequential

things—Luna's latest gardening projects, my cats, Quentin's performance so far—before I hung up with another promise to let him know if we needed anything. I was out as soon as my head hit the pillow.

My dreams were fuzzy, tangled things that faded when the sun came up. I rolled over, wrinkling my nose at the smell of ashes, and peered at the alarm clock. The first digit was a five, which was all I needed to see; groaning, I buried my head under the pillow and went back to sleep.

The sound of knocking hauled me back to consciousness about six hours later. I pulled my head out from under the pillow and glared at the door. The knocking continued. Knowing hotels, the knocking would probably be followed by someone from the housekeeping staff deciding to come in and start dealing with the sheets. I was too bleary to remember whether I'd thought to put up the "Do Not Disturb" sign.

Some people like to sleep naked; me, I like to sleep in a knee-length T-shirt. Nudity wasn't the issue. The issue was that my human disguise had dissolved at sunrise, and I didn't have time to weave a new one.

"Come back later!" I shouted, sitting upright and trying to finger-comb my hair over my ears. I could pass for human long enough to slam the door, if I could get my hair to behave. "I'm not decent!"

The sound of muffled laughter drifted through the door. "I didn't know decency was a requirement for breakfast."

"Alex?" I lowered my hands, scooting out of the bed and reaching for the hotel robe. "What are you doing here?"

"Currently? Shouting through your hotel room door. I brought breakfast."

"Yes, but what are you *doing* here?" I shrugged into the robe, tying it shut as I moved to open the door. "I don't remember ordering room service."

Alex smiled, holding up a paper bag that smelled of

eggs and melting cheese. He had a tray in the other hand, with two large paper coffee cups prominently displayed. My stomach rumbled. "Ordering, no, but needing to? Definitely yes. I told you I'd see you at breakfast."

"I guess you did," I said, and held the door wider. "Come on in." I was taking a chance by asking a man I barely knew into my hotel room, but somehow I doubted that anyone who could be incapacitated with a cafeteria door was going to be much of a threat. If he'd been a pureblood, I might have thought differently. I'd take my chances against another changeling, even one whose bloodline I couldn't quite put my finger on.

"Nice digs," said Alex, walking past me. I watched him as I closed the door. He was clearly one of Faerie's rare morning people, making a tidy contrast to my own bedraggled and half-awake self. I was in robe, oversized T-shirt, and socks, with my uncombed hair raked unevenly over my ears. Suddenly, I found myself wishing desperately for some excuse to sneak off for a shower and a change of clothes.

"Luna booked our rooms," I said, giving my hair another swipe with my fingers. "I probably wouldn't have asked for anything this nice."

"Well, then, my compliments to the Duchess." Alex put the tray down on the desk, opening the bag. "Egg and ham croissant, or egg and sausage croissant? Please don't tell me you're a vegetarian. I'd die of embarrassment."

"I am definitely *not* a vegetarian. Can I get the egg and ham?"

"Egg and ham it is." He tossed a waxed paper-wrapped breakfast sandwich toward me, and I caught it easily, sitting down on the edge of the bed as I did. Alex beamed. "Nice reflexes. How do you take your coffee?"

"Black is fine."

He walked over to offer me one of the cups. "Sleep well?"

"Fairly," I said, sipping the coffee. It was hot, strong,

and about the most wonderful thing I could have wished for. I let my shoulders relax. "You?"

"It was a good night." He walked back to the desk, picking up the second cup.

Sipping at my coffee again, I watched him. He looked perfectly comfortable. Whatever was bothering Jan, it didn't seem to have touched him at all. "So how're things back at ALH?"

"Oh, the usual. Mornings are essentially downtime—once the graveyard shift goes home, things slow down. I probably won't get paged to fix anything for a few hours."

"What is it that you do, exactly?"

"System maintenance. I'm a code monkey." Seeing my blank expression, Alex explained, "I tell the computers what to do, and when they do something they're not supposed to, I correct their instructions."

"And Terrie? She does the same thing?"

"Pretty much. She works nights and I work days, but our jobs are essentially the same." Alex quirked a smile, one eyebrow raising. "Just so we're clear, has breakfast suddenly turned into a game of twenty questions? Because if it has, I think it's only fair that we both play."

"Meaning?"

"I'll answer yours if you'll answer mine."

"Fair enough." I put my coffee down next to the clock, unwrapping my sandwich. "Start from the top. January O'Leary. What do you know about her?"

"A lot, considering I've been working for her for about twelve years. She's focused. I mean, scary-focused. Once she starts a project, she sticks with it until it's finished or until she's managed to beat every possible solution into the ground. She can get a little twitchy when she doesn't have a handle on things, but she means well. Do you have a boyfriend?"

I nearly choked on my sandwich. Swallowing, I managed, "What?"

"I answered one for you, now you get to answer one for me. Do you have a boyfriend?"

"Not right now," I said, cheeks starting to burn. I coughed to clear my throat and said, "Elliot. He does what around here, exactly?"

"He's the County seneschal. He does administrative stuff, like the bills and talking Riordan's people out of challenging us to single combat in the middle of the local computer store. He's been with Jan for like thirty years. What's the deal with your sidekick?"

"Quentin's a foster from Shadowed Hills. Duke Torquill asked me to bring him along, since this is a pretty straightforward diplomatic job."

A shadow crossed his face, there and gone before I could identify it. "Straightforward," he said. "Right."

"Is it going to do me any good to ask what that look was for?"

His grin was only a little bit forced. "Nope. Your question."

"All right: April."

Alex blinked. "April?"

"Sylvester didn't say anything about Jan having a daughter. What's the situation there?"

"April is . . . a special case. She's adopted. Sort of." Seeing my blank expression, he shrugged, and said, "She's a Dryad."

This time, there was no "nearly"; I literally choked on my coffee, coughing for several minutes before I managed to croak out a startled, *"What?"*

"She's a Dryad."

"How does that even *work*?" Most Dryads are sweet, reclusive bimbos who avoid people whenever possible, preferring the company of woodland fauna and other Dryads. They're not the sharpest crayons in the box. Most of them probably don't even realize the box exists.

"It's a long story, and it happened before I got here,

so it's sort of secondhand . . ." Alex looked at my expression and continued without missing a beat, "But I guess I can try. April was an oak Dryad. She lived in a proper Grove and everything, with about a dozen others. Then some developers bulldozed the place—including her tree—to put up condos."

"That's horrible."

"The Dryads thought so, too. Most of them sealed themselves away and waited to die, but not April." Alex shook his head. "She grabbed the biggest branch she could carry and ran like hell."

"So what happened?"

"She got lucky. She found Jan." Alex picked up his own coffee, turning the cup in his hands. "Jan loaded her into the car and drove home. From what I understand, she paged Elliot while she was en route—they've been friends forever—and sent him to look for survivors. All he found was kindling. He cursed the land and came back to see what was going on."

"And?"

"Jan was up with her all night. No one knows exactly what she did, but April lives in an information 'tree' inside one of the Sun servers now, and she's doing fine."

I paused. "You're telling me you have a Dryad living in your computers."

"She's happy there. She doesn't get sluggish in winter like most Dryads do, she doesn't need clean water or fresh air, she's pretty much indestructible—she's happy."

Jan moved a Dryad from her home tree into an inanimate object all by herself? I shook my head. "How does that work?"

"I'm not sure. You'd have to ask Jan."

These people kept managing to get weirder. "What does April do in there?"

"She acts as the interoffice paging system."

This time, I wasn't trying to swallow anything. I gaped at him. "*What?*"

"Have you ever been on one side of a building and needed to talk to someone on the other side?"

"Yes." That was why Shadowed Hills had a small army of pages on continuous duty.

"That's what April does. She finds you, relays the message, and goes back to whatever she was doing before you called. She doesn't seem to mind, and Jan doesn't stop us, so we use her to make sure people are where they need to be."

"You're using the Dryad who lives in your computers as an intercom."

"Basically, yes."

"You're all nuts."

"Yes, and we're cute, too." Alex winked. My cheeks burned red. Now clearly amused, he walked over to sit down beside me on the bed. "I believe that makes it my question."

"I believe you're right."

"*Why* don't you have a boyfriend?"

"Ask the insulting questions, why don't you?" I took a large gulp of coffee, ignoring the way it burned my throat, and shook my head. "It's complicated. There just hasn't been time."

"So that means you're available?"

I gave him a sidelong look. "I think that's two questions."

"Maybe." Alex grinned. "Is that a complaint?"

"Three questions." I could feel the heat coming off his skin. He hadn't dropped his human disguise, and this close, I could smell the clover and coffee of his magic beneath the brisk cleanness of his shampoo. "No, I'm not seeing anyone, and yes, I might be available. After I'm off duty."

"Good." Leaning over, he plucked the coffee cup from my hand, set it on the floor, and kissed me.

Privacy and familiarity make a big difference where I'm concerned. I pressed myself against his chest, returning the kiss without hesitation. The state of my hair and clothing was forgotten in favor of the much more interesting question of how close we could pull each other without one of us actually winding up in the other's lap. He'd been talking with his hands since the moment we met, and now, tangled in my hair and cupping the back of my neck, they sang.

Alex was the one who pulled away first, leaving me out of breath and wide-eyed. "After you're off duty?"

Not quite trusting myself to talk, I nodded.

"Good." He brushed his lips across my forehead as he stood, walked back to the desk and picked up his own discarded breakfast. "I'll see you at the office?"

That was an easier question. I swallowed, and answered, "Yeah."

"Great." Grinning, he opened the door, and he was gone.

I stared after him for a long, stunned moment before I groaned, flopping backward on the bed. The smell of coffee and clover still lingered in the air, and I had the not entirely unwelcome feeling that things had just gotten a lot more complicated.

EIGHT

ALEX LEFT SHORTLY AFTER TWELVE, but it was half-past two by the time I managed to get Quentin moving. More things you only learn when you spend a lot of time with someone: Quentin was even less fond of getting up early than I am. I'm normally the one being hauled out of bed, not the one doing the hauling. I was in too good of a mood after my unexpected breakfast date to get grumpy about it; I just got myself ready to go, ordered more coffee from room service, and let him take his time.

It was already a warm day outside, but I wore Tybalt's jacket anyway, combining it with my T-shirt and jeans in a way that Tybalt would probably have found positively slovenly. The faint scent of pennyroyal still clung to the leather. It was comforting, somehow, even if I didn't want to examine that thought too closely.

On the plus side, our late departure meant we missed most of the traffic. Spending rush hour in a car with a half-awake teenager isn't an experience I'm in any hurry to have. We reached ALH a little after three o'clock, sailing free and easy all the way.

The gate cranked upward as we approached. "That's more like it."

Quentin yawned, damp dandelion-fluff hair still plastered against his head. "You even scare the landscape."

"It probably remembers us from yesterday and doesn't want to be enchanted again. The inanimate can have a surprisingly long memory." It really was a beautiful day. I was almost humming as we pulled down the slope to the parking lot and into the first available space.

A little girl appeared on the sidewalk ahead of us. There was no transition or warning; one second the sidewalk was empty, and the next second she was there, hands shoved into the pockets of her jeans, watching us with the clinical interest of a cat watching a bird through a closed screen door.

"That's . . . different."

"Toby? Do you see that?"

"You mean the little blonde girl on the sidewalk?"

"Yeah."

"Then, yes, I do." I unfastened my seat belt, climbing out of the car. "Let's go say hello." Quentin followed close behind as I started across the lot.

The girl wasn't as young as I'd assumed; she was probably closer to thirteen than ten, although Quentin still looked a few years older. There was a strange blankness to her features that created the illusion of her being a much younger child—a certain lack of information, of the experience you'd expect from a girl in her early teens. She was wearing jeans, sneakers, and a gray T-shirt, and her only visible adornments were the rabbit-shaped barrettes that kept her shoulder-length blonde hair from falling into her face.

Everything about her was yellow, from the faint golden tan of her skin to her wide yellow eyes, shadowed by the green frames of her glasses. Her irises matched her hair with eerie exactness. She had the Torquill bone structure; whatever she'd started out as, she was definitely her mother's daughter now.

"Hi," I said, stopping a few feet away. Quentin stopped beside me, but didn't say a word.

"Hello," she said. Her voice was neutral: it was like talking to a recording. She could have been Daoine Sidhe—her stance and the shape of her ears suggested it—but I didn't think so. She didn't feel like one of the Daoine Sidhe. She didn't feel like anything.

"I'm—"

"You are October Daye, Knight of Shadowed Hills. And this is Quentin, currently fostered at Shadowed Hills from parts unidentified." It wasn't a question.

Great. All-knowing kids aren't my idea of a good time. "Yes, I'm Toby, and this is my assistant, Quentin, and we're from Shadowed Hills."

"I'm April."

"Pleased to meet you," I said.

"Shouldn't you be inside?"

"Why? Does your mother want to see me?"

A quizzical look crossed her face, marring her neutral expression. "My mother is occupied with greater concerns. I thought you had come to view the body."

There are a lot of ways to get my attention. Saying the word "body" is near the top of the list. "The what?" Quentin gaped at her.

"The body. Colin has suffered a hardware failure and fallen out of synch with the server. Everyone is greatly upset; they're running in circles, just like last time, and they're not getting any work done. There is still testing to complete, you know." She said the last almost peevishly, like the world was creating bodies just to spite her.

"No, I didn't know," I said slowly, thinking, *Just like last time?* "Where's the body?"

"Inside, through the glass doors, at the center point of the cubicle maze. Everyone is there. You should go there as well. Then you can worry about it for them, and they will all go back to work." There was a sharp snapping sound, like an electrical cable breaking, and April vanished. Ozone-scented air rushed into the space where she'd been standing.

That's not something you see every day. I stared at the empty air.

"Toby . . ."

"I know," I said, shaking myself out of it. "Come on." Turning, I ran for the door.

This time, I was expecting the transition into the Summerlands, and I took note of the moment when it happened, already wondering how many other ways there were to move between the two sides of the building. Quentin pulled ahead and opened the door into the hall, pausing as he waited for me.

I could smell blood mixing with the processed air as soon as the door was open. Strange as April was, she'd been right about at least one thing: something was very wrong.

"Behind me, Quentin," I said, stepping past him.

"But—"

"No buts. If things look dangerous, you run."

Quentin hesitated before falling in close behind me. Being a page teaches you how to shadow people without being underfoot; that's part of being a good servant. Now he was getting the chance to see how it also prepared you for combat. If anything attacked us, his position meant he was already balanced to fight back.

Elliot, Alex, and Peter were standing at the center of the cubicle maze, arranged in an unconscious parody of the way we'd first seen them. Their fear was so strong it was almost something I could reach out and grab hold of. Peter's human disguise shimmered around him, casting off sparks as his almost-hidden wings sent up a panicky vibration that made my teeth itch. I moved closer, close enough to see what they were staring at.

Colin was sprawled on the floor, eyes open and staring, unseeing, up into the darkness of the catwalks. I didn't need to check for a pulse or ask if they'd tried CPR. I know dead when I see it.

The ground around the body was clear, with no signs of a struggle. Discreet punctures marked his wrists and throat; there were no other injuries. I glanced back at Quentin. He was standing a few feet behind me, wide-eyed and pale as he stared at the body. I couldn't blame him. The first time you see real death is hard.

"Out of my way," I said, stepping between Peter and Elliot. There are times when I have a lot of patience, but there are things that don't get better, or easier, when you let them wait.

"Toby . . ." Alex began.

"Now," I snapped. "And stay here. I need to talk to you." They moved without any further protest. Elliot, at least, looked somewhat relieved. I'm half-Daoine Sidhe; that means people assume I know how to deal with the dead. After all, of all Titania's children, only the Daoine Sidhe can "talk" to the dead, using their blood to access their memories—often including the memory of how they died. We're like the fae equivalent of CSI. Some races got shapeshifting or talking to flowers, and we? We got borrowed memories and the taste of blood, and people washing their hands after we touch them. Not exactly what I'd call a fair trade.

I'm half-Daoine Sidhe; I'm also half-human. That does a lot to damage my credibility, but being the daughter of the greatest blood-worker alive in Faerie makes up for my mortal heritage. Lucky me. I've been trying to live up to my mother for my entire life. Because a crazy, lying idiot is the perfect role model.

The Daoine Sidhe didn't sign up for the position of "most likely to handle your corpses," but we didn't have to. Most fae don't have much exposure to death, and they're grateful when someone—anyone—is willing to play intermediary. Death doesn't really bother me anymore; somewhere along the line, it just became a part of who I am. Coffee and corpses, that's my life. Sometimes I hate being me.

I dropped to my knees next to the body. "Quentin, come over here."

"Do I have to?"

I paused, almost reconsidering. Sylvester asked me to let him follow me around for a while; he didn't ask me to start teaching him the gruesome realities of blood magic. Then again, I don't believe in hiding the truth from our children. It always backfires.

"Yes, you do," I said.

Anger and fear warred for ownership of his expression before he sighed, moving to join me. The habit of obedience was stronger than his desire to rebel. Faerie trains her courtiers well.

"Good," I said, and turned my attention to Colin. Maybe it's a sign of how many bodies I've seen over the past year, but I felt no disgust: only pity and regret. I sighed. "Oh, you poor bastard."

I was aware of the men behind us, but they didn't matter anymore. All that mattered was the body and what it had to tell me.

Colin's coloring was normal under the lines of his henna tattoos, showing no signs of lividity, and his eyes were still moist, almost alive in their blank regard. He'd died recently. He looked startled but not frightened, like whatever happened was a surprise without being unpleasant. At least until it killed him.

"Toby . . ."

"Yeah?" I lifted Colin's hand, frowning at the ease with which his elbow bent. He was cold enough that rigor mortis should have set in already, but his joints were still pliant. That wasn't right. There's a point at which rigor mortis fades, replaced by limpness, but he wasn't suffering from that, either; his body had normal muscle resistance. He just wasn't in it.

"What *happened*?"

"I don't know yet. Hush a minute, and let me work." The punctures on Colin's wrists were nasty, but not enough to be the cause of death. The skin around them was only slightly bruised; the trauma of whatever killed him wasn't enough to rupture many of the blood vessels. There's a lot of blood in the average body, but most of Colin's was still inside where it belonged.

The third puncture was nestled below the curve of his jaw on the left side of his head, surrounded by a ring of jellied blood. There were no other visible injuries. There was something else wrong with the body, but my eyes seemed to slide off it when I tried to look more closely.

I frowned. "Quentin, look at the body. What's wrong with it?"

"You mean besides being dead?" he asked, with an odd half-stutter in his voice.

"I know it's hard. It was hard for me the first time, too. But I need you to look closely, and tell me what you see."

The first time—ha. My first time was one of Devin's kids, back when I still worked there. He overdosed in the bathroom an hour before his shift in the front was supposed to start, and he wasn't even cold when we found him. I helped three older boys carry him behind the bar and leave him for the night-haunts, and I was sick three times before morning. Devin still made me stand my watch, because duty was duty. I've never been that cruel a taskmaster . . . but Devin was my teacher, and I learned a lot from him. One of his most important lessons was that the hard things are best done quickly: face what you're afraid of and get it over with, if you can. It hurts less in the long run.

Quentin swallowed and looked down, scanning the body. He frowned, confusion breaking through his disgust. "Is there something wrong with his hands?"

I looked down. Colin's hands were webbed, like a Selkie's should be, curled at his—

Oh, no. Oh, root and branch, no. Stiffening, I said, "Yes, Quentin. I think there is."

The fae don't leave bodies. That's a lot of how we've stayed hidden all these years. When we die, the night-haunts carry us away, leaving behind illusion-forged mannequins to fool human eyes. The signs of Colin's heritage should have been gone, replaced with apparent humanity by the night-haunts. They should have been gone . . . but they weren't. His fingers and toes were webbed, and his eyes were brown from edge to edge. Except for the punctures at his wrists and throat, he could have been playing some sort of tasteless joke.

But he wasn't joking; he was dead, and something was very wrong. The night-haunts never leave a body long enough for the blood to chill. So why hadn't they come for Colin? Why was he still here?

"Toby?"

"It's okay." I patted him on the shoulder with a suddenly clumsy hand, aware of how cold the comfort must seem. "I think this may be why Sylvester sent us here."

"I don't think he knew . . ."

"I know." I pulled my hand away. "Go see when Jan's getting here." I didn't want him to see what I was going to do next. I may not like lying to the young, but even I have my limits.

Quentin nodded and stood, trying to hide his relief as he turned toward Elliot. "Sir? Where is your lady?"

"April went to get her," Elliot said, voice low and numb.

"How long?" I asked, without looking around as I dragged my forefinger across the wound on Colin's left wrist. Sometimes being Daoine Sidhe is the most disgusting thing I can imagine. Those of us with skill at blood magic can taste a person's entire past in the weight of their blood. It makes us excellent counselors and better detectives; it also means we spend a lot of money on mouthwash. After a while, the taste of blood never really goes away.

The blood clung to my finger. I stared at it. The last time I rode the blood, I wound up so bound to a murdered pureblood that I almost followed her into death. A little paranoia was natural. Careful not to glance behind me—I didn't want to know if Quentin was watching—I slid the finger into my mouth and waited.

Nothing happened. The blood was sour and curdled, and there was nothing in it that spoke of life or death or anything else. I leaned forward, Quentin and the others forgotten. The existence of a fae corpse was jarring and unnatural, but not being able to ride the blood was just plain wrong. Nothing I'd ever heard of could empty blood of its vitality like that. This time I used the first three fingers of my right hand, dipping them into the blood at his throat and sucking them clean. Nothing. Colin's memories, his self, the things that should have been waiting for me, those were gone.

There was no possible way for this to be good.

I looked up to find Quentin staring at me, expression somewhere between horror and fascination. I met his gaze without blinking, deliberately licking a wayward drop of blood from my lower lip. He was going to have to deal with some of the less attractive aspects of being Daoine Sidhe one of these days. After all, he was one, too.

Peter blanched when I licked the blood away, but Alex just watched, seeming fascinated by the gesture. I flushed, fighting the urge to duck my head, and looked to Quentin. "Have you had any training in blood magic?" I asked.

"A . . . little," he admitted. "I've never . . . not with someone that had . . ."

"There's a first time for everything. Come down here." He shook his head before he could stop himself. I nodded firmly. "Yes. I need you to confirm what I'm getting from him. You're supposed to be helping me. So help."

He knelt reluctantly, asking, "What do I . . . do?"

"Touch his right wrist. Get some blood on your fingers." That was the only wound I hadn't tried yet. Amandine may have been the most powerful blood-worker in the country, but I'm still just a half-blood. It was possible that Quentin, even young and half-trained as he was, would be able to pick up on something I'd missed.

He did as I told him, shivering the whole time. I put a hand on his shoulder to steady him. "It's all right. You're doing fine. Now put your fingers in your mouth." He shot me a terrified look. "It's okay. I'm right here."

"But what am I supposed to *do*?"

"You're supposed to put your fingers in your mouth." He flinched, and I continued, "Then you're supposed to swallow. The blood can't hurt you; it's just a conduit for the magic."

"All right," he said. Screwing his eyes closed, he shoved his fingers into his mouth, and swallowed. There was a pause before he opened his eyes, licking his lips automatically, and said, "When does the magic start working?"

That was what I'd been afraid of. "You didn't see anything?"

"No. I just . . . it was just blood." He frowned anxiously. "Did I do something wrong?"

"You did just fine, Quentin. It's not your fault." I looked toward Elliot. "Did you people move *anything* in here? Touch *anything*?"

Elliot flinched, replying, "No, we . . ."

"Good. Who found the body?" Peter raised his hand. I nodded. "When?"

"About fifteen minutes ago." His voice was steady, but I could still hear the low humming of his unseen wings. He was close to panic.

"Were you alone?"

"For about five minutes. Then Alex came in."

"Did you see anything unusual when you entered?" When he shook his head, I turned to Alex. "How about you?"

"Nothing. I got here, we called for April, and she went for Elliot."

"Now she's getting January. I want this area closed off. Who else is in the building?"

"April and Jan, and Gordan." Elliot's eyes lingered on my bloody fingers. The Daoine Sidhe have always had a lot of control over the leadership of Faerie; I think it's largely because the other races want to keep us where they can see us. People who can talk to the dead are sometimes hard to trust.

"And no one else?" My conviction that they knew more than they were telling me was rising. The men in front of me looked upset and nauseated . . . but not surprised. They weren't surprised by what had happened to Colin.

Something was lying in the shadows by the water cooler. I frowned and started in that direction, even as Elliot began to answer.

"We've been a little light on staffing recently."

At least he had the good grace to sound embarrassed by the lie. I shot him a sharp look, saying, "Well, looks like it's getting lighter, doesn't it?" as I crouched by the water cooler and reached into the shadows, pulling out a well-oiled sealskin. I ran it between my fingers, checking it for damage, and stood, brandishing it as I turned back toward the group.

"This is Colin's skin," I said. "Have you ever heard of someone killing a Selkie and *not* stealing their skin? Because I haven't." Selkie skins can be transferred from person to person, turning the almost purely mortal into full-fledged Selkies. They get passed down in the same families for generations; a stolen Selkie skin is worth its weight or more in gold.

"No," Elliot said, voice growing quiet. "I haven't."

"I didn't think so."

Peter swallowed hard, asking, "Is he . . . ?"

"Yes. Very." I allowed myself a small, hard smile. "Trust me on this one."

"But his hands . . ."

"And his eyes," I said. Peter looked away. I was finding it hard to dredge up sympathy for his squeamishness—after all, he wasn't the one with blood on his lips.

Quentin tugged on my arm, and I looked toward him, asking, "You okay, kid?"

"I think I'm going to throw up." He managed to sound both humble and embarrassed about the idea. Not a bad trick.

I tried to sound reassuring as I said, "That's okay, it's normal the first time. Elliot, where's the bathroom?"

"Down the entry hall, to the left," Elliot said, sounding shell-shocked.

"All right. Come right back, okay?" Quentin nodded and took off at a run, heading for the promised bathroom. I just hoped he'd make it in time. His pride would never let him forgive himself if he didn't.

I waited for his footsteps to fade before turning back to Elliot, saying mildly, "If anything happens to him, I'll hurt you in ways you've never imagined. You know that, right?"

"Of course. Is the boy . . ."

"He's my assistant." I wiped my lips with the back of my hand, looking at the smear left behind. If I didn't know better, it would have looked like lipstick.

Sometimes I wish I didn't know better.

"You're Daoine Sidhe, aren't you? Both of you?"

No, we just like the taste of blood, I thought sourly. Unfortunately, some races in Faerie would mean that. "Yes, we are. His blood is purer than mine, but I'm Amandine's daughter." He nodded at my mother's name. I felt a pang of regret. Mother would have been able to coax the secrets from Colin's blood. I was sure of it.

"Can you tell us what happened?"

"No. His blood isn't telling us anything." I leaned down and closed Colin's staring eyes, letting my fingers rest on the lids. "Nothing at all."

"Nothing?" Peter whispered. The Daoine Sidhe don't brag, because we don't need to. My mother was so strong she could taste the death of plants. She could never stomach maple syrup; she said it tasted like trees screaming. The blood should have told me something, even if it wasn't anything I could use. For it to tell me nothing at all was impossible.

"Nothing." I stood, resisting the urge to wipe my hands on my jeans again. It wouldn't get them clean, or take the taste of blood out of my mouth. "The blood's empty."

"But why didn't the night-haunts come?"

"I don't know." The obvious next question was "so what good are you? " and I didn't know what my answer would be.

He didn't get a chance to ask. Jan rushed into the room, clipboard clutched against her chest, with a tiny white-haired woman following a few steps behind.

"Elliot!" Jan cried, voice shrill and angry. "Elliot, what happened?"

He turned toward her, expression grim. "They got Colin, Jannie," he said. "I'm so sorry. They got Colin."

She stopped, raising a hand to her mouth. She was either one of the best actresses I've ever seen, or she hadn't done it. "Colin?" she said, anger fading, replaced by sudden, bleak despair. "Oh, no. That can't be right, Elliot, it can't; I refuse. Look again. You have to be wrong."

"I'm sorry, Jannie," he said, and opened his arms. She threw herself into them, shuddering, and they clung to each other. My presence was forgotten; I had no place in the landscape of their grief. Even Alex and Peter looked away.

The white-haired woman stepped around them and stopped in front of the corpse, studying it for a long moment before she said, "He's dead."

"Yes," I said flatly. Sylvester said he was worried about his niece not checking in. He never said anything about people getting killed.

"How?"

"I don't know," I said, studying her. Most people are upset when their friends die; this woman looked interested, and not all that surprised. That was unusual. She was roughly five feet tall, with a blaze of white hair cut in spikes that did nothing to hide the squared-off tips of her ears. Her figure matched her height—slight, lissome, and easily overlooked. Judging from her scowl, that happened pretty often; it wasn't the sort of expression you master in an instant, even when your friends are dying. Lines cut through her face like scars through granite. They weren't wrinkles; she wasn't old enough for that. They were just lines, indelibly ground into the shape of her.

"Damn," she said, raking her hands back through her hair. "I liked him."

I glanced to Jan and Elliot, and frowned as I saw that she was sobbing on his shoulder. What a great thing to see in a leader: hysterics. I shook my head, looking back to the white-haired woman, and asked, "Who are you?"

"What?" She looked up at me, her scowl deepening until the lines on her face became caverns. "I'm Gordan. Who the hell are you?"

"October Daye." I don't normally flex my titles, but this time I added, "Knight of Shadowed Hills. I'm here by order of Sylvester Torquill, the Duke—"

"Duke of Shadowed Hills, yeah, we know the drill,"

she said, interrupting. "We're not totally uncivilized out here in the boonies, you know. Have you got any credentials on you?"

"What?"

"Can you prove it?"

"I've already shown my credentials to your Countess, but given that you've got a corpse here—an impossible corpse—do I really need to prove it? I'm Daoine Sidhe, I'm a licensed PI, and I don't exactly see you getting any better offers."

"So you're here to fix all our problems? Well, that's just peachy, princess. What the fuck took you so long?"

"What do you mean?"

She gestured to the body. "This started last month—Colin's the third death we've had. What took you so long? Were you waiting for an engraved invitation? 'RSVP for murder?' "

I stared for a moment before I got my mouth working again. "The *third*?"

"Yeah."

"I . . . see. Excuse me for a moment, please." I turned toward Jan, eyes narrowing. She had straightened and was wiping her face with one hand, teary-eyed and sniffling. And I didn't care. "Ms. O'Leary? May I have a word with you?"

She looked up, golden eyes wide. "Huh?"

I'll normally forgive a certain degree of shock after a major trauma, especially when I'm dealing with purebloods; most of them see so few deaths that they don't know how to cope. Considering what Gordan had said, however, I wasn't inclined to be charitable. "A word, Ms. O'Leary. I need to have one with you."

"W . . . why?" She glanced at Elliot, and he looked away. I think he knew what I was going to say. "This isn't the best time. I . . ."

"Why didn't you tell me that people were dying?" I

demanded. Bluntness isn't usually an asset among the fae, but it's served me well over the years.

Jan gaped for a moment before she recovered, snapping, "You can't just stroll in here and expect me to dump all our problems on you! What kind of a Countess do you take me for?"

I hauled my temper to heel, forcing myself to take a deep breath as Quentin walked up to stand behind me. "Did you call your uncle last night?"

She nodded. "I tried. No one answered."

"Well, he answered for me. He's worried. Now answer me this: do you want these killings to stop?"

Jan stared at me. "How can you even ask me that?"

"I am one changeling with a half-trained page to back me up," I said, levelly. "Whether I'm telling you the truth or not, there's not going to be that much damage I can do. But what I also am is a trained investigator sworn to your uncle's Court. Let me do my job. If you think I'm lying to you at any point, you can deal with me."

"I don't know . . ."

"When your car breaks down, do you fix it yourself, or do you send for a mechanic?"

The change of topics was apparently a little too fast for her. She stared at me for a moment, befuddled, before she said, "I send for a mechanic."

"The principle here is the same. When people are dying, you don't fix it yourself. You send for a mechanic." I looked her in the eye, forcing myself not to start yelling again. It wasn't easy. "I'm the mechanic."

Jan froze, trembling with fear and anger. It was a long moment before the fire in her eyes dimmed and her shoulders began to droop, making it briefly clear just how young she was. The purebloods seem ageless, but they aren't; they're young and stupid once, just like everybody else, and if nothing forces them to grow up, they can stay that way for centuries. Jan was more than a century old, but she was still younger than I was where it counted. Voice low, she said, "Can you do it? Can you make this stop?"

I smiled sharply. It's not my most pleasant expression, but with a fae corpse lying just a few feet away, it didn't need to be.

"My lady," I said, "you only ever needed to ask."

NINE

"TOBY, WAIT UP! PLEASE?"

I stopped briskly, turning to glare at Alex. Quentin did the same, his own motions possessing a semimilitary crispness. His terror was translating into a level of formality that I hadn't seen out of him since the night we met. I didn't care for it, but I honestly couldn't blame him. I was scared, too, and I had a lot more experience than he did.

"What is it?" I asked. "Got something else you neglected to tell me? More bodies? Giant spiders in the attic? Because I'm pretty much out of patience, and you didn't bring me anywhere near enough coffee to excuse hiding a murder."

Alex stumbled to a halt a few feet in front of us, his hands hanging limply at his sides. They weren't singing arias now; for the first time since I'd met him, they were motionless. "It wasn't like that."

"Three people are dead, Alex. Two of them were already dead when we got here. What exactly *was* it like?"

"I . . ." He stopped, shoulders sagging, and sighed. "I'm sorry. I wasn't supposed to tell you anything. I didn't know anyone else was going to get hurt."

I raised an eyebrow. "Who told you not to talk to me?"

"Only one woman here with the authority." Alex quirked a small, bitter smile. "You want to know what's going on, you talk to Jan."

"All right; I will. Take us to her."

To Alex's credit, he didn't argue or try to defend himself further. He just turned, gesturing for us to follow, and led us down the hall.

We'd been searching the buildings of the knowe for almost half an hour, forcing me to admit that Colin's killer or killers left us nothing to find. There were no footprints or signs of forced entry; all the blood was on Colin himself, and there wasn't much blood even there. He hadn't struggled at all. Whatever happened to him, it happened fast. His skin was under the front seat of my car, where no one would tamper with it, but I couldn't figure out what it meant, if anything. Who kills a Selkie and doesn't take the skin? I had three victims, a crime scene that told me nothing and offered escapes into two barely connected versions of reality, and a Countess who said nothing was wrong when she knew that people were dying.

There wasn't enough coffee in the world to make this bearable.

Alex led us to a closed door, where he knocked. "Who is it?" called Jan from inside.

"Alex," he said. "I have Sir Daye and her assistant here. They'd like to speak with you."

There was a pause—long enough that I began to wonder whether the illustrious Countess O'Leary had decided to go out the window—before the door swung open to reveal Jan, looking utterly weary, standing on the other side. "Okay. They can come in. Alex, if you could . . . ?"

"Got it," he said, with a sardonic half-salute. "This is a discussion we peons don't need to be a part of. Quentin, Toby . . ." He hesitated. "I'm sorry. That's all. I'll see you soon." Not waiting for us to reply, he turned and walked rapidly off down the hall.

I watched him go before turning to Jan, not saying a word. She stepped out of the way, letting us pass.

The office was Elliot's, according to the nameplate on the desk; like all the offices, it was located in what I was coming to recognize as the knowe's main building. It was as tidy as I would expect a Bannick's office to be, with carefully sorted baskets of paper sitting atop the filing cabinets and a small collection of bonsai trees on shelves around the room. There were several blank spots on the walls, showing spaces where frames had recently been removed. Elliot himself was sitting on a folding chair to one side of the desk, shoulders slumped, still looking shell-shocked.

Jan closed the door behind us, starting to pace almost immediately. She was so clearly her uncle's niece when she moved that way that it was hard to see how I'd ever been able to miss it. "We found the first body last month," she said, punctuating the words with a sharp gesture of her hand. "We thought—oak and ash, we thought it was Dreamer's Glass. We thought it was just some kind of screwed-up scare tactic gone wrong."

"So why didn't you call the Queen?" I leaned back against a clear patch on the wall, watching her. "If Riordan had somebody killed, even by accident, she broke Oberon's first law. You could have brought charges against her."

"No proof." Jan raked her hair back, frustration briefly beating back anger. "We don't even know for sure that it was her. Who's ever heard of the night-haunts leaving a body behind? What the hell was I supposed to do? Go to the Queen's Court and be all 'excuse me, Your Majesty, but Duchess Riordan maybe had one of my people kidnapped, or somehow had her killed in a way that doesn't make sense, and anyway, I don't know any of this for sure, but can you make her stop?' It wasn't going to work."

"You could have told someone."

"I *tried*." Jan sighed. "Whether you believe me or not, I've been leaving messages for Uncle Sylvester since this started. I wanted his advice. But he never called me back."

Sylvester thought she'd stopped calling; she thought he'd stopped answering. I didn't know what it meant, but it couldn't be anything good. "The night-haunts didn't come for the first victim?"

"They haven't come for any of the victims," said Elliot. "All three of them just . . . stayed, exactly like they were before they died."

"And we're sure they died." Jan kept pacing. "There would be demands by now . . . or *something*. Or someone would have managed to get loose, if they'd been kidnapped and replaced with some sort of mannequins."

"Kidnap victims don't always escape on their own," I said.

"The first victim—Barbara—was a Cait Sidhe Queen of Malvic's line. The cats have been in mourning ever since." She fixed me with a steady look. "Don't you think they'd know if she were still alive?"

I winced. Malvic is one of the Cait Sidhe Firstborn. Most of the Kings and Queens of Cats are his descendants, and he wouldn't be happy when he heard about this. Neither would Tybalt.

"All right, so we know she's dead," I said. "Where did you find her body?"

"In the cafeteria."

"The cafeteria. The cafeteria where you left us alone?" She nodded. "Right." They ditched us in a place where somebody died. How sweet. "I assume that means you didn't close the scene after the body was found?"

"We tried, but . . ." Elliot waved his hands.

"It was upsetting people, and there wasn't anything to find," said Jan.

I bit back a groan. Being largely in denial about the existence of death means most purebloods never learn thing one about proper police procedure; when they find evidence of a crime, they're likely to clean it up just so they won't have to look at it. They probably destroyed any evidence before the body was even cold, oblivious to the fact that this could be a bad idea.

"Was there anything that stood out about the first victim?" I asked.

Jan laughed bitterly. "How about the part where she was dead? Exactly like Colin. We left her where she was for almost a day to give the night-haunts time, and they never came."

That wasn't a good sign. Twice is enough to start looking like a pattern. "How about the second victim?"

"She looked like she was sleeping," said Elliot. His voice was bleak. "She was just . . . she looked like she was sleeping. But she never woke up."

"Her name was Yui Hyouden," Jan said, putting her hand on Elliot's shoulder and squeezing. He stared down at his feet. "She was a Kitsune. She worked in software testing."

I looked away from Elliot. "Where was she found?"

"On the lawn outside. She hadn't come through the reception room; she was still in the mortal world."

The statement made my skin crawl. Kitsune can be beautiful, but it's not human beauty. If the night-haunts hadn't come for Yui's body . . . "When did you find her?"

"Just after sunrise."

"Right." That made it less likely that anyone had seen her, especially since none of the local tabloids had been running the story. It was also no help at all. A body found "just after sunrise" could have been there all night, hidden by an illusion that dissolved at dawn. "She was killed the same way as the others?"

"She was," Jan agreed. "That's when people started leaving. They couldn't handle the idea that they might be next."

"But you didn't go because . . . ?"

Her smile was grim. "This is my County. I leave it, I'm probably not getting it back without a lot more lives lost. I'm staying as long as there's any chance we can save what we've been building here."

"Oberon save me from the idealists," I muttered. Louder, I said, "I need to know everything. Where the bodies were found, who found them, who might have had access to those areas before the bodies were discovered, everything. Photographs would be good, if you have them." I'd be surprised if they didn't have security cameras, given the rest of the knowe.

"Whatever you need," Jan said. "Of course, you realize that if it somehow turns out you've found a way to mimic someone else's magic and you're not who you say you are, I'll have you tried for treason."

"And I'll applaud it. Did anyone photograph the bodies? I want to compare the wounds."

Elliot looked sickened. Jan squeezed his shoulder again, saying, "No—"

"Damn."

"—but we have the bodies, if you'd like to see them."

I stared. "What?"

"We have the bodies." Jan looked at me levelly. "They're in the basement."

The cafeteria was an unmarked murder scene and the basement was full of bodies? Cute. On the other hand . . . a firsthand examination might give me something to go on, and I needed it. Colin apparently died of three small punctures, none of which hit a major artery, and some minor blood loss. That wasn't a good sign.

"Have you taken Colin there?" I straightened, gesturing for Quentin to come. He moved to flank me, silent.

Jan nodded. "Peter and Gordan will have finished moving him by now."

Those two were toting bodies down the stairs while the full-sized people sat around? Oh, *that* was a fair division of labor. "Good. Let's go."

"Go where?" Elliot asked. It was clear he knew the answer but was hoping to be wrong.

Tough. "The basement. I need to see the bodies."

"Right." Jan straightened, taking her hand off Elliot's shoulder. "Follow me."

"Can I stay here?" Elliot's voice sounded shaky. "I don't want to go down there." Jan gave me a pleading look, and I nodded. With the way the morning was going, he'd throw up on the bodies. I'm no forensics expert, but even I know that vomit doesn't usually improve the evidence.

"You can stay here," I said. When he brightened, I continued, "I want you to get me everything you have on the victims. Personnel files, medical records—anything."

"I can do that," he said, tone almost painfully grateful.

"I'm going to want to search their offices and work spaces. I'll also need to examine the murder scenes." There might be *something,* unlikely as it was starting to seem. "All right?"

"No trouble at all."

"Good. Jan, Quentin, let's go."

"All right." Jan looked over her shoulder, asking, "Elliot, will you be okay?"

"No. But I don't think it matters right now. I'll cope." Elliot stood. "Take them to the basement. I'll start finding the stuff they need."

"Do you need anyone to help?" They spoke like equals, but there was an underlying unease there—I got the feeling he was usually the one taking care of her, not the other way around.

"I'll call April if I need help," he said, forcing a smile.

"All right, Elliot." She moved toward the door. We hurried to catch up.

"What do you think?" I murmured to Quentin.

"I think we should leave a trail of bread crumbs," he replied.

I barked a humorless laugh and picked up the pace.

The route followed a series of twisting halls over what the windows indicated to be multiple floors. I was learning not to trust my eyes at ALH. By the time we stopped, I was so disoriented that I didn't know if we were on the roof, the ground floor, or the island of Manhattan. The last hall was lit by dim fluorescent bulbs, with a floor covered in industrial gray linoleum. The only door in sight was painted dull orange, trimmed with yellow. A sign at eye level read "Warning: Hazardous Materials. Keep Out."

Jan saw me eyeing it. "It's a joke. It's been hanging there for years. We didn't put it up because . . ."

"Fine," I said, more sharply than I'd intended. "Can we get this over with?"

"Right."

The stairs descended almost vertically into a large, well-lit room. Judging by the stacks of computer parts and desk furniture lining the walls, they used it for storage before it became a makeshift morgue. The air was cold and tasted faintly bitter, like machine oil and carpet cleaner. Three army cots sat in the center of the room, covered by white cotton sheets with unmistakable shapes beneath them. The dead have their own geometry.

Jan stopped at the base of the stairs. I gritted my teeth and walked past her.

"Jan?"

"Yes?"

"Come here. Quentin, you too." No sense coddling

him now—he was going to have to face the reality of our situation sooner or later.

They walked over to me, both frowning. Quentin was trying to look stoic; Jan just looked sad. I held my hand over the sheet, asking, "This is . . . ?"

"Barbara," Jan said. "She was the first."

"Right." I studied the shape through the sheet, trying to get an idea of the body before I disturbed it. Under normal circumstances, I leave the dead to the night-haunts and the police . . . but the night-haunts had opted out, and I couldn't exactly call the police when the bodies belonged to clearly inhuman creatures. That left me. Reaching down, I folded the sheet away from Barbara's face. Jan turned away. Quentin put a hand over his mouth, eyes going wide.

Alive or dead, Barbara was beautiful. Roses bloomed in her cheeks, and her lips were naturally red, making her look like every Disney princess that's ever graced the silver screen. Her hair was a long, toffee-colored tangle, and bands of matching fur tipped her sharply pointed ears. The only marks on her were the punctures at her wrists and neck, identical to the marks I'd seen on Colin: clearly missing the major arteries and just as clearly fatal.

"Toby . . ."

"I know, Quentin. Jan?"

"Yes?"

"You know who we're supposed to be looking at. Is this Barbara?"

"Yes." She sounded strained.

I knew how she felt. "When did she die? I need a time frame."

"Sometime over Memorial Day weekend. She stayed late on Friday—she had a deadline to meet—and that was the last time anyone saw her alive. Terrie found her on the cafeteria floor when she came in on Monday."

"Barbara was already dead?" I bent, prying her left

eye open, and stared into the jade-green iris. Her pupil didn't contract. I let go.

"She was . . . like this."

"Did Terrie check for a pulse or try to perform CPR?"

"She said Barbara was cold and didn't respond when her name was called." She grimaced. "Terrie couldn't call the ambulance. She couldn't spin an illusion that would last long enough to fool the paramedics if the night-haunts didn't come."

"Don't you have security cameras?" I raked both hands through my hair. "Is there a way we can get a better idea of when this happened?"

"We have cameras, but they weren't running."

I dropped my hands, turning to stare at her.

"We don't know what happened. All the records were wiped."

"So you have no idea when this woman actually died, and a four-day window for the event." Jan nodded. I groaned. "Lovely. Terrie works nights, right? When does she get in?"

"She works from nine at night until six in the morning, usually. She'd taken the weekend off for a convention—she stopped in Monday morning to turn on the lights and make sure the place was still standing."

"So Terrie wasn't expected?"

"No."

"And what time did she find the body?"

"4:52 AM." The exactness of the answer startled me. I blinked at her, and she shrugged. "She paged us—Elliot and I—as soon as she realized Barbara was cold."

"How did she page you? Alex said the phones here don't work normally."

"Most of us have modified cell phones. There are also pay phones in the cafeteria and near the third-floor bathrooms, and most offices have landlines. Any of those can dial outside the knowe, if you press nine first."

"All right. When did you get here?"

"About five-fifteen. I don't know exactly. All the gate time stamps after Friday afternoon have been wiped."

I frowned. "I see. You say you got here around five-fifteen. Where do you live?"

"Here, mostly—we have some offices that we've converted into bedrooms—but I maintain an apartment for storage and so I can get my mail. We're not zoned for residence." She shrugged. "It's about three miles away. I came straight over."

"Had you recently lost any employees who might have been angry enough to try for revenge? Anyone you might have fired or otherwise pissed off?"

"No one. We haven't had any personnel changes in the last three years, except for the recent departures, and those came after the killings began, not before."

"I see. Quentin, come here." He stepped over to join me, looking less than pleased. I knelt, patting his shoulder in what I hoped was a reassuring fashion, and studied the wound in Barbara's neck. I didn't know what I was looking for, but that's never stopped me before.

"Look at this," I said, turning her arm over to show the underside.

"What about it?" he asked, uneasily.

"The color's wrong." I indicated the skin between Barbara's elbow and shoulder. "Blood seeks the lowest point in the body after death; it should be pooling here. But it's not."

"Why not?"

"I don't know." I lowered her arm, my frown deepening. "This is all new ground, Quentin. I always knew fae bodies wouldn't decay, but I assumed at least a few systems would break down. Jan? Have there been any changes in the bodies since they were found?"

"No." She scrubbed at her face with one hand, knocking her glasses askew. "At first, we thought they weren't really dead, just sleeping. We were waiting for them to wake up."

"But they didn't," said Quentin.

"No. They didn't. We moved Barbara down here after a week, to keep her cool. We didn't know how long . . ."

"How long it would take her to start to rot?"

She sighed. "Yeah. But she never did."

"Well, you don't need to worry about that."

"What?"

"She's never going to start to rot." I rose, crossing to the second cot. Quentin followed. "Is this Yui?" I asked. Jan nodded. "Right," I said, and pulled back the sheet.

Yui could have been a normal Japanese woman in her late twenties, if it weren't for her four tails and her pointed, red-furred ears. Her hair was braided, exposing the puncture wound on her throat. This wasn't good. Kitsune express their power in the number of tails they have, ranging from the usual one or two up to seven or eight. Keiko Inari, their Firstborn, supposedly has nine. The Duchess of Shadowed Hills only has three, and there's not much that could take her without a fight . . . but Yui looked as calm as the others. Unless we were dealing with someone the victims knew, we were looking at something big and mean enough to take down a four-tailed Kitsune before she had a chance to get angry.

I didn't like that idea one bit. "She didn't struggle."

"Well, why not?" asked Quentin.

"It's possible that she was so surprised that she didn't have time to react. It's also possible that she knew her killer." I looked up. "Three weeks between Barbara and Yui. How long between Yui and Colin?"

"Two weeks," Jan said.

"Either somebody's enjoying themselves, or something's hungry."

She flinched.

I sighed. "I'm just trying to get the facts straight. We'll move on, for now. Do you have any paper cups?"

"What?" It was an odd enough request to make her stop looking upset and start looking confused. It was an improvement.

"Small cups, made of paper? You'd probably find them in the cafeteria."

"Oh. Yes, we do. Why do you—"

"Great. We'll need four of them, filled halfway with lukewarm water." I pulled the sheet back over Yui, saying, "Quentin and I are going to try waking their blood."

"Will that work?" Jan asked. Quentin looked at me out of the corner of his eye, expression telegraphing the same question.

"Probably not, but I don't have any better ideas," I said. "Do you?"

"Guess not. I'll be back." Jan turned and walked up the stairs. We watched her go, and then Quentin looked back to me, obviously getting ready to ask what the hell was going on.

I cut him off. "The bodies aren't decaying because they're still fae. The night-haunts haven't come."

"What?" he said, frowning.

"Do you know why we have the night-haunts?"

"To keep humanity from finding out about us."

"Partially. And partially because fae flesh doesn't rot." I shrugged. "Look, purebloods don't age, right? So why would they decay? I'm not sure what would happen to a changeling body without the night-haunts, but they take the purebloods so they won't just be lying around for the rest of time."

"Oh," Quentin said, looking toward Barbara. Then, slowly, he asked, "So why haven't the night-haunts come?"

"That's the eight-million-dollar question, kid. I'm hoping these three can tell us," I indicated the cots, including Colin in the gesture, "because I'm not sure who else can."

"Oh," he said again, and looked away.

I watched him for a moment. "Beyond the obvious, what's wrong?" He mumbled something I didn't quite hear, and I frowned. "Try that again?"

"I said, I want to stay." He turned to face me again. "Please?"

"Really." I raised an eyebrow. "And what makes you think . . . ?"

"That's always what happens. Something happens, and all the kids get sent away." A sour look crossed his face. "I've been here before. I want to stay."

He was a foster, after all. Maybe there'd been a reason for his posting at Shadowed Hills. I tilted my head, considering him. "Why should I let you?"

"Because Sylvester sent me to learn. How am I supposed to do that if you send me away when things get dangerous?" He shook his head. "I've never even tried blood magic before—not when it mattered. You have to let me stay. I need to know these things."

"You're just a kid; you don't have to . . ."

"If I don't do it now, I'm going to grow up to be one of those useless courtiers you're always complaining about," he countered. "At least this way, you can keep an eye on me."

He had a point. "All right. You can stay until it gets too dangerous. But then you go."

"Understood." He grinned, looking very young, and heartbreakingly joyful.

That sort of look has never led to anything good. I raised a hand, cautioning, "You're going to do what I tell you to do. No heroics. No investigating strange noises because you think they'll lead you to something interesting. Got it?"

"Yes, Toby."

"Screw around on me and I'll send you back to Shadowed Hills so fast you won't have time to blink."

"I'll do whatever you say."

"Damn straight, you will. Now shut up and let me think." I leaned against the wall, standing quietly as we waited for Jan to return. Quentin did the same, imitating my posture either unconsciously or by design. We'd just had time for me to start becoming really uncomfortable about the bodies when the door at the top of the stairs opened, and Alex stepped uneasily inside.

"Jan said you wanted these?"

He was balancing four paper cups on a small tray. He looked understandably unhappy about being there; the basement had become the company morgue, and these had been his friends. His expression of unhappiness deepened when he saw my scowl.

"Where's Jan?" I asked.

"April called her to help Elliot with something. She said I could . . . look, what do you want me to do with these? I can go. I just . . ." He sighed. "I wanted to help."

He looked so contrite that I thawed a bit, and motioned for him to come down, ignoring Quentin's deepening scowl. "Fine. Bring those on over here."

"Sure," Alex said, giving the room another uneasy glance before descending. Quentin met him at the base of the stairs, taking the tray away and leaving him blinking. No one does imperious quite like a Daoine Sidhe. "Is that everything you needed?"

"For the moment." I took the first cup from the tray, gesturing for Quentin to follow me over to Barbara's body. Having Alex there served at least one purpose; Quentin didn't like him, and that meant he'd be too busy standing on his own dignity to argue when I told him what to do.

"What are you going to do with the water?"

"We're going to try waking the blood." I started scraping dried blood from Barbara's wrist and adding it to the water. Quentin stiffened, but as I expected, he didn't protest. Dignity is a wonderful tool sometimes.

Alex swallowed, looking sick. "Why?"

"The blood has to be awake for us to ride it." The water had taken on a pink tinge. I returned the cup to the tray and picked up the second. "If it works, we may be able to see the killer."

"And if it doesn't?"

"We try something else."

"Why can't Jan do it?"

"Because Jan isn't the daughter of the most powerful blood-worker in Faerie, so she probably couldn't wake the stuff up in the first place." I tried to focus on what I was doing. "My mother could do this without breaking a sweat."

"Right," said Alex. "So were you able to . . . get anything . . . from Colin's blood?"

"No, because there was nothing for us to 'get.'" I passed the second cup of bloody water to Quentin. "Here."

Alex frowned. "Nothing?"

"Nothing. The blood was empty." I grimaced. "And before you ask, no, it's not supposed to work that way."

"So how do you know this time will be any different?"

"I don't. I'm a half-blood and Quentin's untrained, and this blood is old enough that I might not get anything under normal circumstances . . . but it's worth trying." Pinching my nose, I gulped down the contents of my cup. Quentin did the same with his.

All I got was the bitter, watery taste of diluted blood. There wasn't a flicker of memory.

Quentin coughed and dropped his cup on the tray. "There's nothing there."

I sighed, putting my cup next to his. "It must have been too old." He didn't have to know that I was lying. I crossed to Yui's cot and folded the sheet back, saying, "Maybe three weeks will make the difference."

"You're going to try again?" Alex asked.

"Have you got a better idea?" I picked up the third

cup, scraping the blood off Yui's right wrist. "If so, please share. I'm all out of good ideas."

"Not really. I just . . . I want this to stop."

"Yeah, well, if I were you, I'd have left by now. Gone somewhere safer." Like the middle of a minefield.

"I can't."

"Why not?" I handed Quentin his cup, started preparing my own.

"It's a little hard to explain."

"Doesn't Terrie want to go?" I asked. Quentin looked up at the mention of Terrie's name, suddenly interested.

Alex flinched. "Not really. That's part of it."

"Have you tried explaining that staying here might be fatal?"

"We don't see each other much," he said, uncomfortably. "It makes it hard to explain things."

"She works the night shift, and she found the first body, right?"

"Yes," he said, sounding startled and a bit wary. Not a good sign. "How did you know?"

I looked at him blandly. "Jan told me."

"Right." He sighed.

"If you see her, let her know I want to talk to her."

His eyes widened. "Why?"

I expected his reaction: no one wants to hear that someone wants to talk to their relatives as part of a murder investigation. What I didn't expect was the expression on Quentin's face—for a moment, he looked like I'd slapped him.

"Calm down," I said, directing the statement to both of them. "I just want to ask her a few questions. I'm not accusing anyone of anything." Yet.

Alex calmed marginally, saying, "If I see her, I'll let her know."

"Good." I sipped the bloody water instead of gulping this time, trying to linger. Quentin saw this and did the same. Not that it did any good; the blood was as empty as Barbara's. I spat it back into the cup. "Well, *that* was useless."

"Nothing here, either," said Quentin. He was starting to look green around the edges. The magic wasn't working, but he was still tasting the blood.

Alex peered at us. "Are you going to throw your cups at me if I say you look like hell?"

I considered for a moment, finally saying, "I won't."

"I might," Quentin said.

"I'll risk it. You look like hell. Have you had anything to eat since breakfast?"

"No," I admitted, and sighed. "I'm still mad at you."

"I know. But that doesn't mean you don't need to eat. Come on. We can hit the cafeteria and get some food into you. The cooks are gone, but the vending machines still work."

"That's probably a good idea," I said, grudgingly, as I dropped my cup back onto the tray. There wasn't any blood on my fingers. They just felt that way. I wiped them against the legs of my jeans, trying to be casual about it. "Is there a phone in the cafeteria?"

"Yes," said Alex.

"I'm not hungry," said Quentin.

"Is there coffee?" I asked.

"You can have a pot to yourself."

"I'm sold." I looked toward Quentin. "Come on. I'll buy you a soda."

"I'm not *hungry*."

"You're a teenager. You're always hungry." I was hungry, whether or not Quentin was, and I'd focus better after a sandwich and some coffee. "Can we get an escort to the cafeteria?"

Looking amused, he asked, "You two need a native guide?"

"Please. Unless you think you have enough staff left to send search parties."

"The place isn't that bad."

"Uh-huh." I spread the sheets back over Barbara and Yui. Maybe they wouldn't care, but I did. Quentin was tossing the cups into the garbage can, not bothering to empty them first. "Have you ever been to Shadowed Hills?"

"No, I can't say that I have."

"Amateur," Quentin muttered, and started up the stairs.

"Quentin . . ." He didn't stop. Sighing, I followed.

Alex came along behind me, pausing to close the basement door. It didn't lock. "So what's the big deal about Shadowed Hills?"

He was clearly trying to get back into my good graces. I considered the sincere unhappiness in his expression, and gave in, saying, "Shadowed Hills is just about as bad as this place. I guess the Torquills just have a family grudge against linear space. I'm practically a native, and I still get lost there."

"This place is confusing at first, but it gets better. You'll catch on."

"I hope so." Quentin was ten feet ahead. I called, "If you don't know where you're going, stop." He glared back at me, but stopped, letting us catch up. "That's better. Come on."

Alex led us through the halls, choosing what I assumed was the best route through rooms that connected without attention to the laws of architecture or common sense. I was sure the physical buildings were more sanely constructed, but we weren't *in* the physical buildings: we were in the knowe. Quentin walked in sullen silence, but Alex made up for it by chattering wildly, pointing out interesting quirks of the knowe's construction and cracking bad jokes. I didn't pay attention to a word. People were dying.

"Are we there yet?" Quentin demanded.

"Patience, young one!" Alex said. Quentin glared, and he amended, "Almost. The cafeteria's just ahead." Then he turned to wink at me, smiling broadly. I smiled back, almost unintentionally. It was hard to stay mad when he was working so hard at winning my approval.

"Good," Quentin said.

We turned a corner, bringing the cafeteria door into view. Quentin sped up, dashing through, with Alex following at a more sedate pace. When he reached the door, he stopped, opening and holding it for me.

"After *you,*" he said, with exaggerated gallantry.

"After Quentin, you mean." He was obviously trying to make me feel better. It was almost working. All this would make more sense once I'd eaten. Food would settle the queasiness in my stomach and my head; if it didn't, it would at least cover up the taste of blood. This looked like it was going to be a long day, and I needed whatever help I could get.

"Right," he said, and followed me inside.

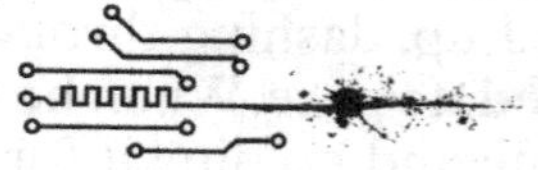

TEN

AFTER GETTING MYSELF a cup of coffee, I made my way to the pay phone mounted on the wall. There was no dial tone. I frowned at the receiver before remembering what Jan said about outside lines, and dialed "nine." Success: the familiar buzz began. I punched in the number for the Japanese Tea Gardens, pumped in quarters until the prerecorded operator stopped prompting me, and waited.

The ringing went long enough that I was starting to lose hope when a soprano voice picked up with a breathless, "Hello?"

I relaxed. "Hey, Marcia. How far did you have to run?"

"Other side of the—Toby? Is that you?"

"That's me," I confirmed.

As a quarter-blooded changeling, Marcia is proof that Lily has a generous soul; most purebloods would never think of employing someone like her. She's too human to have any real magic, too fae to want to live in the human world, and too flaky to do much beyond sitting around and looking decorative. Still, she'd been nice enough, after we got past the part where I introduced myself by enchanting her into letting me in without paying.

"Did you want me to get Lily?" she asked.

"No, actually, I was calling for you. I wanted to ask a favor."

Now her tone turned wary. "What kind of favor?"

"I know the Court of Cats doesn't have a phone. Can you go find Tybalt and tell him I need him to call me at ALH Computing? I have the main number, and I need to talk to him."

"Go find Tybalt? How are you expecting me to do *that*?"

"I don't know. Get a can of tuna and go around the Park calling 'Here, kitty, kitty'?" I sighed. "Look, you know I wouldn't ask this if it weren't important. Please?"

"All right," she said, dubiously. "But if he guts me . . ."

"If he threatens you, tell him to take it out on me instead."

"I will."

"Good." We talked for a few minutes, Marcia chattering about the latest gossip while I sipped my coffee and made interested noises at the right places. When she started winding down, I said good-bye and hung up, immediately dialing again. Shadowed Hills, this time; I wanted to keep Sylvester posted.

My call rang straight to voice mail. I frowned, recorded a quick, curt message, and hung up again, turning to look for Quentin and Alex.

Quentin was buying bags of chips from a vending machine, while Alex was loading a plate with donuts from the counter. Ah, the eating habits of the young and healthy. Alex had to be an exercise junkie: there was no other way he could maintain his figure, which definitely didn't betray the fact that he appeared to live on starch and sugar.

Pulling my attention away from Alex, I surveyed the rest of the cafeteria. There was only one more person present, head bowed over a heap of disorganized-looking notes. I frowned thoughtfully and moved to fill a tray before starting in her direction.

"Mind if I sit down?"

Gordan grunted assent, not looking up. Putting down my tray, I sat, taking the opportunity to study her more carefully. I still couldn't identify her bloodline; her eyes were throwing me. They were dark gray speckled with flecks of muddy red, like rusty iron. There's no race in Faerie with those eyes. I'd already pegged her as a changeling—more fae than human, but human enough to be mortal—and those eyes confirmed it. The only question was what her bloodline *was*.

She looked up, scowling. "Coblynau."

I lowered my coffee mug. "What?"

"You were going to ask—I saw you staring. My mother was Coblynau; my father wasn't." Her brows knotted together. "And yes, he was half-human. Happy now?"

"Oh. Sorry." I felt the blush run up the back of my neck. I hadn't realized how obvious I was being.

"Yeah, you better be. You corpse-lickers having any luck with the dead?"

"Better than you would, metal-whore," I replied, genially.

There are derogatory terms for every race in Faerie; it would be more surprising if there weren't. What *is* surprising is how rarely most of them are used—but then, the fae usually get insulting with spears and siege engines. "Corpse-licker" is one of the more pleasant insults. The less civil ones delve into the nature of the night-haunts and exactly where we spend our nights. Those are fighting words. "Corpse-licker" is just casual profanity.

The Coblynau are the best smiths in Faerie. They can

trap enchantment in living metal, creating spells that last for years; they're artists in a world with little art that it doesn't steal, creating beauty for the joy of it. They're also tiny, twisted, ugly people, scarred by the iron that stains their blood. Some spend their lives in darkness, pretending they don't care what goes on above, while others come to the faerie markets and barter their masterworks for the types of favor only Faerie's more beautiful children can provide. They're metal's whores. Supposedly, it's a fair trade on both sides. Sometimes, anyway.

Gordan's scowl vanished, replaced by a grin that transformed her face into a mask of cheerful wrinkles. I couldn't help wondering what her mother paid for the pleasure of bearing a mixed-blood child. "All right, you can stay," she said.

"How nice of you," I said. Quentin walked up, expression curious, and I nodded to the seat next to me. He put down his tray and sat, moving with an almost exaggerated care.

"I thought so." Gordan's smile faded when Quentin sat, hardening into something less pleasant. "Who's the pretty boy? We have sheltered jerks in town already—you didn't have to bring your own."

I looked at her impassively, not rising to the bait. "Quentin, meet Gordan. Gordan, this is my assistant, Quentin. He's a foster at Shadowed Hills."

"Ooh, a *courtly* pretty boy." Her lips pursed in a moue of distaste. "How much did they pay you to baby-sit? Because it wasn't enough."

Quentin bristled. I put a hand on his shoulder. "They're not paying me. He's here because Duke Torquill thought he might be able to learn something from working with me for a while." I nodded toward his tray, and he started picking at his lunch, still glowering.

"Huh," said Gordan. "Looks like you got screwed on *that* deal."

"Maybe, maybe not," I said, shrugging. "What are you working on?"

She held up her notebook, shooting a sour look at Quentin as she displayed a snarl of notes interspersed with thumbnail sketches of machine parts. It looked like an illustration from *Alice in Wonderland* interpreted by Picasso. "I'm rebuilding one of the routers."

"Okay . . ."

She sighed, recognizing my feeble reply as an admission of ignorance. "Look. Routers move information—data—around. I think I can change the hardware, and make that data move twice as fast."

"Right," I said, nodding. "I think that makes sense."

"Good." Her tone shifted. "Do you two morons have any clue what you're doing?"

"What do you mean?" said Quentin.

Gordan leaned back in her chair, splitting her attention between us. Her eyes were cold. "Either Jan's uncle sent you, like you say, or you're here for Riordan and lying about it. I don't care. What I want to know is whether you're going to make people stop dying. Do you know what you're doing, or are you going to string us along until you can run?"

An interrogation over lunch—just what I always wanted. "We're here by order of Duke Sylvester Torquill, and yes, we're staying until it's over."

"Brave souls. Stupid, but brave. How long before your little boy runs back to the nursery? We probably don't meet his lofty standards."

"At least I *have* standards," Quentin snapped.

"Quentin, be quiet. I don't see you going anywhere, Gordan. Why should we?"

She smiled again, bitterly this time. "Where would I go? This is my home." She had a point. That didn't explain why she was being so nasty to Quentin.

"You're right," I said. "So, since you're a native, care

to share any ideas you might have on who could have done this?"

"What?" She laughed. "Not one. I'd blame Yui if she hadn't been the second one down—the little fox always had a vicious turn of mind. But no. We're down to the dregs, and none of the chumps we have left would have the brains to start killing people."

"Not one of them?"

"No." She put her notebook down, looking disgusted. "Let's guess. You're expecting me to think for a minute and then go 'Hmmm, Alex is very quiet except for his collection of ice picks and hammers,' aren't you? You hoping to get this wrapped up before the commercials?"

"Actually, no. I just wanted your opinion."

"My opinion? Fine: you're wasting your time if you're looking for a killer in this company. We're a family."

"Does that go for the ones that have run out on you?"

"Maybe they ran, but that just means they had something to live for. It doesn't mean they betrayed us. If you want to find a killer, look outside. Or don't bother, and die here with the rest of us." She picked up her fork, jabbing it into a piece of cantaloupe. "Send the kid home if you decide to do that. Dying would mess up his hair."

Quentin glared at her, but focused on his chips. Good boy. I picked up my coffee, saying, "You're a little pessimistic."

"Am I? Wow, I'm sorry. Try having all your friends die or run and see how cheery *you* are." Her eyes narrowed. "You come down here with your little pureblood squire and say you want to 'help.' Yeah, right. That won't last. In the end, you'll run scared like the others."

"Maybe. Maybe not." I shrugged. "And he's not my squire, just my friend."

"Funny taste in friends." Gordan stood, tucking her notebook under her arm. "I hope you're a better judge of murder scenes than you are of people." She turned and stalked away, not bothering to say good-bye.

"That's not fair," Quentin said. "She's the one insulting us, and she gets to walk away?"

"Dramatic exits are the last refuge of the infantile personality," I said. "Now drink your soda and help me think of nasty names to call her next time she shows up."

"All right." Not even being insulted could make him lose his appetite: he was eating his chips with astonishing speed and was starting to filch pieces of fruit cocktail off Gordan's abandoned tray. Good for him.

"Told you that you were hungry," I said, earning an amused snort from Quentin. I ignored my lunch in favor of propping my chin on my knuckles and sipping my coffee. Gordan disliked Quentin on sight. She might just be prejudiced—some changelings really hate purebloods—but that didn't explain how she justified working for Jan.

Alex reached the table, pushing Gordan's now-empty tray aside to make room for his own. "Whoa!" he said, spotting our expressions. "Was the coffee that bad?"

"We just had a nice talk with Gordan," I said.

"Gordan, huh?" Alex sighed, brushing his bangs back with one hand. They immediately flopped back over his eyes. "I'm sorry. She's always been a little . . ."

"Nasty?" Quentin said.

"I was going to say 'sharp,' but if you want to go with nasty, we can work with that. It's not her fault."

"So whose fault is it?" I asked. "The Tooth Fairy?"

Alex shook his head. "No, I mean it—it's *not* her fault. Barbara was her best friend. Losing her . . . I'm surprised Gordan's holding up as well as she is. That's all."

Some information has the effect of making me feel like a total jerk. "Oh," I said.

Alex's statement didn't seem to hit Quentin the same way. He scowled, asking, "Why does that make it okay for her to act like I'm the bad guy?"

"She was a little harsh," I said. "If she didn't work for Jan, I'd assume she was racist."

"She is, a little," Alex said. "Being a Coblynau kid isn't easy. She got knocked around a lot before she hooked up with Barbara, and I think she holds a few grudges. I mean, she was working here for over a year before she stopped being nasty to the purebloods on staff."

"So why . . ."

"Because she's good, and because she was the only Coblynau who needed the work. Jan needed somebody who could handle iron, at least until we got all the systems fully working. By the time her first contract was finished, she was hooked, and she stayed." He shrugged. "She's the one who convinced Jannie to hire Barbara. So, I mean, she does settle down."

"Well, if she listens to you, you might try telling her we're just doing our jobs."

"We want to help," Quentin added, wounded pride overcoming his dislike of Alex. I was sure that would be temporary.

Alex sighed. "I know you're coming into this cold. I'll do whatever I can to help."

"You've been a lot of help so far," I said.

"It's not a problem," he said. "We've been milling around like a flock of sheep—it's nice to have something to do. And I'm really, really sorry I couldn't say anything earlier."

"Right," I said.

"What I'm saying is that if you need help, go ahead and ask me." Alex grinned. I grinned back, at least until Quentin "accidentally" kicked me in the ankle. I shot him a warning glare. He smiled angelically.

". . . and besides," Alex said, "if I have actual work to do, I can always leave it for Terrie."

Quentin brightened. "When does Terrie get here?"

"Good question," I said, more slowly. "When does she get in?"

"What?" Alex blinked.

"Your sister?" I said. He was a lot less attractive when he looked that confused. "When does she come on shift?"

"Oh. Uh . . ." He looked at his watch, then at the window. The gesture looked habitual, like he wasn't sure he could trust the time. "She usually shows up a little past eight."

Quentin asked, "Does she come find you, or what?"

"Oh, no. I'm gone by the time she gets here."

"It must be hard, never seeing your sister," I said.

"What?" He looked nervous—he didn't like us asking about Terrie. I hoped it didn't mean anything. I was really starting to like him. "Oh, yeah. I mean, no. I mean . . . we're not close."

"Okay." I changed the subject, watching his expression. "What can you tell us about the people here?"

Quentin looked like he was going to protest the change of topic, and I took great pleasure in "accidentally" kicking *him* in the ankle. "Ow!"

"What was that, Quentin?" I asked sweetly.

"Nothing," he said, glaring. He wasn't going to question me in front of Alex, and we both knew it. Knowing the weaknesses of your friends matters as much as knowing the weaknesses of your enemies.

"Keep eating." I shoved my tray over to him and turned to Alex. "You were saying?"

Alex was staring at me, dismayed. "You think it was one of us. Why?"

"Yui."

"What?" Alex said. Quentin looked up from my lunch, frowning.

I didn't blame them for not getting it; I would have missed it, too, fifteen years ago, but time has given me a new distance from Faerie. Sometimes that's a good thing. "Yui was a four-tailed Kitsune. That means she was strong, fast, and had pretty powerful magic, right?"

Alex nodded. I continued, "Whatever killed her took her by surprise—we know she didn't struggle. We also know she was strong enough to defend herself: she could have fought back, and the amount of power she had would have stopped most people. It would *definitely* have stopped someone like me. That means one of two things. Either her killer was something so nasty that it could take down a four-tailed Kitsune without a fight, or . . ."

"Or it was someone she knew," Alex said, horrified. "I didn't even think of that."

"Most people wouldn't." Most people don't spend as much time dealing with death as I do. Lucky them.

"If it was a monster, would the bodies have been there?" Quentin asked.

"That depends on what it eats. The best answer is 'probably not'—we could be dealing with something that killed in self-defense, but killing for food is more likely, and I've never heard of something that can kill a Kitsune but wouldn't eat the body. Have there been any unexplained disappearances in the County that you haven't reported to the Crown?"

"What? No. We report all deaths and disappearances to the Queen's Court."

"Up until this most recent batch, you mean," I said.

"Yes. No. I . . . Jan tried to report those!"

"To her uncle, not the Queen, but whatever. I'm not going to fight with you. I'm just going to trust that if you think of any deaths I'm missing, you'll tell me. Have you found any unusual tracks or spoor? Animal markings? We might have a shapeshifter on our hands."

"Not that I've heard of." He leaned forward, putting his hands over his face. "I can't believe one of us is doing this. I just can't."

"I'm sorry," I said, and I meant it; it hurts when your family betrays you.

"You could be wrong," Alex said, through his fingers.

"We could be," I agreed. "How long has the company been here?"

Alex lifted his head. He wasn't crying, but it was only a matter of time. "Seven years."

"Where was the company before it was here?"

"Uptown, near the Dreamer's Glass border. We found land we could connect to the Summerlands about eight years ago, and we wanted to get farther away from Duchess Riordan, so we started construction."

"But you could only open a Shallowing?"

"The ley lines weren't deep enough to allow for anything else."

"Maybe you woke something up, and it just took a while to realize dinner was right above it. If you did, a lot more people will die before we find out what it is and how to stop it." I wasn't pulling punches. There's a time for mercy, but it's never on the killing grounds.

"If it was one of us," he said, slowly, "the worst thing you're facing is . . . one of us."

"That, or a shapeshifter impersonating one of the employees." I took a sip of my coffee. "I'm not happy with either choice, but they're the options we have." Quentin had fallen silent again, eating my sandwich as he watched Alex.

"I see," Alex said.

"Now. What do we need to know?"

Alex was quiet for a long moment. Then, taking a deep breath, he said, "ALH was Jan's idea—she provided the working capital and hired the original crew. We're part of the County, but that's a formality; we get paid for working here, we all have steady jobs, and the last time we held Court was at the company barbecue back in May."

"Was she already a Countess when she founded ALH?"

"Yes. She was titled but landless until we broke away from Dreamer's Glass."

"So how long have you worked here?"

"About twelve years. Terrie and I came from Cincinnati when Jan held the first inter-Kingdom job fair, and I've—we've—been here ever since."

I frowned. From the way he said that, I wasn't sure Terrie *had* been there the entire time. Resolving to get my hands on her personnel files, I asked, "Has Jan been a good leader?"

"One of the best." Alex leaned forward, suddenly earnest. "She doesn't think like most people. She's still good at what she does. You just have to give her a chance."

I don't usually give chances when people are dying. On the other hand . . . I once made a similar speech before the Queen's Court, when a Royal Commission was reviewing the actions of a local Duke. I said they had to give him the benefit of the doubt: that they couldn't judge him when they didn't know him. Sylvester didn't do things the way people expected, but he did well. If Alex gave Jan the same testimony, I had to give her a shot. And maybe he was right. Maybe Jan and Sylvester shared more than just the color of their eyes.

I just hoped she wasn't going to disappoint us all.

"So Jan called you here," I said. "Is there anything else I should know?"

"I don't know what you consider a 'should know.' Jan does her job. Normally, she has Elliot to take care of the details, but he's been shaky lately. Death isn't his strong point."

"It's not a strong point for a lot of people."

"You handle yourselves okay."

Quentin gave him a disbelieving look. I shook my head, and said, "I've had a lot of practice," hoping that my bitterness wouldn't show. I was sure it would. "Is there anyone else you think I should know about?"

"Huh." He tilted his head to one side. "You've met Gordan, Elliot, and Jan—Peter's locked in his office working on a deadline, and Terrie's on the night shift."

"And then there's April."

Alex almost smiled, agreeing, "And then there's April. I take it you met?"

"Blonde kid, glasses, talks like the Oracle at Delphi when she was in junior high. Yeah, we met."

"She's creepy," Quentin added.

"Dryads generally are," I said, offhandedly, and paused. "That's how she disappeared." Dryads are one of the only races that can teleport entirely on their own. The normal ones need to be close to their trees, but if April had been integrated with the company network, she probably just needed to be close to a power outlet.

"Exactly," Alex confirmed.

Quentin looked at me, wide-eyed. "She's a Dryad?"

"It's a long story. Alex—"

The rest of my question was lost when April appeared next to the table, sending an electric shock through the air. I jumped, and Quentin yelped.

April looked at him. "Are you all right?" The concern sounded rehearsed.

"I'm fine," Quentin muttered.

"You . . . surprised us," I added.

"Mother is looking for you," she said, feigned concern dissolving. "She wants to talk to you and has asked me to find you." She made it sound like being out of Jan's sight was a crime.

"So I guess we should go to her, hmm?" said Alex, grinning. She looked back at him, unimpressed: it was the first genuine expression I'd seen on her face. "Is she in her office?"

April considered for a moment before she nodded, saying, "Currently."

"Let her know we'll be right there, okay?"

"You will come directly?" Her tone implied we'd get distracted and wander off, leaving her to take the blame.

"Yep."

"Excellent." She vanished. The air rushed into the place she'd been with a gentle popping sound, leaving the smell of ozone behind.

"Sounds like that's our cue. Quentin, come on." I stood, finishing my coffee. Grumbling, Quentin did the same, my half-eaten sandwich in one hand. I looked to Alex. "Come on, native guide. Lead the way."

"My pleasure," said Alex, and grinned as he led us out of the cafeteria.

The knowe remained convoluted, verging on labyrinthine, but Alex didn't miss a beat, turning corners and navigating halls I would've sworn weren't there earlier. It wasn't that surprising; he'd been working there long enough to have adjusted to the fact that the ground floor was on the roof and could only be reached by going down three flights of stairs. It didn't take me that long to learn how to park in San Francisco, and that's arguably worse.

Jan's door was propped open with a brick. She was seated on the desk inside, laptop balanced on her knees. Drifts of paper littered the floor, knocked aside by her fidgeting.

I rapped on the doorframe. "Hello?"

Her head snapped up. "What—oh. It's you." She relaxed, smiling. "Hi, Toby, Quentin. Hey, Alex."

"Hey," Alex replied. He didn't enter the office.

"April said you wanted us?" I stepped inside, Quentin stuffing the last of my sandwich into his mouth, swallowing, and assuming his usual "I am in the presence of nobility" stance. He was definitely developing a working definition of teenage expedience: I've never seen anyone swallow that much ham and cheese without chewing before.

"Yeah." She slid off the desk, putting her laptop aside. "Alex, could you excuse us?"

"No problem—I was sort of expecting it. Toby, if you

need me, ask Jan to show you my office." He waved and left, closing the door behind himself.

I watched him go, then turned toward Jan, looking at her speculatively before I spoke. "April looks like you, if you ignore the hair."

"She does, doesn't she?" Jan smiled. "She was protean at first—changed her face every time she appeared—but then she decided I was her mother and started looking like me. It's a good thing she identifies as blonde, or we'd get really confused."

"Alex told me what you did," I said. "How did you . . ."

"She had a living branch when she escaped the grove. I thought 'Dryads live in trees, but nothing says they have to live in physical trees'—they're physical manifestations of the spirits of trees *anyway,* so why do they need wood?" She gave a one-shouldered shrug. "I cracked a server box and worked bits of the branch she was carrying into the circuitry before the sap dried. When she started to vanish, I closed the box and restored the power—and when it came back on-line, so did she. Instant cyber-Dryad."

"Impressive." There was a new sharpness in her eyes and voice when she talked about April's rescue; it was almost like talking to someone else. I was starting to understand how most people felt when they dealt with Sylvester for the first time. It was easy to assume that outward flakiness equaled stupidity. People have died making that assumption about Sylvester; I wasn't going to make the same mistake about his niece.

Quentin was also watching her, frowning. The kid caught on quick. "Why did you call us here?" he asked.

Jan paused, enthusiasm dimming. "I needed to talk to you."

"We're here," I said. "Talk."

"I've got those files you asked for—and I wanted to know what you found in the basement."

"Nothing." I shook my head. "Quentin and I both tried, and we didn't get anything. Maybe my mother could work with their blood, but we can't. We're not strong enough."

"Is there anything else you can try?" she asked.

"Not without access to a police lab. Forensics isn't my strong suit, and without proper equipment, it's practically impossible."

"We can't involve the police."

"I know." The Fair Folk have it pretty good these days; no one believes in us anymore, and so we're free to live our lives. It wasn't always like that—there were bad times before we were forgotten, centuries filled with fire and iron. Not even the truly insane members of the Unseelie Court want to go back to that . . . but give the mortal world three fae corpses and we wouldn't have a choice. That much proof of our existence would bring the old days back, whether we wanted them or not, and I'd face down Oberon himself before I'd let that happen.

Jan sighed. "I tried calling my uncle again."

"And?"

"And nothing." She shook her head. "I can't get a person. I left another message."

"I left a message for him, too, and one for the San Francisco King of Cats. I'm hoping he can help me figure out what would have been able to get the jump on Barbara."

Jan nodded. "Keep me posted?"

"Of course."

"Good. Is there anything else you need?"

"Yes, actually," I said. "I want a list of the people who had access to the cafeteria when Barbara was found. If there are any security cameras that *didn't* have mysterious breakdowns just before the killings, I'll need to see what they recorded. I also want the places where bodies have been found roped off until Quentin and I can go over them—that includes the lawn outside the knowe."

"Done and done. Do you have any idea what could be behind this?"

"I don't think it's a 'what.' I think it's—" I stopped as the overhead lights flickered and died. The computers along the back wall went dark, and something started beeping stridently.

"This isn't right," said Jan. Her posture had shifted, reflecting tightly controlled panic.

"You don't get power outages?" Dim light slanted through the room's single window, outlining the desks. I walked to the window, pulling the drape aside and looking out at the grounds. "Quentin, check the door."

I'll give him this: he moved with admirable urgency, taking up a blocking posture next to the door. He wasn't letting Jan out until I said he could.

Jan didn't seem to have noticed. "No, we don't. The power never goes out."

"The electric company does it to me all the time." There was no one on the lawn; just the standard assortment of cats.

"We have generators that kick in before the lights even flicker. We can't *afford* to lose power." She started for the door. "We have systems that should never go offline. April—"

"Jan, stop." She froze. "Give me a second. Where are the generators stored, and who has access?"

"They're in a room next to the servers, and everybody's got access. I don't even know if the door locks. What's going on?"

"I don't know." I started for the door. "We need to go check the generators."

"Follow me." She reached for the doorknob. I nodded to Quentin and he stepped aside, letting her lead us out of the room.

The halls were even stranger in the dark, filled with shadows that didn't quite match the objects casting them. Jan strode through them without flinching. Quentin followed close behind while I dropped back, taking the rear. Maybe we weren't going to be attacked, but I refused to count on that when Jan was so *sure* the power couldn't go out. She knew her company.

Jan stepped into the generator room and screamed.

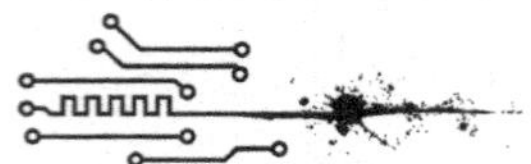

ELEVEN

I ONLY CAUGHT A GLIMPSE of what was in the room before I yanked Jan back into the hall, slamming the door behind her. "Peter," she said, staring at the door. "That was Peter."

"I thought you didn't have any night vision. How can you be sure?"

"No one else in this company has wings."

"Damn." I looked back toward the door. "I need to go in there."

"Are you sure that's wise?" Jan asked, frowning.

"Without backup?" asked Quentin.

"I need to see the body, and that means I need to get the generators back up. How do I do that?" Death doesn't bother me, but murder makes me edgy, and my lack of weaponry suddenly felt like a potentially fatal mistake. If we got back to the hotel alive, I wasn't coming here again without my knife and the baseball bat. And maybe a tank, if I could find one fast enough.

"Right." Jan sighed. "There's an orange switch on the second box inside the door. If there's any gas left in the generators, you should be able to force them back on-line by flipping the switch, waiting thirty seconds, and flipping it again."

"Okay." Looking to Quentin, I said, "Stay here. If you see anything out of the ordinary or anyone acting strangely, grab Jan and run; I'll catch up. Understand?"

"Yes," he said. If he disapproved of my orders, he wasn't showing it.

Jan looked like she was going to argue, but quieted when I glared at her. She was starting to display signs of sense.

"Good," I said, before opening the generator room door and stepping inside.

The room was dark, lit only by a small, thick-glassed window, and looked deserted. That didn't mean there was nothing in the room with me—just that anything that might be hiding in those shadows knew how to be quiet. Sometimes I wish I wasn't such a positive thinker.

I paused, scanning the shadows while my eyes adjusted. I caught a flicker of motion out of the corner of one eye and whirled. There was nothing there. The "motion" was just the late afternoon sunlight slanting through the window and glinting along the edge of a steel girder. I stopped, taking a shuddery breath.

Finding the second generator from the door wasn't hard: I inched along the wall until my thigh hit something sharp, stepped back, and then inched forward again until I hit something else. I wasn't willing to move away from the wall; Peter was a dark blur at the center of the floor, and I didn't want to step on him by mistake.

I was jumpier than I thought. I groped around until I found the panel with the switches; figuring out which one to flip was harder. The longer I stood there, the shakier I was getting, and Jan and Quentin were in the hall alone and unarmed. Time mattered. I settled for flipping the largest switch I could find, waiting thirty seconds and flipping it again. My heart thudded in my ears like a steel drum until the sound of the generator revving drowned it out. The engine coughed twice, turned over—and the lights came back on. I almost immediately wished that they hadn't.

Peter was on his back, barely recognizable as the man we met when we arrived. Death had finally removed his human disguise. He was four feet tall, with delicate antennae and feathered gray hair, lying on a blanket made by his own gray-and-green wings. He'd been a Cornish Pixie, almost the only pixie breed large enough to interact with the bulk of Faerie as an equal.

Well, he wasn't going to be doing anything as an equal anymore: he wasn't going to be arguing about whether Klingon was a language, or confusing visiting changelings by wearing a human disguise when everyone else had shed theirs. It was starting to look like the ALH retirement plan was "get found dead in the back room." Punctures broke his skin at the wrists and throat, dispelling the illusion that he was only sleeping. He was never going to wake up.

I knelt, touching his throat, and winced as I felt the lingering warmth of his skin. Blood and a thin film of dust covered my fingers: pixie-sweat. That gave me a time of death. Pixies stop "dusting" when they die, and the glittery traces they leave behind dissolve quickly. He couldn't have been dead when the lights went out, or the pixie-sweat would have already faded.

The lights came back up too easily to have been sabotaged, but it made no sense for whoever had killed Peter to have also killed the power. The body would have gone undiscovered for hours, maybe even days, if we hadn't needed to restart the generator. The killer could have had time to make a clean run of it . . . unless they knew that turning off the generators would lead us to the body, and were hoping to lead me—or maybe Jan—straight to Peter. This could have been a trap or a sick display. And, either way, someone wanted us to find the body.

Things were *not* looking up.

I pressed my fingers to my lips, sampling the blood. Pixie-sweat masked the normal copper taste in a veil of ashes and burnt sugar, cloying, but no more unpleasant than usual. I wasn't hoping for much, and I wasn't disappointed. There was nothing in the blood—no life, no memory, nothing. It was empty.

The room only had the one door, plus the small, heavy-glassed window: logically, no one could have left once I was inside. Unfortunately, we were in a faerie knowe, where logic didn't always apply. I stood, backing out of the room and closing the door behind me. Peter could wait a while—the dead are patient. "Quentin?"

"Here," he said.

Good. I hadn't left them to be slaughtered. Pulling the door shut, I turned. "He's dead."

Quentin nodded. "Now what?"

"Now we start to work." I turned toward Jan. "Is there any other way into this room?"

"No," she said, shaking her head. "Just the one door."

"Could April have gone inside without using it?"

"Not while the power was out," said Jan firmly.

"Right. Quentin, set the wards." He turned to blink at me, surprised. I smiled thinly. "Call it practice." Practice, and avoiding a headache. As a pureblooded Daoine Sidhe, Quentin's wards would be stronger than mine, and they'd cost him a lot less.

Nodding with sudden enthusiasm, Quentin stepped over to the closed door and raised his hands. The smell of steel and fresh-blooming heather rose around him, and the outline of the door flashed red, then white. Lowering his hands, he turned to look to me, as if for approval. I flashed him a thumbs-up, and he beamed, looking briefly, deeply, pleased. That was apparently exactly what he'd wanted. At least one of us was happy.

I turned my attention back to Jan. "We're going to need to move the body, but we can't do it alone. Let's go find Elliot."

"All right," she said, nodding.

We'd only gone about ten yards when we heard someone running down the intersecting hall ahead of us. I pulled Jan to a stop, signaling for Quentin to get her against the wall, and started forward alone. It could be just another of the locals—but it could also be something worse, and none of us were armed. The best I could do was try to find out without getting us killed.

I had almost reached the corner when Gordan ran into the open, skidding to a stop as she spotted us. She'd obviously left whatever she was doing in a hurry; grease stains smeared her shirt and arms. "What are *you* doing here? And what are you doing to Jan?"

"Keeping her out of the basement," I snapped.

"Gordan, it's all right," said Jan. "I don't want to be wandering around alone."

Gordan's hands were clean, unlike the rest of her. "What *happened*?" she demanded. She was glaring, but the bulk of her fury seemed reserved for Quentin. Poor kid.

"Peter's gone," Jan said. Gordan's scowl collapsed, eyes going wide in a suddenly young face. I couldn't ignore the question there, no matter how much I wanted to.

"He's dead," I confirmed, moving to join Jan and Quentin against the wall. "We found him in the generator room just after the power went out. The killer wanted him found."

"And what are you going to do about it?" Her voice had gone shrill and brassy. "That's two of us since you got here! There's almost no one *left*! Why haven't you stopped this?"

I put my arm out to stop Quentin even as he started moving forward. "Down, boy."

"But, Toby—"

"I know. Calm down. I'll handle it." He glowered. I

turned to Gordan. "We can't do *anything* until we know what's going on. If you're not going to help, I suggest you leave."

Gordan stared at us, shivering. I stared back, outwardly calm and inwardly seething.

Finally, Gordan shook her head. "You're right. But these are our friends . . ."

"And we'll do our best. But I need to know that we'll have whatever help we need."

"You will," said Jan. Stepping forward, she took Gordan's hand with surprising tenderness and led her down the hall.

"Come on, Quentin," I said, and followed, Quentin half a step behind. That was how we progressed through the knowe: Jan at the lead with Gordan leaning on her arm, me just behind, and Quentin following. Three of us jumped at every shadow, while Gordan just walked blindly on. Two deaths in a day seemed to have been a bit too much for her.

Terrie was in the cafeteria when we arrived, standing by the vending machines. Her hair was tousled, and she was yawning, still marked by sleep. Quentin perked up, smiling and waving as if we hadn't just found a body on the floor of the generator room. I repressed a bolt of bitter irritation, aimed more at her than him. How dare she rest while people were dying?

Jan let go of Gordan's arm, calling to Terrie, "Peter's dead. Stay here while I reboot April and get Elliot." She turned and left, moving too quickly for me to tell her to stop.

I considered the value of running after her and shouting. It didn't seem likely to do any good. "You people and the walking blithely into certain danger. It's got to be something in the damn water."

Terrie stared after her. "What?" She turned toward us, repeating, "What?"

"Peter's dead," I said, walking over to get a cup of coffee. Gordan moved to a table and sat, burying her face in her hands.

"But—what—when? How?"

"During the blackout," said Quentin.

"They cut the power, killed the generators, and then killed him. Probably to get our attention." I sipped my coffee. "They got it."

"Oh," whispered Terrie, eyes wide. "Are you sure?"

"I'm sure. I know what dead looks like."

"Oh, Maeve, Peter . . ." she said. "He was such a wonderful engineer . . ."

I opened my mouth to snap, and stopped as I saw the look on Quentin's face. He was watching Terrie with utter adoration, caught up in her pain. That made even less sense than my anger. He'd been temperamental but sane through this whole ordeal, facing everything with calm equanimity. So why was he getting involved *now*? They'd flirted, but they hadn't had time to fall in love, and something in his expression reminded me uncomfortably of my own when I was looking at Alex.

I was saved from following that thought to its logical conclusion when the door swung open and Jan and Elliot stepped into the room. Elliot was shaking and glassy-eyed. At least his voice was steady: he answered when I asked if they'd seen anything in the hall. They hadn't. Not a damn thing.

Explaining what we knew didn't take long; there wasn't much to tell. Elliot crossed the room and put his hands on Gordan's shoulders, but didn't interrupt. Jan nodded, confirming my story, then offered some useful information—I hadn't thought to check the generators for loose wires, or realized that their internal systems would record and time stamp the power outage.

Elliot, Quentin, Jan, and I went back to the generator room, leaving Terrie and Gordan behind. Even with the power on, the knowe didn't seem any friendlier. Some kinds of darkness have nothing to do with whether there's light.

The wards on the generator room were undisturbed. Quentin released them, and I stepped inside, taking a moment to study the scene before I let the others in. Peter was still intact; the night-haunts weren't coming. The forensic tests I could perform—checking for footprints, tracks, and blood trails, noting the wounds and their locations on Peter's body—took only a few minutes. Jan ran the tests on the equipment; there were no loose wires, and the generators time stamped the power outage at 7:49 PM—not exactly the witching hour. No leads there.

I looked to Jan, frowning. "Could he have turned the generators off as he fell? Could this have been a coincidence?"

"No way," Jan replied. "You have to trip three breakers and press a button on the back of the main generator if you want to shut the system down. Failsafes."

"Why do you know that?" She'd rattled off that chain of actions a little too glibly for my tastes.

Tiredly, Elliot said, "Jan does a lot of our hardware maintenance, especially now that we're on a skeleton crew. She has to be able to kill the power in case of an emergency."

"Plus, I designed a lot of these systems," Jan said.

Elliot smiled wearily. "That, too."

"Right," I said, raking my hair back with both hands and sighing. "So it was intentional."

"Looks like it," Jan said. "Unless a dying man knows what fuses to pull."

"Okay. Let's get moving."

The four of us wrapped as much of Peter's body as we could in a sheet, careful not to break his wings, and we carried him down to the basement, clearing off a counter before laying him down. Elliot shuddered the whole time. He was starting to look rumpled; I was worried that our Bannick was going to pieces.

"What do we do now?" he asked, not looking at me.

"Now we hunt," I said. I looked to Jan, expecting an argument, but she nodded. "Elliot, you're with me; Quentin, with Jan. If you see anything, don't investigate. Just run."

"All right," said Quentin. And we were off.

The halls of ALH were snarled like Möbius strips, bending back on themselves in strange and implausible ways. Some rooms were brightly lit, while others were illuminated only by the dim light lancing in from outside. We searched room by room, hunting through closets and cubbyholes and finding more secret routes than I wanted to believe. Tracking anyone would have been a nightmare, but tracking a native—and that was what we had to be looking for—was going to be all but impossible. Thanks to the recent personnel losses, I couldn't even be sure that the person we were looking for was one of our known suspects.

We found nothing. And I kept thinking of Terrie's exaggerated mourning and Gordan's too-clean hands.

Elliot and I had just stepped into the reception room when Quentin and Jan came around the corner. They stopped when they saw us.

"Anything?" I asked.

"Nothing," said Quentin.

"Right." Whoever killed Peter was cocky, and the cocky are frequently good; that's how they live long enough to *get* that way. Unless our killer could walk through walls, we were finished. "Come on, Quentin. We're going back to the hotel."

Elliot stared at me, eyes shell-shocked and pleading. "Can't you stay?"

"Stay in groups. No one's been attacked when they weren't alone. Quentin and I need to go back to the hotel and get our things." Mainly, we needed to get my weapons. "We'll be back before dawn."

"Be careful," said Jan.

"We will," I said. Somehow, I couldn't be angry with them anymore. Their world was falling apart, and they knew it. "Quentin, come on."

We walked into the cool night air together, letting the door slide closed behind us. We were halfway to the car when Quentin said, "Toby?"

"Yeah?"

"Are we coming back?"

"Yes, we are. We have a job to do. Are you holding up okay?"

"I'm scared." He said it like he expected me to yell at him.

I shook my head. "So am I, Quentin. Believe me, so am I."

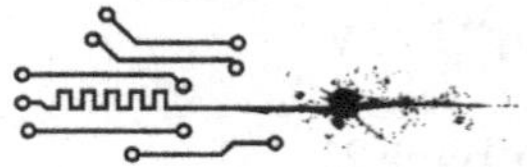

TWELVE

THE DESK CLERK CRINGED when we stormed through the lobby. Quentin had crafted his human disguise during the drive from ALH, and I'd slammed mine into place in the parking lot. It wasn't very well sealed, but I didn't care. It was just there to keep us out of the tabloids until we'd reached our rooms and taken what we needed. Colin's sealskin was slung over my arm, disguised to look like a slightly dingy towel; I wanted to keep it out of harm's way, so that it could be returned to his family when everything was finished—if we survived.

We could probably have done without the disguises; the desk clerk was the only one in sight, and he was a pale, worried man who'd never have recognized what we really were; a child of the modern world, raised to think of faeries as pastel creatures dressed in flower petals and bathing in moonbeams. If he saw us undisguised, he'd think he was looking at a kid playing Star Trek games and a giant Tinker Bell knockoff with PMS, and he wouldn't understand why he wanted to run away. I glanced at him as we passed, and he flinched. Looking away, I shook my head. It never gets better. I don't think it ever will.

The humans aren't stupid, no matter what the purebloods say; they're just blind, and sometimes, that's worse. They put their fear in stories and songs, where they won't forget it. "Up the airy mountains and down the rushy glen, I dare not go a-hunting for fear of little men." We've given them plenty of reasons to fear us. Even if they've almost forgotten—even if they only remember that we were beautiful and not why they were afraid—the fear was there before anything else. There were reasons for the burning times; there's a reason the fairy tales survive. And there's a reason the human world doesn't want to see the old days come again.

Neither do most of the fae, myself included. Faerie didn't need changelings to bridge the worlds in those days: her children ruled the night, and they were going to live forever. It didn't last—it *couldn't* last—but they didn't know that then. Time made Faerie weak while it made the humans strong; that's the reason people like me can exist. Faerie is finally weak enough to need us. So, no, I don't want the dark years back; I don't want to rule the night or cower in the dark, and those would be my choices. But there are times when I want to drop the illusions and say, "Look, I'm a person, just like you. Can we please stop hiding from each other? We have better things to do."

I want to. But I never will.

Quentin and I stepped out of the elevator on the fourth floor. "What now?" he said.

"Get what you need—some clean clothes, any weapons you have. You did bring some kind of weapon, didn't you?" He shook his head. I sighed. "What are they teaching you?"

"Etiquette, heraldry, how not to offend visiting dignitaries . . . that sort of stuff," he said.

"Unless you're planning on dining with Kings and Queens on a regular basis, none of that's as important as having something sharp to put between yourself and whatever's trying to kill you. Understand?" When I got done shouting at Sylvester, we were going to have words about Quentin's education. Shadowed Hills had plenty of knights; one of them would be able to start teaching Quentin to fight properly. Etienne, maybe. I'd have to talk to him, assuming we made it back.

"Sorry, Toby."

He looked so repentant I couldn't stay annoyed. It wasn't his fault they weren't teaching him properly. Shaking my head, I said, "Get your things and meet me in the lobby in ten minutes. We'll see what we can do about getting you something resembling a weapon."

"Got it," he said, and headed off down the hall at a fair clip. I watched him go, shaking my head. If nothing else, we could raid the cutlery section at the local all-night grocery store or something. There's always an option if you're willing to be creative. When he was out of sight, I turned and walked the short distance to my own room, digging the key out of my pocket.

Housekeeping had been through while I was out, replacing the wet towels with fresh ones and folding down the covers on the bed. It's nice to have someone play Brownie for me—that's one faerie service changelings can't sign up for, and I really need it. The word "slob" doesn't even start to cover my household skills.

My duffel was on the floor of the closet. I dropped the sealskin and scooped the bag onto the bed, rummaging through my wadded-up clothes until I found the velvet box at the bottom under my spare jeans. The ribbon fell off as I pulled the box free; not that it mattered. I'd been using it to keep things closed. It was time to open them.

We don't get to redo the past just because we don't like the way things turned out. Dare died for me. It was up to me to survive for her.

I pulled out the knife she gave me, sliding it into my belt and anchoring the hilt through one of the loops before tugging my shirt down to cover it. It was a standard faerie fighter's blade, hardened silver sharpened to a killing edge. It was also the best talisman I had. Silver doesn't burn the way iron does, but it comes closer than anything else.

The baseball bat was under the bed, tucked away where it wouldn't upset the cleaning staff more than was necessary. I picked it up, hefting it thoughtfully, and let out a breath I'd barely known I was holding. Being armed always improves my mood, especially when something's been killing people. Maybe a dead girl's knife and a stick of aluminum aren't "mighty weapons," but they'd have to do.

I picked up the phone after cramming my clothes into the bag, dialing the number for Shadowed Hills. Melly answered on the second ring. "Shadowed Hills, how may I be of service?"

"Is Sylvester there?"

She paused. "October? Child, you sound exhausted. What's the matter?"

The sound of her voice—of any voice that meant I had a chance of reaching my liege—was like sunlight through the clouds. I sat down on the edge of the bed, closing my eyes. "Just put Sylvester on, Melly. Please. It's sort of urgent."

"All right, dear, all right. Just hold on a moment."

"I'll be right here."

There was a click as she put the call on hold; Sylvester picked up less than ten seconds later, tone vibrating with concern. "October?"

I took a deep breath, letting it rush out before I said, "Hey. Did you get my message?"

"What message?" He sounded honestly perplexed. "I've been waiting for you to call. Is everything all right? What's going on?"

"No. Everything's not all right. Everything's not even a little bit all right. Listen." And I told him what was going on. There was a lot of ground to cover, especially since he kept breaking in with questions. I did my best to answer them. In the end, there was a moment's silence, both of us waiting to hear what the other would say.

Finally, subdued, Sylvester said, "I want to call you home more than anything. You know that, don't you?"

"But you can't. I know that, too."

"No, I can't. Toby . . ."

"I want to send Quentin back to Shadowed Hills. It's not safe."

He hesitated. "If this is some sort of political attack, as you say January fears, it isn't safe to send him back alone. I'll have to find someone who can come and collect him without angering Riordan. Can you make sure he stays alive until then?"

I laughed bitterly. "I'm not sure I can keep *myself* alive until then, but I'll try."

"Do what you can," he said. "Just do me the favor of being careful?"

"I will. Check your phones, okay? I don't know why our messages aren't getting through, but it's freaking me out."

"I'll keep someone by the phone night and day. Call every six hours."

"Or what?"

He was quiet for a moment. Then, flatly, he said, "I'll think of something."

There was nothing to be said after that. I made my good-byes and hung up, shoving Colin's skin into the bag before leaving the room. Quentin was waiting in the lobby with his backpack over one shoulder, leaning against the wall by the elevators.

"What took you so long?"

"Nothing," I said. "Come on. We need to find you something to hit people with."

"What, we're going to go steal me a brick?"

"It's an idea." I started for the door. The desk clerk winced as we passed; apparently, our appearance wasn't improved by the addition of an aluminum baseball bat. I was just glad my knife was covered—he'd have had an aneurysm. I offered a genial nod, and he smiled tremulously. I was suddenly glad that we weren't checking out. His nerves weren't up to the strain of actually talking to us.

Getting to the car meant going through the garage, where the flickering overhead lights made too many shadows. I hurried us to the car. Quentin moved to the passenger side, and I caught his eyes as we peered through our respective rear-door windows. We shared a brief, wry smile. There are worse things I could do than infect the kid with a healthy sense of paranoia—for one thing, I could leave him thinking nothing in the world was ever going to hurt him.

The car was clean. I unlocked my door, leaning over to open the passenger side before tossing my things into the back. Quentin clambered in, settling his backpack between his knees.

"Any idea where we can get you a meat cleaver or something?"

"Grocery store?" he offered.

"You're on."

We pulled out and headed for the city's main drag. If anything was open, it would be there. I glanced at Quentin as I drove; he was staring pensively out the window. Shaking my head, I turned back to the road.

The hero's journey has suffered in modern years. Once we could've gotten a knight in shining armor riding to the rescue, pennants flying. These days you're lucky to get a battered changeling and her underage, half-trained assistant, and the princesses are confused technological wizards in towers of silicon and steel. Standards aren't what they used to be.

THIRTEEN

IT WAS ALMOST MIDNIGHT when we reached ALH. Quentin slid his bargain-bin carving knife back into its cardboard sheath, watching the streets scrolling by outside the window. I hadn't told him I was sending him back to Shadowed Hills. I couldn't figure out how.

"It's so dark," he said.

"Everyone's gone home."

This time, the gate didn't open at our approach. I rolled down the window and leaned out, calling, "It's Toby and Quentin. Come on, let us in." There was no answer. I was about to get out of the car and try enchanting the controls again when the gate began cranking upward.

"Maybe it's still confused from the power outage?" said Quentin.

"I guess so." I started the car again.

We were halfway through the gate when the portcullis froze above us, making a horrible grinding sound.

"Toby, what's it . . . ?"

It creaked. And then it fell.

It's funny, but they never mention the incredibly offensive design of the portcullis in those old movies about knights and castles and kings. That suddenly seemed like a glaring omission, because those spikes were sharp, heavy, and headed straight for us.

"Toby!"

"Hang on!"

Too much of the car was through the gate for me to back up; we'd get impaled if I tried. I took the only option left, slamming my foot down on the gas so hard that something snapped. There wasn't time to find out whether it was my ankle or the car. My little car did its best, the engine screaming a mechanical battle cry as it leaped forward. On a good day, it could have raced the wind.

The portcullis was faster.

The spikes at the bottom pierced the roof behind our heads, slowing us to a crawl. Quentin screamed. The portcullis was still descending, peeling back the roof as it went. It was going to lodge in the back seat, slamming up against the rear end, and we were going to wind up pinned.

The rear end. "Unfasten your belt," I snapped, taking my hands off the wheel.

"But—"

"Do it!" The gas tank of the old-style Volkswagen Bug is in the back of the car, not the front. I'm not a mechanic, but I'm not stupid; I know rupturing your gas tank isn't a good idea.

Quentin's eyes widened as he fumbled with his belt. I pulled mine off and tried the door—jammed.

I reached back and grabbed my baseball bat, shouting, "Duck!" Quentin ducked. I swung the bat, hitting the windshield as hard as I could. It cracked but didn't break. Safety glass. It's a great idea, until it's keeping you in a car that's about to get shish-kabobbed by the world's biggest cooking fork. Swearing, I fumbled the glove compartment open, pulling out a spray bottle of marsh water mixed with antifreeze. I'd used it for a case two weeks earlier that required a little breaking and entering, along with the usual assortment of small misdemeanors. Fortunately for me, Barrow Wights aren't really in much of a position to press charges.

"Toby, what are you—"

"Quiet!" I squinted my eyes closed, chanting, "Apples-oranges-pudding-and-pie! Can't find the door and nobody knows why!" I pulled the top off the spray bottle, flinging the liquid across the glass. The smell of antifreeze filled the car, overwhelming the sudden copper and cut grass flare of my magic. The windshield trembled, going milky with fractures before it imploded and showered us with shards. I threw the bat out the window, twisting around to face Quentin.

He was straightening, wide-eyed, fragments of glass glittering in his hair. "What—" he began, words dissolving in a startled squawk as I grabbed his shirt and tossed him onto the hood of the car. He landed on his shoulder, rolling out of sight. I braced my hands against the steering wheel, boosting myself up and diving after him.

Hitting the ground hurt more than I thought possible. I rolled with it, trying to ignore the glass shards cutting my back and sides. The hilt of my knife was digging into my waist, but at least the blade was staying in place—bruises would be much easier to deal with than accidentally gutting myself.

Dimly, I hoped someone had taught Quentin how to fall.

Inertia pulled me to a stop. I raised my head, tensing to run. The car was pinned about eight feet behind me. The engine was still screaming, but now it sounded strained and strange, and there was a sharp, almost pensive ticking running underneath it. I'd never heard a car sound like that before.

That wasn't the worst of my problems. Quentin was sprawled on the ground a full body length back, facedown, not moving. His newly purchased knife was next to him, blade bent nearly double from the force of the fall. It hadn't defended him after all.

There's nothing wrong with my reflexes. I scrambled to my feet, ignoring the glass cutting my hands, and sprinted toward him. "Quentin!" When he didn't react, I grabbed his upper arms, dragging him upright and slinging him over my shoulders in a fireman's carry. My back and knees screamed with pain, but I didn't slow down. I needed to get some distance between us and the car.

Cars don't catch fire easily: that's a device used for dramatic effect in the movies and on television. I know that. But I also know that security systems, even ones built using the "medieval wonderland" blueprints, don't usually attack visitors. Knowing something is or isn't true doesn't change what actually happens.

I made it about ten yards before the ticking stopped. They say that when the music stops the rest is silence. That's true. What they *don't* tell you is that the silence is probably going to be painful. I kept running, stumbling as a charge raced through the air, sending a warning screaming through my bones. I know magic when I feel it. I tried to reach for the spell's source, looking for the person behind it, but it was already too late; the charge grounded itself in a spray of half-visible sparks, obliterating the caster's magical signature.

The car exploded.

The wave of heat came first, racing ahead of the shrapnel and knocking us both to the ground. Quentin was jolted out of my hold, landing about four feet away. I let forward momentum carry me into a roll, ignoring the pain reawakening in my shoulders, back, and knees. I had more pressing problems, like the question of whether or not my hair was on fire. A chunk of the hood embedded itself in the ground a foot from my head, and I amended that idea; burning hair wasn't nearly as much of a problem as being decapitated by the flying remains of my car.

Momentum gave out and I rolled to a stop, tucking my head under my body and listening to the debris raining down around me. There were a few soft thuds, then silence. The air stank of gasoline, smoke, and melted tar, but no one was screaming; I decided to take that as a good sign. Even so, it was several minutes before I raised my head.

The remains of my car were smoldering in the gate, pinned by the portcullis. The vegetation on all sides was charred and broken, but the gateway itself wasn't even scratched, and the stones were clean. Whatever spells they'd built into that thing were holding.

"If this was part of the alarm system, I'm going to kill them," I muttered.

Quentin was where I'd dropped him, head resting on his arm. None of the debris seemed to have hit him; that was a small blessing. I walked over and bent to check his pulse, noting the scrapes scoring his arms and neck. He looked like he'd taken less damage than I had. His pulse was fast, pushed up by panic and adrenaline, but it was there, and it was strong.

"You're lucky as hell, kid," I said, brushing the glass away and rolling him onto his back. My hands left bloody prints on his shoulders and upper arms. I straightened, despite the protests from my back and knees, and turned to face the parking lot. And I waited.

I didn't have to wait long. People are pulled to explosions by an instinctive desire to see something forbidden, and that goes double for the fae. Only a few minutes passed before I heard running footsteps and Jan shouting, "That's Toby's car!"

"Well, it *was*," I said, even though none of them were close enough to hear me. My hands were starting to seriously hurt. That would have to wait. There'd be time to worry about how badly I was or wasn't injured later, if I was lucky—time was turning into a limited commodity, and if Quentin and I were targets, it was running out.

Jan crested the rise separating us from the parking lot, Terrie running close behind her. Terrie was panting, one hand pressed against her chest, gaping at the wreckage.

"Oh, my . . ."

"Yes. The car exploded. Can someone pick up Quentin? I'd do it myself, but my knees are killing me." My desire to get Quentin to safety was warring with the need to collapse into hysterical laughter, and I didn't think that was a good idea. At least not before I got the two of us inside.

"What *happened*?"

"Your security system tried to kill us." I paused, remembering the charge that raced through the air just before the explosion occurred. "Or somebody else did."

"Are you all right?" Jan ran across the debris-strewn driveway, skidding to a stop a few feet in front of me. Her eyes were enormously wide behind her glasses, making her look more like an overgrown child than the Countess of her own fiefdom.

"I'm better than Quentin. At least I'm awake." Something was running down the side of my face. I raised my hand to my cheek, touching the dampness. My fingertips came away slick with a mixture of blood, ash, and broken glass. I can't stand the sight of my own blood. I added the urge to vomit to my already long list of suppressed reactions. "Oh, yeah, I'm fine," I said, wiping my hand across my lips. "I do this every day."

Jan moved to take my arm. "Let's get you inside."

I licked my lips, grimacing at the taste of blood. "We have to take care of Quentin."

"Terrie's got him. It's all right."

The taste of my own blood—which was nowhere near empty—seemed to be focusing my thoughts. I frowned, pulling away from Jan, and said, "No. I'll take care of him."

"No, you won't," said Jan, reclaiming my arm. "You're barely upright. Let Terrie."

Grudgingly, I allowed her to guide me, shooting a poisonous look back toward Terrie. "I know how badly he's hurt. If he's any worse, we're going to have words. Understand?"

She looked stunned, but nodded, moving to scoop Quentin off the ground. I watched until I was sure she had him, then turned to Jan, asking, "Has this happened before? This kind of reaction from the security system?"

"No." She shook her head. "The gate's Coblynau design. It's perfectly weighted. This can't have happened."

I looked at her flatly, asking, "Just like the lights can't go out?"

"Yes! Just like . . ." She stopped, staring at me. "You can't be serious."

"I can. I've said as much to Alex. Whatever's doing this isn't a what—it's a who, because this has to be an inside job." I gestured to the gate, trying to ignore the blood drying on my cheeks. "No monster did that. Monsters aren't that subtle. This was a trap."

"Oh." Jan closed her eyes. "Oh, oak and ash."

"Yeah."

Someone tried to kill us; the gate proved it. Even if the fences were under a "no damage" enchantment, they should have been dirtied when the car blew up—should have, but weren't. There was no reason to put that sort of spell on a building fixture. A normal accident would have attracted the police and been covered by their insurance. Mine wasn't normal, and I was willing to bet that if the police were called by one of the neighboring businesses, they'd be quietly sent away. This was a duck hunt, and neither Quentin nor I was the one holding the rifle.

"Looks like someone didn't bother filing for their hunting license," I muttered.

"What?" Jan flashed me a pained look.

"Never mind." I know how it feels to realize that

someone in your family is a killer. Devin and I were family once. "Family" really means "the ones that can hurt you the most." So yeah, I understood; I would even have pitied her, if I'd had the time. There's never time for sympathy when you need it the most.

"Your car . . ."

"It's not important," I said, with a small shake of my head. Terrie and Quentin were long since out of sight. "I'm going to be fine. Let's just get inside before Quentin wakes up and thinks he's been kidnapped."

Exhaustion was rolling over me in a wave. I just wanted to crawl into a bed—any bed—and stay there until this was all over. Maybe I'd get lucky and somebody else would show up to take care of everything. If I was lucky, I wouldn't have to lift a finger to bring us to a simple, happy ending. Unfortunately, the sinking feeling in my stomach said my luck had finally run out.

FOURTEEN

"STOP SQUIRMING," GORDAN SNAPPED, dabbing at my cheek with a cotton swab. She was holding a pair of stainless steel tweezers in her other hand. I eyed them warily. "You've got glass ground pretty deep in here. Do you want me to get it out, or do you want to spend the rest of your life looking like an order of meatloaf surprise?"

I glared at her, struggling to hold still. It was turning into a pitched battle between my nerves and the pain. The pain was winning. "That *hurts*."

"Suck it up," Quentin said. Gordan had already treated him, snickering about how much fun it was to watch a pretty boy mop the road with his face. It didn't seem to have affected her work; she'd sterilized and bound his wounds quickly, even while she was mocking him. He was sitting on the counter, a cup of soup in his hands and a swath of gauze taped across his forehead, pushing his bangs up in a jagged line. He looked like he was recovering from his first bar fight.

I didn't care; I was just glad he was awake. "Don't make me come over there."

"Gordan wouldn't let you."

"He's right for once; I wouldn't." She smiled, showing the points of her teeth. "And you should be glad this hurts. The only way it *wouldn't* hurt is if you were already dead."

"Just be careful," I said, hunching my shoulders. I still suspected her; I had no logical reason not to, save for the fact that I couldn't figure out why she'd have killed her own best friend.

"I am," she said. She put down the tweezers, selecting a strip of gauze. Her fingers were gentle as she bandaged my cheek, avoiding the spots where the skin was torn. For all her hostility, she knew what she was doing. "You'll heal, but I don't recommend sliding down any more driveways on your face."

"I'll keep that in mind," I said, dryly.

"Good. This was fun and all, but I don't want to do it again." She started to pack the kit with neat, rapid motions, tucking away gauze, ointment, and those awful sharp-edged tweezers. "Get some coffee or something. You look like the dead."

"The soup's good," Quentin said, hefting his mug.

"You're that worried about my welfare all of a sudden?" I looked at Gordan.

"Stuff it," she said, not unkindly. "I just don't want you upsetting Jan even more."

"Right," I said, standing and crossing to the coffeemaker. The pot was half-full; good. I didn't want to bother brewing more. The bandages on my hands were light enough that I could handle it easily—I hadn't lost any manual dexterity, and that was even better.

We were alone in the cafeteria, and the doors were locked with a warding charm of Jan's design. I'd tried to open the door once, just out of curiosity, and found myself pushed gently but firmly back into the room. The seal was good. After dropping us off with Gordan, Jan and Terrie had disappeared to find Elliot and take care of the mess blocking the front gate.

"Toby?"

"Yeah?" The coffee was hot enough to be worth drinking. I took a long swallow and topped the cup off again. I was sure to need the caffeine.

"What are they going to do with the car?"

"Small questions, small minds," Gordan muttered.

Ignoring her, I said, "Well, either they're going to put up a really *big* illusion while they search for a giant can opener—"

"Yeah, *right,*" Quentin said, wrinkling his nose. Gordan snorted.

I settled next to him. "Like I said, either it's giant can opener time, or they've got themselves a forklift." My poor car.

"Will they call the cops?"

Gordan snorted again as I said, "Jan's not going to call the police when she has a basement full of bodies." That was good, since none of us wanted to be arrested for murder or carted off for dissection by the nice government men. That's the kind of hospitality I can skip.

"Oh." Quentin considered this. "What about our stuff?"

"Fireballs aren't generally polite enough to leave everyone's spare jeans intact."

He sighed. "Great."

"I know this is hard for you," I said, fighting to keep from smiling, "but human teenagers wear the same clothes two days in a row all the time and it hasn't killed any of them yet." Quentin was doing the impossible: he was cheering me up. Well, him and the coffee.

Quentin wadded up his napkin and threw it at me. "Jerk."

"Completely," I said. "Besides. I spoke to Sylvester, and he said he was going to send someone to help." And to take Quentin back to Shadowed Hills, although that could wait until he wasn't still riding the adrenaline high of his very first auto accident. "So whoever it is, they'll have a car, and they can get you some fresh clothes."

"That won't make trouble with Duchess Riordan?"

"Kid, at this point, she can cope."

Gordan glared, opening her mouth. Whatever she was going to say was lost as the wards dissolved and the door swung open, letting Jan, Elliot, and Terrie into the room. Jan's shoulders were squared and her chin was up; she looked like every other hero in Faerie, getting ready to strap on her shining armor and ride off to fight the dragon. That might be a problem, because the world has changed, and the heroes haven't. Oh, they're still the perfect solution when you're dealing with dragons or damsels in distress—I figure that's why Faerie keeps making heroes—but there's a distinct shortage of problems that straightforward. Giants and witches, fairy-tale monsters . . . those are for heroes. For everything else, they have people like me.

All of us, even Gordan and Quentin, fell silent as we watched Jan walk to the coffeepot and fill a large mug, draining it dry before she turned toward me. Elliot tapped the top of the machine, which promptly started refilling the pot. Hearth magic has its uses, even if I couldn't quite see how "making magic coffee" fell under the usual Bannick suite of abilities.

"So you think it's one of us," Jan said, without preamble.

How far can we push you before you snap, little hero? I wondered. Aloud, I said, "It's the only answer that makes sense." I felt Gordan's glare on the back of my neck. Sorry, kid. Sometimes you have to tell the truth, even when you're talking to heroes. Maybe especially when you're talking to heroes.

Jan's expression was bitter. I've seen that mixture of resignation and hopelessness before; it's usually in my mirror. "You're sure?"

"As sure as I can be." I stood. I knew I was falling into

a subservient posture, but I couldn't help it. Half of me is fae, and the fae know how to obey their lords. "Monsters don't lay that kind of trap."

"I see." She looked down at her hands. Her nails were bitten to the quick. "I trust everyone that works for me. I can't imagine who would do this."

What was I supposed to say? I exchanged a glance with Quentin. Jan built herself an ivory tower to keep the wolves out; she never dreamed they were already inside.

"I'm sorry," I said. I meant it: no matter how much of an idiot she'd been, none of them deserved this. "We'll do what we can."

"I know."

"And we'll figure out what to do about the bodies." I shook my head. "I still don't understand what's going on with them."

"The night-haunts always come," said Quentin.

"Maybe they aren't really dead." Jan looked at me, suddenly hopeful. "Can you bring them back? Wake them up?"

"No." I didn't know how to tell her how dead they really were. Jan hadn't tried riding their blood; she hadn't tasted the absence of life like sour wine. Quentin and I did, and we knew they were gone. Worse than gone: their blood was empty. Blood is never empty. It remembers all the little triumphs and tragedies of a lifetime, and it keeps them for as long as it continues to exist. Their blood remembered *nothing*. Whatever lives they'd lived and whoever they'd been, it was lost when they died. They took it into the darkness with them, out of Faerie forever.

Jan sighed. "I see. I . . . oak and ash, Toby, I'm sorry. You should never have gotten wrapped up in all of this."

"My liege sent me, so I came." I shrugged. "I'm not leaving until this is over."

"And Quentin?" asked Terrie, biting her lip.

Quentin shot me a worried look. Clearly, he'd been wondering the same thing.

It was going to come out eventually. "Sylvester is sending someone to get him. Until then, we just need to keep him safe."

"Toby—"

"She's right," said Terrie. "This isn't your fight, Quentin. You don't have to stay."

"I want to," he said.

"Hey, I say we let him," said Gordan. "At least if the killer picks him, we get to live a little longer. Call it a learning experience." You have to respect self-interest that focused. Most people at least try to pretend your welfare matters as much as their own.

"Gordan, that isn't fair," said Jan.

"Fair isn't the point, and this isn't a discussion. Sylvester's calling him home. He's going," I said. Quentin's expression was one of sheer betrayal. Tough. I wasn't going to be responsible for getting him killed. "I'll be here until this is over. You can't get rid of me that easily."

"I don't think anyone ever has," Gordan muttered. She'd given up glaring: now she just looked sullen.

"In the meantime," I said, ignoring her, "we're going to need all the things I asked for. The information on the victims, access to their work spaces, everything. I don't want any of you going anywhere alone. Is it possible for you to go somewhere else in the County until this is fixed? Someplace outside the knowe?"

Jan shook her head. "No."

"Jan—"

"April can't leave." The words were simple, quietly said, and utterly without hope. "I don't have a portable server set up for her. If we went, we'd have to leave her behind. She'd be defenseless. I won't leave my daughter."

"And we won't leave our liege," said Elliot.

"If everyone dies, you lose the County. Let me call Sylvester. Let him help."

"Dreamer's Glass will see it as a threat."

I eyed Jan. "Is there *any* way for us to get help without going to war?"

"No," she said, simply. "There isn't."

"Maybe that's what they want." Gordan stood, crossing her arms over her chest. "How do we know Sylvester sent them? Maybe they're here to make *sure* we don't figure things out."

"Gordan—" Jan began, and stopped, glancing toward me. They didn't know. With the lines down between them and Shadowed Hills, there was no way they could. Much as I was coming to dislike her, I almost had to admire the way Gordan's mind worked. She wanted us out, and she'd found one of the fastest ways to get what she wanted: calling our credentials into question. She was smirking now, visibly pleased.

"That's crap," snapped Quentin.

"He's right," I said. "If you want to work yourselves into a paranoid frenzy, go for it. Whatever. Just understand that it's not my damn problem. The dead are my problem."

Elliot had the grace to look embarrassed. "I'm sorry. It's just that politically . . ."

"Politically, it would be a good idea to send saboteurs. We're not them."

"I believe you," said Jan. Behind her, Gordan scowled.

"Good." I walked to the coffee machine, aware of the eyes on my back. Let them stare. I needed to regroup before I started screaming at them. I'd been trying to ignore the political aspects, but they still mattered. No one should die for land. Oberon believed that: he fought to keep the playing field even. Some people say that's why he disappeared—he saw what Faerie was becoming and couldn't bear to watch. I wasn't sure I could bear it, either. I didn't have a choice.

"One way or another, I guess we'll know your motives soon," said Terrie.

I toasted her with my coffee cup. "Same to you."

"We know the risks," said Jan. Before the fae grew soft and secretive, the look in her eyes would have sent armies to die. There's no stopping that kind of look; all you can do is stand back and hope the casualties will be light. "So where do we go from here?"

I met her eyes, and sighed. She wasn't going to back down; we both knew it. The people that were going to leave were already gone, leaving only the loyal ones, the heroes, and the murderer. I'm not a hero; if I'm lucky, I never will be. I just do my job.

"You're going to have to do everything I say," I said.

"Of course," she said, and smiled. It was a victor's smile, and she was right to smile that way. We were staying at ALH, and they were counting on me to win their war. I just didn't see a single way to do it.

FIFTEEN

"ANY ANSWER?"

"None." Quentin dropped the phone back into the cradle, looking disgusted. "I've tried calling eight times, and no one's picking up."

"Sylvester said he'd keep someone by the phone. So we've got two choices. Either he forgot . . ."

Quentin snorted.

"My thoughts exactly. Which means something's stopping the calls from going through. How much do you know about the phones at Shadowed Hills?"

Quentin shrugged, putting down the folder he'd been pretending to read. "They're ALH manufacture. They were installed shortly before I was fostered with Duke Torquill."

"Uh-huh. Ever had any problems with them?"

"No. Never."

"But no one's picking up, and none of Jan's messages got through, even though we were able to call just fine from the hotel." A nasty image was starting to form in my mind. "Give me the phone."

"What?"

"Give me the phone." I held out my hand. "And keep

reading. We need to know whatever there is to know about these people."

"I don't understand why I have to do this," he grumbled, handing me the receiver. "You're making me go home."

"Because I said so. Now shut up, and read." Half-holding my breath, I punched in the number for the Japanese Tea Gardens, and waited. Shadowed Hills was a knowe. Shadowed Hills had a Summerlands-based phone system. The Tea Gardens . . . didn't.

After our discussion in the cafeteria, Elliot had taken us to what had been Colin's office, where I could get started on the investigative side of things while keeping Quentin out of trouble. It was a small, boxy room, with surfing posters on the walls and Happy Meal toys cluttering the shelves. The single window looked out on an improbably perfect, moonlit beach. That was a Selkie for you. He'd found a way to work inland and still be close to home.

We searched the office thoroughly, but found nothing to justify murdering the man. There was a small Ziploc bag of marijuana behind the fish tank, and a large collection of nudie magazines which caused Quentin to forget he was mad at me for almost ten minutes while he snickered. A herd of miniature Hippocampi swam from side to side in the tank, eyeing us suspiciously. The largest was no more than eight inches long, a stallion whose perfect equine upper half melded seamlessly into the scales and fins of his bright blue tail. His mares came in half a dozen colors, as brilliantly patterned as tropical fish.

The phone kept ringing. I sighed, and was about to hang up. There was a clatter and a shout of, "Dammit!" as the receiver was slapped out of the cradle on the other end. Breathless, Marcia said, "Hello?"

"Marcia?"

"Toby? Oh, thank Oberon. I found Tybalt for you. He's—"

"Marcia, I don't have time for this right now. I need you to do me a favor, okay? I need you to go to Shadowed Hills, and tell Sylvester I need help. I'm in Fremont, and there's something wrong with the phones here. I can't call Shadowed Hills."

"Fascinating. Do go on." The voice was dry, amused, and distinctly *not* Marcia's.

I paused. "Tybalt?"

"Did you expect that you would call for me, and I would refuse? Perhaps you did. Much as I appreciate your deciding to provide me with an afternoon's amusement, I must say . . . 'here, kitty, kitty'? Did you really expect this to have any positive result?"

"Tybalt, this is really not the time."

"What did you want to discuss with me that was so vital you had to send a handmaid begging at the bushes?" His tone sharpened, turning dangerous. "I don't take kindly to being toyed with."

I rubbed my forehead with one hand. "All right, look, my methods were maybe not the best, but they got you to wait on my call, didn't they? I'm guessing you didn't do anything to Marcia?"

"She assured me her activities were entirely your fault."

"Good." Quentin was giving me a quizzical look. I turned away from him before he could distract me, and said, "Did she tell you why I'm in Fremont?"

"No. I assume that honor was being left for you. I do hope you're giving my counterpart the troubles you normally reserve for me."

Oh, oak and ash. That was what I'd been hoping not to hear. Keeping my tone light, I said, "Your counterpart. I assume you mean Barbara Lynch, the local Queen of Cats?"

"None other." The danger bled out of his voice, replaced by amusement. "She must not know you've elected to phone me. We're not precisely on good terms, she and I. Silly little thing should never have taken a throne. Why, with her delicate sensibilities—"

"She's dead, Tybalt."

Silence.

"She died last month."

Now he spoke, voice a low, harsh rasp that was closer to a snarl: "How?"

"We don't know. That's the problem." I closed my eyes. "You didn't know."

"How would I have known?" The bitterness and anger in his tone were undisguised. "She held a crown without a kingdom, thanks to that Riordan bitch."

That was new information. "What do you mean, 'a crown without a kingdom'?"

"There were no true Cait Sidhe in her domain, only our feline cousins and their changeling children. The others left long ago, when it became clear that Riordan held no respect for Oberon's word."

Oberon established the Court of Cats, gave them a political structure outside the standard Faerie Courts and Kingdoms. They ruled themselves, and no political power in Faerie had any say over them. There have always been rulers who didn't want to listen to that ancient declaration. They try to tax the Cait Sidhe, subvert them, recruit them into their political reindeer games. It wasn't much of a surprise to hear that Riordan was one of those.

Still . . . "You can talk to my cats."

"Your cats are my subjects, and subject to my laws. The cats of Barbara's Court weren't. They couldn't reach me."

"Where did all the other Cait Sidhe go?"

"My fiefdom. Others. But Barbara remained, stubborn to the end." His tone turned more bitter still. "I think she liked the perversity of it. Bowing at the knee to a daughter of Titania."

"She's not bowing anymore," I said, with a sigh.

"I'm sorry to be the one who told you. And I'm sorry about the 'here kitty, kitty' thing. It just seemed like the best . . ."

"Wait. She died in Fremont, and you don't know what killed her."

"Yes."

"And you're still there."

"Yes."

"Are you in danger?"

I considered lying. Only for a few seconds, but still, the urge was there. Pulling his jacket closer around me, I said, "People are dying. Sylvester's sending someone to get Quentin out, but I'm staying until we know what's going on. I can't run out on them."

Again, silence.

"Tybalt?"

"You really are a little fool, aren't you?" His tone was distant, almost reflective. "You still have the jacket I left with you?"

"I do," I admitted.

"Good. I'll be wanting it back."

"I'll try to stay alive long enough to return it. Can you put Marcia on? I need to ask her for a favor."

His tone sharpened. "What favor?"

"Something's wrong with the phones, and I can't get through to Shadowed Hills. Someone needs to tell Sylvester we're in trouble. Big trouble. Someone just tried to kill us, and they came pretty close to succeeding." I paused. "He can probably call me from the pay phone in the parking lot. He should station someone there."

"Consider the message relayed," said Tybalt, in that same distant, thoughtful tone.

"What are you—"

The phone buzzed in my ear. The line was dead; he'd hung up on me.

Groaning, I turned and dropped the receiver back into the cradle. "Whatever's wrong with the phones, it's specific to Shadowed Hills. I got through to the Tea Gardens just fine."

Quentin was once more pretending to review the employee files. He slanted a sidelong look my way, and asked, "What did Tybalt want?"

"To give me a headache. Still, he wouldn't take the message if he wasn't planning to deliver it." I leaned over to take the folder from his hands, scanning the first page, and wrinkled my nose. Maybe the company dietitian cared about the fact that Barbara liked her field mice alive, but I didn't. "Change of subjects. Does it say anything in here about where her office is?"

"Nope. Did you know that Colin had a doctorate in philosophy?"

I looked up. "What year, and where from?"

"Nineteen sixty-two. Newfoundland."

"Any of the others have degrees from Canadian colleges?" I flipped through Barbara's folder, stopping at the sheet labeled "education." "Babs didn't—her degree's from UC Berkeley. Women's Studies and English."

"Peter taught History at Butler University in Indianapolis, and Yui's file says she used to be a courtesan in the court of King Gilad."

I looked up again, eyeing Quentin. "*Please* tell me you know what that means." He turned red. "Good. I didn't want to explain it. So we have basically no connections."

"None."

"And of the four victims, two have offices that don't seem to exist." We'd done Peter's office before Colin's. It was almost empty, containing a desk and an assortment of office supplies. The few personal touches we found dealt with football—a Butler University pennant on one wall and a foam-rubber football that he probably tossed around when he was bored. There was nothing that provided us with a visible motive for murder, and that worried me.

"One at least—I mean, no one's actually said Barbara had an office."

"Right." I dropped myself into the chair by the fish tank. The Hippocampi fled to the far end, the tiny stallion swimming back and forth in front of the rest as he "protected" them from me. "Maybe she worked out of a broom closet, I don't know. No offices means no leads. Not that we're getting much from this place unless you like weed."

"What?"

"Never mind." I shook my head. "So they were telling the truth about the turnover rates. It doesn't look like they'd lost an employee in a long time before this started."

"So where does that leave us?"

"It leaves 'us' nowhere, Quentin. You're leaving as soon as your ride gets here."

"And what if I won't go?" He crossed his arms, jaw set.

"Sylvester's orders, kid. You'll go."

"Why are you so determined to get me out of here? I want to help. I want to—"

I grabbed the collar of my shirt and pulled it down, exposing the scar on my left shoulder. Quentin stopped talking, and gaped. I held the collar down long enough to make sure he got a good look before tugging it back into place, glaring at him.

"That was made with iron." His eyes were wide, and scared.

"Good to see they've taught you what iron damage looks like."

"How did you—"

"I lived because I got lucky, and because someone was willing to pay a lot to keep me around a little bit longer. Most people don't get lucky."

He swallowed, and stood. "I'm going to feed the Hippocampi."

"Good idea," I said, and reached for the stack of folders. I didn't want to scare him—he was making more of an effort to do the right thing than most purebloods twice his age would bother with—but he needed to realize that this wasn't a game. This was real, and he was going home.

The Hippocampus food was on the shelf beneath the fish tank. Giving me one last sidelong glance, Quentin opened it, shaking bits of dried kelp and barley into the water. The tiny horses flocked to the food, their wariness forgotten as they chased it around the tank. I smiled faintly and flipped the first folder open.

They liked records at ALH: everything from employment history to diet and heritage was recorded, like they were trying to paint portraits of their employees on paper. Even though was it helping us research, I couldn't figure out why they'd bothered in the first place.

The first page of Colin's file included a listing of family members. I found myself wondering who was going to have to tell them he was gone. Disgusted by the thought, I slammed the folder down on the desk and pushed it away. "This isn't helping."

Quentin looked up from feeding the Hippocampi. "What do you mean?"

"They were normal." I indicated the folder. "All were purebloods less than three hundred years old, all lived human at some point without cutting their ties to the Summerlands—nothing out of the ordinary. Barbara was local, and Yui was from Oregon, so there's a West Coast pattern . . . only Colin was from Newfoundland, and Peter's last listed residence was in Indiana."

"So what connects them?" Quentin asked, returning the Hippocampus food to the shelf where he'd found it.

He was obviously expecting some ingenious, Sherlock Holmes-like gem of wisdom, and I hated to disappoint him. Unfortunately, I had no other options. "Nothing but ALH." That worried me. Unless our killer was basing his moves on a factor I couldn't see, we were dealing with someone whose only motive was "here." That didn't bode well. For one thing, it was a strong indicator that we might be looking for a crazy person.

Insanity is dangerous. All fae living in the mortal world are at least a little nuts; it's a natural consequence of being what we are. We have to convince ourselves that we can function in a place that's run by people whose logic looks nothing like our own. When we do it well enough, we're even right. The problem is that eventually, the lies stop working, and by that point, it's generally too late to run.

"Oh," said Quentin, sounding disappointed.

"Yeah," I agreed, "oh."

Something crackled in the air behind me. I didn't pause to think; I just whirled, scattering file folders in my rush to put myself between Quentin and any potential threats. April's outline flickered as the papers passed through her, fluttering to the floor. She watched impassively as they fell, finally asking, "Are you well?"

"Don't *do* that!" I said, dropping shakily back into my seat. Quentin looked as shocked as I felt. Good. That made him less likely to laugh at me later.

"Why not?" She tilted her head, showing a flicker of curiosity. The fact that I'd just thrown several sheets of paper through her upper torso didn't seem to bother her. Dryads are weird, but April was going for the grand prize.

"Because it's not polite to startle people."

"I see." April looked to Quentin. "Is she correct?"

Wordlessly, he nodded.

"I see," April repeated. After a moment's consideration, she asked, "Is it my materialization you object to, or my doing so outside your immediate range of vision?"

Quentin and I stared at her. She gazed back, bland curiosity in her yellow eyes. Now that I was looking more closely, I could see that her irises lacked normal variation; they looked almost painted-on. Her lack of small detail was making her seem more and more like something that was created, not born. That probably explained a lot about her, even if it didn't change the fact that she'd just tripled my heart rate by deciding not to use the door like everybody else.

"I object to having you appear behind me without warning," I said.

Quentin nodded. "That's, um, pretty much my problem, too."

April smiled, an expression that looked entirely artificial. "Acceptable. I will refrain from abrupt materialization in your immediate vicinity without prior notification of my arrival."

It took me a moment to puzzle through that one. "So you won't appear suddenly?" I guessed. I wasn't going to make assumptions with someone who seemed to view silly things like "physics" as a mere convenience.

"Yes."

"Good." I glanced back toward Quentin, and saw that he was starting to relax again. "Can I help you with something?"

"Mother says you are going to assist us."

"We're going to try."

"Mother says you are here about the disconnection of the residents of this network."

Silence was becoming a major punctuation in this conversation. I looked to Quentin, who shook his head and spread his hands to show that he hadn't understood it either. "What?"

"The ones that have gone off-line. You will determine what has caused them to remain isolated from the network."

Oh. She was talking about the murders. "Yes. We're going to find out why people are being killed."

She frowned, looking puzzled. Then the expression faded, and she asked, "Why?"

I shrugged. "Somebody has to."

"That makes no sense," she said, frowning again.

"I rarely do. It's one of my best traits."

Quentin snorted, trying not to laugh.

"Gordan does not trust you," April said.

"I knew that, actually."

"Mother trusts you." She shook her head. "I still do not know whether I trust you."

"I'm glad you can be honest about that," I said. She was starting to unnerve me. There were too many little inconsistencies in the way she behaved and the way she was made, and it was getting harder to resist the urge to wave my hand through the space her body appeared to occupy just to find out whether or not she was there.

"Honesty is the only sensible option."

Maybe for computer-powered Dryads, but the rest of Faerie seemed to be having a bit more of a problem with it. Slowly, I asked, "Why are you here?"

"Mother requested that I notify you if any company personnel exited the presence of their assigned partners."

"And?"

"Gordan and Terrie have departed from one another's company."

Swell. "Message received. Where are they?"

"Gordan is located in her cubicle. Terrie is located in the cafeteria."

"All right. Why don't you go take care of whatever else you need to do, and I'll see if I can explain to them why this isn't okay, all right?"

April gave me a long, measuring look, expression alien as ever. It was like watching an anthropologist trying to figure out a foreign culture—and who knows? Maybe that's what she was doing. "Understood," she said finally, and vanished in a flicker of static and ozone.

"Right," I said, eyeing the space where she'd been before turning to pull the keys out of my pocket and toss them to Quentin. He caught them without pausing to think; good reflexes.

He gave me a bewildered look. "What are you giving me these for?"

"I need to go knock some heads together. Repeatedly. I want you to lock yourself in."

"Uh." Quentin's eyebrows rose, expression turning dubious. "Have you never seen a horror movie in your entire life? Splitting the party is never a good idea."

"I got that. I also got the part where if I'm creeping around the knowe worrying about you, I'm even more likely to do something stupid. Stay put. Lock the door, and don't let *anyone* in, even if they sound like me, unless they know the password."

"April isn't going to use the door."

"I don't really think April is particularly dangerous, unless you're threatening her mom. Maybe you should see if you can get her to come back. Asking her some questions might be good for you."

"Toby—"

"Just do it."

He looked like he was going to keep arguing. Then he sighed, shoulders sagging, and asked, "What's the password?"

I managed a fleeting smile as I rose and walked toward the door. "How about 'do your homework'?"

"Catty," he said, forcing a smile of his own.

"Exactly," I said, and stepped out of the room. I waited in front of the door while Quentin closed and locked it, throwing the bolt with a decisive "click." That done, I started down the hall.

SIXTEEN

I WAS STARTING TO FIND MY WAY AROUND. The hall where Colin's office was located led to a larger hall, which led in turn to a pair of wide double doors that opened on the company lawn. A dozen cats were splayed on the grass, distributed around the door like spokes radiating from a wheel. They lifted their heads when I stepped out, watching my approach. I frowned. They'd come because of Barbara—if Tybalt was to be believed, she'd been the only true Cait Sidhe in Fremont—but they'd stayed for reasons of their own.

That's the thing about cats: they remember a time when there were true faerie kings for them to look at, not just Kings and Queens of Cats and the imitations we have today. Cats watch from corners and hearths, and they see history happening, and they never forget a minute. Some people say cats are the memory of Faerie, and that as long as there's one cat that remembers us, Faerie will never die. People say some weird things, but sometimes, there's truth there that we can't see. They can say whatever they like about the cats of Faerie; I still say most of them are damned nuisances. And that includes mine.

I crossed the lawn, stepping around cats as I walked toward the main building. They watched me intently, and I paused, frowning. Despite the feline population explosion on the grounds, I hadn't seen a single cat inside. "You guys have a problem with enclosed spaces?" I asked. They didn't respond, making no move to either follow or move away. "Right."

Shaking my head, I went inside.

The emptiness of the main building was even eerier now that I knew what was happening. My footsteps echoed as I walked along the hall, heading toward the cubicle maze. More than anything, I wanted to evacuate the place—send the survivors home, or even back to Shadowed Hills, and figure out who our killer was without hanging around in this giant technological crypt. But that wasn't going to happen.

Jan and Elliot were in her office with the door open, passing a pencil back and forth as they bent over a set of incomprehensible blueprints. I paused to watch them. Jan raised her head, a silent question in her eyes, and I waved her off, resuming my patrol. She didn't need to know that her people weren't obeying the rules. Not unless they refused to listen to me when I told them off for it.

The air-conditioning was off, and the hall lights were low as I walked back into the room where we'd first met the people of ALH. The catwalks were a series of smudges overhead. It looked like the sort of place frequented by brainless blondes in cheap horror movies; considering the number of bodies we'd found in the area, that wasn't a bad comparison. Fortunately, I've never been inclined to wander down dead-end alleys in my underwear. Keeping my footsteps light, I started into the maze.

I can't move as silently as my mother—another consequence of my mortal blood—but years of practice have taught me a few things about being quiet. I stopped paying attention to where I was putting my feet as my eyes adjusted, concentrating on listening instead.

A faint sound was drifting out of the maze to my left. Typing. I turned.

Following the sound of Gordan working down the rows of cubicles did more to bring home what ALH had lost than every personnel file in the world. The desks were personalized with little touches; small toys, photographs, clusters of dried or dying flowers. A nameplate caught my eye, and I stopped. "Barbara Lynch." The office we hadn't been able to find.

"*There* you are," I breathed.

The desk was covered in drifts of paper scribbled with complex calculations, while a pile of origami roses offered silent testimony to her preferred form of stress relief. Most of the papers tacked to the cube wall were work-related, with the exception of a poster of a kitten with the motto "hang in there" written in large, cartoony letters, and a photograph of a smiling man with white-blond hair. I removed the tack, turning the picture over to read the inscription on the back. "To my dearest Babs; a cat may look at a king. May I look at a cat? Love, John."

Oh, damn. I smothered a sigh as I put the picture down. There weren't any other photographs, which struck me as a little strange; if Gordan had been her best friend for as long as Alex seemed to think, I would have expected to find some sign of their relationship—a picture, a card, something. But there was nothing to indicate they'd ever met outside a professional context. I started shuffling through the papers littering the desktop, frowning. Most of what I found seemed fairly mundane; notes on troubleshooting the company's latest software offerings, bug reports, documentation of program glitches.

Barbara hadn't been very highly ranked in the department; aside from her glaring lack of an office, the memos I could understand seemed to indicate that she'd been at the bottom of most of the corporate food chains. Whenever something went wrong, it seemed like Barbara took a lot of the blame. More tellingly, a lot of the blame was coming from Gordan. "Maybe they had a little falling-out," I murmured, starting to test the drawers. Most opened easily.

The top drawer was locked. Frown deepening, I knelt and peered at it. Jan would give me the key if I asked, but I wanted to think about it first. There was probably a perfectly logical reason for Barbara's drawer to be locked; maybe someone kept stealing her pencils.

Or maybe she was trying to hide something.

Breaking cheap locks is just one of the fun skills I've picked up in my day job. It's astounding how many divorces you can finalize with things that were protected by a fifty-cent tumbler in a standard-issue desk. I scanned the desktop until I spotted a paper clip. It took only a few seconds to straighten it out, and I bent back over the lock, makeshift lockpick in hand.

Desk locks generally don't take more than a minute to pop. This one was no different. After three sharp twists of the wire the tumblers slipped, and the drawer came open with a loud "click." The sound of Gordan's typing stopped for a moment, then resumed, just as rapid as before. With bated breath, I eased the drawer out of the desk and sat down on the floor, starting to sift through its contents.

The top layer was fairly generic: announcements of company-wide events, torn envelopes, old pay stubs and blank steno pads. I flipped through them and set them aside, continuing to dig downward. More papers, more debris, none of it more complicated than the layers of silt that build up in every desk in the world. Her checkbook was buried at the bottom. I started to flip through it, noting the cute kittens on her checks before I reached the log of deposits and withdrawals. I stopped there, suddenly cold.

Half the deposits were credited to "payday": those were decently sized, indicating a respectable, if not show-stopping monthly income. Nothing suspicious about those. The other deposits, though . . .

The labels said "contracting bonus." They were almost as common as the payday deposits, and each was easily three times bigger. I may not know much about the computer industry, but I understand logic. If Barbara was making that much as an independent, she wouldn't have needed ALH; the contracting payments alone covered her withdrawals and expenses. Whatever those payments were for, it wasn't contract work.

Tucking the checkbook into my jacket pocket, I started going through the drawer again. The remaining contents were nothing remarkable, and I quickly found myself at the bottom, with a heap of papers and office supplies on the floor beside me. I frowned, glancing from the debris to the empty drawer. When I broke into the desk, the top drawer was so full it was in danger of overflowing. Now, with the contents even less organized, I had a pile three inches shorter than the drawer was. Something was missing.

Reaching into the drawer, I slid my fingers around the edges until I hit a dip in the back left corner. Jackpot. It only took a few minutes to pry the false bottom loose, leaving me free to study the rest of the drawer's contents. I looked inside and stopped, eyes widening. At the top of the tidy pile of paper I'd just revealed was an envelope watermarked with the stars and poppies crest of Dreamer's Glass.

The envelope was unsealed. Careful to touch the paper as little as possible, I shook the contents into my hand: an uncashed check for an amount that matched the "contracting bonuses" listed in Barbara's checkbook and a note that read "Enclosed please find payment for May's activities. June's report will be expected at the same time and place." It was signed with the vast, looping squiggle of Duchess Riordan's signature. If the crest hadn't already told me what was going on, that would have cinched it.

"Guess you won't be making June's report," I said, and picked up the drawer, leaving the unnecessary pieces scattered on the floor. I needed to go through what I'd found more thoroughly, after I'd spoken to Jan and gotten back to Quentin. Tucking the drawer under my arm, I walked onward toward the sound of typing. I briefly considered the fact that stalking the sound of typing through a computer company just because I assumed it was someone I knew might not be my best idea ever—after all, if I were trying to attract computer programmers, I'd probably do it with an innocuous sound. Like typing.

That disturbing train of thought pulled into the station as I turned the corner and found myself at Gordan's cubicle. It was more devoid of personality than the others I'd passed, but I could tell who it belonged to: the fact that she was still sitting there was a pretty big clue. She raised her head and scowled as I approached, hitting a key at the top of her keyboard. Before the screen went dark, I caught a glimpse of a diagram as complex and snarled as one of Luna's knitting projects. "What do *you* want?"

The evidence I had under my arm was enough to prove that her best friend had been working for the opposition before she died. Feeling oddly exposed, I said, "April told me you were here. You know you shouldn't be alone."

"You don't know who the killer is. What makes me safer staying with *them?*"

Touché. "I'm trying to do my job." I was going to be nice if it killed me. She was probably as scared as I was, if not more. After her, it was her company under siege.

"And it's doing so much good." She snorted. "I can see the improvements since you got here. What was I thinking?"

My good nature only goes so far. "That's not fair. We're doing our best."

"It's not? Gee, I'm sorry. I didn't realize. I guess it's perfectly fair for you to suck face with Alex while my friends die?" I flinched. Gordan answered with a mocking smile, saying, "Honey, it's obvious what you've been up to. Doesn't it get cold out there on that hillside?"

If the sarcasm got any thicker, I was going to need a shovel. "Maybe if you'd try to help instead of attacking me all the time, we'd get better results. What's this about a hill?"

"Maybe if you knew what you were doing, you wouldn't need my help!" She glared at me. I glared back. Maybe she'd just lost her best friend, but that didn't excuse her behavior; trauma only works as an excuse for so long. There's a point when you have to take back the responsibility for your own actions.

"You're riding us pretty hard for someone that doesn't have any answers. It's a little suspicious that the things that keep going wrong are all Coblynau technology."

"You got a reason I shouldn't ride you hard? You come here with your little pretty boy, sucking up to Jan, acting like it's going to be okay now that your precious liege is involved—weren't we good enough to save before he cared?"

"We didn't know you were in trouble. No one told us what was happening here."

"That's not good enough!"

"It's going to have to be good enough, because it's the truth. I'm sick of you treating me like crap, and Quentin even worse, just because you're scared."

"You should have known something was wrong. Your precious purebloods should have figured it out." Her eyes were bright with past hurts and anger. "Isn't that what they're for?"

"You don't like the purebloods much, do you?"

"What was your first clue?" She turned her face away. "I'm just returning the favor."

It's not unusual for changelings to be resentful. Hell, *I'm* resentful. Our immortal parents get the best of Faerie and take what they want from the mortal world, and we get the things they let us have. Even so, the level of her resentment was unusual. She almost burned with it. "Mind if I ask why?"

"Yes," she said, curtly. Then, in a quieter voice, she said, "Mom was pureblooded Coblynau. Dad was a changeling, and I was an accident. I'm just mortal enough that the mines won't have me, and I'm not mortal enough for the mongrel workshops. You want to spend your life getting screwed? Try mine on for size."

I winced. "You're right. That sucks."

The Coblynau make their homes in deep mines, deeper even than the Dwarves and the Gremlins. Being a changeling made Gordan unsuited for a life lived entirely at those depths. Being more fae than human, on the other hand, would make her too sensitive to iron to deal with the changeling workshops, and get her eyed with suspicion in the border communities. It was a tough break, no matter how you wanted to slice it.

"You have no idea."

"That's where you're wrong." I felt sorry for her. That wasn't stopping me from getting annoyed. "I'm Amandine's daughter. You knew that, didn't you?" When she nodded, I continued, "Well, *everyone* knows that. I'm just a changeling. I'm not even as fae as you are. But her reputation precedes me everywhere I go, and I spend every damn day failing to live up to it. So don't tell me I don't know how hard it is to deal with the hand your parents dealt you. My cards may be different, but they're just as bad."

Gordan glared at me. I glared back, and she was the first one to look away.

I relaxed marginally. Victories, even small ones, are good things. I'm petty enough that they matter to me, and as long as that's the case, I'm still human enough to stand a chance. "It's okay to be mad," I said, as gently as I could.

She shrugged. "Is it?" she asked. I took that to be her way of getting choked up. The Coblynau have never been very visual with their feelings.

"Yes, it is," I said. "I've been mad since I got here. People don't help when they say they will, they keep wandering around on their own . . . I'm pissed."

"So why are you here?"

"Why?" I shrugged, settling on the truth. "Sylvester asked me to come, and you need me."

"You don't care if we die," she said, tone turning bitter. She looked back at me, eyes narrowed. "You're just here because your liege ordered you to be."

"He didn't order, he asked. And you're wrong."

"What do you mean?"

"I *do* care if you all die, because Faerie cares. I care because no one needs to die, and," I raised one hand in mock melodrama, "Sylvester will kick my ass if I don't care."

It worked. She bit back a smile, half-turning to keep me from noticing. Ha; too late. I can be pretentious sometimes, but I know it, and knowing your flaws means you can exploit them. "This would work better if we weren't fighting," I said.

She looked back. "You're right," she conceded, "it probably would."

"You don't have to like me. I mean, April doesn't."

Gordan grinned. "April doesn't like a lot of things."

"I noticed. Why is that?"

"She's distanced."

"Distanced?" I asked. I wanted Gordan to relax, but I had a job to do, and part of it was learning everything I could about the remaining inhabitants of Tamed Lightning. Most of them were probably nice folks, but one of them was a killer.

"She used to be a tree. She did tree things—she drank water, absorbed nutrients from the soil, photosynthesized—the good stuff." She leaned back in her chair, now on familiar ground. "You want to talk 'cycle of nature,' trees have it down. Everything nature does is in a tree."

"True enough."

"So she's a tree. Only suddenly she's *not* a tree, she's a network server. It's cold there. It does server things, not living things. Instead of sunlight, she has electricity. Instead of roots, she has cables. It's stuff she didn't need before. So she starts to learn these new things—how to be a good machine—and she forgets about sunlight, and water in her roots, and photosynthesis."

"Oh," I said, realization dawning. "The Dryad is the tree."

"Right. The more she knows about being a machine, the less she knows about being anything else."

"But she still likes some people."

"No, she likes *Jan*. The rest of us are tolerated as functions her 'mother' needs to remain operational." Gordan shrugged. "It's no big deal. We're used to her."

"Doesn't it seem a bit . . . strange?"

"Have you ever met anyone with a cat they'd adopted from the pound?"

I blinked, a little thrown by the conversational shift. "Yes."

"Let me guess: the cat was devoted to them and hated everyone else. Am I close?"

"Yeah," I said, thoughtfully. Mitch and Stacy adopted a kitten from the SPCA once. It was a little ball of fluffy feline evil, set permanently on "kill." Every time Shadow saw me—or Cliff, or even Kerry—he launched himself for whatever tender bits were closest to hand and started trying to remove them. But he never stopped purring when Stacy was around.

He died of old age two years before I came home. According to Mitch, he never mellowed: even when he was toothless and half-blind, he kept trying to savage anyone who came to visit. Good for him.

"It's like that for April and Jan. April was the lost kitten at the pound, and Jan was the one who brought her home. It makes sense for April to be totally devoted. Personally, I'm amazed you can ever get her to stop following Jan around."

"So they're always together?"

"Not always. But if Jan snaps her fingers and says 'jump,' you can bet April will be right there to make sure you're asking 'how high.'"

"I see."

"Do you?" Gordan fixed me with a stare. "I may not be big on the purebloods as a whole, but there's a lot of loyalty around here. You might want to watch who you're pointing the finger at."

There's no arguing with a statement like that. "I need to be getting back. You shouldn't be here on your own."

"I'm a big girl." She held up a small black box. "This is my panic button. Anything comes for me, I push this, and the server failure alarm goes off. Don't worry about me."

I frowned. "Why doesn't everyone have one of those?"

"We've never needed them before."

"We need them now."

"I'll see what I can do." She looked at me impassively, adding, "I'm not moving."

"I got that." I sighed, rising. "Don't die."

"Not intending to."

I walked away into the darkness, feeling her eyes on my back until I turned the corner back onto the main pathway. I wasn't comfortable leaving her alone, but I was even less comfortable staying, and I wasn't going to fight with her. Not until I'd had the chance to go over Barbara's papers and figure out what, exactly, they meant.

Thanks to the air-conditioning being off while we were on generator power, it was actually cooler outside the building. I squinted up at the moon, and then glanced to my watch. Almost four o'clock; the sun would be up soon. Just one more complication for the list.

Walking from the open spaces outside into the enclosed halls was like walking into a science-fiction ghost town; I was just waiting for the aliens to attack. The windows showed conflicting views of the landscaping outside, seeming even more disparate than they had earlier. A window on the third floor—if you could judge by the apparent distance to the ground—showed a perfect nighttime view of the lawn, complete with cats sprawled on the moonlit path.

Jan's office was two rooms over at the end of a long hallway. The door, which had been propped open before, was closed. Frowning, I put a hand on the knife at my belt as I walked up and knocked. "Jan? Are you in there?"

"Coming!" There was a series of bumps and clatters as Jan made her way across the office and swung the door open. I glanced past her. Elliot was gone.

"Where's Elliot?"

"He had to go get something. But I haven't left this office—I'm totally safe, I was working on . . . actually, never mind what I was working on. I can't explain it, and you wouldn't understand it." There was no insult in her tone—she was almost certainly right. Tilting her head to the side, her expression turned concerned. "Are you okay? I mean, you're all pale. Have you eaten? Or slept?"

"That isn't important," I said, cursing inwardly. Why had she picked *now* to start paying attention? I felt like hell, but that didn't mean I wanted it pointed out.

"How do you know the killer won't come to you? And if you're 'totally safe,' how do you know *Elliot* isn't in trouble?"

"I . . ." She paused, looking at me sharply. "Are you trying to scare me?"

"Yeah, I am. If you get killed, your uncle will have my skin for a throw rug."

"You're probably right. It's just weird to think anyone would want to hurt me."

"You realize that if this is politically motivated, you're in more danger than anyone else here?" I held up the drawer from Barbara's desk. "I have information. Can I come in?"

Jan eyed the drawer. "What is that?"

"Evidence that Barbara was screwing you." I brushed past her into the office. She closed the door, following me to her desk, where I put the drawer down atop a pile of papers. "That's not the most important thing. I know why you can't reach your uncle."

"What?" Her eyes went wide. "What do you mean?"

"It's the phones." I outlined my conclusions, including the fact that calls placed from outside the knowe, or to phone numbers ALH hadn't installed, worked just fine. I left out my discussion with Tybalt. It didn't seem like something she'd need to know.

At first, Jan just stared. Then her eyes narrowed, expression going cold. "It really was one of us," she said, in a soft, dangerous voice. I'd heard that tone from her uncle. It generally meant it was time to look for cover.

"I think so," I said, and handed her the envelope I'd found in Barbara's desk, with the seal of Dreamer's Glass turned upward. "It looks like Barbara had a second job."

She stared. "She was working for Riordan?"

"She was taking bribes. I don't know any more than that—not yet, anyway. I will. There was a secret compartment in her desk. I also found her checkbook; if the dates are accurate, she's been receiving payments from them for at least a year."

"Barbara was a spy?" She hoisted herself onto the edge of the desk and crossed her legs, reaching for her laptop. "If Elliot ever calls me paranoid again, I'm going to *spank* him." Flipping the screen open, she started to type.

"Uh, Jan?" I tucked my hair back behind one ear, bemused. "What are you doing?"

"Here at ALH, we pride ourselves on respecting the privacy of our employees' personal lives," she said, briskly. Then her tone changed, becoming more cynical as she added, "But if we have reason to believe they've been spying for the skank next door, I get to crack their computers like eggs and play with the gooey goodness inside."

"Huh?"

"It's called 'hacking.' Well, it would be if I didn't own her computer. But I do, so it's called 'taking an interest in network security.'" Jan continued to type, fingers moving in sharp, vicious jabs.

"The computer was off," I said, hoping I didn't sound as lost as I felt.

Jan looked up, and actually grinned. At least one of us was enjoying this. "That might matter if we were, y'know, in the mortal world. But getting electricity in the Summerlands is hard enough that it never works quite right, so we have to deal with kludges. Generators instead of ground power, lights on timers . . . computers that don't realize they're supposed to forbid network access when they're turned off." The laptop made a sharp pinging sound. "We're in."

"In what?"

"Barbara's computer. I have full access."

Now we were getting somewhere. "Can you do some sort of search for things that might have to do with Dreamer's Glass?"

She looked at me, amused. "I can make this computer dance the polka if I want it to." Her typing picked up speed, only to stop when the laptop pinged again. "And . . . whoa."

"Whoa? What whoa?" I craned my neck to see the screen. "What did you find?"

"Only everything," she said, mouth compressing into a thin, hard line. She tilted the laptop so that I could see the screen; it was covered by a list of file names so long that it scrolled off the bottom. "This is what I get when I search for files with the words 'Dreamer's Glass,' 'report' and 'confidential.'" She tapped the screen with the tip of one finger, and the first title lit up for a moment before a word processing program took over the screen, opening the file. "She was a busy little girl."

"Yes," I said. "It looks like she was."

The file Jan had opened was a financial overview of the company, the County, and their performance over the last few years. It was annotated, showing where Barbara had interfered with the County to the advantage of Dreamer's Glass. I glanced to Jan.

"We couldn't figure out where the money was going," she said. "Another two years and she'd have closed us down."

"Would someone have killed her over this?"

"Possibly," she admitted. "I might have strangled her myself. But . . ."

"But you wouldn't have killed the others. Can you print Barbara's records for me?"

"Of course." She shook her head, frowning. "This is so . . . wow. Babs was our *friend*."

"She was a cat. The Cait Sidhe have never followed the rules." I shoved my hair back again. "Would Dreamer's Glass have anything to gain by killing you all?"

"Just the land."

"There's nothing special about the knowe?"

"Not a thing. We dug the Shallowing ourselves."

"Great." Another dead end. "Make those printouts, and we'll keep working. Just be careful. Getting yourself killed won't bring anyone back."

"Don't worry. I won't storm over to Dreamer's Glass and confront the Duchess." Her smile was mirthless. "Although when this is over, I'm kicking her ass."

"Totally fair." I paused. "Is there any chance Gordan was working with Barbara?"

"No, not really," Jan said. "She got Barbara hired on, and she was always worried about her doing something stupid. They were working on a project together, and they'd been fighting for months."

"What about?"

"I was never quite sure. They seemed to be sorting it out between themselves."

"Good to know," I said, and hefted the drawer. "I'm going to go back to Quentin and start shuffling through this stuff. See if there's something else in here that we can use."

She blinked. "You left him alone? After telling us to stay together?"

"I left him with a locked door between him and the rest of the knowe," I said, feeling suddenly uncomfortable about that decision. "He's got the keys, and I needed to do some hunting."

"Well, at least it paid off." She looked up at the ceiling. "April, could you come here?"

The air in front of her flickered, and April was there, delight transforming her face into something bright and real. I looked at her, remembering what Gordan told me. April loved her mother. No one could see them together and deny it.

Jan looked down, and smiled. "Hey, sweetie. I hope I'm not interrupting anything?"

"Nothing of importance, Mother. May I assist you in some way?"

"Please. Do you remember Quentin?"

April's nod was immediate. "Yes. He is located on the first floor, in office A-3."

I stared at her. Either she'd just been visiting him, or she knew where he was without thinking about it. If it was the latter, the killings *couldn't* have been an outside job—she'd have spotted an intruder before they could do anything. "You watched us get here, didn't you? That was you in the woods," I said, before I fully realized I was going to.

"Yes," April replied. "I watch all entrances."

Right. Unless our killer was somehow invisible to April, we were dealing with a person, not a thing. "Have you seen anyone strange coming or going right around the murders?"

"Only you."

"I see. Will you be available later? I'm going to want to talk to you." I just needed to figure out what I was going to ask her.

She slanted an anxious glance toward Jan. "Mother?"

"Do as Toby says, sweetie; it's all right." April made an unhappy face. Jan smiled. "I know you don't want to. Tell you what: I'll come to your room and watch a movie with you tonight, real-time, okay? We can snuggle."

"Will there be popcorn?"

"Popcorn and cartoons."

"Acceptable," April said, and vanished.

Jan looked toward me, a tired smile on her lips. "Normally, she watches movies straight from the file server, but she'll watch them slow if it means I do it with her." She removed her glasses, rubbing her eyes with the back of her hand. "Motherhood is exhausting. What was I thinking, saying I could handle a County and then adopting a kid? I must've been crazy."

"Jan . . ."

"This whole thing is crazy." Sighing, she put her glasses back on. "I'm sorry we were so weird when you got here. We've been running scared for a while now."

"I'm sorry," I said, and was surprised to realize that I meant it. "We're doing our best."

"I know you are." A flicker of something like anger crossed her face. "It's almost ironic. What we're trying to do here . . . people shouldn't be dying. That's the last thing that should be happening."

"What *are* you trying to do here?"

"Nothing big. Design better computers. Get the Summerlands onto a decent phone plan. Save Faerie." She waved a hand vaguely, like she was brushing off a fly. "The usual nonsense. What are you going to do now?"

"Go back to Quentin, and go through the rest of this paperwork." I picked up the drawer, tucking it under my arm. "I need you to be more careful. All of you. Gordan's in the cube maze, alone. Elliot is Oberon-knows-where, alone. Cut it out."

"I'll talk to them," she said.

"We've reviewed the information you gave us and searched the offices we could find. Did Yui have an office?"

"Yeah—she just hid it really well." She pursed her lips, looking momentarily unhappy. "When Elliot gets back, I'll ask if he can lead you there. He can usually find it."

"Elliot? All right. We can't find anything the victims had in common, other than working here. I'm going to have a second look at the places where the bodies were found, but I don't expect to find anything."

"They were hired from a lot of different places, for a lot of different reasons," Jan said, almost apologetically. "Colin . . . well, we needed a Selkie for some of our integration testing. It's difficult to explain, but race really mattered. Peter was a history teacher with a specialization in folklore—that wasn't just human folklore."

"Faerie historian?"

"Genealogist."

"Why did you need a genealogist?"

"Market research." Jan shrugged. "You can't use the same sales pitch with a Daoine Sidhe and a Centaur. It's not going to work. Yui was our team alchemist. She could make just about anything compatible with anything else, if you gave her time."

"What about Barbara?"

"Friend of Gordan's, hired in a nonsecure position. She was from San Jose. That probably explains why . . ." Jan stopped.

"Why she betrayed you? Yes, it probably does."

"Don't the bodies tell you anything?"

"Nothing. They died of some internal trauma; I have no idea what it was, but the external wounds can't have killed them. Maybe I'd know if I were more of a forensics expert, but I don't, and I'm not." The fae have never needed forensics training; that's what the Daoine Sidhe are for. Unfortunately, that means we don't have many options when the blood fails us.

"Maybe you're too weak to ride their blood," Jan said, slowly. "Changelings are weaker a lot of the time, aren't they?"

"Quentin tried, too. Nothing."

"We can't get you a forensics expert. We can't get the police involved."

"I know," I said. "Unfortunately, the dead aren't talking."

"But why are they like that?" she asked. "Why didn't the night-haunts come?"

"I have no idea." I raked my hair back with both hands, trying to hide my exasperation. "You'd have to ask the night-haunts."

"Well, can you do that?"

I paused. "Can I . . . ?"

Could I ask the night-haunts? Were they something you could *ask*? I'd never seen them, and neither had anyone I knew; they came in the darkness, took the bodies of our dead and were gone. They weren't something you saw . . . but *could* I see them? Was there a way to summon them—and more importantly, could they tell me what I needed to know? The Daoine Sidhe know death, but the night-haunts *are* death. They might have the answer. I owed it to Jan to try.

Jan was watching me. I nodded, saying, "It may be possible; I don't know. I've never heard of it being done. Maybe they can be summoned without a body." I paused. If there was anyone who would know how to call the night-haunts . . . "I'll have to get back to you on that."

"Please."

"I'm going to head back to the office, go through these files, and try to figure out whether it's possible. And get coffee. I really need coffee. Will you be okay until Elliot gets back?"

"I'll be fine." She pushed her glasses up with one finger. "I'll lock the door and check in with April every few minutes."

"Okay." I inclined my head in the bare outline of a bow, tucked the drawer up under my arm, and walked back out into the hall. I had a lot to think about.

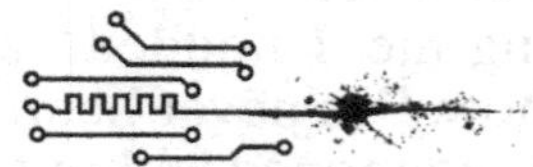

SEVENTEEN

VOICES RAISED IN faint argument were drifting through the door of Colin's office. I sped up. Quentin's safety was the one thing I wasn't willing to risk. That's why I wanted him to stay in the office in the first place: better paranoid with a locked door between him and the rest of the knowe than following me when I wasn't sure I could protect him.

"—and I'm telling *you* that if they focused more on telling a good story, the graphics wouldn't matter! How many explosions do you *need* in the first ten minutes of a movie?" That was Quentin. He sounded annoyed, but not like he was being threatened.

"Your argument is specious," countered the second voice. April, who sounded like, well, herself. Not quite bland enough to be a machine, but close. "You are a teenage male. Teenage males like explosions."

"Generalize much?"

I relaxed before leaning forward and knocking, noting impassively that my brief terror seemed to have helped my exhaustion. The voices went quiet. Then Quentin called, "What's the password?"

"Do your homework. Now let me in."

He unlocked and opened the door, revealing April in my abandoned seat. The Hippocampi were clustered at the end of the tank, apparently as unhappy with the Dryad's presence as they'd been with mine. I looked between them and raised an eyebrow.

"I tested that 'pager' thing," Quentin said. "I just said her name and she showed up. And then we started talking about movies."

April disappeared from the chair, reappearing next to Quentin. "His taste in plot and construction is contrary to that of most teenage males and does not make sense."

"Chalk it up to his archaic upbringing," I said, not bothering to smother my grin. "You two about finished? I need to update Quentin."

"I have duties which I can attend to," April replied. Looking toward Quentin, she said, "We will resume at a later point," and vanished.

"Looks like someone has an admirer," I said, and closed the door. "She open up at all?"

"Not really," he said, sitting down again. "I learned that she likes AC current but DC tickles, she likes rabbits, and she thinks computer games are good exercise programs. Oh, and she doesn't approve of people dying, because it disrupts the production schedule."

I put the drawer from Barbara's desk down next to the tank of Hippocampi. "So she doesn't know anything?"

"If she does, it's not anything I can get out of her."

"Great." I shook my head. "Not exactly useful, but you tried. Good for you."

"Did you find anything?"

"Well, Barbara was spying for the Duchess of Dreamer's Glass; I found her files. Everyone in this County has a death wish and insists on hanging out alone. And I need coffee. Get your things, we're heading for the cafeteria."

Quentin stood, nodding. "Do we know when my ride's going to get here?"

"Ready to leave?"

He grimaced. "Ready to not be sitting in this office anymore."

"I need to make a call anyway; we'll call Shadowed Hills afterward, see if we can get a status." I was assuming Tybalt had actually given Sylvester my message, and that someone would be waiting by the pay phone.

"Who are you calling?"

"Jan's asked me to try summoning the night-haunts."

Quentin froze, staring at me. "Can you *do* that?"

"We'll never know until we try." I was glad he hadn't asked who I was calling. We'd both be happier if he didn't know that part of things until he had to.

"Will they be able to help?"

"I have no idea." The night-haunts live on the flesh of Faerie. They might decide I was an ideal midnight snack and rip me into pieces . . . but they might also decide to answer my questions. They had to have a way of knowing when anyone with fae blood died; they arrived too quickly not to. If they were capable of thought, they'd have a reason for their actions. They could share it with me. There was a chance that I'd get myself killed in the process, but that's always a risk; if it worked, it would be worth it.

He watched my face as we left the office, starting down the hall toward the cafeteria. "Toby?"

"Yeah?"

"Is this a good idea?"

"Absolutely not. But it's the only one I've got just now, so we're going to run with it."

"Right," he said, with a sigh.

We walked the rest of the way to the cafeteria in silence. I opened the door to reveal Elliot sitting at one of the tables, staring into his cup. He looked up and smiled when we entered, trying to look like he wasn't worried. It wasn't working. "Hey."

"Do we need to have a talk about what 'keep someone with you' means?" I asked, heading for the coffee machine. My exhaustion was fading, replaced by a sense of general irritation with the world. "Why are you here by yourself? Jan's alone in her office."

He sighed, putting down his cup. "You're mad at me."

"I'm mad at everyone." I poured myself a cup of coffee as Quentin walked past me to the soda machines. "You're the third person I've found alone. Are you *trying* to make this harder than it has to be?"

"No, I'm not. I'm sorry."

"Forget about it," I said, and took a long gulp of coffee, relaxing as I felt the caffeine starting to hit my system. "Quentin, get something nutritious to go with your soda. A Snickers bar or something." Peanuts have protein, right? Topping off my coffee, I walked over to the pay phone.

"Dial nine for an outside line," said Elliot.

"I don't think that's going to be an issue." I put down my coffee, picked up the receiver and pressed my palm against the keypad, hitting all the numbers at once. The smell of grass and copper rose around me, almost cloyingly strong as I chanted, "Reach out, reach out and touch someone." Quentin and Elliot were looking at me like I was nuts. That was all right; maybe I was.

The silence gave way to clicks, which faded and were replaced by watery ringing. Then a familiar, irritated voice was on the line, saying, "Hello?"

There are times for pleasantries; this wasn't one of them. "Luidaeg, it's Toby. I need to summon the night-haunts." Elliot stiffened. Quentin dropped his soda. Well, they recognized the name.

The Luidaeg was silent so long that I was afraid she'd put the phone down and walked away. Then she snarled something in a language I didn't recognize before demanding, in English, *"What?!"*

"I need to summon the night-haunts." Repetition is

sometimes the best way to deal with the Luidaeg: just keep saying the same thing over and over until she gets fed up and gives you what you want. All preschoolers have an instinctive grasp of this concept, but most don't practice it on immortal water demons. That's probably why there are so few disembowelments in your average preschool.

"Why?"

I outlined the situation as quickly as I could without leaving anything out. Dealing with the Luidaeg is a bit like juggling chainsaws, except for the part where you can't master the trick. A chain saw won't flip randomly in midair and dive for your throat: the Luidaeg might. Worse, if she thought I was holding back on her, she could refuse to help.

Elliot paled as I described what I'd found in Barbara's desk, but kept listening, horrified and fascinated. Quentin gave me a wounded look and turned away. It wasn't that I was calling for help: it was that I was calling the Luidaeg, who had every reason to hurt me after she helped. Almost everyone's heard of the Luidaeg; she saw most of Faerie born, and she may see it die. Even for people who are supposedly immortal, that kind of age is scary. Some people say she's a monster. I just say that she's got issues.

When I finished she said, "And that's why you want to summon the night-haunts?" She didn't sound angry; just tired, and a little bit exasperated.

"Yes. I'm hoping they can tell me why they haven't come for the bodies."

"What if they won't tell you? What if they don't know?"

"I don't know," I said, opting for honesty before cleverness. "I'll think of something."

The Luidaeg snorted. "I'm sure you will. How many of the people you're 'guarding' will die while you think?"

That stung. "I'm doing the best I can."

"Is it good enough?"

"Are you going to help or not?" Across the room, Quentin winced. The Luidaeg's had millennia to learn how to piss people off. It was probably always a natural talent, but at this point, she can pack a world of insult into a single word.

"I shouldn't, but I will," she said. "Mostly because if I don't, I'm sure you'll try anyway and get yourself killed while I'm not there to watch. Do you have a pen?"

"Yes," I lied, and gestured to Elliot, making scribbling motions in the air. He handed Quentin a notebook and pen, and Quentin brought it to me, quickly. I nodded to him, saying into the phone, "Go ahead."

"Ask me the question first."

"Luidaeg, I—"

"You know the rules. Ask me, and I'll tell."

"How do I summon the night-haunts?"

"Good girl. Now, here's what you'll need . . ." And she started rattling off ingredients and ritual gestures the way most people assemble shopping lists. Fortunately, I take good shorthand. Quentin watched, grimacing as I wrote out more and more elaborate instructions. I ignored him, continuing to write until she finally stopped, snapping, "You got that?"

"I think so. First, you . . ."

She cut me off, saying, "Good. Remember, don't get cocky, and be sincere. It's the intention they'll be listening to, not the shape; if you don't believe in what you're saying, the night-haunts have the right to demand you go with them as a sacrifice." She paused. "I should set up a deal like that. Bother me and I get to eat you."

"Luidaeg?"

"Yes?"

"Will this work?"

"Follow my instructions and it will. Do you understand what you're summoning?"

"I think so."

"Good. You do this alone. They won't answer if they feel the calling isn't unified."

I glanced at Quentin and Elliot, wincing. They weren't going to like this. "All right. I understand." I'd have to explain while we prepared.

"Understand this, too—that was your last question. My debt to you is paid. I don't owe you anymore." The line went dead.

I set the receiver back in the cradle, saying, "I know, Luidaeg. I know." She'd owed me one true answer to any question I cared to ask. She didn't owe me anymore. If I survived ALH, I might be coming home to my own execution.

Is there a law that says life can't be simple?

"Toby? What's wrong? What did she say?" Quentin sounded like he was on the verge of panic. It's not every day you watch someone call the monster under your bed for help.

"She said . . ." *That she's going to kill me.* I took a deep breath, suppressing the thought, and started again with, "She said I could do it. I can call the night-haunts."

"You're going to do what?" Elliot asked, eyes wide.

I turned to look at him. "Weren't you listening? I'm going to summon the night-haunts so they can tell me why they haven't been coming for the bodies."

"Are you sure that's wise?" Elliot looked more worried than Quentin. Between the two of them, I could tell which one actually had an idea of what the night-haunts could do.

"No. But the Luidaeg told me how to do it, and I guess I should follow her directions."

"How can you just *call* the Luidaeg?" Quentin demanded, somewhere between awed and afraid.

"It helps to have the number." I sighed, looking at my hastily-written list of ingredients. "Elliot, is there a florist near here?" The ritual the Luidaeg outlined was a gardener's nightmare, demanding dried samples of all the common fae flowers and about a dozen of the uncommon ones. It made sense, from a symbolic standpoint. From the perspective of obtaining the flowers, it was just annoying.

"Yes . . ." he said, slowly.

"Great. Would you do me a teeny little favor?" Anyone who knew me would have known better—when I ask for favors, run, especially if I'm using words like "teeny." Cute phrases and I don't meet often. Stacy and Mitch would've been out the door as soon as I opened my mouth, heading for a sudden appointment in Tahiti. Fortunately, Elliot didn't know any better. The sap.

"Sure. Uh . . . what do you need?" He looked nervously at the phone. Considering what he'd overheard, he was probably expecting me to ask for a live chicken and a boning knife.

"These." I flipped to a clean page, copying the list. "Dried is better, dead will do. The florists may not want to sell you dead flowers—you may have to dumpster dive." I ripped out the page, handing it to him. "I need them to construct my circle. The ritual starts at sunset."

I have to give him credit: he took the idea in stride. "I'll get right on it," he said. "Is there anything else you need?"

I consulted my notebook. "Half a pound of sea salt, six unmatched candles—preferably ones that have been burned before—juniper berries, a mandrake root, and some raven's feathers." It sounded like I was getting ready for a supernatural Girl Scout Jamboree.

"Oh." He considered. "There's sea salt in the kitchen, and about a dozen candles in the earthquake preparedness kit." Most California fae keep earthquake kits. Immortality's not that useful when the earth opens up and swallows you whole.

"Really? That helps."

"Hold on . . ." Elliot pinched the bridge of his nose.

"Do they need to be feathers from a real raven, or will skin-shifter feathers do?"

I paused. Selkies are the most common breed of skin-shifter, but there are others, including the Raven-men and Raven-maids. "I can't tell the difference," I said, finally, "so they should work."

"Our last receptionist was a Raven-maid, and she left a lot of feathers in her desk. They should be in the storage closet in front."

I looked at him quizzically, but it was Quentin who asked, "Do you people ever throw anything away?"

Elliot shrugged. "Not really."

"That's everything but the juniper berries and the mandrake root," I said. "Is there an herbal specialty shop or a New Age supply store near here?"

"I didn't see one," Quentin said.

Elliot looked at us for a moment, expression unreadable, and then turned to the door. "Come with me." Quentin and I followed, exchanging a bemused look.

We walked through a series of short hallways, stopping at a row of dark, closed offices. The nearest was marked with a small brass nameplate reading "Y. Hyouden." I glanced at Elliot. "This is Yui's office," I said. "We couldn't find it earlier. We were looking."

"It's hard to get here if you don't know the way," he said, pressing his palm against the door. "She liked her privacy."

"Jan mentioned that. She said you could lead me here."

"And I have," he said, voice soft.

"Why are we here?" Quentin asked. "I mean, other than the hunting for clues part."

"Because she always said she could stock an occult store out of her desk." Elliot closed his hand into a fist, leaving it against the door. "She was so smart . . . but she couldn't stop whatever it was that took her away." His voice was full of raw, angry longing.

I blinked, startled. I shouldn't have been: in any community as insular as ALH, some ties would be bound to run deeper than "coworkers." "Elliot?" I said. "Are you all right?"

"We were going to be married this fall," he said, like I hadn't spoken. "We were waiting for the leaves to turn. She wanted . . . she wanted to be married when the world was on fire."

The blows just keep coming. "I'm sorry." The words weren't enough. Words are never enough.

"It doesn't matter. She's gone, and you're going to find out who took her from me." He shrugged and opened the door, motioning us inside. I studied him, and then nodded, walking into the room. Quentin followed a few steps behind me, and Elliot brought up the rear, turning on the lights as he came.

Quentin stopped as the lights came on, eyes widening. "Neat . . ."

The office *was* neat, in an eclectic sort of way. It was decorated in a mix of "modern electronics" and "traditional Japanese," with red walls and soft lighting. The computer was on a raised platform surrounded by cushions, and a more standard drafting desk with deep, wide drawers was centered on one wall. Framed prints occupied three of the four walls; the fourth was dominated by a corkboard covered in glossy photographs.

"Toby, look," said Quentin, pointing toward the photo at the center of the display. It was the largest picture there, obviously situated in a place of honor, surrounded by smaller, more careless snapshots.

"I see it," I said, glancing toward Elliot. The picture showed him with Yui, dressed in summer clothes, smiling at the camera. He had one arm around her waist. Both of them were shining with that perfect, fragile happiness strong men have died trying to achieve; a happiness that was gone now. I think it must be worse to find it and lose it again than never to find it at all. Elliot walked over to stand in front of the picture, eyes filling with quiet tears.

If it were up to me, I'd have let him do his mourning in peace. Unfortunately, the Luidaeg's instructions were precise, and we were on a time limit. "Elliot . . ."

"Check the desk," he said, not taking his eyes away from the photograph.

I *do* know how to take a hint. I walked over to the desk and opened the left-hand drawers. Quentin followed, doing the same on the right. Peering inside, I let out a long, low whistle. "Wow."

Yui wasn't exaggerating when she said she could stock an occult supply store with the contents of her office. The drawers were packed with jars, bottles, and packets of herbs, wedged alongside bundles of feathers, dried flowers, and stranger things—all the necessities of life. I started to rummage. "Quentin, find the juniper berries."

"What will they look like?"

"Dark purple pebbles. Sort of leathery."

"Got it."

The mandrake was in the second drawer I checked. I slid it into my pocket, shuddering as I felt the power leaking through its white silk covering. It had been gathered properly, wrested from the ground beneath a full moon; that was the only explanation for the way it was radiating strength. The preparation meant that it would work better, and more reliably . . . but I still didn't like it. Mandrakes are used for the creation of doubles and Doppelgangers. They're tools for people darker and creepier than I've ever wanted to be, but the Luidaeg had made it clear that there were no substitutions allowed.

I was just glad Yui's mandrake was an infant, barely six inches long; I could never have handled a three foot long adult. It would have been too much for me and might have seized control of the casting. Letting a mandrake root take control of a blood magic ritual is a quick and easy way to die. Quick and easy; not painless.

"I've got the juniper berries," Quentin said, holding up a glass jar.

"And I've got the mandrake. Elliot?"

"What?" he asked, finally looking away from the picture.

"You said you had feathers?" I continued to look through the drawers as I spoke, taking note of their contents. Many Kitsune are herbal alchemists, using plants and minerals to strengthen their magic. Some of the things Yui had were powerful, like the mandrake, but none of it was suspicious; it was just a Kitsune's tool kit, designed to let her work her magic with as little effort as possible.

"Yes—I'll send them with April after I've checked with Jan and arranged for the flowers. What are you doing?"

"Checking the office," I said, and closed the desk drawers, moving to the drafting table. Elliot stared at me, dismayed. I sighed. "We've searched the offices of all the other victims, Elliot. I'm sorry about Yui, I really am, but we still need to do our jobs."

"I . . . understand," he said slowly, and leaned against the wall, tugging his beard. "Please, continue."

"We'll be as quick as we can," I promised, and pointed to the prints on the walls. Quentin nodded, moving to start taking them down and checking the backs for hidden papers. I concentrated first on the drafting table, then on the computer and the cushions on the floor around it, turning things over and looking beneath them, hoping for another find like Barbara's office, and half-dreading it at the same time—I did *not* want to be the one to tell Elliot that his fiancée had sold them out.

Fortunately for my sanity, I didn't have to. We searched for twenty minutes and found nothing but a stack of half-completed projects, some technical manuals, and a book of handwritten sonnets that we surrendered to Elliot without thinking twice. Eventually, we admitted defeat, and I moved toward the door.

"There's nothing here. Quentin, come on."

"Can you find your way back without me?" Elliot asked. I could hear the promise of tears in his voice.

I didn't want to leave him alone. I didn't want anyone to be alone in this death trap of a company. And yet, somehow, I couldn't deny him the right to grieve. "Sure," I said.

Elliot nodded once. "I'll meet you there." He turned to exit the office, shoulders bowed. We watched him go, silent. What was there for us to say? I couldn't promise justice. If there'd been justice in the world, I could have given him Yui back. As it was, all I could do was try to avenge her.

He was barely past the doorway when April appeared, her arrival sending the smell of ozone and electrical fire washing over the office. Elliot stopped, turning back to face her, but her attention was focused on me.

"Are you available to receive a message?"

I blinked. "What?"

"Are you available to receive a message?" she repeated, tone exactly the same.

"That means you're being paged," said Elliot. "Yes, April, we're available."

"There is a visitor at the front gate."

I glanced to Quentin. "Sounds like your ride's here. April, who is it?"

"Identity presented as Connor O'Dell. Purpose presented as 'beat Toby's ass until she agrees to get the hell out of this death trap.'" April's neutral expression didn't flicker. "He is currently held at the front gate. Shall I permit him to enter?"

"Please. Quentin, come on." I grinned, unabashedly relieved. "We're getting you out of here."

EIGHTEEN

"WHAT MADE YOU THINK you should come without a car?" I stared at Connor, aghast.

He shrugged, spreading his hands in apology. "I thought you'd let us take yours."

"Ignoring the part where you just assumed you could commandeer my only means of transport, is there a *reason* you didn't ask the cab to wait until you'd checked with me?"

Connor shrugged again, looking helpless. "I didn't think you'd let me in if I had a mortal cabbie with me."

"He's right," Jan said, looking between us. "We wouldn't have."

I rolled my eyes heavenward. "Great. Just great."

Connor's arrival had triggered an impromptu assembly in the cafeteria; after notifying us of his arrival, April had gone off to tell her mother, who had, quite naturally, summoned Gordan. Recent events meant that it wasn't a good idea for nonresidents to walk around without an introduction. Only Terrie and Alex had failed to show up, which Jan attributed to the coming end of Terrie's shift. Quentin looked unaccountably disappointed by Terrie's absence. I might have been upset over missing

Alex, but Connor's announcement that he'd been planning to take my car had quashed that emotion, covering it with irritation.

"I couldn't have known that you were planning to blow up your car!" Connor protested.

"I wasn't *planning* to blow up my car! It just happened!"

Connor blinked at me. I blinked at Connor. Then, almost in unison, we started laughing. The absurdity of it all was too much. People were dying, Quentin's ride came without a car, I was exhausted and preparing to summon the night-haunts . . . my choices were "laugh" and "cry." Laughter seemed healthier.

Jan and Elliot exchanged a look before she cleared her throat and asked, "Should I be concerned by all this? Because if you're going to have hysterics, I'm going to scream."

"I think this is normal," said Quentin, uneasily. "I mean. They're always like this."

"Shadowed Hills must be a fascinating place," said Elliot.

Quentin sighed deeply. "You have no idea."

I wiped the tears from my eyes, getting myself back under control. "I'm fine. Honest. Connor's a moron—"

"Hey!"

"—but I'm fine." I dug my wallet out of my pants pocket, flipping through it until I found Danny's business card. "Well, you can't take my car, since it's sort of ashes right now, but we can call for a nonmortal cabbie. It'll just take him a little while to get here." I smiled, rather sharply. "You can tell Sylvester why we had to put a round trip from San Francisco on his tab."

"Doesn't anyone here have a car that I can borrow?"

"I rode my bike," said Jan, apologetically.

"I need my car," said Elliot. "I've been asked to raid the local florists, and that's difficult to do on the bus."

Connor blinked. "Raid the local florists for what?"

"I'll explain later," I said.

"Toby's summoning the night-haunts," said Quentin.

". . . or not," I said, as Gordan and Connor exclaimed, in unison, *"What?!"*

"You can't be serious." Connor looked alarmed as he stepped toward me, raising one hand to brush the bandages on my cheek. "You're already hurt. What if they go for you?"

"The Luidaeg gave me a ritual to keep them from hurting me."

"This is supposed to calm me down because . . . ?" he asked. "She's ancient and oh, right, crazy. She's going to get you killed."

I reached up, catching his hand and holding it firmly. "I trust her. It'll be fine."

I'm a good liar—I've had years of practice—and I've been lying to Connor longer than I've been lying to almost anyone else. He searched my face for a moment, and was apparently reassured by what he found there, because he squeezed my fingers, raising our joined hands to rest his knuckles very lightly against my cheek.

"You look like shit, Daye."

"You don't look so good yourself." I was lying again, but at least this time I didn't feel bad about it. Connor O'Dell is capable of a lot of things. Looking "not so good" isn't one of them.

He was tall, lean, and still managed to be fairly compact; if Alex was the magazine cover-model version of the California surfer, Connor was the real thing, right down to the calluses on his hands and the cut of his hair—long enough to be attractive, short enough that the waves wouldn't plaster it down over his drowningly dark Selkie eyes.

"Yeah, well. When His Grace decides to ship me off to Fremont at a moment's notice, I get a little worried." He held my hand where it was for a moment more before releasing it and turning to offer Jan a wry smile. "It's good to see that she doesn't just cause collateral damage at home."

"It's been educational," Jan agreed, holding out her hand. "Toby, you want me to call that guy for you?"

"Please." I passed her Danny's card. "Tell him it's for me, and he'll come. I mean, he'll bill through the nose once he realizes I'm not going to be the one in the cab, but that's why Sylvester has a bank account, right?"

Jan grinned. "Right."

"If you'll all excuse me, I'd like to get started on those errands," said Elliot. "The sun should be up any moment now, which will herald the opening of the flower shops. Gordan, would you mind accompanying me?"

For a moment, Gordan looked like she was looking for an excuse to refuse. Then she shrugged, scowling, and said, "Better than hanging around this mortuary."

"April will stay with me," Jan said. "That way, I can get some work done, but I won't be alone. Fair?"

"Fair," I allowed. "If you see Terrie or Alex, tell them we're setting up base here in the cafeteria. We'll just get my things from Colin's office." I didn't want to try cramming Connor, Quentin, and myself into the relatively small office for any length of time; someone would wind up with a bloody nose. Since it would take Danny at least half an hour to get to us, we needed to move to a bigger space.

"Got it," said Jan, giving me a small half-salute. And with that, we scattered.

For once, I was awake at dawn and didn't really mind that much. The sun came up when we were halfway down the hall, and Quentin, Connor, and I stopped where we were, leaning on each other's arms until the moment passed and we were able to breathe again. Connor grinned goofily, taking a little longer than was necessary to let go of me as he straightened.

"Remember that time we almost got caught out, and you pulled the blue eye shadow out of your purse and smeared it on your cheeks so you could tell people we were on our way to a *Star Trek* convention?"

Quentin blinked at him. I bit back a groan.

"Embarrassing stories later, paperwork now, please," I said, and herded them toward the end of the hall with Connor snickering all the way.

His snickering stopped when we entered the office. He took in the posters on the walls and the tank of Hippocampi before turning to me, asking, "Whose office is this?"

"Was. Colin Dunne's." He paled. I cocked my head to the side. "You knew him?"

"Not well, but, yeah, I did. How . . . ?"

"Same way as everyone else here: under circumstances we don't understand just yet. We're working on it. That's why you're getting Quentin the hell out of here, remember?"

Connor nodded, very slowly. "Where's his skin?"

His . . . oh, oak and ash. Groaning, I put a hand over my face. "It was in the car."

"The car."

"Yeah."

"Which exploded."

"Uh-huh."

"With Colin's skin inside it." He was starting to get angry; I could hear it in his tone.

I dropped my hand to see Quentin looking back and forth between us in utter confusion. Poor kid was probably fostered from a landlocked state. He wouldn't understand the succession laws of the Selkie families.

"It wasn't intentional. The car seemed like the best place at the time. It just—"

"How the hell am I supposed to tell his family that not only is Colin dead, but his skin's been lost? 'So sorry, you're down a member, forever?' Oberon's *teeth,* October, do you understand what a big deal this is? Did you even think—"

"You need to take some sort of sedative," commented Alex from the doorway. "Valium, maybe. Or just weed. Colin was a big smoker, there's probably a dime bag somewhere in here." He was rumpled, like he'd just gotten out of bed, wearing jeans and a black T-shirt that read "Mathematicians Do It by the Numbers."

I smiled. I couldn't help it. "Alex. Hey. We missed you last night."

"Sometimes, even I must go off duty." He entered the office, walking over to offer Connor his hand. "Alex Olsen. Pleasure to meet you."

Connor didn't take the hand. He just scowled at him. "I'm not sure your opinion was asked for."

"True, it wasn't." Alex dropped his hand, looking entirely unbothered by Connor's reaction. "Toby, you need me to help carry anything? Jan said you guys were setting up in the caf, and I just wanted to see if you needed any manual labor."

"Here." I passed him the drawer I'd taken from Barbara's desk. "Where's your sister?"

"Asleep in her office," said Alex. "Don't worry. Nothing's going to happen to her."

"You're sure . . . ?"

"Terrie's safe as houses." He smiled. "Nothing bothers her when she's sleeping."

"If you're sure. Quentin, Connor, get the rest of those folders. You're staying where I can keep an eye on you until Danny gets here." United by their apparently mutual irritation, they nodded, picking up the folders and heading for the door. Connor "accidentally" hit Alex with his elbow as he passed. I raised an eyebrow. "Behold the maturity."

"I get it a lot," said Alex, with a shrug. "After you."

I considered him for a moment and then nodded, following Connor and Quentin into the hall. "We'd better be quick, before they get themselves lost forever."

"Would that be such a shame?"

"Don't tempt me."

The brief ease we'd shared was gone, washed away by the tension. I eyed Quentin and Connor as we walked into the cafeteria, dumping my own share of the files on a table before heading to the pay phone. "Make yourselves useful and start putting those in alphabetical order."

"I'm your secretary now?" Connor asked, still looking annoyed.

"Consider yourselves the clerical pool," I snapped back, and dialed.

My suspicions about the phones were justified; the phone barely managed to ring before it was snatched up, and Sylvester's voice was saying, "October? Is that you? Are you there? Are you all right?"

"Whoa—I didn't think you'd be the one on phone duty." The image of Sylvester spending the night standing by the pay phone, waiting for news, was funny and tragic all at the same time. He couldn't help. I was miles away with his niece and his foster, and he couldn't do a thing but wait.

"What's going on? Is Connor there?"

"He's here, but, well . . . he didn't bring a car. We're calling for a cab, but it'll be a little while. Your Grace, I need to tell you what I'm planning. I'm going to summon—"

"Don't worry about that; I don't need to know. I trust your judgment. There's been a change of plans."

I blinked. "What?"

"It's not safe for them to be on the roads. Tell Connor that he's to stay with you until your business there is done, and you can all return to Shadowed Hills together."

"With all due respect, Your Grace, I don't think you

quite understand just how bad things are getting over here. We've got a lot of dead bodies in the basement, for a start, and that never strikes me as a good sign."

"There's nowhere safer than by your side."

I couldn't decide whether his faith in me was touching or insane. "Your Grace—"

"Just tell him to stay with you. Please, October. This will all be over soon."

"I don't think this is a good idea."

"Trust me."

That was that. Sylvester was my liege; if he wanted me to keep Connor and Quentin in Tamed Lightning, I didn't exactly have a choice. I set the receiver back in the cradle, turning to face the trio who had watched curiously throughout the call.

"There's been a change of plans," I said, slowly. And with Oberon as my witness, I had no idea what I was going to do about it.

NINETEEN

"TOBY?" SAID QUENTIN HESITANTLY.

"What?" I was sitting at one of the cafeteria's many tables with my head in my hands, fingers buried in my hair, trying to figure out what to do next. Recognizing my mood, Alex and Connor had been walking on eggshells since I got off the phone. Alex had even gone so far as to scrounge a box of donuts from somewhere in the kitchen before going off to tell Jan to call Danny and tell him not to come, while Connor brewed a fresh pot of coffee. Maybe more than one; every time someone refilled my cup, I drained it, making it impossible to judge exactly how much caffeine I'd had.

"If we're staying, does that mean we get to help you summon the night-haunts?"

"No." I raised my head, giving him a stern look. "It means Connor gets to keep an eye on you while I deal with them."

He frowned. "But if I'm here . . ."

"Quentin, look." I sighed. "If it weren't for the part where they're as likely to kill and eat me as they are to answer my questions, I might say yes. But the Luidaeg said that it's a solo summoning. If it comes from more than one person, it's not solo."

"Hang on." Connor lowered his half-eaten donut, eyeing me. "Kill and eat you? No one said anything to me about killing and eating. I am not in favor of you being killed and eaten."

"We need to talk to them, and this is the only way. Believe me, I don't want to. I'm scared stiff." I wasn't exaggerating. I was terrified, but it was too late to do anything about it. I was committed to summoning the night-haunts.

"I don't think this is a good plan," Connor said, reaching out to grab my wrist. "Get a better plan. A plan with less inherent death."

"Weren't you mad at me a little while ago for crisping a Selkie skin?"

"It'll be hard to be mad at you when you're dead, Daye." He tightened his grip, holding on for just a beat too long before he let me go. The warmth from his fingers lingered on my skin, reassuring me.

"Look, guys. This is going to happen, whether any of us like it or not. We may as well just try to do it right." I rose, taking my cup as I moved to check the cupboards near the coffee machine. They were a jumbled mess, but the third one yielded an almost full container of sea salt. "Elliot was right." I put it down on the counter before turning back to Quentin and Connor. "I'll have all the supplies I need to make this as safe as possible. Connor, I don't care what Sylvester says. If it looks like things are getting worse—"

"I take Quentin and run. Got it."

I risked a smile. Maybe having him around wouldn't be so bad after all. I'd still worry about Quentin, but Connor provided a layer of backup that I'd been missing since leaving Shadowed Hills. All I had to do was keep myself from looking into his eyes long enough to remember why it wasn't a good idea for me to be alone with him. "Good. Are there any chocolate donuts left in that box?"

"Saved you two," he said, and grinned.

"Excellent."

I was halfway through the second donut when Alex came rushing back into the cafeteria, the color high in his cheeks: a man on a mission. "Toby!" he called. "Jan wants to see you."

"What's up?" I put my donut down on the counter, then, regretfully, put my coffee down beside it. "Connor, Quentin, wait here. *Do not* go anywhere alone. I mean it. If one of you needs to pee, you go together and you leave a note. You got me?"

"Yes, ma'am," said Connor, mock meekly, before shooting a glare at Alex. Quentin just snorted.

"I'm taking that as agreement, Quentin," I said. "Alex, lead the way."

"Gladly."

Alex led me out of the cafeteria and down the hallway to a door I didn't recognize. Not that that meant much; I was learning some of the landmarks, but I'd given up on real navigation. He pushed it open, and I stepped through, onto a patch of lawn shaded by spreading elm trees.

I blinked, first at the lawn, then at Alex. "Where's Jan?"

"Not here." He grinned, sunlight slanting down through the trees and sparking highlights from his hair. Then there was no more talking, because he had his arms around my waist, pulling me close as he kissed me.

The first time I kissed Alex, it was a pleasant surprise. The second time was less surprising, if no less pleasant. The third time, it was like someone had just set my hormones on overdrive. I relaxed into his arms, plastering myself against him, returning the kiss with interest. His hands came up, snarling themselves in my hair, pulling me closer still as the smell of coffee and clover rose around us, almost overwhelming the green smells of the outdoors.

Coffee and clover. In my hotel room, I'd taken the smell to be an aftereffect of the illusion that made him look human. Here, standing on the lawn, neither of us was wearing a human disguise. Neither of us was casting any sort of spell at all. So why could I smell magic?

Startled, I pushed myself away from him so fast that I bit my lip, breaking the skin and spreading the taste of blood across my tongue. Alex stared at me, poppy-orange eyes wide in something that looked first like confusion—and then, as my shock and outrage spread across my face, like shame.

"Oh," he said softly.

"Oh?" His arms were still around my waist. I pushed him again. He didn't let go. I pushed harder, sending him stumbling into the nearest tree as I took a few rapid, stuttering steps backward. The smell of coffee and clover was getting thicker, hanging in the air like cheap perfume. "What are you doing, Alex?"

"Nothing! I—I'm not doing anything. Come on, Toby. Please." He held out his hands toward me. "You just need to calm down. Come on over here."

I wanted to. Oh, oak and ash, I wanted to. It was like a small voice in the back of my head was saying, *It's all right. He's not a bad guy. You want this as much as he does. You'd have wanted this anyway. Don't be silly. Just go.*

I took a shaky step forward before I caught myself. Biting my lip again, I clung to the hot taste of my own blood like it was a lifeline, and hissed, "You stop that right now, Alex, or I swear you won't be worrying about mysterious murderers anymore. What. Are. You. *Doing?*"

"What do you mean?" he asked, eyes going wide and innocent. The smell of clover was cloying, overwhelming the coffee and threatening to overwhelm even the taste of blood.

"You know what I mean. Stop it. I don't want this."

"Does it matter? If you feel it, does it matter?" He was almost pleading.

I didn't care. "Yes!" I balled up my hands, digging my nails into my palms and focusing on the pain. "I refuse to be in love with you!"

"Are you sure?" he asked. He took three long steps, put his hands on my shoulders, and kissed me again.

There was a moment of bewilderment before I realized what he was doing, and by then it was too late. The smell of coffee and clover rose, stronger than ever, and I melted into him, my body refusing to let me do anything else. I was trapped. The worst of it was that I couldn't figure out who'd betrayed me more—him, by being whatever he was, or me, for being stupid enough to get myself caught. His hands slid down to the small of my back, pulling me closer as the taste of coffee threatened to overwhelm the taste of blood.

It was getting harder to think about anything but kissing him. Dimly, I understood that if this didn't stop now, it wasn't going to stop at all. We'd wind up going places I didn't want to go, and I'd say yes every step along the way.

Mustering what control I had left, I pulled back, only half-pretending the need to catch my breath. He loosened his grip, and I twisted my head to the side until I couldn't see his eyes before biting down hard on my tongue. Blood filled my mouth, washing away the clover and coffee, and suddenly I could think again.

Alex pulled away from me, sensing the danger in my sudden stiffness, and I shoved him back as hard as I could. For the second time, he went stumbling into the tree; this time, he stayed where he was, watching me warily, not advancing.

"You *bastard*!" I drew Dare's knife from my belt, holding it in front of me. I didn't intend to use it, but I didn't want him coming near me again. "What are you?"

"Toby . . ." His eyes flicked from me to the blade and back again. "It isn't . . ."

"Shut up." Showing an unexpected degree of self-preservation, he did as he was told. I narrowed my eyes. "Now, I'm asking you again. What are you?"

"Scared," he said, softly. "I'm scared, Toby. I want someone to hold me and say it's going to be all right. Don't you want that, too? Just for a little while?"

For a moment, he almost had me. Then I swallowed, blood coating my tongue, and he lost me again. "Not like this. Never like this. Is this some sort of game? Do you and your sister try this routine on everyone who comes here? What kind of glamour are you using?" I was shaking, and not entirely from anger. Part of me wanted to dive right back into his arms, but I wasn't giving in.

He sighed, seeming to deflate. "It's not a glamour, exactly. I'm sorry. We can't help it. It just . . . comes naturally."

"And the way you act? Kissing me? That comes naturally, too?" Whatever bloodline they descended from, I never wanted to meet a pureblood.

"It does. Toby, believe me, this isn't something I do to every woman who comes along. I really like you. And—"

"Don't talk to me. You make me sick. And tell your sister that if she touches Quentin—if she comes *near* him—we're leaving. Sylvester will understand when I tell him why. You got that?"

Paling, he nodded.

"Just so we understand each other. What are you?"

"Toby . . ."

"What *are* you?"

"Please."

I looked at him for a moment before sliding my knife back into my belt. "If that's the way you want it. I'll ask Jan. Now go find your sister and stay with her. I don't want you anywhere near the rest of us."

He looked at me bleakly. For a moment, I thought he was going to argue—but the moment passed, and he turned, walking inside without another word. I waited until he was gone before sitting down hard on the grass, sticking my head between my knees. The world seemed to be spinning with a nauseating mix of adrenaline and magically induced attraction. What had I been *thinking*?

That was an easy one to answer: I hadn't been thinking at all. Alex had been doing it for me. If it hadn't been for the blood, I might not have figured it out. I might have just gone along, thinking it was my own idea. I shuddered and shook the thought away, lifting my head.

Half a dozen cats had appeared on the lawn around me, watching me with unblinking eyes. "What?" I demanded. They didn't reply. Taking a slow breath, I stood, catching myself against the nearest tree when the world spun around me.

I was so tired I didn't even want to think, but that didn't matter; Alex wouldn't come near me again, and I was pretty sure he'd warn Terrie away from Quentin. They had to be at least that smart, and for the moment, I needed to put them aside and get back to work.

Connor and Quentin looked up when I stepped back into the cafeteria. Quentin paled while Connor bolted to his feet, crossing the floor in five huge, ground-eating steps. "Toby? What happened? You're bleeding!"

It was too much. People were dead, Sylvester wasn't letting me get Quentin out of harm's way, I hadn't slept in over a day, and we didn't have a vehicle capable of getting us out under our own power. No matter how I looked at things, we were screwed.

I put my arms around Connor, put my head on his shoulder, and cried. He raised one hand to stroke my hair, somewhat unsteadily. I saw Quentin out of the corner of my eye, pretending not to see us. That's another thing they teach courtiers young: discretion.

It took a few minutes for me to get control of myself. I straightened, wiping my eyes and sniffling. I'm not pretty when I cry. My nose goes red and the skin around my eyes gets puffy. Mom gave me blood magic, Dad gave me the ability to cry myself into disreputability.

"You okay?" asked Connor. "Do you need to sit down? Or put an ice pack on your lip?" He paused, expression darkening. "It was that Alex guy, wasn't it? Did he hit you?"

The image of Connor going off to avenge my honor was just ludicrous enough to kill the urge to cry again. I giggled helplessly instead, moving to sit down in one of the uncomfortable plastic chairs before my giggles turned into full-fledged laughter. Quentin and Connor watched with wide eyes and almost matching baffled expressions, which just made me laugh harder.

"Does she do this often?" asked Quentin, cautiously.

"Not often, no," said Connor. "Toby? Does that mean I don't need to go hit him?"

"He's six inches taller than you," I managed, between gales of laughter. "He'd smash you."

"Yes, but I'd be smashed with honor," said Connor.

That set me off again, and it was several minutes before I calmed down enough to clear my throat, wipe my eyes again, and say, "Okay, guys, serious now."

"Serious," said Quentin, still eyeing me with suspicion, like he expected me to burst into a new flavor of hysterics at any second.

"Alex didn't hit me." Connor relaxed, only to tense again when I said, "I hit myself."

"Toby . . ."

"I needed the blood." I looked between them. "Look, I don't know what he and his sister are—he managed to talk me out of making him tell me—but whatever it is, they've got some sort of fucked-up glamour going on, and it's a strong one. I nearly had to chew a hole through my tongue to keep myself from—" *Going off with him and not showing back up until morning.* "—kissing him. Even though I knew I didn't want to."

Connor's eyes widened. "You're kidding."

"I'm not. You see a dark-haired lady with orange eyes, you don't go anywhere with her alone. You'll find yourself allowing liberties that Raysel probably won't approve of."

He reddened, looking away. Quentin frowned, looking thoughtful. "Does it count as being unfaithful to Katie if I wanted to be with Terrie?"

"No. It might if you'd actually done anything, but you can't help being enchanted." I hoped he'd believe me, because I honestly wasn't sure. You can't really get away with saying "magic doesn't count" when you're living in Faerie. Still, it was a good question.

My answer appeared to reassure him, because he nodded. "All right. What do we do?"

Seeing that look on his face—the look that said he knew I'd have all the answers, and that if he asked the questions right, I'd share them—made me want to run for the hills. I stood, ignoring the unsteadiness in my legs. No matter how shaken I was, I needed to keep moving. "All right, it's what, one-thirty? Two o'clock?"

"Two fifteen," said Connor.

"Close enough. We're going to get some work done."

"Work?" Connor raised his eyebrows.

"Work." I moved to the pile of folders covering one of the cafeteria tables. "Quentin, you've got A through L. Connor, you've got M through Z. I want you to pull anything that looks even a little bit weird."

"What are you going to do?" asked Quentin, even as he started to do what I'd asked.

"Go through these." I lifted Barbara's desk drawer. "There may be something here that tells us where to look next."

"I didn't know I was coming to play secretary," grumbled Connor.

"Then you should've brought a car."

The next several hours passed in the sort of mind-numbing grind that was so familiar from past cases. We shuffled files, looked for connections, made more coffee. Rearranged papers, checked time stamps, made more coffee. Jan wandered through, accompanied by April, to drop off a fresh pile of folders and get a candy bar from the machine. I acknowledged her presence with a grunt and a vague wave of one hand, too deeply engrossed in the tangled list of names that represented the company's lifetime employee tracking to realize I was missing the opportunity to ask her about Alex's heritage. That realization came later.

And time rolled on.

"Toby?"

"What?"

"It's four."

I looked up. "In the afternoon?"

"Yes." Quentin nodded. Connor was still bent over his own pile, grumbling. "When are you supposed to . . . ?"

"Sunset." I rose, closing the binder. "Time to get to work."

"What can we do?"

Get the hell out of here before something happens to you. "You still have those juniper berries?" He handed them to me silently, and I walked over to the counter, putting the mandrake root and juniper berries down next to the sea salt. "Elliot should be back with the flowers soon. It was a pretty big list, but there must be plenty of local florists."

A faint buzz in the air warned of April's approach before she appeared, clutching a small plastic bag. I didn't flinch this time. Connor did the flinching for me, recoiling so hard that his chair went toppling over.

I smothered a snicker. "Hey, April."

"I was instructed to monitor for signs of ritual preparation. I have brought you candles and feathers." She offered me the bag. I took it. "I have also been instructed to inquire regarding further needs." She paused. "Do you have further needs?"

"Actually, there's something I wanted to ask." Seeing that she wasn't going to react until the question was asked, I continued, "Do you know who was nearest Barbara when she died?" It was a shot in the dark, but one worth taking: if April knew where everyone in the knowe was at all times, she might be able to tell me.

April frowned. "Define 'died.'"

I paused. She'd never used the word "dead" in conjunction with any of the bodies. "Was removed from the network?" I ventured, trying to use words she'd understand.

"The time of removal is not recorded." Her voice was calm, like she was reporting something of no real consequence. Maybe, from her perspective, she was.

"I thought you knew where everyone in the company was at any given time?"

"Yes. I am aware of current locations. I am not aware of past locations unless I have had reason to take note of them." She shrugged. "Do you require anything further?"

"No; you can go." I needed to think about this—but later, after the night-haunts had come and gone. Assuming I was still thinking about anything by that point.

"Noted," she said, and vanished in a spray of sparks.

"What the . . ." Connor began.

"Dryad who lives in the local computer network," said Quentin, sounding disinterested. I had to smother another snicker. The kid was definitely learning about playing blasé.

"She's Jan's adopted daughter," I said, bouncing the bag she'd handed me to check the weight before I looked inside. It contained candles and feathers, just like she'd said. Normal Dryads can't take things with them when they teleport. The Tuatha can, but their method of teleportation is more direct—they open doors between places, rather than actually disappearing and then reappearing somewhere else. The fact that April could move physical objects said a lot about just how much Jan's procedure had changed her. "Take a look at this, will you?"

Both of them walked over to me, but it was Quentin who reached for the bag. I let him take it. He looked inside, then up at me, asking, "What about it?"

"Does it seem normal to you?"

"Um . . . yeah. Why?"

"Because April brought it with her when she teleported in."

Connor frowned. "Weird."

"Just like everything else about this place." I reclaimed the bag, putting it down on the counter. "You guys want to help me move the tables?"

"Just tell us where," said Connor, and smiled.

I smiled back. "Get 'em up against the walls." Moving to an empty table, I started to push. Connor and Quentin nodded before doing the same.

The tables proved to be surprisingly light; plastic is a wonderful thing. We worked in comfortable silence for a while, moving the tables against the walls and stacking the chairs in tidy piles. I was going to need a lot of space if I wanted to make a circle large enough to be secure.

We were almost done when Elliot pushed open the cafeteria door, Gordan close behind him. Both of them were carrying armloads of dried flowers; Gordan had almost vanished behind her heap of foliage, leaving nothing but the white-topped crest of her hair visible.

Looking up, I nodded. "Great. Put those on the counter."

"I'm sorry it took so long, but your list was very specific, and—"

"It's all right. We still have . . ." I glanced up at the clock over the door. "Almost an hour before the sun goes down. That's plenty of time to set up the circle." I straightened, planting my hands in the center of my back as I stretched, then walked over to pick up the sea salt. "Quentin, get the candles. Connor, the juniper berries." They nodded, moving to do as they'd been asked.

Elliot and Gordan watched me draw a wide circle of salt in the center of the cafeteria floor, making it large enough for me to sit in comfortably. Quentin followed me, handing me candles whenever I reached back toward him. I arranged all but one around the rim of the circle, using small piles of salt to hold them up. The last candle went into the circle just before I sealed it. There was no need to speak; Quentin understood the basics of ritual magic as well as I did, and he could see the shape of what we were making.

Finally, Gordan asked warily, "What are you going to *do*?"

"Connor?" I held out my hand, and he pressed the jar of juniper berries into it. I began walking around the circle, scattering berries as I went. "Well, most likely, I'm going to get myself carried off by the night-haunts. If that doesn't happen, I'm going to find out why they aren't taking your dead."

"What?!" Elliot stared at me.

Even Connor eyed him strangely for that outburst. I put my free hand on my hip, saying, "You knew I was calling the night-haunts, Elliot."

"You never said anything about them carrying you away!"

"What, you thought the night-haunts would be friendly? They don't like to be disturbed, but the circle should protect me, if I've done it right." I moved to pick up the silk-swaddled mandrake. "This is the sacrifice. Connor, get the feathers, would you?"

"Got 'em."

"What are the feathers for?" asked Gordan.

"They're the lure." Connor handed me the packet

of feathers, and I shook them loose, tossing them into the air. They landed helter-skelter all around the circle's edge, but not a one crossed the barrier of salt. "Ravens are psychopomps. They have a connection to dead things. So their feathers will help me get the attention of the night-haunts."

"And the flowers?"

"They're more death that used to be something beautiful." I knelt, placing the mandrake root in the circle, next to the last candle. "Before you ask, they need to be dried because otherwise, they're too close to being Titania's, and the night-haunts might be offended."

"Are you sure the night-haunts will come when you call?" Elliot again. He didn't look happy about the idea. That was all right; neither was I.

"I have the things I was told to get and a ritual to follow," I said, straightening again. "Now I just need it to work. All of you, help me get the flowers piled around the circle. Don't scuff the salt."

Working together, the five of us were able to get the flowers arranged as needed with time to spare. Not much time, but time. I measured the circle with my eyes and said, "You can go now. I'll take it from here."

Connor put a hand on my shoulder. "Are you sure you're going to be all right?"

"I'll tell you later, okay?" I ducked out from under his hand and walked to the coffeemaker, pouring myself a cup with surprisingly steady hands. "Keep an eye on Quentin for me."

"Toby . . ." Quentin protested.

"No, really. You have to go." I looked back at him, smiling wanly. "It'll be okay. I'm pretty tough, remember?"

"I don't like this."

"Again, neither do I. Now go, all of you." My expression hardened. "I need to get ready. Lock the doors when you go." I didn't need to add that what they found when they came back in might not be pretty. We all knew that part.

"I won't forgive you if you die," said Connor sternly, walking over and hugging me.

"Understood." I returned the hug, enjoying the familiar solidity of him almost as much as I enjoyed knowing that my pleasure in the gesture was real; no magic required. What I felt for Connor was genuine in ways that Alex could never understand. "I'll be fine."

"Don't lie. Just don't die on me, either."

"I promise it's not a goal."

He released me, turning to follow Elliot out of the room. Quentin lingered, looking at me anxiously before ducking out, pulling the door shut behind him. The bolt clicked a moment later. If I survived, I could shout for my freedom.

It was going to be a long night.

I drank my coffee slowly, savoring it, but decided against another cup. When I tired of pacing and worrying about what was going to happen I stepped into the circle, settling carefully into a cross-legged position. Breaking the protective seals wouldn't be the dumbest thing I'd ever done, but it might be the last. Time to wait.

If dawn is human-time, sunset belongs to us. I can't always feel it coming—it's subtler than sunrise—but sitting in the middle of a half-started ritual, I couldn't miss it. It didn't feel like enough time had passed when the air started to tingle around me, signaling the sun's descent. It was time to start. Oak and ash preserve me.

I removed the bandages from my left hand, grimacing at the state it was in—the broken glass had already done a number on it, and I was about to make it worse. Drawing Dare's knife, I placed it across the midpoint of my palm. I hate the sight of my own blood, but the Luidaeg was specific: it had to be the blood of the summoner, or it wouldn't work. I couldn't even choose a less essential extremity. My choices were hand and heart, and of the two, I knew which was more likely to be fatal. I just had to hope I wouldn't need any fine dexterity in the next few days.

Holding my breath, I jerked the knife across my hand.

The blade was sharper than I thought. I dropped it, swearing. It didn't matter; my part of the bargain was fulfilled. Blood was already welling up, running in hot ribbons down my arm. I unwrapped the mandrake shakily with my right hand, letting it roll onto the floor before cupping my hands together, letting my blood pour over it. The root writhed, soaking up the blood as fast as it fell. Drinking it in.

"My name is October Christine Daye, daughter of Amandine, and I am here to petition for your attentions," I said, concentrating. The air hummed with the copper and cut grass scent of my magic as the flowers piled around my ritual circle burst into blue-green flame. The candles lit themselves, and the overhead lights crackled, sending out sprays of sparks before going dark. A stabbing pain hit me behind the eyes. Magic-burn. I was going to pay for this night's work. I just hoped it would be worth it.

The room began to fill with thick, sweet smoke as the flowers burned. I kept letting my blood fall across the mandrake, trying to ignore the way the temperature was dropping, despite the fires. "I've brought you blood and flowers and salt from the sea. All our Courts together here support my plea." The mandrake whimpered. I raised my hand, bringing my bloody fingers to my lips and kissing them. "I bring you life." Reaching down, I pressed my fingers to the mandrake's "head."

The root stopped writhing, opening eyes like chips of summer ice. Before it could dodge or squirm away, I grabbed Dare's knife and drove it through the mandrake's body. The mandrake screamed, outer layers peeling away until a tiny, perfect duplicate of myself was writhing naked on the point of the knife. I slammed my hands flat against the floor, gritting my teeth as I said, "If I could speak with you for a moment . . ."

The room went silent. The mandrake stopped screaming, staring past me in terror, and even the crackle of the flames faded and died. A low buzz crept into the silence: the beating of the night-haunts' wings. I raised my head, barely daring to breathe.

They filled the room, hovering all around my circle. The ones near me had shapes I could name; they were all the races of Faerie, united by their shadowy pallor and their frail, fiercely beating wings. They dissolved into shapelessness as they drew farther away, becoming deep shadows and the fluttering sound of leaves on the wind. I gasped.

The figure at the front of the flock was Dare.

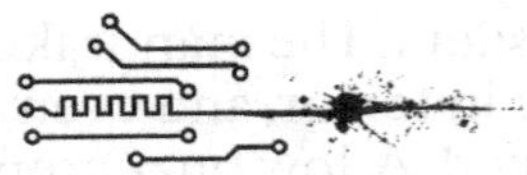

TWENTY

"DARE?" I WHISPERED. It couldn't be Dare. Dare was dead. I watched her die. And at the same time, it *was* Dare, because it couldn't be anyone else.

She was too slim for it to be intentional, underfed and scrawny. Her hair was vivid blonde, contrasting with her apple green eyes. Silver clips tipped her ears, and she wore a gown of dust and cobwebs, making her look like a deposed, despotic princess. The wings were new, blurred shapeless by their constant motion—the wings, and her height. Dare was small before, but now she was Barbie-sized, diminutive enough to stand in the palm of my hand.

There were other familiar faces in the crowd, similarly reduced and remade—Devin was there, as was Ross, the quarter-Roane changeling who died in Golden Gate Park—but most were unfamiliar, smudged to obscurity by the closeness of their fellows. I didn't see any of the people who'd died on the grounds of ALH Computing.

Dare watched impassively as I stared at them, wings beating hummingbird-fast. I wanted to leap to my feet and hold her in my arms and never let go. I wanted to beg her for forgiveness. I stayed where I was.

"You called. We came," she said. "What do you want?"

It was her voice that let me break through my shock. It had Dare's tone and cadences, but lacked the accent and emotion behind the words. She might have Dare's face, but that was all she had. "I called because I need your help," I said.

The night-haunts tittered. The one who looked like Dare tilted her head, studying me, and said, "I know you."

I froze. She continued, "The last owner of my face died with your name on her lips. I remember the feel of it. What do you want, October Daye, daughter of Amandine, who should never have called for us? This gamble is beyond you."

"What?" I whispered.

"Don't play coy. You know my face." Pain bloomed like a flower behind her apple green eyes, making her expression earnest and innocent. "Can I ask you a question, Ms. Daye?" she said, Dare's accent suddenly coating her words. Whatever she was, she wasn't kidding. "You got out—can you get us out, too? Take us with you? Please?"

"Stop it!" I snapped, before I could stop myself. "That isn't fair!"

"Since when has death been fair?" The innocence faded from her face, replaced by calm. "Death is how I know you. How we all do."

Other voices called from the flock, some familiar, some not. "Yes . . ." "I remember . . ." "She has forgotten, and we remember." "They all forget." "Yes." They closed around me, and I realized that my salt and juniper berries were no protection. If they wanted me, they'd have me. The mandrake tugged at the knife, slicing its palms, and I felt a brief flash of pity—maybe we were both trapped, but I had some hope of surviving the night. My newborn double didn't.

"Every death and every drop of blood you've ever touched is ours." Her eyes fixed on the mandrake and she smiled, displaying needle-sharp teeth that bore no resemblance to Dare's. "We know you better than you dream."

"I need your help," I said.

The night-haunt with Devin's face fluttered to the front of the flock. "What do you want from us?" Every word hurt. I'd been trying to summon the ghouls of Faerie, not looking for my own dead.

The night-haunts aren't something we talk about, even inside the comforting bounds of our own knowes. They live in darkness and come for the dead; exactly what they are and why they want the dead so badly is never discussed. Most don't know. I certainly never did. I was starting to understand them, a little bit, and I didn't want to.

"Our help?" said the one with Dare's face. "To what end?"

"There have been deaths here."

The one with Devin's eyes smiled. "We know."

"You haven't come for the bodies."

"That's sort of right. It's also wrong. We've come for the bodies. We just haven't taken them away with us."

"Why not?"

"If you want to know that, you must know us first. Do you want the burden?" He cocked his head. "Most wouldn't. Pay the sacrifice, and we'll go. We'll let you live. I can't make that promise if we remain."

Great: double or nothing. Let them leave without telling me anything, or risk everything to make them stay and tell me too much. For a moment, I wanted to let them go. I could pretend the ritual failed; Jan and the others would believe me, and there would be other ways to find the information I needed. It might work . . . and it might not. I'd paid for the right to question the night-haunts and be answered; the Luidaeg wasn't going to forgive my questioning her if I panicked at the last minute. Faerie has little compassion for cowards.

But even that wasn't what settled the question. Dare did that. I looked at the night-haunt wearing her face, and I imagined Quentin and Connor hovering beside her because I hadn't been willing to listen to what they had to tell me. That was the one risk I couldn't take. Never again.

"I can't do that," I said. "I need to know why you haven't taken this fiefdom's dead."

He smiled. "Then we'll tell you."

The night-haunt that was almost Dare—almost, but not quite—folded her wings and landed outside my protective circle, closing her eyes as she breathed in the smoke. There was no small amount of amusement in her expression when she opened them again. "You've prepared well. Someone told you, I think, how to ready yourself for us."

"The Luidaeg."

"Maeve's whelp? That explains much. Our mother was a sister of her blood; she watched us in our cradles and changed our swaddling cloths before they knew what we would be—before even we knew what we would be, although we suckled on blood from the first. And then we learned our purpose and devoured our mother, and fled the marsh and fen for darker havens."

The figure with Ross' face landed next to her, folding his wings. "We fled to the crevices of the world, and they did not pursue, for they'd been waiting for us. How we came, and when, those were unexpected—but they knew why we existed, and why we must be spared."

I thought of the corpses in the basement. "Faerie flesh doesn't rot."

"Of course not!" The haunt laughed. "It doesn't need to. The fae never die, after all."

"But in this world, they do," said the almost-Dare. "They founder and fall. Someone had to take the bodies, lest they bury the world. The pyres blackened the sky before we came; only fire cleanses the bodies of the dead as well as we do." An amused buzz ran through the flock. "For all that they were never meant to die, they did, and do, with such surprising grace."

"So you exist to eat the dead."

"Yes. But there had to be an incentive—you should know that. Your blood runs close to ours; we take the bodies, but you take the blood. Would you drink the lives of your kin if they brought you no revelations?"

"No."

"Neither would we. We were made to eat Faerie's dead; that doesn't make it pleasant. There are . . . other ways." She motioned for one of the night-haunts from the back of the flock to come forward. It came reluctantly, a translucent, half-drawn shape of mist and shadows, wings visible only when they moved. I could feel it watching me, even though I couldn't see its eyes; it was hungry. "Ways to force our actions, you might say."

"Oh, oak and ash . . ." I breathed.

"If we do not eat, we fade," she continued, ignoring my discomfort. "We learned quickly, and made a bargain with Oberon our father. We no longer touch the living, but the dead are ours. We eat their flesh, drink the memories in their blood, and use their shapes in lieu of our own. That is how it is. That is how it shall be. Do you understand?"

Did I understand that I was surrounded by cannibals who thought they had a divine right to eat my flesh? Oh, yeah. "I think so."

"Good. Then you understand why we do not eat the dead of this place."

Huh? "No."

"The blood remembers, and the memory is what keeps us alive—not just the flesh, but the life that wore it. We drink the memories and they give us shape, for a time. There are always more dead waiting when the memories fade."

The Ross-haunt nodded, snapping his wings open. They made a sound like ripping silk. "We drink their lives and live their hours, and we remember them. It's a small thing, and it ends, but we remember."

"We always remember," said the one with Dare's face.

Understanding hit. That was why their leader wore Dare's face, and why I recognized other members of their flock; they pretended to be the dead because they had no choice. No; that wasn't right. They *were* the dead. "You don't have shapes of your own."

"That's right. And something's beaten us to the bodies of this place. There's nothing here that can sustain us." She shrugged. "We don't work for free."

"Do you know what drained the . . . the memory of the blood?"

"No. This has never happened before." For a moment, she looked almost gentle. "If we knew why, we'd stop it ourselves. There aren't so many deaths in Faerie that we can afford to see them wasted."

"I understand," I said, trying to justify this with what I already knew. The blood was dead; this confirmed that it wasn't supposed to be. The night-haunts are a natural part of the faerie life cycle. If this had happened before, they'd have known.

"Do you understand why no one must know the why and how of what we are?" She looked at me sharply, waiting.

I nodded. "If all of Faerie knew, some people would burn the bodies to keep you from taking them."

"That is so. We would fade to nothing but the sound of leaves on the wind." She fanned her wings, closing them with a click. "Will you keep your silence, daughter of Amandine?"

"I will," I said. I meant it. Faerie has reasons to be the way it is, even if I don't always understand them. The night-haunts have as much right to be what Faerie made them as the rest of us do; if ignorance preserved them, I'd keep their secrets.

"You're wiser than most who deal with us. Is there anything else you would know?"

"No. That's everything I needed. We can end this now."

The night-haunt with Devin's face smiled. "What makes you think we're done?"

I went cold. "What more is there to do?"

"The matter of payment remains." He kept smiling, and I realized he didn't really care whether they took the mandrake or me. He wanted blood—any blood. The night-haunts hadn't survived by being picky.

I pulled the knife out of the mandrake's chest and picked it up. It clung to my fingers. I felt a brief, sharp pang of guilt. It was part of me, blood of my blood, and I was throwing it to its doom. Still, sentimental as I can sometimes be, I'm not stupid; if the choice was it or me . . . "I'm sorry," I murmured, and held it out toward the night-haunts. "Blood is all I have. I'm offering it to you, if you'll leave me my life and leave this place in peace."

"Why should we take it? You reject the blood and all it gives you." The almost-Ross looked at me, eyes cold. "We could take you."

"The Luidaeg wouldn't like it," I said, trying to sound confident. For all I knew, she'd laugh—especially if they meant it when they claimed to be her sister's children.

"She'd think you performed the ritual wrong," Devin's haunt said. "She'd blame you, not us."

Uh-oh. "Are you willing to risk it?" My heart was beating too fast, and I was sure they could hear it. If they decided to take me, there was nothing I could do.

"Take the offering," said Dare's haunt. "Let her dismiss us."

"But—" the Ross-haunt protested.

Dare's haunt moved too quickly for my eye to follow, seizing the larger night-haunt by the throat. It fell silent, watching her. "I found the last kill. I. Remember?" she snarled. The haunt she was holding nodded, sullenly silent. "I brought us blood and bone and memory, and until another kill is found, I rule. Is this not true?" She shook her victim again, glaring at the other haunts. "Is this not true?" They whispered agreement, drawing away from her.

She released her captive. It collapsed to the ground before slinking into the shadows of the flock. "I rule here," she repeated. The whispering night-haunts agreed. She walked back to the circle's edge, holding out her hands. "Give it to me."

Carefully, I reached past the salt, putting the mandrake down even as it scrabbled to hold onto my fingers. It was almost as large as she was. She placed one hand on its shoulder, and it froze, watching her with terrified eyes. "The dues are paid; you have given proper courtesy. We'll let you live."

"Why?" hissed the not-Devin. She turned, and he fell back, cringing.

"Because I said so," she said. "My most recent memories say she is a hero. Not just any hero; *my* hero." She looked back at me. "You will fade from my mind. If we meet again, I may not be so kind—but today, you are my hero. I've had few enough of those, in all my lives. Good luck to you. I'll find your body when you fall, and wear your face with pride." Her smile was small and amused. "It's the greatest gift I can offer."

Then the night-haunts rose as one body, dragging the mandrake into the air with them. It shrieked, voicing its terror. I clapped my hands over my ears, sagging forward in the circle as a shallower, more natural darkness filled the cafeteria. The sound of the fire slowly returned. The night-haunts were gone.

The emergency sprinklers finally registered the smoldering remains of my circle and switched on, dousing the room. I tilted my head back, cradling my wounded hand against my chest as the water poured across my face.

I didn't save Dare, but she'd managed to save me twice. I wasn't a very good hero, but I was the only one she had, and there's power in that. There's power in information, too, and I had all the information I could have wanted. I'd never wanted to know what the night-haunts really were, and I knew I'd never be able to forget. That could wait. For the moment, I sat in the falling water, surrounded by the cloying smell of burnt flowers, and cried.

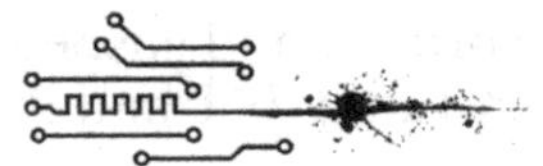

TWENTY-ONE

"TOBY?" THE DOOR OPENED, sending a shaft of light into my damp, comfortable darkness. I wasn't sure when the sprinklers had stopped; I also wasn't sure I cared. Connor called again, more loudly this time: "Toby, can you hear me?"

I tilted my face forward, wincing as my head started throbbing in earnest. Connor was in the doorway, with Quentin casting a dark silhouette on the wall behind him. At least they weren't wandering around alone. "Hey, guys."

"It smells like smoke in here," Quentin said, tone radiating relief. He probably hadn't been sure they'd find me alive. That was all right; I hadn't been sure, either.

"Can we turn the lights on?" Connor asked.

"If they'll work. They shorted out when the flowers caught fire." I forced myself to stand. It wasn't easy. My legs were threatening to abdicate from the rest of the body, and I wasn't coming up with any good reasons why they shouldn't.

Elliot spoke from behind Quentin. "I'll turn on the backups."

Backups. They had backups for the backups in this

place. It was amazing anything had been able to go wrong: they should've had backups for the people, too. "You do that," I said.

Elliot leaned past Quentin, flipping a switch, and a set of yellow-tinted lights came on overhead. All three of them turned toward me and gasped, almost in unison. It would have been funny if I hadn't been so damned tired.

"Toby?" Connor whispered.

"That would be me," I said, wiping the water off my cheek. "In the flesh, as it were."

"You look . . ."

"I know." My hair was plastered to my head. My hands were black with ash. "But I'm still here."

Elliot glanced at the mess covering the floor. "I'm not going to ask."

"Probably for the best," I said. Quentin had pushed past the other two and was approaching, almost timidly. I turned to him, mustering a faint smile. "Hey."

"Hey," he replied. "Are you okay?"

"I'm alive. That's all I hoped for." He still looked profoundly uncomfortable. I sighed. "Look, I'd hug you, but I'd get blood all over you."

"I don't care," he said, and threw his arms around my neck. I slung my right arm around him, letting my unwounded hand rest on his shoulder. Connor followed his lead, hugging me from the other side, and for a moment, the three of us just stood there, holding on to one another.

It was Elliot who broke the silence, saying uncomfortably, "This is . . . rather untidy. May I clean you?"

I pulled away from Quentin and Connor enough to look down at myself. Blood, ash, and streaks of muck stained my clothes and Tybalt's jacket. I was sure my hair looked like a dead animal stapled to my head. Still. Holding up my hand, I asked, "Is it safe when I'm still bleeding?"

". . . no," Elliot said, looking displeased. "We'll have to get Gordan to look at that." He crossed to the kitchen area, opening a cabinet and pulling out a clean towel, which he tossed toward us.

Connor caught it, pressing it into my uninjured hand. "Find her fast, please," he said, expression worried. "I don't like the way her hand looks."

"The way it . . . right." I hadn't really looked at my hand since cutting it. I'd been a little busy. "Guys, let go."

They stepped back, and I looked down, assessing the damage. I had all my fingers, and I could move them, if I was willing to cope with the pain: that was where the good stuff ended. My palm was split from the wrist to the base of the index finger, and when my fingers flexed, I thought I saw bone. Changelings heal fast and thoroughly when the wounds aren't made with iron; my hand would recover if I had it taken care of. It still looked pretty bad.

Starting to feel faintly nauseated, I said, "Getting Gordan in here might be a good idea."

Elliot nodded. "I'll fetch her. You wait here." Then he was out the door, hurrying away from the mess and from the questions he wasn't asking yet. That was fine. I wasn't ready to start answering them, and I didn't trust his self-control to last. I really didn't need him to start cleaning the room while we were still in it.

"Come on, Toby. Sit down." Connor took my arm and led me to a chair, with Quentin following close behind. I didn't fight. Judging by the looks they were giving me, I looked worse than I felt, and that was worrisome.

I collapsed into a sitting position, sticking my head between my knees. Connor began rubbing my back in slow, soothing circles, fingers shaking. The room was starting to spin. That's never pleasant. My headache wasn't helping. My magic isn't strong to begin with, and I'd just performed the largest blood-ritual of my life. In a way, it was a miracle that I was still coherent enough to hurt.

"Toby?"

He sounded worried enough that I forced myself to look up. "Yes, Quentin?"

"Did they come?"

I sighed. "Yeah. They came."

"Wow." Quentin sat down in the chair next to mine, shaking his head. "I . . . wow. Did you talk to them?"

"As much as I could, yes."

"Oh." We were silent for a while, Connor still rubbing my back, Quentin watching worriedly. Finally, voice meek, Quentin asked, "Are you going to die?"

"What?" The question was unexpected enough to get my full attention.

Swallowing, he said, "You've seen the night-haunts. Are you going to die?"

"I don't think it works that way. They don't cause death. They come after death happens. I'm not going to die because I saw them." I might die for other reasons, but I was fairly sure the night-haunts wouldn't have anything to do with it.

"Oh," Quentin said, relaxing. "Good."

We sat quietly after that. I was glad to have the company; even knowing the night-haunts weren't coming back, I didn't want to be alone. Both of them were clearly bursting with questions, but they kept their peace, letting me rest. I needed the chance to breathe.

Elliot came back after fifteen minutes. "Gordan and Jan are on their way."

"Peachy," I said, sitting up as Connor stepped back. "Got any painkillers?"

"Gordan doesn't want me to give you anything until she's seen your hand."

I decided to hate her. "Why not? It's my *head* that's killing me."

"Because we don't know how much damage you've

done to yourself." He gestured toward the remains of my protective circle. "It looks like you held a war in here."

"I almost did," I said.

"Care to explain?"

"Give me the painkillers and I will." Connor almost managed to hide his smirk—almost. He knew Elliot was fighting a losing battle; if stubbornness were an Olympic sport, I'd be a gold medalist.

"Right." Elliot sighed. "We wait."

I glared. "That was supposed to make you give me the pills."

"I know." He bared his teeth in a humorless grin. "I'd just rather have *you* mad at me than Gordan."

"Why?" Quentin asked.

"I'm pretty sure I could outrun you at the moment, but Gordan knows where I sleep."

"You sleep?" I said dubiously. "When?"

Elliot shrugged. "Popular opinion holds that's the reason I have a house."

"Right," I said, fighting back a wave of dizziness. I let myself lean backward, into Connor. Sleep sounded like an excellent idea. I would have liked it better if I was certain I'd wake up. "I guess that's understandable."

"Did they . . ." Elliot glanced at the circle again. ". . . come?"

"The night-haunts?"

Elliot nodded, expression telling me he didn't really want to know.

I answered anyway. "Yes." In retrospect, I hadn't wanted them to. There's that damn hindsight again.

"This can wait until everyone else gets here," said Connor firmly.

I offered a wan smile, sending a silent thanks to whoever might be listening. "Good idea. I don't want to go through all this more than once, anyway."

"Fine," Elliot said disgruntledly and turned to watch the door. I sighed. I was too tired to deal with clashing personalities and sulking locals. All I wanted to do was curl into a ball and sleep until the pain went away.

"Elliot . . ." I began, only to be saved from further discussion by the door swinging open. Gordan stepped into the room, first aid kit in her hand and a scowl on her face, closely followed by an anxious-eyed Jan. Oh, root and branch. How could I tell her what was going on when I still didn't understand myself?

Gordan gaped at the bloody mess that was my left hand, planted her own hand on her hip, and demanded, "What have you done to yourself *now*?" The cafeteria's acoustics caught her voice, bouncing it off the walls until it became an invasive presence. My headache announced its displeasure, leaving me even dizzier.

"Please stop shouting," I moaned. I wanted to yell, but I didn't dare. My head might explode.

Quentin stood, moving to stand a half step in front of me. Even through the pain, I was amused; he was learning how to be protective. "Shut up!"

"Oh, the pretty boy thinks he's gonna be a big man now, does he?" Gordan said. "If you're so tough, why is it *her* blood I keep having to mop up? You too good to bleed?"

"You little—"

"Stop it! Both of you!" Jan snapped. Quentin stopped mid-word, while Gordan snorted and looked away. Glaring, Jan shook her head. "You should be ashamed. Did you stop to think for a *second* that you weren't helping her recover by fighting? Huh?" Neither answered. Jan sighed and knelt in front of me, lifting my chin with one hand. I didn't fight. Connor tightened his hands on my shoulder, and waited.

Jan tilted my head to one side, then the other, studying my eyes. Whatever she saw there didn't please her, because she frowned as she let go and stood. "The next person who yells is going to regret it. I don't know whether whatever she did worked, but it's left her with a pretty vicious case of magic-burn."

Gordan turned to glare at her. "She's the idiot that pushed her limits. Why do we have to be nice?"

"She was trying to help *you*!" Quentin snapped.

Jan sighed. "I know, Quentin. Gordan, can you please take a look at her wounds without being snotty about it?"

"I'll try," she muttered, and sat down in front of me, ignoring the dirty water covering the floor. "Give me your hand." I did as she asked; it was easier than fighting her.

Gordan grabbed my wrist, twisting my palm toward the ceiling. The cut looked even worse in direct light. Jan gasped, while Quentin made a small gagging noise. Gordan just frowned, asking, "What did you do, argue with a lawnmower?"

I swallowed, vowing not to faint until she was done hurting me. "Silver knife. Summoning ritual. I didn't mean to cut so deep."

"You're an idiot," she said, sounding almost impressed. "You'll be lucky if you missed the major muscles. What were you summoning again? Godzilla?"

Hands tightening on my shoulders, Connor said, "She was summoning the night-haunts."

"Oh, right, she's a fucking moron," said Gordan, sounding entirely too cheerful about it.

"Gordan . . ." said Jan warningly. Gordan subsided, grumbling under her breath as she resumed her inspection of my hand. Jan waited for me to relax before asking, "Did it work?" Elliot turned toward me and Gordan glanced up, both waiting for my answer.

"Yes," I said. "They came. Sorry about the floor."

"No big deal," Jan said, waving it away. "Did they . . . did they tell you anything?"

"Some, yes. We were wrong when we thought they

weren't coming. It's just that the bodies aren't any good to them, so they've been leaving them behind."

"Why aren't they any good?"

"For the same reason Quentin and I can't get anything out of the blood. Whatever's been killing your friends has been somehow stealing the . . . vitality that should be left in their bodies."

"It's stealing their *souls*?" Elliot asked, sharply.

I shook my head, wincing as it throbbed. "It's not stealing their souls; it's stealing their memories. Your life is stored in your blood, but the blood here is empty. Their memories are gone, and the memories are what the night-haunts need."

"Why?"

"I don't know." I told the lie without flinching. I'd promised the night-haunts I'd keep their secrets, and I meant it.

"It's stealing their *memory*?" Jan said, putting an odd stress on the last word. Something flitted across her face, there and gone so fast I wasn't sure I'd seen it at all.

"Yes."

"So the night-haunts are leaving the bodies here . . ."

"Because they just don't care," said Gordan, and grabbed my fingers, yanking them down. The pain was incredible. I screamed.

What happened next was a little blurred. Jan shouted. I tried to jerk to my feet, and Connor pushed me back down, keeping me where I was. Quentin started to move. Suddenly, my hand was free and Gordan was on the floor with her hand pressed against her cheek. Quentin was standing between us, fists raised.

"Don't *touch* her!"

Gordan pushed herself up, glaring. Quentin towered over her; she didn't seem to notice as she spat, "I ought to kick your overprivileged ass!"

"You want to try?" Quentin asked.

"Stop it!" Jan said. They ignored her. Whatever internal rivalry they'd created, they seemed intent on finishing it.

"I think maybe I will," Gordan said, stepping forward.

I took a deep breath, steadying myself, and stood. This time, Connor let me. The wet floor didn't make it easy, but I managed to keep my balance. "Are you two going to cut this out, or do I need to go somewhere else?" I asked.

Quentin turned, looking mortified. "Toby, sit down, you shouldn't be . . ."

"Gordan, back off," Elliot snapped.

She glared. "He hit me."

"You deserved it," Jan replied. "Now, if we're done being jerks? Toby, sit. Quentin, cool it. And, Gordan—was there a reason you just tried to take Toby's hand apart?"

"Yes," she said sullenly, rubbing her cheek. "I needed to see if she had feeling in her fingers."

"Well, now you know. So don't do it again." Gordan started to speak, and Jan raised her hand. "Please, I don't want to hear it. Yes, he hit you, and yes, you earned it. I'd like to get the rest of this story *today*."

"Right." I sighed, and sat again, leaning back into Connor. He returned his hands to my shoulders, lending silent support.

Grumbling, Gordan knelt in front of me. Quentin backed off, not taking his eyes off her. If she made one wrong move, she was going to regret it. Jan folded her arms, watching; Elliot was standing just behind her. I squinted at them, realizing how bad this looked. I was dizzy and sick from a combination of exhaustion and magic-burn, and now I couldn't even control my assistant. How was I supposed to help these people when I was barely standing up?

"Try not to squirm," said Gordan, slathering antibacterial sludge onto my palm.

I gave Quentin a sharp look, hoping he'd get the point and stay where he was. "The night-haunts aren't avoiding this place. There just isn't any reason for them to take the bodies."

"But what are we supposed to do with them?" Jan asked.

"We'll have to burn them; that's what we did before the night-haunts came." I shrugged.

Jan paled. "Oh."

"That can wait—right now, we need to figure out what's going o—ow! Gordan!" She'd tightened a loop of gauze around my hand, mashing the edges of the wound together. Quentin started to step forward. I held up my unwounded hand, motioning for him to stop. "That hurt!"

"So sorry," she drawled, and kept wrapping. My fingers were going numb; I couldn't see how that was a good thing. "I don't have the facilities to give you stitches without them turning septic, and I've got to stop the bleeding before you need a transfusion. Unless you want to try telling some human doctors what you've done to yourself?"

"Right," I muttered, and huddled against Connor, trying to distract myself from the pain. It wasn't working. My headache was making it hard to think straight.

Elliot looked at me, saying, "Jan, she met with Alex just before she did . . . whatever it is she did. I think she might need to lie down for a bit."

There was that expression again, flickering over her face and vanishing. "Are you sure?"

"I asked Terrie."

"What are you talking about?" I asked. Neither would meet my eyes. I looked down at Gordan, and saw that even she was focusing on my hand, not looking at me. "What am I missing? What does Alex have to do with anything?"

"It's nothing you need to worry about now," Jan said.

I eyed her. She sighed. "I promise. You just need to rest for a while."

"And you'll tell me what's going on when I wake up?"

"I will. You have my word."

I looked at her. She looked back. Finally, I shook my head. "Quentin? Connor?"

"Yeah?"

"I'm going to take a nap. I want you two to stay together. Wake me if there's any sign of trouble. Understand?" Reluctantly, they nodded. "Good. And, Quentin, I don't want to hear about your fighting with Gordan while I was asleep." *Even if she deserves it,* I added silently.

"But, Toby—"

"No buts. I don't care if she's the one starting everything. I'm too tired to deal with this on top of everything else."

He sighed. "All right."

Jan fixed a stern eye on Gordan. "The same thing goes for you. Both of you behave."

"Whatever," Gordan said, taping the gauze on my hand before starting to repack her first aid kit.

I eyed this and asked, "Can I have some painkillers first?"

Jan smiled, almost sadly. "Gordan?"

"Yeah, she can have some Tylenol." She pulled a bottle from the kit, tossing it to Jan, who removed the cap with a flick of her thumb. I held out my unwounded hand, and she placed three small white pills on my palm as solemnly as if she were handing me the crown jewels of India. I popped them into my mouth, dry-swallowing them in a single convulsive gulp. I don't know how we dealt with magic-burn before we had over-the-counter painkillers, but I think there's a reason the faeries in the old stories are so incredibly cranky.

Gordan snatched the bottle out of Jan's hand, scowling. "Be careful," she said. "Your hand will be weak for a while, and you should really have stitches. Don't strain yourself if you don't want to lose a finger."

"Got it," I said, nodding.

"Don't mention it." She raked a hand through her spiky hair, shooting a glare toward Quentin. He glared right back. "I sure won't."

"Gordan . . ." Jan began.

"Whatever," Gordan said. She turned, shaking her head, and walked out of the room.

Quentin scowled as he watched her go. "What a—"

"Stop right there," I said, levering myself to my feet. Connor moved to support me. "I know she is, okay? You don't need to stress. Just don't hit her again."

"Fine," he said. The tips of his ears were red, although I couldn't tell whether it was from anger or embarrassment.

Elliot sighed. "That went well."

"It could've been worse," I said, as diplomatically as I could.

"I'm sorry, both of you," Jan said.

"It's all right. We're all stressed." I forced a smile, leaning on Connor. "If you don't mind, I need to fall down until my head stops hurting."

"Of course." Jan looked away, but not before that strange, half-aware expression had crossed her face a third time. What the hell was going on? "Elliot, are you coming?"

"Sure."

I kept leaning on Connor as we left the cafeteria and made our way down several of the knowe's endless halls. Quentin took up the rear. We stopped at a small room containing a futon, a table and an ancient color television. Ignoring the TV and the fact that I was almost definitely showing how vulnerable I was, I collapsed on the makeshift bed, closing my eyes.

"Toby?" Quentin said.

"Stay with Connor," I said, eyes staying closed. "If you get bored, ask April to come talk. You like April. Don't . . . make trouble . . ." I was more tired than I'd thought: I was already starting to drift away.

"All right," he said. "Sleep well."

Connor bent over me; I felt him brush my hair back, fingers lingering against my skin before he whispered, "Don't you dare bleed to death."

I smiled, not opening my eyes. "I'll just work on that."

"You'd better. Don't you leave me again." Then he was gone. I heard three sets of footsteps leave the room. I stayed quiet, waiting.

I didn't have to wait long. Jan stepped closer, sneakers scuffling on the carpet, and said, "Toby? We haven't—*I* haven't told you everything, and I think it's important for you to understand what we're really working on. Promise you'll come find me when you wake up?"

"I'll find you," I mumbled. I wanted to make her tell me now, but I couldn't find my legs, much less make them work. We all have our limits, and I'd exceeded mine.

"Okay. What you said about the memory? This may explain. And I think it's important that you know." She sighed. "I need you to know everything."

"Promise . . ." I said. Something in me was screaming for answers, but the fog didn't care. I don't remember how long she sat there or when she left; all I remember is the fall into darkness and the half-dreamed sound of the night-haunts' wings.

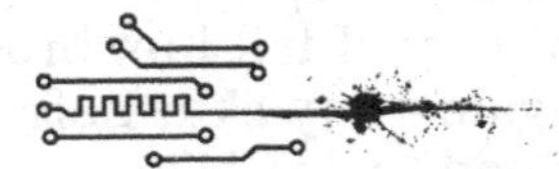

TWENTY-TWO

MY DREAMS WERE A TANGLE of twisted snapshots. April disappearing in front of the building in a hail of sparks and oak leaves; Gordan shouting in a dozen languages as she ran down an endless hall; Alex and Terrie, bloody hands intertwined, laughing. Pale-faced knights and maidens littered the ground, and I was looking for the birds. I had to find them. A phrase kept repeating, scrawled on walls and bulletin boards: ". . . and no birds sing." Why did it matter whether or not the birds were singing? And above it all there was the faint, constant buzzing of the night-haunts' wings, and a voice saying, "You were my hero. I've had few enough of those."

"What about the birds?" I shouted. The walls were falling, leaving me scrambling for purchase on the dissolving ground. "I have to find the birds!"

"Do you think that they will sing for you?" the voice asked, almost gently.

The world continued to fall. Someone I couldn't see was shaking me. I thought it was part of the dream and swung wildly, only to find my arm caught. Alex's voice broke through the remains of my dreams, vibrating with barely restrained terror: "Toby, wake up. *Please.*"

Panic is a wonderful stimulant. I pulled my arm free and sat up. "What's wrong?" I was too busy processing the situation to get mad at him for touching me. Yet.

"We can't find Jan." He looked haggard but alert; at least someone had been finding time to rest. Connor was asleep next to me, and Quentin was curled up on the floor, using his coat as a pillow. I must have been asleep for hours if they'd both gone down, and asleep *hard* if I didn't even hear them coming in.

"When did you last see her?" I stood. Dizziness washed over me. I caught myself against the wall.

"About an hour after sunrise."

Oh, oak and ash. "What time is it now?"

"Almost eleven-thirty."

I stared. "Why the *hell* didn't you wake me sooner?" I demanded. Quentin made a small grumpy noise and rolled over, still asleep. That wasn't going to last long.

"Elliot said to let you sleep until we were sure she was gone. Gordan just got back from checking her apartment. He said it was time to wake you." Catching my expression, he added, "He's her *seneschal,* Toby. Whether or not it was a good idea, he's allowed to make the call."

"I know. I know." I took a deep breath, trying to calm down. "Is her bike still here?"

He paused. "I don't think so."

"That's a good sign. Everything we know about has happened on company grounds, so if her bike's gone, she's probably okay. You go check; I'll wake the guys and be right there."

"Can you find your way out?"

I felt the irrational need to comfort him, and glared. He put his hands up.

"I'm not doing it on purpose, I swear. I'm just nervous. It happens when I get nervous."

"We can find it. Now get out." I was willing to believe he couldn't help it. That didn't mean I wanted him near me. "Go see if her bike is there."

"All right." He shut the door as he left, and my thoughts cleared almost immediately. I shook my head, disgusted.

My dislike of Alex didn't have anything to do with the matter at hand. Jan was missing. Oberon help us all. Bending over the futon, I shook Connor's shoulder. He muttered something unintelligible and opened his eyes.

"Get up," I said. "Jan's missing."

Connor sat up almost as fast as I had, swinging his feet around to the floor and kicking Quentin in the shoulder. Quentin staggered to his feet with eyes still half-closed, looking dazedly around the room.

"What happened?" asked Connor.

"I don't know. They just woke me." I put out an arm, steadying Quentin. "Wake up. Jan's missing."

The sleepiness cleared from his face like I'd flipped a switch. "What do we do?"

"Follow me, both of you. And stay alert." I crossed the room in two long steps, Connor close behind me, Quentin bringing up the rear.

The halls were amazingly straightforward, running in almost straight lines. We found our way to the parking lot without a single wrong turn, bursting out the door. Elliot was outside, staring into the underbrush. He ran over when he saw us, grabbing my hands. I winced at the pressure on my wounded palm but managed not to scream or pull away.

"Please, you have to find her," he said. "Please."

"We'll do our best," I said. Anything less would have been unfair; anything more would have been a lie. Unless she'd gone off-site or locked herself in an empty office to get some work done, she was probably dead. I'm enough of a realist to know that . . . but I also knew that wasn't the kind of reassurance he was looking for.

"That's all we can ask," he said, and dropped my hands. He looked smaller somehow, deflated. He'd already given up. I couldn't blame him; he'd lost his lover, and now we both knew he'd lost his liege as well. It would have broken anyone. It would have broken me.

Alex wasn't far away. He was standing to one side, staring at his hands. I didn't have to ask to know whether he'd found her bike. The tears running down his face told me everything.

"Toby . . ." Quentin said.

"I see him." Turning, I walked to the main entrance with Connor and Quentin behind me. No one followed; no one saw us go.

The halls were empty, and our footsteps echoed as we walked. It was like walking back through time to Shadowed Hills right after Luna disappeared . . . only this time we weren't expecting to find the missing regent pruning roses in a garden somewhere. This time, we weren't expecting to find the missing regent at all.

Connor's hand found mine, fingers slipping into place. "Where do we start?"

"We're not starting anywhere," I said. "We're going to let the knowe show us the way."

"What?" asked Quentin.

"Just follow me." This wouldn't have worked earlier, while Jan was alive and controlling the knowe with her expectations. It might not work now. It was the best idea I had. Turning the first corner we came to, I walked.

Knowes shape themselves to fit the subconscious desires of their keepers. That's why Shadowed Hills has so many gardens; that's why my mother's hall never had any mirrors or locks on the doors. I was counting on that to take us to the body. I would never have tried it with a moving target or with anyone less tied to the County than Jan . . . but the King is literally the land in Faerie, and if she were dead, the knowe would want us to find her.

We didn't pass anyone as we walked. I was following the patterns in the tile and the directions indicated by careless arrows on bulletin boards, trusting anything that looked like it could be a sign. It seemed to be working. Our route was leading us through more and more places that I recognized, taking us onto familiar ground.

Quentin looked at me as we walked, asking, "Is she dead?"

"Probably." I studied our surroundings, finally starting for the door that seemed most aligned with the scuff marks on the floor.

"Why didn't they wake us sooner?"

"Because that would have made it real," said Connor. We both looked toward him, and he shrugged. "As long as they were looking on their own, it wasn't happening."

The door led to the cafeteria kitchen, revealing a second entrance previously concealed by the cupboards on that wall. The cafeteria was spotless, all traces of my ritual circle and its messy results wiped away by Elliot's magic. I wondered how long we'd been asleep before he gave in to the urge to clean.

"Come on," I said. "We're getting closer."

"But what are we doing?" Quentin was looking increasingly frustrated.

"We're letting the knowe lead us. Jan was Countess, and the land will be in mourning if she's dead. It'll want us to find her." I stepped into the hall, noting without surprise that we were only a few doors down from Jan's office. There wasn't much chance of finding her there—they'd almost certainly looked there first—but it was a start. Even endings begin somewhere.

"How can that even *work*?" Now Quentin looked perplexed. From his expression, Connor got it, but was willing to let me be the one to explain.

"The King is the land, Quentin. That's all. That's how it's always worked in Faerie." The door to Jan's office was standing ajar. Someone inside was crying. I pulled my hand out of Connor's, signaling him and Quentin to stay where they were. When the sound didn't change, I pushed the door open and stepped inside.

The office lights were off and the shades were drawn, casting the room into an artificial twilight. I squinted. "Hello? Jan?" The sobbing continued, bitter and brokenhearted. "Jan?"

"That's not her," said Quentin, as he and Connor stepped into the room.

I paused, listening. He was right. The voice was too high to be Jan's. "No," I said, and started toward the desk, stepping carefully. Heaps of paper had fallen to cover the walkway, creating minor avalanches that would probably never be cleaned up. That hurt. The difference between clutter and chaos is control, and Jan's control had been broken.

Her notes on Barbara's connection to Dreamer's Glass were stacked on the desk chair. I knelt, pushing it aside to reveal April, compacted into a ball with her hands over her face, weeping.

"April?" I put my hand on her shoulder, or tried to; it passed through and hit the back of the desk. It was like reaching into a fogbank. I withdrew my hand. "Can you hear me?"

She shuddered, sobs fading as she chanted, "She's gone she's gone she's gone . . ."

"Who's gone? April, where's Jan?" I kept my tone calm. The last thing I wanted to do was upset her more.

"Mommy's off-line. No more reboots." She raised her head. Tears were falling in straight lines down her cheeks, like they'd been drawn on. It would have been unnerving under normal circumstances, but her distress made it even worse. "She's not supposed to go off-line. She's supposed to take *care* of me."

I blanched. I knew what "off-line" meant to April. Carefully, I asked, "Where's your mother, April?"

"Like the others now. Gone." She shuddered and began rocking back and forth, arms wrapped around her knees. "Off-line. Out of service. Yanked from the router."

"Gone," confirmed a voice. I looked up. Alex was in the doorway next to Connor, hands limp by his sides. It was the first time I'd seen him so still. "Gordan found her. She's gone."

"Where's the body?" I asked, suddenly, crushingly weary. How could I have lost her? How could I have been stupid enough to believe that we had time?

What was Sylvester going to say when he found out I'd failed him again?

"She's in one of the server rooms. It looks like she went to check on a glitch in router four, and whoever it was . . ." He stopped, looking away. "Maybe you'd better come see for yourself."

"You're right. We should. April . . ." I reached for her and she whimpered, disappearing in a crackle of static. I stood. I could find her later; for the moment, her mother needed me more. Oberon help us all.

None of us spoke as Alex led us through the empty halls. He didn't need to say anything; his posture was accusation enough, and in the face of that accusation, the rest of us had nothing to say. Connor took my hand, and clung, both of us trying to take strength from the contact. We failed. After everything we did or tried to do, we couldn't keep Jan safe. What was the point, if we couldn't save the people we were trying to defend?

Alex stopped at an unmarked door. "She's inside."

Either his glamour was more voluntary than he wanted to admit, or I was too sick with failure to be affected. "So we go in."

He didn't say another word. He just opened the door.

The server room lights were on, and I was suddenly glad I hadn't had any breakfast. Quentin made a muffled choking sound, clapping his hands over his mouth. Connor went pale. My own nausea was easier to swallow, replaced by a crushing sense of loss.

Oh, Jan, I thought. *I am so sorry.*

She was crumpled like a discarded rag doll, head bent at an impossible angle, with a series of uneven gashes splitting her torso from waist to shoulder. Another gash cut across her throat. Her eyes were open behind her glasses, staring at nothing. Blood pooled on the floor around her, dried brown and ugly; she could never have lived after losing that much blood. Bloody handprints climbed halfway up a rack of stacked machines and trailed down the wall beside it.

The others died without fighting, but not Jan. Several cables had been yanked loose in the struggle, and the machines they connected to were beeping, telling us that power had been compromised. That wasn't all that had been compromised. She had time to try to get away. That meant she also had time to suffer.

"Toby . . ." Quentin said unsteadily.

"If you need to be sick, do it in the hall." I moved toward the body, studying the blood splatters on the floor. The footprints were all hers—wait. No, not all. There were smaller prints around the body, made by doll-sized feet. The night-haunts had been and gone, and they're not normally clumsy enough to leave signs of their passing behind; this was a message. *There is nothing for us here.* Jan's body was still fae, her unnatural beauty left intact. Whatever hunted the dead at ALH, it took her, too.

Quentin's retreat was followed by the sound of retching. I ignored it, kneeling next to the body. The wounds on her chest and throat were the most obvious, but they weren't the only ones; she'd been hamstrung, probably while she was still moving. Whoever cornered her took no chances. I turned her head to the side, exposing her neck. The expected puncture was there, on the other side of the larger, more garish wound, and similar punctures marked her wrists. This wasn't a second killer; Jan had surprised our original murderer into breaking his pattern.

Three of her fingernails were torn, and one sleeve of her sweater was ripped nearly off. Whatever she did, it was almost enough. "Good for you," I whispered, and pressed my fingers to her cheek, pulling them away slick with blood. It was cold; she'd been dead since shortly after she disappeared. That's when she'd have been easiest to catch—morning, when people would be most distracted by exhaustion and the dawn. I brought my fingers to my lips, licking them, and scowled. The blood was empty, just like all the others.

Alex shifted his weight, saying, "Well?"

"Let her work," snapped Connor.

I ignored them, looking over my shoulder toward the door. "Quentin, come over here."

Still pale, he stepped back into the room, walking over to stand next to me. He avoided the blood on the floor. Good boy.

"Now what are you going to do?" said Alex.

"Look, can you just give us a minute? We need to work."

"Haven't you had enough minutes?"

I looked at him calmly, too exhausted and heartbroken to be angry. "Connor, get him out of here. We need to concentrate."

"I'm not leaving!"

"Yeah, dude, you are." Connor hooked his arm around Alex's throat, catching the taller man by surprise. While Alex was coughing, Connor continued, conversationally, "Now, we can stand here until you stop breathing and I drag you out, or we can go out to the hall. You'll like the hall. It comes with oxygen."

Alex managed to gasp, "Hall," and Connor smiled. "Clever. Toby, shout when you need us."

I offered a half-salute. "Got it. Now get out." I bent forward, concentrating on the body until I heard the door close. Without looking up, I asked, "They gone?"

"Yes," said Quentin. I looked up.

"I know this is hard, but we don't have a choice. I need your help. Can you do that?" When he nodded, I forced myself to smile. "Good. What's wrong with this picture?"

He frowned. "Her wounds are different. She had time to struggle?"

"Right." I removed Jan's glasses, sliding them into my pocket before gently closing her eyes. I didn't need to worry about tampering with the evidence: in a very real sense, Quentin and I *were* the forensics team. "Can you tell me what that means?"

"Um. Is the blood still . . . like the others?"

"The blood in her body is." Straightening, I walked over to the server rack, studying the smeared blood for patches that hadn't quite dried.

Quentin's eyes widened. "You think her killers didn't get it all?"

"It would make sense if they hadn't, wouldn't it?" I glanced back at him. "You think there was more than one killer. Why?"

"She's . . . well, she's split open. I don't think one person could do that."

"I'd agree with you, but remember, some races are stronger than others." I've seen Tybalt kill an adult Redcap with no weapons but his own claws. "I'm a lot more interested in the fact that all the footprints are Jan's, or from the night-haunts."

"I've never heard of the night-haunts leaving footprints," said Quentin.

"I think they did it on purpose, so I'd know they'd been here." I'd have to consider what that meant, later; if I had a personal relationship with the ghouls of Faerie now, I wanted to know about it.

"Why?"

"So I'd know they came, and they chose not to take her."

"Oh." Quentin dipped the first fingers of his left hand

into the blood on Jan's neck, studying them. He was starting to learn; adult Daoine Sidhe usually go for the blood before anything else, because a solid answer can prevent years of debate. I didn't stop him. He'd have to learn sometime, and now was as good a time as any.

Something glittered on the lower shelves. I ran my fingers across the spot, pulling them back gooey with congealed blood. I glanced back to Quentin and saw him put his blood-covered fingers into his mouth, tasting the blood I already knew was empty. I waited for his grimace, and then asked, "Anything?"

"Nothing," he said, spitting into his hand.

"We'll get some water in a minute. Hang on." I raised my hand, sucking the blood from my fingers.

I knew the blood was vital as soon as I tasted it. Then Jan's memories overwhelmed my vision, and I didn't know anything beyond what the blood was telling me.

Warning bells in the server room; need to make sure everything's okay, we have enough problems already. The lights are out. That's no good. Can't see in the dark, never could, stupid eyesight, stupid glasses. Feel around, find the switch, where's the switch—

Pain pain pain, *pain like burning, pain everywhere, why's my shirt wet? Reach down, feel the blade where it meets my chest—the fire ax from down the hall? Why is the fire ax in my chest? I . . . oh. Oh, I see. Shouldn't I be upset? Shouldn't I be crying? It hurts. It hurts so bad. But all I feel is confused. Why is this happening . . .*

"Toby?" Quentin's voice cut through Jan's memories.

"Be quiet," I said, and swallowed again, screwing my eyes closed. I'd already learned something vital: we were right when we assumed it was a "who," not a "what." Monsters don't generally use fire axes. The magic stuttered, trying to catch hold, and started again. . . . *here? I grab the ax handle, and pull, trying to free myself. I don't want to die like this, I don't want to die without answers . . .*

Something's behind me, it's too fast to see (the room's too dark too dark to see), grabs the ax out of my hands. Turn to run, run run run, too late, steel hits flesh, shoulder hits the wall, look for purchase, grab hold, flailing, losing blood so fast. It hurts, but I'm angry, so angry—how dare *they hurt my friends, my family, my world—I catch the blade and they gasp, it's a person, a* person, *not a monster, can't see who, I can't see . . .*

The blade pulls free. I scream—so angry, so helpless—and the ax hits again and again, and it's getting hard to breathe. Can't see. Can't taste anything but blood. Force the air through the lungs, out the lips, "Why?"

No answers. The ax hits again, and there's a new feeling, a cold new feeling . . .

That was when the memories in the blood ended; my best guess was that she fell and died after that, while that "cold new feeling" drained the vitality from the blood still in her body. I shook myself, gasping, back to the present. "She fought," I said, aware of how dazed I sounded.

"Toby?"

"It's okay, Quentin. I'm okay. I just . . ." I looked at my bloody fingers, and shuddered. "I found part of what we've been looking for."

"Did she see the killer?"

"No. Jan wore glasses, remember?" I allowed myself a bitter chuckle. "She had no night vision."

Quentin deflated, saying, "Oh."

"At least she had a chance to fight. That's more than the rest of these poor slobs got." I wiped my hand on my jeans—a little more blood wouldn't make a difference one way or the other—and started for the door. "Come on. We need to get moving."

"What are we going to do now?" Quentin asked, following me.

"First we're going to move her down to the basement. I want all the bodies in one place."

"And then?"

"Well, then, we're going to find the others, and I'm going to call Sylvester." I offered him a small, grim smile. "I think I'm done avoiding a diplomatic incident, don't you?"

TWENTY-THREE

THIS TIME, THE PHONE RANG five times before it was answered: Sylvester again, out of breath and anxious, sounding almost terrified. "Hello? Who's there?"

I paused. "Sylvester?"

"Toby! Oak and *ash,* October, why didn't you call before? We've been waiting. Your hotel says you haven't been checking messages there, either. What's going on? Where are you?"

"What . . . what are you talking about? You know where I am! You told us to stay here."

Now he sounded wounded; more than that, he sounded scared. "I did no such thing! Tybalt came to tell us you were worried about tampering with the phone systems, and I've been waiting here ever since. When it wasn't me, it's been Etienne, or Garm. Even Luna's taken her turn. You haven't called."

Oh, Oberon's blessed balls. Gritting my teeth, I said, "The problems with the phones may go a little bit past tampering."

"What do you mean?"

"I mean, I called you right after Connor got here, and you said we should all stay put."

He paused. "Do you mean . . . ?"

"Uh-huh. Connor and Quentin are still with me."

"Oh. Oh, October. That's not good."

I glanced over my shoulder toward the boys. Quentin was leaning against one of the soda machines, while Connor was making himself a cup of tea. I've always been wary of men who don't drink coffee. Tea's just such an inefficient way of getting your caffeine on. "No," I agreed. "No, it's almost certainly not."

Something in my tone must have telegraphed how serious things had become, because there was a pause before he asked, "Are you hurt?"

"A little bit. Nothing I can't handle." My head was pounding, my hand felt like hamburger, and the cuts on my face had barely started to scab. Oh, yeah. I was in top condition.

"What about Quentin?"

"He's scraped up, but he's fine. We had a minor accident with the car." It was technically true. We were already out of the car when it exploded. "Connor got here after that; he's fine, too."

There was another pause before he said, more quietly now, "Not everyone's fine, though, are they? I can hear it in your voice."

"January," closing my eyes and letting my forehead rest against the cool metal of the pay phone. "She's dead."

"Ah." There was a world of pain in that single tiny syllable; a world of mourning that he didn't have time to give in to. "How?"

"We're still not sure. She didn't die like the others, though. Her death was more . . ." I hesitated. Somehow, I couldn't quite bring myself to say "violent." Not when I could already hear Sylvester crying. Lamely, I finished, ". . . disorganized. Either she wasn't the intended victim, or it was more personal than the others were. I don't know yet."

"I see." He was silent for a long time. I held the line, waiting until he said, "If she's dead, I suppose Riordan's wishes don't matter as much anymore. Can you stay alive until I can get there?"

Before Luna, before peace and Shadowed Hills and developing a reputation as a sweet, slightly bewildered man who just happened to run the largest Duchy in the Bay Area, Sylvester was a hero. A real one. He was one of the lucky ones—he survived long enough to quit—but that didn't change where he'd started out.

Almost crying from relief, I nodded. "We can. How long will it take you?"

"Not long. Tybalt's already on the way."

I jerked upright, eyes snapping open. *"What?"*

"You didn't really think he'd sit out this fight, did you?" A flicker of dark amusement crept into his tone. "Not once you told him a Queen of Cats had died."

"Oh, Maeve's *tits*." I glanced back at Quentin and Connor again. This was going to make things even harder to deal with. Just what I needed. "Any clue when he'll get here?"

"Not a one. I'll see you soon. Stay safe."

"Always do," I said, voice bright with artificial cheer.

"You're a terrible liar."

"I know. Just get here."

"As quickly as I can. Open roads, all of you. And Toby . . . thank you for trying." He hung up before I could say anything about his thanks—and more, before I could say good-bye. I understood that all too well. He didn't want to hear it when it might just be forever.

"You, too," I whispered, and set the phone back in its cradle.

"What did he say?" asked Quentin.

"He's on his way, and he's bringing in the cavalry. We just need to keep ourselves alive until he gets here." I looked at him, seeing how much of the calm, arrogant facade he tried to project had collapsed since our arrival. He was pale and drawn, and the only reason I couldn't say he'd gone white was that the bandages on his forehead were still whiter. My company wasn't doing him any favors. "If it looks like I can't do that, we'll hot-wire a goddamn car and go meet him at the Interstate."

Connor walked over, his tea in one hand, a cup of coffee in the other. He handed me the mug, smiling at my grateful expression, and asked, "So now what?"

"I don't know." I sighed, sipping my coffee. "If the killer had a political agenda, I think they've accomplished it. Jan doesn't have any kids but April, and I don't think April knows what an heir is, much less how to be one. Dreamer's Glass will swallow Tamed Lightning. In a decade or two, nobody's even going to remember that this was a County. That's how it works."

"That doesn't work," said Connor, now frowning deeply.

I turned toward him. "All right: tell me why."

"Because from a political standpoint, there was no need for the other deaths. They just made Jan paranoid and harder to kill. Once she's dead, the game is over. So why draw it out so long? Why risk that many violations of Oberon's law?"

"Huh." I sipped my coffee again, considering what he'd said. Maybe he was right. Maybe we'd been looking at things the wrong way. "Okay. Assume it wasn't political. The politics are a red herring, they don't matter. Where does that leave us?"

"And what about Barbara?" asked Quentin.

I paused. Barbara was spying for Duchess Riordan . . . and she was the first one to die. "Barbara's what proves that it *wasn't* political," I said finally. "Her cover was never compromised. So why kill her?"

"Someone who was loyal to the County found out, and . . ." Quentin dragged a finger across his throat, making a disturbingly suggestive sucking noise.

"You have been watching *way* too much television, dude," said Connor.

"Besides, it still doesn't work," I said. "You kill Barbara out of County loyalty—why kill the others? You've stopped your spy. No, I think the politics were a factor in the paranoia, but not in the deaths. What does that leave?"

"Power?" suggested Connor. "Maybe somebody here wanted to be in charge."

"That feeds back into politics. Without Jan, they lose the County. It doesn't work."

"All right, revenge, then."

"On who, the company? Maybe." I paused. "And there's the way Jan died."

Quentin blanched. "You mean the mess?"

"The other killings were quick, but Jan had time to fight back. Why?"

"Well, didn't you tell Sylvester that Jan might not have been the target?" asked Connor.

"Maybe . . ." I stopped, frowning. The reflections on the soda machine next to Quentin were moving. Whatever was casting those shadows was behind me—and there were no windows on that side of the room. We weren't alone. "Guys?"

"What?" asked Quentin. Connor sipped his tea, giving me a puzzled look.

"Hang on." Whatever was moving had to be mostly hidden or he'd have seen it; judging by the reflection, Quentin had a clean line of sight. It very well might have been invisible, using an illusion spell that wasn't properly set up to include mirrors. Never trust anything that skulks around invisible in a building where people keep dying. "Actually, Quentin, come over here a second." It had too clear of a line on him. I didn't like it.

"Why? I'm already right here." He stepped forward, saying, "I don't—"

The reflection started moving again. *"Get down!"* I

shoved him as hard as I could, grabbing a handful of Connor's shirt and diving for the floor as the gun went off.

Two shots echoed through the room, almost drowning out the sound of Quentin shouting.

The first hit the wall where I'd been standing a moment before, flinging bits of tile in all directions. I didn't see where the second hit. I was too busy flattening myself against Connor and trying to see behind me, searching for our invisible assailant or assailants.

There was no one there.

The kitchen door we'd discovered during the search for Jan's body was standing slightly open. It swung shut as I watched. There would be no more shots, but I'd missed the shooter. As the rush of adrenaline faded, I realized that a chip of flying tile had opened a cut along my left cheek. I'd landed on my wounded hand, and blood was soaking the gauze. Just what I needed: more pain. I don't like being shot at—it makes me cranky—but I liked what the shots implied even less. None of the victims were shot. This was either someone new trying to get revenge for our failure, or the original killer was trying to scare us away. Neither option was good.

"Connor?"

"I'm fine. I'm fine." He laughed unsteadily as I pushed myself off of him. The color was high in his cheeks. "I forgot how exciting hanging out with you can get."

"Yeah, well. Quentin? You okay over there?"

He didn't answer.

I turned to face him, and froze. "Oh, oak and ash."

He was sitting with his back against the soda machine, left hand clamped high on his right arm. Blood ran between his fingers, coming way too fast. His face had gone whey-white, bleached by shock. "Not really," he mumbled.

"Oh, *crap,*" whispered Connor.

I scrambled over to Quentin, reaching for his arm. "Let me see."

"See what?" he asked, eyes wide and glossy.

"Your arm. Move your hand and let me see." Gunshot wounds require medical attention, no matter how minor they seem. The shock waves a bullet sends through the body are nothing to screw around with.

"Oh." Still dazed, Quentin let go. I grabbed his arm just above where he'd been holding, squeezing hard. Blood loss was my first concern. If he lost too much, we'd lose him, no matter how bad the wound was.

"Toby—"

"I know, Connor. Quentin? This may hurt a bit, okay?"

He frowned and closed his eyes, saying, "It already does. Never been shot before. Don't like it."

"You're being very brave. Now hang on." Keeping the pressure on his arm firm, I pulled the gauze from his forehead and used it to start wiping away the blood. The bullet had passed straight through, which was good. It appeared to have broken his arm in the process, which wasn't.

"Hurts . . ." he mumbled. His head was starting to loll forward, and the blood wasn't slowing down.

"Hey. Stay awake, you. Stay awake, and stay with me."

"Don't want to," he said, in a reflective tone. "Tired now."

"I know you don't want to. I don't care. I'm ordering you to stay awake!"

"Are you pulling *rank* on me?" he asked, sounding oddly amused.

"If that's what it takes, yes." I leaned harder, putting more pressure on his arm. "Connor, get over here. I can't hold this tight enough."

Connor was almost as pale as Quentin by that point, but he nodded, scooting over to slide his hands under mine.

The blood slowed when he clamped down, and I helped him slide Quentin over until he was flat on the floor.

"Connor, get his arm up above his heart."

"Got it," he said, keeping his hands tight on Quentin's arm as he lifted.

"Okay, good. Quentin? Come on, kiddo," I touched his cheek. "Don't you leave me."

"'M not going anywhere," Quentin whispered.

"Liar." I didn't want to leave the boys alone; not with Quentin injured and Connor preoccupied with keeping the blood inside his body. Looking up, I shouted, "April! Come to the cafeteria *right now*!"

I wasn't sure she'd come; she could have been too sick with grief to listen. Then the air crackled and she was there, confusion fading into wide-eyed shock as she saw us. It was the first time I'd seen her speechless.

There wasn't time to enjoy it. "April, get us something we can tie around Quentin's arm. Then get Gordan. Tell her it's an emergency. You got that?"

"Yes, but—"

"No buts! *Go!*"

She disappeared.

"Toby . . ." Connor sounded worried. I turned back to Quentin, and winced.

He'd grown paler, and the blood between Connor's fingers was getting darker. Both of us were soaked to the elbows. How much more did Quentin have to lose?

"Hey." I put my hand on Quentin's shoulder, squeezing. "No sleeping, you. Open your eyes. Come *on,* Quentin. Open your eyes. Please. Please? Please . . ."

April reappeared, holding a strip of white cotton. "Will this work?" she asked, sounding honestly worried. Things were starting to get through to her.

"Yes." I grabbed the fabric, edging Connor's hands aside as I tied it around Quentin's upper arm. The cotton was red by the time I had it in place, but the bleeding had stopped.

"Quentin, wake up." I shook his shoulder. He made a small, grumpy noise, and I did it again. "Wake up."

"No," he said, opening his eyes.

"Tough," I said, managing not to start crying in relief. He was alive. He might not stay that way, but he was alive.

The cafeteria door slammed open, and Gordan came running into the room, first aid kit in her hand. "Holy *crap*!" she exclaimed, skidding to a stop. "What the hell happened in here?"

Now I did start to cry, slumping against Connor. Quentin stared at me, and then he started crying, too. It was just too much. We'd lost Jan, and I had no idea how badly Quentin was hurt, and . . .

Everyone has a breaking point. I was starting to wonder how close I was to mine.

TWENTY-FOUR

IT TOOK GORDAN TEN MINUTES to splint Quentin's arm and get a pressure bandage in place. I helped as much as I could, holding his head when she had him stretched out on the floor, fetching and carrying things from her first aid kit. I've never been interested in emergency medicine, but I was starting to think I needed to learn. The people around me get shot too often.

I couldn't keep the image of Ross out of my head. Just like Quentin, he was shot when he was with me; unlike Quentin, he took the bullet in the head. All that saved Quentin from the same fate was the fact that my paranoia wouldn't allow me to ignore a glint of motion in a supposedly empty room. If I'd been paying less attention—if I'd been just a little bit more self-absorbed—I'd have lost him.

Oak and ash. That was too damn close.

April watched for a long time before she asked timidly, "Is he leaving the network?"

"What? No! No." I glared. I couldn't help myself. "He's going to be fine."

"I am glad," she said, voice grave. "Do you require further assistance?"

I looked at Quentin's silent, tear-streaked face—when did he get that pale? How could he be so pale and still be breathing?—and said, "Can you go get Elliot for us, please? We're going to need help moving him."

"Yes," April said, disappearing.

When I raised my head, Gordan was staring at me. "What?"

"I told you he didn't belong here." She tied off another strip of gauze. "Guys like him are too delicate for this kind of thing."

"Don't start, Gordan." I pushed my hair back, ignoring the way it caught at my blood-tacky hands. I was filthy. For the moment, I really didn't care. "It's not his fault someone decided to pick us off."

"So whose is it? Yours?"

Her words stung more than I wanted to let them. "No. It's just the way it is."

"Uh-huh. Let me tell you about 'the way it is.'" Her finger stabbed toward Quentin's chest. "You see how he's breathing? He lost a lot of blood. I mean a *lot* of blood. I can't do stitches, and I can't do blood transfusions. You're going to get that boy to a healer or a hospital, or he's going to die. So pick one. Or is that too much like accepting responsibility?"

"I'm not listening to you."

"Of course you're not. I suppose you're not going to listen when I tell you that you can't take him to a hospital, either." She started cramming bloodstained first aid supplies back into the box. "Get out of here, or he's a casualty. That plain enough for you?"

"What the fuck do you want from me? Sylvester's already on the way. I can't get us out of here any faster without a flying carpet!"

"Sorry, I left mine at home," Quentin said, his voice a faint croak.

"You're awake," I said, bending over him again. "Don't try to move."

"Wouldn't," he said, and smiled—very slightly. "See? I follow orders."

Connor barked an unsteady laugh. Gordan snorted. I shot her a warning look, saying, "April's getting Elliot, and we're going to move you."

"Can't leave."

"Quentin . . ."

"No." He opened his eyes. They were pained but clear. "Let me wait until His Grace comes. We'll never avenge them if you leave now."

"I can't keep you here." I knew how ludicrous we looked—both of us covered in blood, arguing. Never let it be said that fate doesn't have a sense of humor.

"Can't risk moving me, either." He closed his eyes again. "Put me in a room with a lock. I'll be fine."

"Suicidal jerk," Gordan said. I looked up. This time she met my eyes. "Are you going to let him decide whether or not he stays and dies?"

"Why not? I let the rest of you." I stroked Quentin's hair back with one hand, and looked to the door. There were footsteps coming down the hall. "Of course, unless that's Elliot, it may be a moot point." Connor's hand found mine, and took it.

"Ha ha. Very funny." Still, Gordan turned to watch the door, shoulders tense, and didn't relax until Elliot stepped inside, followed by Alex. April appeared in her usual burst of static, standing several feet away from the new arrivals.

"I have brought him," she said. It almost sounded like she was seeking approval.

"You did good," I said, and stood. Elliot and Alex had both stopped just inside the door, eyes wide, staring at Quentin. I cleared my throat. "Hi."

"Toby!" Elliot turned. "What happened?"

"Someone tried to kill us," I said.

I couldn't have gotten a better result if I'd tried. Elliot staggered, and Alex stared. "What?" he said, blankly.

"Kill us. Someone tried to kill us." I shook my head. "There were two shots. The first missed. The second got Quentin."

"He's a lucky bastard," said Gordan, standing. "They shattered the bones, but missed the artery. A little further and he would've bled to death before I got here."

I shuddered, unable to hide it this time, and said, "We've already gone over why I can't take him to a hospital. Does the room where I was napping earlier have a lock?"

"Yes . . ." Elliot said.

"Good. We're going to move him there. Connor will stand guard. Sylvester's on his way; I'm going to call and tell him to hurry, but I don't know whether he'll have left already. If he's not here by sunset, I'm taking your car, and I'm taking Quentin home." I looked at Elliot. "I refuse to let him die here. Do you understand?"

"You'll abandon us?" Alex asked, horrified. I felt the half-familiar tickle of desire kindle in my stomach, and shoved it down again as hard as I could. He might be a master of glamour, but I was a Daoine Sidhe covered in blood, and few things are harder to control.

"I'll come back, but yes. If it's a matter of saving Quentin's life, I will leave." I looked to Gordan. "Is it safe to move him?"

"I'd recommend it," she said. "This place is trashed."

"And infection's always a risk. Got it." I stepped over, and knelt by Quentin's head, asking, "Quentin, can you hear me?" There was no reply. I watched him for a moment to be sure that he was breathing. "Okay. He's out."

"I don't think—"

"Elliot, shut up." I said.

"I've got him," said Connor, moving to Quentin's other side.

"Good. Elliot, come get his feet. Connor, you've got the unhurt arm—just slide your hands under him. One, two, up." The three of us lifted together, getting Quentin safely off the floor. "Alex, get the door."

"I don't think this is a good idea," he said, but moved to push the door open.

"And what would be? Leaving him here? Going back to Shadowed Hills? Tell me, O wise one." I glared at him, shifting my grip on Quentin.

Alex sighed. "I don't think there are any good ideas left. Come on. It's this way."

We made a funny parade. Alex led the way, with April appearing and disappearing beside or ahead of him. Connor, Elliot, and I took the middle, fighting not to jar Quentin any more than we had to, and Gordan brought up the rear. We were all jumpy, even April, and we flinched from the slightest noises.

Nothing attacked.

Gordan took charge again in the break room, barking directions as we settled Quentin on the futon and tucked a pillow behind his head. The tattered, filthy condition of his clothes brought a fresh scowl to her face. Eyes narrowed, she targeted on Elliot. "This is an infection risk," she said.

"What do you want me to do about it?" he asked. He didn't sound defensive; just tired.

"Take care of it. Them, too." She jerked a thumb toward me and Connor. "Infection risk. Also, they smell lousy."

"Of course." He sighed, turning toward us. "Embarrassed as I am to ask under these circumstances . . . may I clean you?"

"Sure," said Connor.

"Of course," I said. I was still bleeding, and that was probably going to hurt, but that wasn't as important as getting Quentin taken care of. Anything that reduced the risk of infection was all right by me. "You have my consent for Quentin, too."

"April, you should go now; this is bad for your circuits." The Dryad vanished. Elliot raised his hands. "If you would please cover his nose?"

"Got it." I put my hands over Quentin's mouth and nose, closing my own eyes. Heat and moisture surrounded me, accompanied by the feeling of hundreds of small, scrubbing hands. The cuts on my face stung like fire, but I held myself firmly in check, keeping Quentin's face covered. I just had to hope he wouldn't wake up and panic in the middle of the process.

The dampness abated. I opened my eyes, straightening. Quentin looked almost infinitely better, clean, groomed, wearing clothes that seemed almost new. Connor and I had received the same treatment, and even the dressing on my hand had been repaired, becoming smooth and snowy white. That's Faerie for you, split between psychopaths and people who can steam clean your entire body with a thought.

Gordan bent to adjust the bandages on Quentin's arm. "He needs sleep. You should check him once an hour, at least, and get him to a healer as soon as you can."

"I will," I said.

"Great. I'm going back to my desk." She started for the door.

I cleared my throat. "Not alone."

"What?"

"You can't go alone."

"I'll go," said Alex, looking from me to Quentin and back. "I have stuff to do anyway."

"Fine," said Gordan sullenly, and stepped out of the room. Alex gave me a mournful look and followed her. Neither one said good-bye.

I sat on the edge of the futon, jerking a thumb toward the door. "What's *his* problem?"

"Other than being one of Nature's grade-A assholes?" Connor asked, stepping over next to me. He didn't sit, for which I was grateful; we didn't want to jostle Quentin.

"He likes you, and he feels that he's upset you," Elliot said, moving to close the door.

"He *did* upset me. Has he pulled this 'you must love me' stunt with anyone else, or am I lucky?" Connor shot me a startled look, which I did my best to ignore.

Elliot sighed. "Would it matter if I said he can't really help it?"

"Not when he tried to take advantage of me." There's room in Faerie for everything. That doesn't mean I need to put up with it. "He kissed me. After I told him not to."

"Now I want to hit him even more," Connor said darkly.

"Sometimes Alex has . . . poor impulse control," said Elliot. "I apologize."

"I don't care. If he touches me again, I'll break his face. We clear?"

"We're clear." Elliot looked from me to Connor, and asked, "Did you need a phone?"

"Please. I need to call Sylvester." It was obvious he didn't want to continue the discussion. Fine. I meant what I'd said; if he didn't want to listen, that was his problem.

"I'll get you one of the modified mobiles." He raised his hand, adding, "And I'll call for April. I won't go alone."

"Good," I said. "We'll wait."

"Of course." He stepped out of the room, closing the door.

"Toby—"

"Hang on a second, Connor, okay?" Twisting around to face Quentin, I asked, "So, how much of that did you catch?"

He opened his eyes, blinking. "How did you know?"

"You think I've never played possum? You breathe differently when you're awake."

"I woke up a while ago," he admitted. "I just thought it'd be a good idea not to react."

"Good plan. You feeling okay?"

"My arm hurts like . . ." He winced. "It hurts a lot."

"That's normal with gunshots, I'm afraid. It'll heal."

"Good."

"Elliot's bringing a phone. I'm going to let Sylvester know what's going on, see if they can get here any faster. And if he says they can't, I'm calling Danny. He must know someone with a cab around here."

"This is such a goddamn mess," said Connor, shaking his head.

"Hey." Quentin managed a wan smile. "The Duke wanted me to learn some stuff."

"Well, you're learning." I returned his smile, doing my best to make it look genuine, and stood. "Connor, you're not going to like this—"

"If you're about to say what I think you're about to say, you're right."

"—but I need you to stay here with Quentin."

"You're right," he said, grimly. "I don't like it. Reasoning?"

"I don't want to leave him alone."

"So *you're* just going to wander off on your own?"

"I'm not badly wounded enough that I can't do my goddamn job."

"Yeah, well, you seem determined to change that if you can." Connor glared, eyes dark and angry. "This isn't a good idea."

"So you'd rather I left Quentin here by himself?"

"I'd rather you didn't go anywhere at all!"

"I have to," I said, with sincere sorrow in my tone. "People are still dying."

Connor looked at me, anger fading. I glanced toward Quentin. His eyes were closed again, shutting out our argument. He was staying put, no matter what we decided.

Closing the distance between Connor and me was easy. Closing the distance between his lips and mine was the work of years. He kissed me like he was a drowning sailor instead of a Selkie, pulling me as close as he could. I returned the favor, plastering myself against him until the scrapes on my hands and the bruises on my knees protested. I ignored them in favor of the salt-sweet taste of his skin and the feeling of his heartbeat filtered through his chest into mine, running faster for the longer that we held each other there. It had been so long since we touched each other. Somehow, our bodies still knew the way.

Finally, regretfully, we let each other go, neither stepping back for a few seconds. Both of us were breathing just a little too fast.

"Don't you dare die," he hissed, forehead almost touching mine before he stepped back. I hadn't known how much comfort I was taking from his heartbeat until I couldn't feel it anymore.

"Do my best." On that uninspiring note, I left the room. The lock clicked home behind me almost as soon as the door was closed, and I leaned against the wall, groaning.

This mess kept getting deeper. I'd kissed Connor. Rayseline would kill me if she ever found out. And at the moment, that was the least of my problems, because someone in the building with me was a much more immediate threat. It couldn't be April—she was too upset when Jan died—and I could eliminate Elliot the same way. Gordan would have been in the running if it weren't for Barbara, but I couldn't see Gordan killing her best friend, even if they were fighting. Who did that leave? I knew where everyone was during at least one murder, even Alex . . .

Everyone but Terrie. Terrie, who found the first body. Terrie, who hadn't lost anyone who seemed to be particularly important to her. Terrie, whose mourning verged on parody, even when people were dying all around her.

Most damning of all, Terrie, who'd been nowhere to be seen during the search for Jan.

I started to pace, looking for an explanation that didn't leave Terrie as our killer. I wasn't finding one. By the time Elliot returned, I was so deep in my own thoughts that I didn't hear him approach. He cleared his throat. I jumped.

"Don't *do* that!"

"Sorry," said Elliot, grimacing, and held up a portable phone. "I had to find one that was modified *and* charged. My battery died yesterday, and the charger's at home."

"It's all right," I said, getting my breath back. "I'm just jumpy."

"I think we all are," he said, handing me the phone. "I'm glad you're staying."

"Quentin's out of here as soon as the cavalry comes, but I'll be here as long as I can. We need to stop this while some of us are still alive."

He smiled bitterly. He'd already lost everyone he really cared about. Someday I'll learn to think before opening my mouth. "Do you have any ideas?" he asked.

"Does anyone here have a gun registered in their name?"

"Barbara did."

"Well, somebody stole her gun." I sighed. "It's a local. Monsters don't use guns." He flinched. "It's the only answer I can see. I'm here to save you if I can. Not to coddle you."

"I know. I just can't believe one of us would do this. That one of us would kill Jan, or my Yui. Why would they do this?"

"I don't know—I'm trying to find out. But I have a pretty good idea of who it was."

"Really? Who?"

"Terrie."

Elliot sputtered. For a moment I thought he was trying not to laugh. Then he got himself back under control, and said, "I don't think that's plausible."

"If she has an alibi, she hasn't shared it. She found the first body, and she didn't join the search for Jan. It doesn't look good."

"There were reasons for all those things, Toby," he said.

"I doubt they're good enough. Everyone else has an alibi."

"Actually, you might find these reasons quite . . . legitimate."

I folded my arms across my chest. "Try me."

He looked at his watch. "It's four-thirty. You'll have an answer at sunset."

I raised an eyebrow. "Which is when?"

"Seven o'clock. Terrie won't be here until then."

"If her excuse isn't good enough, I'm taking her into custody for breaking Oberon's law. When the sun goes down, the game's up. Got that?"

"Yes," he said, sadly, "I rather suspect I do."

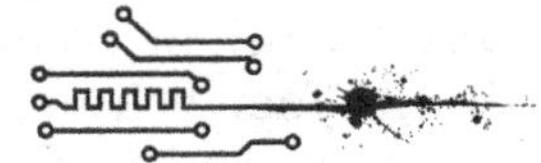

TWENTY-FIVE

THERE WAS NO SIGNAL IN THE HALL. I snapped the phone closed, glaring at it like it had done this just to spite me, and moved toward the futon room door. "I need to go outside and find a signal. Just let me tell Connor where I'm going."

My knuckles hadn't even hit the door when April appeared, expression—for her—distraught. My arm was going straight through her throat. I yelped, jerking backward.

"Quentin is sleeping. Connor is monitoring his condition. Please do not persist in your attempts to disturb him. His batteries must recharge if he is to remain on the network."

I glanced at Elliot, bemused. He looked as bewildered as I felt. "All right, April. I didn't mean to upset you."

"Apology accepted. Leave now." She vanished, the smell of ozone hanging in the air.

"That was weird," I said.

"She seems to have taken a shine to your assistant. Maybe it's just that he's the age she appears to be. Shall I show you the way outside?"

"Please."

The simplification of the knowe had continued while I slept; Tamed Lightning was in mourning, just like the rest of us, and there was no reason to complicate the halls. It had nothing left to hide. The more I see of our world, the more convinced I am that everything in Faerie is alive. April was a sentient computer, and one of my pets is a rosebush with feet. Why shouldn't the places where we live be just as awake? In Faerie, the land can hold opinions.

Elliot respected my obvious desire for silence, pulling a few steps ahead of me as we approached what was presumably the door to the outside. He undid the lock and pulled the door open—only to squawk in surprise and vanish, yanked out the door by the hand that had suddenly latched around his throat. Swearing, I broke into a run, rocketing out the door only a few seconds behind him. Then I stopped, clamping a hand over my mouth, and stared.

Tybalt was holding Elliot a foot off the ground. He'd shown at least a little bit of mercy, letting go of Elliot's throat in favor of grabbing his collar. While this seemed less likely to rip Elliot's jugular open, it wasn't doing him any favors in the "breathing" department; Elliot was thrashing, face turning a worrying shade of plum. Every cat in the place seemed to have gathered around them, turning the lawn into one teeming, furry mass.

"Tybalt?" I said, lowering my hand.

He turned toward me, and dropped Elliot. "October?" His eyes flicked from my pristine condition to the scrapes on my cheek and the bandages on my hands before narrowing, attention swinging back to Elliot, who was huddled in a graceless, gasping heap. "Is this one responsible for your hands?"

"What? No! No, I did it myself." I was smiling, irrationally relieved by his arrival. Tybalt doesn't normally move me to smile, but somehow, having additional firepower didn't strike me as a bad idea. "I sort of had to."

"How do even you wind up in a circumstance where you 'sort of have to' slice your hands open?" Tybalt prowled toward me, Elliot clearly dismissed. "Did you also 'sort of have to' do whatever it is you've done to your face?"

"No, that happened when I jumped out of my car to keep myself from being inside it when it decided to explode." I shrugged. "It'll heal."

"If you don't die."

"If I don't die," I agreed.

He gave me another up and down look, finally saying, "Nice coat," before turning back to Elliot, who shrank back. "You. The cats say you're one of the people in charge here."

Elliot glanced at the cats surrounding him like he was looking for support. A fluffy orange tomcat flattened its ears, hissing. He winced. "I . . . I suppose I am. Can I help you?"

"You can begin by explaining why no notice of Barbara's death was sent to the other Regents of the Court of Cats," said Tybalt, sounding almost bored as he hoisted Elliot back to his feet. "Then, you may explain why my subjects tell me that any who enter that building," he indicated the door with a jerk of his chin, "never come out again."

I raised an eyebrow. "Elliot?" Elliot didn't answer, being preoccupied with once again turning a rich, slow shade of purple. I sighed. "Tybalt, most people can't answer questions when they can't breathe. Put him down." After a pause, I added, "Gently."

Tybalt lowered Elliot's feet to the ground, not letting go of his shirt. "Speak," he growled.

"We didn't tell you because we didn't have any way to *reach* you! There aren't any other Cait Sidhe in the County! Jan said her uncle knew you, but we couldn't get through to him, and people kept dying!" Elliot was babbling, words spilling over one another as he fought to get them out before Tybalt cut off his air again. "We weren't hiding it from you!"

"And the cats?" Tybalt asked, in a tone that seemed much more relaxed, and was likely much more dangerous. I didn't mind. I wanted the answer to that one, too.

"I . . . the cats were Barbara's responsibility," Elliot said. "I really don't know."

Tybalt released his shirt and knelt, not taking his eyes off Elliot. A calico hopped onto his shoulder, meowing, and he nodded, expression grave. The cat jumped down again as he straightened. "The cats agree with your story." The words "luckily for you" didn't need to be spoken. They were already all too present. "You may take me inside now."

"Wait." I raised a hand, remembering why we'd left the building in the first place. "I'd rather not be left alone out here, and I still need to make a call. Can you two hang on?"

"Of course," said Tybalt, in a dry tone. "I came entirely to wait on your pleasure, not to avenge a dead Queen of my line at all."

Ignoring the sarcasm, I smiled. "Excellent. This won't take long."

I meant that seriously. What I didn't expect was how accurate my words would be. I dialed the pay phone in Paso Nogal, waiting until a winded Melly answered the phone, managing to gasp out, "Hello?"

"Melly?"

"October! Ah, child, it's good to hear your voice."

"Melly, is Sylvester still there? I need to—"

Melly cut me off, saying, "His Grace has already ridden out, along with most of the knowe, I'm afraid. Even Her Grace went along. Is it . . . is it true that dear January's left us?"

The image of Luna attacking a killer with an army of rose goblins was interesting, but not useful. "I'm afraid so."

"Oh, that poor lamb," she said, with a deep, wounded sigh. "Just take care, if you would. There's been death enough."

"I will," I said, before hanging up. I'll give Elliot this much; of the pair of them, he was the only one pretending not to listen. "Sylvester's on his way. He'll get Quentin out of here."

"Good," said Tybalt. "*Now* may we go inside?"

"Of course," said Elliot.

Tybalt fell into step beside me as we followed Elliot into the knowe, saying quietly, "I would have come straight to you, but the place is warded. None of the Shadows would open."

"They have a Coblynau on staff."

"Ah." He nodded. "That would do it. Why are you so concerned with what becomes of this 'Quentin'? Is he a new swain of yours?"

"First, Tybalt, no one says 'swain' anymore. Secondly, no. He's a foster at Shadowed Hills, and he's been injured. Someone was trying to shoot me, and they got him instead."

His eyes narrowed. "Who?"

"I don't know." I paused. "But you might. Elliot, take us to the cafeteria."

"Why?"

"Because we just got ourselves a bloodhound," I said, smiling thinly. Tybalt snorted at my comparing him to a dog, but didn't object. The news that I'd been shot at seemed to have disconcerted him more than I expected. If it made him agreeable, well, *I* wasn't going to argue.

The cafeteria was empty. Wherever the surviving denizens of ALH were spending their day, it wasn't here, perhaps because they were avoiding the grisly sight of Quentin's blood, which had dried to a dirty, unpleasant brown on the floor all around the soda machine. Elliot stiffened at the sight of it. "No," I said, before he could ask. "You can't."

He shot a glance my way before turning, shoulders tight, to walk over to the coffee machine. Fine. If it would keep him occupied, he could make all the coffee in the world. "I take mine with cream, sugar, and pain-killers," I called. "That's where Quentin was shot, Tybalt. You think you can find the gun?"

"How, precisely, should I do that?" The look he gave me then was very nearly amused. "Shall I simply wave my hands and call, 'Here kitty, kitty'?"

"No." I shrugged. "Follow the smell of gunpowder."

Tybalt blinked, and then nodded. "Worth trying."

"At this point, everything is," I said, without humor. "Elliot, stay here. Get Tybalt anything he asks for. I'll be right back for my coffee."

The look Tybalt gave me then was anything but pleased. "Where are you going?"

"To check on Quentin," I said, and slipped out of the cafeteria, heading down those newly linear halls toward the room where I'd left Quentin and Connor.

Connor cracked the door open on my second knock, peering out into the hall before opening the door all the way and stepping out. "Hey," he said, voice soft. "Everything okay?"

"Sylvester's on his way, and Tybalt's here," I said. "How is he?" I didn't need to specify which "he" I meant. There was really only one candidate.

"Asleep." A brief smile crossed his lips. "April brought him the Hippocampi from Colin's office a little bit ago. Tank and all. I think she's trying to make him feel better, she just doesn't know quite how."

"And they're still alive?"

"Frisky as ever."

"Huh." If April could teleport living things, she had definitely become something very different from your average Dryad. "You holding up okay?"

"Sure, for now. What are you doing wandering around alone?"

I leaned over to hug him, briefly. "Just checking in. Stay safe."

He kissed my cheek. "You, too."

"Trying," I said, and turned to return to the cafeteria. Once he was out of sight, I raised my hand, touching the spot where he'd kissed me. If Raysel had reason to hate me before . . .

There'd be time to worry about that later, when we weren't dead. I stepped back into the cafeteria and into a tableau strange enough to stop me in my tracks, just blinking.

Three mugs of coffee and the last box of donuts were sitting in the middle of one of the tables, as decoratively placed as any tea party preparations. A bottle of Tylenol was sitting next to one of the mugs. Elliot, sleeves rolled prissily up to keep them from brushing the floor, was kneeling next to an open vent, peering into it. Tybalt was nowhere to be seen.

I cleared my throat.

Elliot looked around, and said, "Your coffee's on the table," before returning his attention to the vent.

"What's going on?" I didn't let my confusion prevent me from heading for the coffee. It was still hot. Blessed caffeine. Better yet, blessed caffeine with a side order of painkillers. Maybe mortal medicine can't beat fae healing, but it comes close, and it's a damn sight more reliable.

"He believes he's found a trail."

As if on cue, a burly tabby-striped tomcat popped out of the vent, looking disgusted. The smell of pennyroyal and musk rose around him, and Tybalt was seated on the floor. "Nothing," he said, sounding disgusted. "What a charming place this is."

"Have some coffee," I suggested. "You'll feel better."

"Will it bring back the dead?"

"No. But it may save your sanity."

"Excellent." He stood, moving to join me before turning baleful eyes toward Elliot. "What have you people been doing here?"

"Nothing," said Elliot, looking uncomfortable.

"Dying," I said. "Tybalt, come on with me. I'll show you Barbara's work space. Maybe you can find a trail there."

He looked at me, clearly trying to decide whether I was simply trying to distract him, before finally offering an imperious nod. "Very well."

"Elliot—"

"I'll get April to escort me to Alex's office. He and I have some things to go over, anyway."

"All right." I held up the phone. "I'm keeping this."

"Excellent. I'll have you notified at once if Sylvester shows up."

"Good. Tybalt, come on."

He gave me a dubious look, but followed me out of the cafeteria and back into the halls. It was almost five-thirty; sunset was still hours away, and Sylvester was Maeve-knows-where.

I just hoped he'd get here soon. We were running out of options.

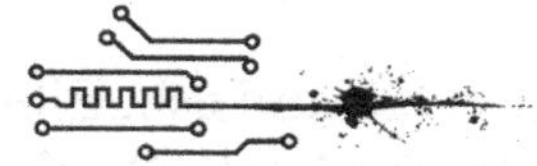

TWENTY-SIX

SPENDING SEVERAL HOURS WITH TYBALT was surprisingly easy, maybe because we had a common task to focus on: sorting through Barbara's personal effects. When I asked, hesitantly, why she left her files in a place where they'd be so easy to find, Tybalt laughed, replying, "She was a cat, October. Where would the fun be if she hid them?" There was the Cait Sidhe mind-set in a nutshell.

I became a PI because I was good at focusing my attention and shutting out the things that wanted to distract me from the task at hand. I was so preoccupied with studying the contents of Barbara's desk, trusting Tybalt to notice any threats that might arise, that it was a genuine surprise when Elliot walked up, saying, "It's time."

"What?" I looked up. "Oh. Elliot. Sunset, already?" I frowned, glancing toward the wall like I expected a window to appear. "Sylvester's not here yet?"

"No. But you should come with me, please. Terrie will be here soon."

"Right." I put down the papers I'd been holding and moved to follow him, Tybalt silently trailing us.

Elliot glanced at me as we walked, and said, "We haven't been entirely honest with you."

"I noticed," I said. "You've never embraced 'full disclosure' around here, have you?"

"In more ways than you know. Alex will meet us in the cafeteria."

"Alex?" I stared. "Oak and ash, Elliot, I don't want to accuse his sister of murder in front of him!" I didn't like the man, but there are limits.

"Don't worry." He smiled regretfully. There was something I needed to know in that expression. I just couldn't tell what. "She never gets here before sunset."

"What are you talking about?" I paused. "If she's some sort of bloodsucker and you haven't told me—" Faerie has its vampires, sort of, and most of them can't stand the sun.

"That's not it," Elliot said, stopping at the cafeteria door and pushing it open. "After you."

Alex was sitting at one of the tables, wearing a denim jacket over a white cotton shirt and a pair of leggings. He looked exhausted. Glancing up, he saw me and paled. "Uh, hi, Toby. Elliot. Dude I don't know."

"Tybalt," I supplied. As for Tybalt, he had moved closer to me, starting to snarl almost silently. I glanced at him, surprised.

"Uh," Alex said. "Right."

"It's almost sunset, Alex," said Elliot. "Toby needs to talk to your sister."

"What?" Alex sounded almost frightened. I narrowed my eyes, watching him. "She's not here. You know that."

"We need you to stay until she comes." Elliot shook his head. "I'm sorry."

"Elliot . . ." Alex began.

"Toby," Elliot said, not looking at me, "please tell Alex your suspicions."

I took a breath. "I don't think that's any of his business." Tybalt's growl was getting louder, distracting me.

"It's important that he know why he needs to stay." Elliot sounded serious.

I frowned. "If you're sure . . ."

"I am."

"All right." Turning to Alex, I said, "I think your sister is involved with the murders."

He made a startled squeaking noise. "Really?"

"I don't know what her motives are, but she has no alibis, she hasn't participated in any of the searches, and she was alone when she found the first body. She may not be guilty. She may have good reasons for everything. But it doesn't look good."

"And now you want to see her."

"I do. There've been too many deaths. We can't just let this lie." If I didn't find someone for the nobility to punish, they'd choose someone on their own, and they tend to be a lot less picky than I am. They might take all of us, on charges of obscuring justice.

"Elliot?" Alex looked toward him, eyes wide.

Elliot shook his head. "This one's yours." His smile was bitter. "You should have been more careful. I've told you before not to play games."

That seemed to mean something to Tybalt that it hadn't meant to me. His snarl became suddenly louder, and he all but pounced on Alex, hoisting the other man by the upper arms like he weighed nothing at all. "How *dare* you!" he roared.

I stared. "What the hell—"

"I didn't hurt her!" Alex shouted, his attention fixed on Tybalt.

"You're not going to have the chance." Tybalt released Alex's left arm, pulling back a hand that was suddenly bright with claws.

And the sun went down.

Transformations in the real world never happen the way we expect. The light around Alex blurred as his hair melted from gold to black, the tan bleaching out of his skin, the focus shifting until Tybalt was holding a gasping Terrie off the ground. The change seemed to have disoriented him, because she was able to squirm out of his grip and wobble in place. Women have smaller lungs than men do; sunset had to feel like the worst asthma attack ever.

The change was the piece I needed to answer the question of Alex and Terrie Olsen's heritage, spelling it out in neon letters that made everything else fall into place. Gordan's comments about it getting cold out on that hillside. The speed of our mutual attraction. The way he could make me forget about doing my job, just by smiling. A glamour that kept hitting me, even after I knew it was happening, a bloodline I couldn't identify, and the way I'd hated Terrie, just as quickly as I'd fallen for him. And the birds . . . oh, root and branch.

"And no birds sing," I said, horrified. Keats didn't know much about Faerie, but he knew enough to get some things right. Gean-Cannah—the Love Talkers. I'd never met a changeling Gean-Cannah before, only heard rumors, so I hadn't been able to recognize their blood. True Gean-Cannah were shapeshifters, entirely protean creatures who changed their faces and genders with a thought. Only their changeling children were tied to the movements of the sun, split forever into different people. I should have known when I saw their eyes. I should have known. But I didn't.

Gean-Cannah were common once. They preyed heavily on the mortals. Too heavily. There's never been any shame in hunting humans. The shame is in getting caught. It's all right to be a monster, but it's not all right to be sloppy. The Gean-Cannah took what they wanted, and they were noticed. Oh, were they ever. They were heavy victims of the war with the humans, and the Love

Talkers have never bred fast; they can't stand the company of their own kind, and most fae are too canny for them. They're rare these days. I've only seen a single pureblood, and he was on the other side of a royal Court. Not exactly close enough to learn the attributes of the blood.

The Gean-Cannah will become your perfect lover, and it'll be your last. They pull the life out of you, leaving you drained of everything but the need to keep loving them, to keep feeding them every ounce of strength you have . . . until it's over.

Most affairs with the Gean-Cannah end in suicide.

Tybalt was getting over his surprise, looking even angrier now. I stepped forward, taking hold of his arm while I glared at Terrie. "The night shift."

"I'm sorry," she said, lowering her inhaler. "I would have told him not to, but he didn't leave me a note until it was too late."

"So you couldn't have killed them all."

She shook her head. "I wasn't awake."

"This . . . thing . . . touched you?" asked Tybalt, tone gone dangerously quiet.

"Her day-self did." I looked at Terrie. "Do you have any control?"

"I . . ." Terrie paused, sighing. "You want to know if Alex forced your attraction to him."

"Yes."

She looked away. "Yes."

For a long moment, I just stood there. Then, turning to Tybalt, I said, "Do whatever you want. I'm done." Terrie's head whipped around, eyes gone wide. I ignored her, attention swinging toward Elliot. "You let him."

"Toby, I—"

"Do you know what happens when you lie down with the Gean-Cannah? Do you?" None of them said a word. Not even Tybalt, although the growl was beginning again, low in his throat. "You get tired and your thoughts get fuzzy and you stop thinking about anything but when you'll see your lover again. You lie down on the cold hillside, and you *die*. And you were just going to let me stumble into his arms, without a warning?"

"Toby, it wasn't like that—" Terrie began. I glared at her, and she stopped.

"I don't care what it was like, and I don't care what your reasons were," I said. "This is too much. I'm taking my people, and we're getting out of here." I turned and stalked out of the cafeteria, letting the door swing shut behind me.

They didn't follow. If the look on Tybalt's face meant anything, he wasn't going to let them.

I made it as far as the hall before my knees buckled and I sank to the floor, starting to cry in vast, exhausted gasps. How dare they? How *dare* they? I cried until I ran out of tears. It took a frighteningly long time. It wasn't until I stopped to wipe my eyes with the back of my hand that I realized someone was leaning against me. I froze, realizing I'd just broken my own cardinal rule for surviving: I'd gone off alone. It would be a beautiful, annoying sort of irony if I got killed right after making my dramatic exit.

Whoever it was wasn't making any hostile moves; they were just leaning. Most psychopaths seek blood before cuddling—it's a trait of the breed. And no, I don't think they'd have killed less if they were hugged more. I just think that by the time they start killing, they aren't necessarily looking for a pat on the back.

I looked down. April was huddled against me, eyes closed, tears rolling down her cheeks in fractal patterns. "April?"

She didn't open her eyes. "I didn't think my mother could go off-line."

"Oh, April." I bit my lip, not sure what to say next. It was easy to forget her origins and focus only on her strangeness. Maybe she wasn't normal, but Jan was her mother—probably the only one she'd ever had. Dryads don't exactly come from nuclear families. I settled for the most inconsequential, least hurtful words I could find: "I'm sorry."

"She was supposed to take care of me, but she left the network without me. How could she do that? She has to take *care* of me."

"I'm sure she took good care of you." I winced as soon as I spoke, realizing how patronizing that had to sound.

April realized it too, because she raised her head, expression fierce. "She did take good care of me. She always did." She paused, continuing more quietly, "People said she only cared about me because I was new, and she'd forget me when she found something else new. But they were wrong. She took care of me. When I was hurt or sick or confused or anything, she took care of me. She always . . ." Her voice trailed off.

"She always what, April?"

"She kept my systems operational," she said. "She loved me."

That surprised me more than it should have. I knew April was devoted to Jan. I hadn't realized she understood what love was. Quietly, I said, "I think I understand."

"Do you?" she asked, pulling away. It was hard to get used to the emotion in her voice. She'd been sounding steadily more alive—more "real"—since Jan died.

I only wished her mother could have seen it.

"I think so."

"I would never have let anything hurt her."

"I know."

"I hope so," she said, and shook her head. The tears on her cheeks disappeared like they'd never been. "There aren't many choices left. I have to go now, and you have to think. It's *important*." Then she was gone in a haze of static, leaving me alone.

"April? April, come back—what's important? April!" I stared at the empty air, hoping she'd reappear and explain herself. No such luck. "What was that about?"

Picking myself up off the floor, I raked the fingers of my good hand through my hair, looked toward the futon room door, and turned, with a sigh, to walk back toward the cafeteria.

I couldn't go. I wanted to, and I couldn't. If it had just been Jan, maybe I could have left the mess for Sylvester, but April . . . April needed someone to find out what had happened to her. I owed that to her, and I owed it to her mother.

To my surprise and mild disappointment, the cafeteria was not the site of further carnage. Terrie was gone, and Tybalt and Elliot were at opposite sides of the room, Tybalt glaring, Elliot trying to look like he wasn't uncomfortable about being glared at. Tybalt straightened as I entered, attention refocusing on me.

I moved until I was standing nose-to-nose with Elliot, and said, "We're staying until Sylvester gets here. Not for your sake. For Jan's. And if Alex comes near me again, night or day, I'll kill him. Do you understand?"

He raised his hands, supplicating. "We weren't trying to endanger you."

"You could've fooled me."

"Terrie can't help what she is—it's her nature to make people love her, just like it's your nature to pull answers from the dead." He paused. "I've always wondered why the Daoine Sidhe have that gift. You're Titania's children. Why are you so tied to blood?"

"Because we're also Oberon's, and no one else was willing to take the job. Cut the crap, Elliot. Do you want my help or not?"

He looked at me blankly. "Yes. We do."

"Then you need to follow my rules. Can you do that?"

"I can," he said slowly, like he found the words distasteful. Tough.

"Good." I stepped away from him. "First rule: no one goes anywhere alone, no matter how secure you think the area is or how certain you are that nothing will happen. There aren't many of you left. I'd like to keep the ones we have."

Elliot nodded. "I'll order everyone that's still here to travel together."

"Can you make them listen?"

"I think so."

"Good. Second rule: if I ask a question, I want an answer, not an excuse and not a string of technical terms you know I won't understand. A real answer. Can you promise me that?"

"I promise."

"Swear."

"Toby, do I really need—" He saw the look on my face, and stopped. "Fine. I swear by root and branch and silver and iron, by fire and wind and the faces of the moon. May I never see the hills of home again, if I deceive." He paused. "Will that do?"

"For now."

"And you'll help us?"

"We will. Let's go give Connor a status, check on Quentin, and . . ." I paused. "Where's Terrie?"

"She left," Tybalt said, sounding satisfied. "Best she stays gone."

"So she's alone?" If she wasn't our killer, she might well be a target. I didn't like her. I didn't want her dead.

"I suppose," said Elliot.

"Oh, Maeve's *teeth*. Tybalt? Can you find her?"

He nodded, barely, and took off at a run. I followed a beat behind him. I didn't know that anything was wrong—not really—but I knew that every time I'd gambled with fate in this place, I'd come up snake eyes. The house always wins.

Tybalt hit the door Alex had led me through earlier, rushing out into the warm night air with me and Elliot at his heels. The smell of blood hit me even before I saw Terrie lying loose-limbed and still in the grass. The cats were gone. It was the first time I'd been outside ALH without seeing cats.

"Oh, you poor thing," I said, glancing to Elliot and Tybalt. "Tybalt, go find the cats. See if they saw anything." He nodded. "Elliot . . ." Elliot was pale and shivering, shaking his head from side to side. I sighed. "Stay there."

Tybalt turned, vanishing into the shadows as I walked toward Terrie's body. Kneeling beside her, I turned her head to the side, revealing the puncture just below her jaw. Similar punctures marked her wrists, exactly where I expected them to be. "Jan really was a fluke," I muttered. Our killer was back to the normal pattern.

Terrie's skin was still warm, even warmer than Peter's had been. We'd almost made it in time. Too angry and exhausted for delicacy, I lifted her arm, raised her punctured wrist to my mouth, and drank.

Blood is always different. It has a thousand tastes, spiced by life and tainted by memory. Take away those flavorings and all you have left is copper, cloying and useless. Terrie's blood was empty. I prepared to spit it out, and paused, licking my lips. There was something there. Ignoring Elliot's choked-off gasp, I took another mouthful. Yes; there was definitely something there, something not quite gone. It was just a flicker of memory, a distant whisper of clover and coffee, too faint to tell me anything . . . but it was there.

I sat back on my haunches, frowning. What was different here? What distinguished this death from the rest? The others were purebloods; Terrie was a changeling. Maybe that was it. Or maybe it was the fact that she was two different people . . . and only one of them had died.

"Elliot? What time is it?"

"A little after eight." He hesitated. "Why?"

I smiled, and he blanched. I could feel the blood drying on my lips. "Let's move her to the basement. I want to check on Quentin, and then I'm going to sleep until Sylvester gets here. I need to be alert in the morning."

"Why?" he asked. He didn't sound like he really wanted to know.

Tough. Still smiling, I said, "Because at sunrise, I'm going to wake the dead."

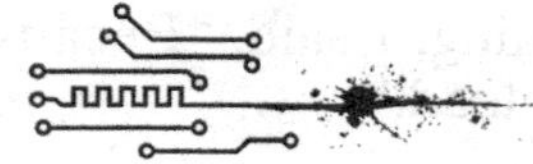

TWENTY-SEVEN

WE WAITED FOR TYBALT to return before moving the body. His mood had grown even worse while he was scouring the knowe for cats; someone, he reported, had driven them away with a high-pitched sound, leaving them skittish and miserable. Someone was going to pay for that if he had any say in the matter.

He and I carried Terrie's body through the knowe together. Ignoring Elliot's disturbed stare, we moved Colin's body to the floor, settling Terrie in his place. I'd need easy access to her body, and Colin wasn't in a position to object. The dead are usually pretty mellow about that sort of thing. The basement was getting crowded. Most of the bodies looked like movie models, too pristine to be real; the only body that seemed even halfway natural was Jan's beneath its mottled sheet of red and brown. I still didn't understand why Jan had been killed so differently from the others. What was I missing?

"You can go," I said, glancing toward Elliot. "Call April, and stay with her. Make her take you to Gordan."

For a moment, he looked like he might argue. Then he nodded, heading up the stairs without another protest. I watched him, trying to ignore the pain in my head and hand. I was so tired. I needed to sleep before the morning's work, or I wasn't going to survive it. And there were still things I had to do.

Tybalt remained silent until Elliot was gone. Then he swung his head around to look at me, asking, "What do you intend to do?"

"Something really, really stupid." He narrowed his eyes, and I shrugged. "Look: Terrie and Alex share a body, but they're not the same person. If Terrie's dead, and Alex isn't, I might be able to jump-start him somehow. That could wake the blood back up."

He paused. "I don't know whether that's brilliant or suicidal."

"That's all right." I offered him the ghost of a smile. "Neither do I."

"Charming." He walked toward me, fingered the collar of the jacket I was wearing, and said, "It suits you, I think. You should keep it."

"Tybalt, I—"

"Not that I would have it back, after the amount of blood you've doubtless shed on it." He pulled his hand away. "You're about to ask me for something. I recognize the look."

"I am." For a moment, I wanted to catch his hand, just to have something to hold onto. The moment passed. "I don't know where Sylvester is, and he shouldn't be taking this long. Can you go and try to find him?"

"Not until I've seen you safe."

I shot him a sidelong look. He looked imperiously back.

Finally, I sighed. "Whatever."

We walked the deserted halls in silence. At the futon room door, I knocked, and Connor let me in, only looking slightly askance at Tybalt. Quentin was asleep, his face pale in the gloom, while the Hippocampi frolicked in their tank, unaware of the dangers around them. Lucky things.

Tybalt nodded to Connor, then to me, before turning and melting away into the shadows of the hall. I closed the door, locking it, and looked at Connor. "Wake me half an hour before dawn or when Sylvester gets here, whichever comes first."

"Do I want to ask?"

"Probably not," I said, wearily. He nodded, hugging me briefly before letting me stretch out on the floor in front of the futon. I fell asleep almost as soon as my eyes were closed.

If I had any dreams, I don't remember them.

"Toby, it's time." Connor's voice, only inches from my ear. I jerked upright, nearly smacking my head into his, and stared at him.

"What?"

"It's time."

"Sylvester—"

"Tybalt can explain." From the grim set of his lips, it wasn't good.

I nodded. "All right. Just a second." I stood, taking my time getting to my feet, and reached over to feel Quentin's forehead. He wasn't hot enough to worry me, and his breathing was even. Infection was a risk—it's always a risk—but he wasn't going to die in his sleep.

Tybalt was waiting in the hall, along with Elliot. Connor stepped out with me, keeping his hand on the doorknob. I looked between them.

"Well?"

"Your monarchs are such charming people," said Tybalt, not bothering to hide his disdain.

I groaned. "Riordan."

"She won't believe Duke Torquill is here for valid reasons," Elliot said. "I called her seneschal as soon as I heard, but . . ."

"But she's stopping them at the border?"

"Indeed." He nodded grimly.

"That's just . . . damn." I sighed. "All right, where's Gordan?"

"In April's room, with the door locked. Everyone's accounted for."

I knew where everyone was. So why didn't I know where to point the finger? April was Jan's daughter. Gordan lost her best friend and Elliot lost his fiancée—who was left? Unless there was somebody else in the building, I was almost out of people, and completely out of suspects.

"Fine. Connor, stay with Quentin. Eliot, Tybalt, come with me." I started for the cafeteria before Connor could object. "I need coffee."

"You're so charmingly predictable," said Tybalt, dryly, and followed.

Elliot looked between us, asking, "What are you intending to do?"

"Just what I said: wake the dead. Don't ask for details. I don't have any."

He stopped, staring at us before managing to ask, in a hushed tone, "*All* the dead?"

Oh, oak and ash. I hadn't intended to make him think that . . . "No," I said. "I can't do that. I'm sorry. I don't have it in me. But there's still a chance for Alex."

Elliot looked momentarily heartbroken, and I wanted to slap myself. I'd been mad at these people for being so damn vague, and now I was doing the same thing to them. "I see."

The bloodstains had been cleaned off the cafeteria floor, and there was already a pot of coffee waiting on the counter. I headed straight for it, snagging a mug.

"I told you she was fond of her coffee," commented Tybalt.

"Observant," I said, approvingly. "Hey, Elliot, why's Gordan in April's room, anyway?"

"Maintenance."

"Maintenance?" I echoed, filling my mug.

"Her server has to be checked every morning. Gordan's the only hardware expert left."

Tybalt frowned. I realized that he hadn't been filled in as to April's nature. "Why does this 'server' require checking?"

"If it breaks down or loses power, April goes off-line." Elliot shrugged. "We have to perform regular maintenance to make sure that doesn't happen."

I paused, mug halfway to my lips. "Repeat the bit about the power."

"If April's server loses power, she's off-line for the duration."

"And off-line means what, exactly?"

"She disappears. She leaves the network and 'dies' until the power comes back."

"And then what? She's fine?"

"Well, yes. As soon as she's been rebooted."

I put my cup down. "Right." No wonder April didn't understand why Jan wouldn't wake up; she didn't understand death, because every time she "died," she came right back to life. She would have been the perfect suspect, the innocent killer . . . if not for Peter, who died during a power outage. How could she kill him when she was "dead" herself? "Can she come here?"

"Not during a maintenance window."

"Right." I started toward Tybalt. "Where's her room?"

"Near Jan's office."

"Okay." I glanced at the clock. The sun would be up soon, and the answers I needed would only be found with the dead. "Do you have a key to the futon room?"

Elliot frowned. "Yes."

"Good. Now listen carefully: don't go anywhere near April's room. I want you to head back to the futon room, and lock yourself in. Don't let anyone in. If April shows up . . ." I paused. "Don't let her open the door."

His frown was deepening. "What are you talking about?"

"Just trust me, okay?" It wasn't Terrie: Terrie was dead. It wasn't Elliot: if he'd been the killer, I'd have been dead as soon as we were alone together. That left April and Gordan . . . and April didn't understand what death was, but could never have been the one to kill Peter.

We had a problem.

Elliot frowned worriedly, saying, "All right," before turning to hurry out into the hall.

"Will he be safe?" Tybalt asked. The question sounded academic; he didn't care one way or the other, and he wasn't bothering to pretend.

"April's off-line and Gordan's busy," I said. "This may be the last time he's safe." I looked up at him. "I'm assuming you plan on coming with me."

He smiled, very slightly. "As if I'd let you risk life and limb alone?"

"Right," I said. "This way."

It was almost dawn when we reached the basement door. I thought about trying to make it down the stairs and decided not to push it. I might make it. I might also be halfway down when the sun came up, and the idea of breaking my neck because I was dumb enough to play chicken with the dawn didn't appeal. Closing my eyes, I leaned against the wall, and waited. Tybalt put his arm around my shoulders, and I jumped, but didn't look. Dawn always passes. That's one of the few things I like about it.

If I hadn't slept, the force of the sunrise would have been enough to knock me out. As it was, my headache was back full force by the time the pressure went away, leaving me queasy and glad that I'd skipped breakfast. I would have been sick otherwise. Tybalt kept his arm around my shoulders the whole time, steadying me. As dawn passed, I opened my eyes and flashed him a grateful look. He turned away, expression unreadable.

Right. For a moment there, I'd forgotten that we weren't friends. I pushed away from the wall and opened the basement door, heading down the stairs into the makeshift morgue.

One small, important detail had changed. If I hadn't known the contents of the basement so intimately, I might have missed it, but as it was, it was like finding water in the desert: too out of place to overlook.

Alex was lying in Terrie's place.

Tybalt breathed in sharply. Apparently, he hadn't believed me when I said something would happen. More fool him.

"Jackpot," I said, with a satisfied smile.

Alex looked like all the others: like he should open his eyes at any moment and demand to know what he was doing in the basement. There was one major difference, however, which became evident when you looked for it; the punctures on his wrists and throat were gone. The dawn had healed as it transformed.

"What in the . . ."

"Two people, one murder," I said, pressing my ear against Alex's chest. There was no heartbeat. I hadn't really expected dawn to revive him—that would've been too easy—but I'd hoped. "Alex's blood is still alive. That's why he changed when the sun came up. Now I've just got to figure out how to wake him the rest of the way."

Tybalt growled, the sound resonating through the basement. "Why not let him rot?"

"It's tempting. But I need to talk to him. Besides, fae don't actually decay." When dawn healed him, it left him with a body that was fully intact and ready to function. I just needed to figure out how to jump-start it.

It had to start with blood. Everything starts with blood. Pulling the knife from my belt, I turned his arm toward me and cut shallowly across his wrist. There was very little blood. It had probably settled in his veins when his heart stopped. That was fine; I could cope.

Bending, I pressed my lips to the cut, and drank.

Down the corridor quick now quick run away run for safety find Toby find Elliot find anyone no not now no not me no I won't die this way I can't I won't so run run get awa—

Gasping, I jerked myself out of the memories and staggered backward, into Tybalt. He caught me easily, eyes gone wide.

"October?"

"Too close," I said, trying to get my breath back. "It starts too close to dying. I can't see who killed her."

"Then find another way," he said, and set me back on my feet.

I blinked at him. "You think I can?"

He smiled, briefly, and reached out to tuck a lock of hair behind my ear. "I believe it. This suits you far better than your silly illusions."

"Oh." I kept blinking at him for what felt like an impossibly long time before wrenching my gaze away, reaching for my knife. "The blood remembers itself. There's nothing but inertia keeping him dead." I paused to smile, grimly. "I'm going to regret this."

"What are you going to do?"

"Not sure. Now hush."

He hushed.

Blood magic is based half on instinct and half on need. There are patterns to follow and rituals that can make things easier, but in the end, it all comes down to instinct and need. I had to have lessons in flower magic and water magic; I had to be taught to spin illusions and mix up physical charms. But blood magic . . . blood magic just told me what needed to be done, and I did it. It's the only thing that's ever come without a struggle, even if it's never been exactly easy.

My mother can make stone sing with a few drops of

blood and a heartfelt plea. I wasn't looking for anything that flashy. Just a little resurrection.

Placing the knife against my left wrist, I cut a careful X, deep enough to bleed but shallow enough that it wouldn't be life threatening if I took care of it quickly. The smell of grass and copper began to rise, crackling in the air as the spell, still half-formed, began to sing. Good. Blood welled up from the cuts, running down my arm. The smell of copper strengthened, overwhelming the grass almost entirely.

Keeping my movements deliberate, I placed my knife gingerly on the counter and turned toward Alex, tilting my arm to let the blood run down my fingers. The gauze covering my hand promptly turned a rich and vivid red. I ignored it; for the moment, it wasn't important. Things felt exactly right. Even the pain wasn't important. All that mattered was the pattern that the blood was telling me to follow.

"October . . ."

I'd almost forgotten that Tybalt was in the room. "Hush," I said again, beginning to drip blood onto Alex's forehead and lips before pressing my hand flat over his heart, leaving a crimson handprint. The magic was catching hold, the pattern so clear I could almost see it . . . and it wasn't enough. The pieces of the spell were there, but the picture wasn't coming clear.

Fine. If the universe wanted to play rough, I'd play rough. Raising my wrist, I chanted, "Oak and ash and willow and thorn are mine; blood and ice and flowers and flame are mine." I pressed my lips to the cut, taking a mouthful of blood and swallowing. It burned all the way down. "Mine in turn are those who hold me, hurt me, bend me to their ends; I have bled and burned here, and I demand the return of what is mine." The scent of cut grass and copper was overpowering. I took a second mouthful of blood and bent over Alex, pressing my lips to his and forcing the blood into his mouth.

The spell shattered in a mist that sent me staggering. My feet slipped on the bloody floor and I nearly fell before Tybalt caught me, holding me upright.

And Alex opened his eyes.

That was the final piece to end the feeling of absolute serenity that had come when the spell caught hold; suddenly, I realized that I was bleeding, dizzy, and my head was pounding. What's more, the taste of blood was coating my throat, making me want to gag. "Damn," I muttered, stepping away from Tybalt to grab the sheet off Yui's cot and start wrapping it around my arm. I'd just raised the dead—technically—and I didn't need to bleed to death as a consequence. I'm not that fond of irony.

"Oberon's balls . . ." whispered Tybalt, in a small, awed voice. I glanced toward him, and he looked away, not meeting my eyes. That hurt.

There would be time to worry about Tybalt later. I wrenched my attention back to Alex, who was sitting up now, eyes unfocused. He didn't look like he was quite all there, and I couldn't blame him. Being dead couldn't have been easy.

"Welcome back, Sleeping Beauty." All that blood was a little distracting. I didn't know whether I wanted to throw up or faint.

"I . . ." Alex raised his hands, staring at the bloody fingerprints running down his arms. "I'm alive?"

"Good guess."

"How . . ."

"You weren't really dead. You just thought you were."

"What?" He looked at me blankly. Out of the corner of my eye, I could see Tybalt doing the same.

I sighed. "You weren't dead." I felt surprisingly lucid, despite the pain and blood loss. I should really learn to recognize when I'm in shock. I can spot it in everyone else, but it somehow always takes me by surprise. "Whatever attacked you tried to drain the memories from your blood. I think that's what actually kills people. They lose themselves." I paused, wobbling. "It got Terrie, but it couldn't get to you. Not at night. So here you are."

Alex's eyes went wide. "Terrie's dead," he whispered.

"I'm sorry." And then everything hit me at once.

Dying probably takes a lot out of you. I wouldn't know—I've never died—but I know how hard blood magic can be on the body. I managed to take a shaky step toward the cot before I fell. Tybalt didn't catch me this time. Alex was shouting, far away, and I angrily thought that I'd told them not to go anywhere alone. What was he doing all the way over there? I tried to tell him to go find the others, but there were no words, just the taste of blood and ashes . . .

And there was darkness.

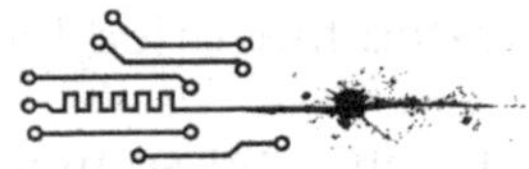

TWENTY-EIGHT

I WOKE SLOWLY, fighting every inch of the way. The more awake I was, the more I hurt . . . but I was alive. That would have to do. I've always run myself hard—it's one of my worst flaws—but I'd never tried two major acts of blood magic that close together before, and I was starting to think I'd blown some sort of internal fuse. My headache was worse than ever. I groaned, raising my right hand to my temple, and the last of the comfortable darkness dissolved, leaving me inarguably awake.

Damn.

"Toby? Are you all right?" I didn't recognize the voice. That wasn't surprising. I barely recognized my name.

"Is she awake?" This voice was higher, although not high enough to be April. I sorted through the possible speakers, settling on Gordan. That wasn't good, given my suspicions.

"Her pulse is steady," said a third voice. This one I recognized: Tybalt. Once I allowed that moment of recognition, I realized I was on my back with my head on someone's leg, and that something cool and damp was pressed against my forehead. Probably a washcloth. "I think we just need to wait."

"I'll wake up fast if someone gets me some coffee," I said, not opening my eyes.

"Toby!" That was Alex. Oh, good. He'd stayed not-dead. "You're okay!"

"No, I'm annoyed. There's a big difference." The inside of my mouth tasted like dried blood. Yuck. "Can I get that coffee?"

Shuffling footsteps on what sounded like tile. "Toby, this is Elliot. Can you hear me?"

"I'm answering you, aren't I?" All this talking was making my headache worse. I was starting to seriously question the wisdom of not being dead.

"She'll be fine if she doesn't do anything else stupid," said Gordan, tone making it quite clear that she wasn't harboring delusions about my intelligence.

I considered my options. Movement was out—my head wasn't allowing any argument—but I could open my eyes if I was willing to deal with the pain. I'd have to do it eventually.

When I worked at Home, I woke up with hangovers on a regular basis. Most of them made me feel like my skull had liquefied. This was worse. The light was too strong, and the colors were too bright. I winced, forcing my eyes to stay open as I looked around. My head was in Tybalt's lap. Elliot and Alex were standing nearby, and Gordan was off to one side, packing things back into her first aid kit.

"How do you feel?" asked Alex.

"Like I've been through a meat grinder. Am I getting that coffee?"

"You lost a lot of blood," said Gordan. "That's twice I've had to tape you back together. Don't make me do it again."

"I'm not planning to." Especially since I was pretty sure she wanted to take me apart herself.

"Good." She picked up her kit and turned, starting for the stairs.

"No going off alone," said Elliot.

She stopped, scowling. "I need to get back to work."

"Take Alex."

"No," I said quickly. "I need to talk to him."

"Well, I have *work* to do." Gordan glared at us all.

"So go do it," I said, hoping I sounded tired enough that she'd believe I was slipping—and that she really was our killer. I wanted to be sure before I confronted her. I also wanted to be able to stand under my own power. "Call April if anything happens."

"Your concern is touching," she said, and flounced up the stairs.

Elliot turned to me once she was gone, frowning. "You let her go off alone."

"Yeah, I know." I tilted my head back, looking up at Tybalt. "Help me sit up?"

Without a word, he slid his hands under my back and scooped me into a sitting position. I pulled away, managing to support myself for almost a second before my arm buckled and I fell back against his chest. He put an arm across my shoulders, holding me there.

"Stay," he said, firmly.

"You got it," I said, looking around the room. We were still in the basement. A thick bandage had been wrapped around my left wrist, streaks of red staining the white. Tybalt and I were sitting on the cot where we'd placed Terrie's body. That made sense. It was available real estate now.

"You were bleeding so much we didn't dare move you," said Elliot. "If Tybalt hadn't told us you did it to yourself, we'd have thought you were attacked. I've never met anyone who cuts themselves open as often as you do."

"It's a talent of hers," said Tybalt.

"Not a good one," said Elliot, picking up a mug and offering it to me. "Drink this."

"Coffee?" I took the mug, peering into it. It wasn't

coffee. Not unless the description had been rewritten to include "green and sticky."

"No," said Elliot. It was good to know that I didn't need to add hallucinations to my list of symptoms. "Just drink it."

"I don't drink green things."

"I made it. Drink it."

That didn't strike me as being an incentive. "What is it?"

"One of Yui's recipes," he said. It was the first time he didn't flinch when he said her name. "It's good for headaches. She used to give it to Colin when he stayed human too long."

I peered into the cup. If it tasted anything like it smelled, I was going to be very unhappy. Still . . . "Does it work?"

"Colin said it did."

"Right." I was an excellent target in my current condition, and I couldn't afford to turn down anything that might help. Squeezing my eyes shut, I chugged the contents of the cup.

It didn't taste as bad as it looked. It tasted worse. Stars exploded behind my eyes as the mug slipped out of my hands to shatter on the floor. For a moment, I was halfway convinced that I'd been poisoned; then my headache withdrew, so abruptly that it left me dizzy. The ache in my wrist and hand seemed to worsen, filling the vacuum, but that was the sort of pain I could deal with. I'm used to it.

I opened my eyes. The world snapped obligingly into focus. "What was *in* that stuff?"

"Pennyroyal, cowslips, and wisteria, mostly," Elliot said. "Are you all right?"

"No, but I'm feeling better." Sometimes I hate our inability to thank each other. Tap-dancing around the phrase gets old, especially when I'm tired.

"Good," said Tybalt, removing his arm.

I leaned back on my good hand, taking a breath. I still felt queasy, but it was nowhere near as bad. Straightening, I turned to Alex. He looked surprisingly good for someone that had recently been dead.

"We need to talk," I said.

He nodded, slowly. "I think you're right. Was I really . . . ?"

"As a doornail. How are you feeling?"

Alex shuddered, saying, "I don't know. It feels like part of me is missing."

"Part of you *is* missing, Alex." I shook my head. "I don't think Terrie's coming back." He looked stricken. I pushed on anyway, asking, "Do you remember anything about what happened?" *You'd better, because I can't do that again,* I added, silently.

Alex licked his lips, looking between me and Elliot before he said, "I don't usually remember what happens to Terrie."

"But this time you do?"

"A . . . a little bit." He grimaced. "She felt awful when you left. So she went for a walk."

"Did she see anyone?"

"Well, yeah." He sounded slightly surprised. "April. She said Gordan wanted me. Wanted Terrie."

"So Terrie followed her?" I asked. I felt Tybalt stiffen beside me.

Alex hesitated. Then, slowly, he nodded.

"Elliot. April is the interoffice pager, right? That's her job?"

"Yes, exactly," said Elliot, starting to look as uncomfortable as I felt. He was connecting the lines. I could see it in his eyes.

"So all of you, you just follow her whenever she asks you to."

"Well . . . yes."

"I see." At least I thought I did, and I didn't like what I was looking at. Maybe April couldn't have been the one to kill Peter . . . but nothing said Gordan had to be working alone. "Where did she take Terrie?"

"The generator room." Alex paused, expression twisting. "Where Peter died."

"Then what happened?"

"I . . . we . . ." Alex closed his eyes, starting to talk more quickly. "She said to wait, and she vanished. And the lights went out."

"Just the lights in the generator room?"

"There were still lights on in the hall. Terrie has . . . Terrie had really good night vision, and she saw something in the shadows. You said not to go off alone. That's when she realized she was alone."

"Is that when Terrie ran?"

"No. She called for Gordan—she's always hanging out in weird places, it could have been her—but she didn't answer, and that was sort of scary. So Terrie ran." He was talking faster and faster, like he could outrun what he was saying. "Whoever it was followed her into the hall, so she kept running. Terrie made it outside." A sigh. "She thought she was safe."

"What happened then?" He started to shake, not answering. "Alex?"

He didn't stop shaking, but started to talk again, voice dull: "Something hit her from behind. There was this pain in her throat and wrists and then in her chest . . . and then it was over." He raised his head. "Then you were kissing me."

Tybalt growled. I put a hand on his knee, signaling him to be still. Things were coming together with fast, fierce finality. April had given me the last piece I really needed; I'd just been too distracted to see it. When she came to Colin's office, she said I was going to find out what caused them to *remain* isolated from the network. And when Jan died, she said there were no more reboots. She didn't want to know why they were dying, because she already knew why.

She wanted to know why they weren't coming back to life.

"Is that everything?" I managed, trying not to let him see how stunned I felt.

"Yes," he said, with a small, unsteady nod.

"All right." I slid to my feet, grabbing the edge of the cot and holding on until the world stopped swaying. Tybalt moved to catch my arm, but I held up my hand, motioning him off. When I was sure I wouldn't fall, I let go and took a cautious step. My balance held. Maybe I wasn't up to running for my life, but I could walk, and that was a start. "Where's April's room?"

"You shouldn't—" Alex reached for my shoulder, and stopped when he saw me glare. Tybalt's snarl probably didn't hurt, either.

"Don't mess with me, okay? I'm so not in the mood."

"Sorry," he said, taking a step backward.

"One more time: where is April's room?" Gordan was supposedly going to work on April's hardware. She'd be there, and we could catch them both before they realized we'd worked things out. This could be over. It could finally be over.

Elliot sighed. "Behind Jan's office."

"Can you take me there?"

"We can just call April," said Alex. "She'll come here."

"She always comes to us. It's time for us to go to her." My arm was throbbing and I was dizzy enough that the world blurred if I moved too quickly. My resources were running out. Whether we solved this thing or not, I was nearly done, because if I went much longer there wouldn't be anything left of me. "This needs to end. Come on."

It was time for us to get some answers. All I could do was hope that we weren't already too late.

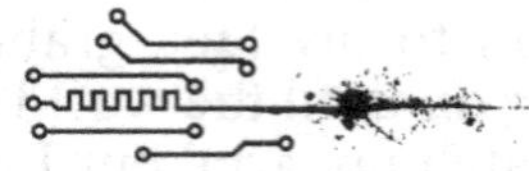

TWENTY-NINE

ELLIOT LED OUR RAGTAG PROCESSION down the halls past Jan's office. Tybalt and I walked in the middle, with me trying to look as if I didn't need his elbow to stay upright—like I was just holding it because it amused me—while Alex dogged our heels. We didn't talk. I was too tired, and I needed to save what little strength I had left for the confrontation ahead.

Tybalt still wouldn't meet my eyes. I didn't want to think about what that meant.

The fact that April was probably Gordan's accomplice terrified me. I'd left Quentin alone with her, and just because she hadn't killed him yet, that didn't mean she wasn't going to. Gordan didn't like him. That was even more reason to confront them in April's room, where I could break her server if I had to. They hadn't killed Quentin. They weren't getting the chance.

Elliot stopped in front of a pale pink door with purple trim around the edges. It looked like something you'd see in a nursery school. "Here," he said.

"Good." I glanced between them. Elliot looked worn out; Alex seemed even worse. Coming back from the dead had revitalized him, but it was a false strength, and it was fading. Only Tybalt looked like he'd stand a chance in a fight. "You three wait here."

"What?" they said, almost in unison. Tybalt's eyes narrowed dangerously as Elliot said, "You're insane if you think I'll let you—"

"You're not stupid. You know why I let Gordan leave, and you know why we're here." He nodded marginally, acknowledging my words. I continued, "I need to see April, alone, and I don't want Gordan sneaking up on me. Three men on the door is safer than one, given Alex's condition. If you see anything funny, scream."

"And if you see anything 'funny'?" asked Tybalt, eyes still narrowed.

"Then *I'll* scream."

"April doesn't know you very well," said Elliot, in a last bid to accompany me. "She won't like you being in her room."

"That's her problem." She came to me when she needed to cry. Somehow, I didn't think it was going to be an issue. "Can you please just wait here?"

"We'll wait," said Tybalt, coldly. That, it seemed, was the end of it; Elliot and Alex looked away, no longer willing to argue.

"Good. Elliot, when I come back out, you're going to tell me what Jan wanted me to know before she died." I turned and stepped through the door, leaving him staring.

April's room might have been better termed a generous broom closet. Most of the floor space was taken up by a tall machine that stood on a metal frame at the center of the room, humming contentedly. Cables connected it to power outlets on all four walls; they weren't taking any chances. It was the sort of thing I'd come to expect. The rest of the room, on the other hand . . . wasn't. I stopped just over the threshold, and stared.

The walls were pink, with a border of stenciled purple rabbits on a white background. A bookshelf filled with computer manuals and kid's books was up against one wall, next to a pink-and-white bookshelf piled with stuffed rabbits of every color imaginable. One of the rabbits was three feet tall, not including the ears, sitting on the floor next to the shelf with a red bow around its neck. A heart-shaped sign hung above the bookshelf, proclaiming this to be "April's Room" in large cartoon letters. Add a bed and a dresser and it would have looked like the room of any normal, well-loved little girl. Damn. Just once, can't the villains look suitably villainous?

No one was in the room. It took me three steps to reach the machine, feeling more like an intruder with every second that passed. I kept noticing details. The picture of Jan and April on the bookshelf, the geometric precision with which the rabbits were piled . . . the baby blanket wrapped snugly around the base of the server. Someone had worked very hard to give this airy nothing a local habitation and a name. Jan had loved her daughter so much.

"You're here." I hadn't heard April materialize, but I was too tired to jump when she spoke behind me. Exhaustion makes you harder to surprise.

"Hey, April." I turned slowly, so as not to betray how unsteady I was. "How are you?"

"Why are you here?" she countered. She was scowling, as annoyed as any teenager finding an uninvited adult in her living space.

"I thought I'd come see how you were."

She narrowed her eyes. "*I* am fine. Why are *you* here?"

"I have some questions I think you can answer," I said, leaning against the wall next to the shelf of plush rabbits. "At least, I hope you can." I reached over to straighten one worn cotton bunny's ear.

"Don't touch that!" April vanished, reappearing next to me with a crackle of static as she snatched the rabbit out of my reach. Glaring over the top of its head, she said, "This is *mine*. My mother gave it to *me*."

"I'm sorry." I held up my hands, palms outward. "I didn't mean to upset you."

"My mother always buys me rabbits." She stroked the bunny's head, looking down at it. "Every time she goes somewhere I can't follow, she brings me another rabbit. I like rabbits."

"I can tell."

"She'll bring me many rabbits this time, because she didn't tell me she was leaving."

"April . . ." I wasn't sure what to say. There was a good chance that she'd been killing people. Was it still a crime if she didn't understand what she'd done? "April, you understand she's not coming back this time, don't you?"

"Of course she's coming back." She looked up, eyes wide and guileless. "We just have to find a way to bring her back online."

"Honey, people don't work that way." I struggled against the urge to comfort her the way I would have comforted Dare or Quentin, and shook my head. "She's gone."

"I work that way, and she's my mother. She's coming back for me."

"I don't think you understand."

She glared. "No, *you* don't understand. It's going to work this time."

That was the opening I'd been waiting for. "You killed those people, didn't you?" I asked, keeping my voice measured and calm.

"I didn't mean to!" April protested, looking every inch the wounded child. "I didn't mean to hurt anyone. It wasn't supposed to go that way."

"But you did hurt them. You took them off the network." I started inching toward the server. If she made any sudden moves, I was going to find out just how fast

I could kick those plugs out of the back of the machine. "We never got around to searching the spots where the bodies were found, but that wouldn't have mattered, would it? What did you do?"

"I didn't know it would happen."

"That doesn't matter, honey. They're still dead. How did they die?"

"It was supposed to be all right! No one was supposed to get hurt!" She clutched the rabbit to her chest, eyes filling with strangely fractal tears. "I didn't know you broke so easily. It was supposed to be an upgrade."

"I need some answers, April," I said, gently. She probably meant what she was saying; she hadn't known what she was doing, and Gordan took advantage of her ignorance. That didn't change what they'd done. "I need to know how you killed them."

"That's why you're here! You're going to fix things! Bring them back on the network!"

"I can't. No one can do that."

"I—"

"You had to know they weren't coming back. April, you killed your mother."

The change in her was incredible. Suddenly furious, she straightened, shouting, "I did not! I tried to tell you! *That wasn't me!*"

I hadn't been expecting that. "What?"

"I wouldn't! I said no! And so . . . so . . . she did it without me. I didn't help. I didn't hurt my mommy!" Her voice broke as she began to sob, burying her face against the rabbit.

I stared at her. April thought she was somehow helping the people they attacked. Jan died differently. Jan had time to fight. Of course April didn't help—she couldn't have done that to her mother. Gordan killed Jan. April might not understand what they were doing, but Gordan did. When April wouldn't do as she was told, Gordan acted alone. She killed Jan, and she was somewhere in the knowe, unguarded . . . and Connor was alone with Quentin, unarmed.

"April, where's Gordan? We need to find her—we need to stop her before she—"

April shook her head, going calm again. "I'm sorry, but I can't help you. I have to bring my mother back. If I stop Gordan, she won't help me reinstall her properly."

"Please. She can't come back. We don't work that way."

"There are flaws in the process and her casing was damaged, but Gordan says the limits of the hardware can be overcome. We can download her to a new server. We can try again."

"April, please, you have to stop. If you help us catch Gordan, I can make sure you're safe. It wasn't your fault. You were used, you didn't understand." I meant it, too. She could be protected. It would be hard, but root and branch, I'd find a way. I owed it to Jan.

"I . . ." She hesitated, eyes more pained than any living eyes should be. "I'm sorry. I never meant to hurt anyone . . . but I need my mother. I don't know how to take care of myself."

"April—" I reached for her, hoping I could hold her, but it was too late: she was gone.

The stuffed rabbit hung in the air for a moment, seeming suspended. Then gravity took hold, and it fell. April didn't reappear. I hadn't really expected her to—she was running away, after all—and that meant I had to run after her. That's my job. Leaving the rabbit on the floor, I bolted for the door, and I didn't look back.

I could have disconnected her server, removed her from the playing field, but without Jan to help us turn her back on, I wasn't sure she'd survive. I wasn't going to avenge Sylvester's niece by killing her only child, no matter how misguided that child's actions had been.

The others were waiting where I'd left them. Thank Oberon for small favors. They all straightened as I reappeared, but it was Tybalt who spoke first, asking, "Toby? What's wrong?"

"April and Gordan are our killers. Gordan convinced her that it wasn't murder, it was an 'upgrade.' Only the process doesn't work, and when April refused to help her kill Jan, Gordan did it on her own." I wheeled on Elliot, stabbing my finger toward him. "What am I missing? What haven't you told me? Talk fast. There isn't much time." I was already starting toward the futon room, taking long, ground-eating strides. "Tybalt, can you take the Shadows?"

"They're warded against me," he said, pacing me easily. "I can't access them."

"Of course they are," I snarled.

Elliot was hurrying to catch up, saying, "Gordan and *April*?"

"Gordan and April," I confirmed. "April couldn't do it alone. Even if Peter hadn't died during a power outage, she didn't understand what death was. You two had better start talking."

"Toby—" Alex began.

"No," said Elliot, cutting him off. I stopped, turning toward him. He met my eyes, not flinching away. "No more stalling. We'll tell you."

"But the project—" Alex protested.

"Is over. Yui's dead, Jan's dead, and the project is over. We failed. Ashes, ashes, we all fall down." Eyes still on mine, Elliot said, "Jan brought us here to save the world."

"Right," I said doubtfully, starting to walk again. "Keep talking."

"I'll need to give you a bit of background. Stop me if it gets too technical."

"Fine."

Alex was staring at both of us, looking scandalized. Elliot caught the look, and snapped, "I'm Jan's seneschal. If April's a murderess, she can't take the County, and

I'm in charge." Alex looked away. Elliot continued, "It started when Jan transplanted April. She didn't know it could be done until she'd done it, but once she had, what she'd found was obvious."

"What do you mean?"

"The way back to what Faerie should be. Isolated, pure, eternal . . . if she had the right tools, she could change the world and save us all." Elliot sighed. "She called us because we were the best Faerie had to offer. We came because we believed her."

"I don't understand," I said.

"Faerie is dying," said Alex. On his lips, it became a statement of irrefutable fact. The sun shines, rain falls, and Faerie is dying. "We die faster than we're born, and the humans are winning. The sun loves them. In the end, we'll be stories for them to forget."

"You're fools," said Tybalt, scornful. "Faerie is immortal."

"The Gean-Cannah are almost extinct," Alex said. I didn't have an answer for that.

Elliot shook his head. "There will always be fae, but Faerie, as a culture and a world, can die. We've already lost our regents and most of our lands. We can't survive like this."

"We've lasted a long time," I said. "Maybe we've had long enough."

"Nothing is long enough," said Elliot. I knew he was thinking of Yui. We could have argued for hours. We didn't have them. We had to reach Connor and Quentin, and the halls weren't helping—they seemed to be continuing to unspool, long past the point when we should have reached our destination. I was trying not to let that worry me. It wasn't working.

"How was a computer company supposed to save Faerie?" I asked, lowering my voice to conserve my breath. I had to be missing something in all the circuitry and strangeness. I just didn't know what it was.

"We were going to take it inside, away from everything that could hurt or change it," said Alex, expression pleading with me to understand. "We were going to save it."

"Inside where?" growled Tybalt.

"The machines," said Elliot, and actually smiled. "April was the key. She's a perfect blend of magic and technology. Whatever you do to her, she comes back whole. We have her on disk. We can bring her back to life a thousand times, and she'll always be the same, and she'll always keep going. Jan looked at her and knew that we could do it again."

"That is *sick,*" said Tybalt, looking disgusted.

I didn't disagree. "You were going to turn us into *machines*?" There's a difference between immortality and stasis. For people who'd been so fast to embrace new mortal technologies, the inhabitants of Tamed Lightning seemed awfully fuzzy on the distinction.

"Not quite. There were problems. We—" Elliot stopped, frowning. "Where *are* we?"

The room was huge, filled with filing cabinets. Conflicting views of the grounds showed through windows on all four walls, and from the skylight overhead. I'd never seen it before, and it definitely wasn't between Jan's office and the futon room. "Elliot . . ."

"This shouldn't be here," Alex said. "That hall doesn't *lead* to the west sunroom. Ever."

Elliot's shock was fading, replaced by resignation. "Jan is dead, and April was her heir," he said. "April is assuming her mother's position. The knowe is changing to suit her."

"Is she doing this consciously?" I asked.

"I doubt it," said Elliot. "The knowe is reacting to her panic. They're still syncing up."

"Great," I said bleakly, staring up at the glass ceiling. If the knowe was reacting to April, I wouldn't be able to sweet-talk it anymore. It had a new mistress, and it wasn't going to listen to some half-blood interloper who owed it no fealty. But somewhere in that changing landscape, my friends were in danger. "Now what?"

Elliot shook his head. "I don't know."

"I think . . ." said Alex, hesitantly. "I think maybe I do."

"So speak," snarled Tybalt.

"We go out the window."

Right.

THIRTY

"ARE YOU SURE THIS WILL WORK?" The only window showing a ground-floor view of the grounds was large enough for us to fit through one at a time, but I didn't trust it not to jump to the third floor while I was only halfway out. Call me paranoid. I'm frequently right.

"We're in a Shallowing," Alex said, hoisting himself onto the windowsill. "We can twist space in knots inside the knowe, but we can't change the shape of the buildings without violating the laws of physics."

"You have eight miles of hallway in a two-story building," I said. "The laws of physics have already been violated. What happens if they decide to press charges?"

"He's right," Elliot said. "The outside stays the same shape and size, no matter what we do in here. The windows connect randomly to the landscaping, but they *do* connect. And they do it from whatever floor they look out on."

"So even though this is a second-floor window, it's actually on the ground floor."

"Yes."

"That makes no sense." I shook my head. "I'll trust you, though—it's not like I have a choice. Which brings me to my next issue—it's night out there."

"Yes," Elliot said. "It is."

I glanced to Alex. "What's going to happen to . . . ?"

"Guess we'll find out," said Alex, wanly, and slid out the window.

It was a six-foot drop to the ground. We heard a thump as he hit the ground, followed by silence. Elliot and I exchanged a wide-eyed glance, rushing to lean out the window. Tybalt stayed where he was and yawned.

"Perhaps he'll stay dead this time," he said, nonchalantly.

"Tybalt," I snapped. He gave me a look, as if to say "what?" then began studying his nails.

Terrie was lying facedown in the grass. I grabbed the windowsill with my good hand and vaulted outside, landing next to her and checking her wrist for a pulse. It was weak, but it was there. "She's alive," I reported, looking up.

Elliot was leaning out the window. "What happened?"

I slid my arms under Terrie's shoulders and stood, balancing her limp form against my knee. "Alex is alive, and Terrie isn't. I guess he's going to be having a lot of early nights."

"We could put her back inside . . ." said Elliot, sliding awkwardly out the window.

"The shock might kill her again," I said. "Tybalt, get down here and help me with her."

"Ah, it's time for the 'here kitty, kitty' again," he said mildly, and jumped from the window, making it look effortless. He grabbed Terrie's legs. "What shall we do with her? Is there a wood chipper available?"

"Tybalt, behave."

"Why?" he asked, sounding honestly interested.

"I don't have time for this. Come on." With Tybalt's help, I was able to shift her into the brush along the building, looking back at Elliot as we got her out of sight. "How is it night out here? The sun just came up."

"The land is suggestible in a Shallowing. If we went back in and came out a door, it would be daylight."

"Right." I straightened, stepping out of the bushes. "Lead the way, and keep talking."

Elliot started to walk. "I mentioned that there were problems, yes? They were mostly in the upload process. We were planning to copy people into the machines without killing them or changing them in any way. We'd just have an extra 'version' of them, and of everything in Faerie, that would live inside our computers."

"How would that save Faerie?" asked Tybalt, pacing me.

"Our ideals and culture would endure, even if nothing else did." He shook his head. "It didn't work. Yui was in charge of magical integration. She said the system refused to release the data. She could make it copy, but she couldn't make it interact."

"It was frozen?" I asked.

"Basically. I don't quite understand where things went wrong—I worked in an administrative capacity, and I never used the actual equipment."

Cats were slinking out of the bushes, falling into formation behind Tybalt. I ignored them, saying, "Somebody might have come up with a new process."

"It's possible."

"Would Yui have volunteered to test it?"

"Absolutely not. Barbara died before Yui; even if her death was caused by the development team, Yui wouldn't have agreed to test a process that had already killed someone."

"What was Terrie's involvement?"

"She worked on the software with Jan, creating the virtual environment. Gordan designed the hardware interfaces."

"Gordan's the one who determined how the machines hooked up to the subjects?"

"Well, yes."

"I see." The pieces of the puzzle were fitting together. I didn't like the results, but they were the ones that fit. "That's where you had the most problems, wasn't it?"

"Yes, it was." Elliot stopped walking, staring at me. "Oh, Oberon's *teeth* . . ."

I glanced to Tybalt, trying to read his expression. It had gone completely neutral, but his eyes were locked on Elliot. Still, I pressed on. "You tried with cats first, didn't you? They remember everything. They were perfect."

"I knew there was a plan to try with feline test subjects, but I was never involved."

"Yeah, well, if you ask the cats, the ones who went to be 'tested' never came back."

Elliot licked his lips nervously. "Barbara was very upset."

So was Tybalt. His shoulders were locked, and the smell of pennyroyal and musk was rising in the air around him. Reaching over, I took hold of his wrist, keeping my eyes on Elliot. "And you never asked?"

"I . . . it didn't seem . . ."

"Did you know that half the cats in a Cait Sidhe's entourage are changelings?"

"No. I never . . . no." Elliot seemed to realize he was on thin ice, even if he wasn't sure how he'd ended up there. "Barbara never said . . ."

"You broke Oberon's law, whether you knew it or not," I said. Glancing up to Tybalt, I asked, "Is the Court of Cats going to demand recompense?"

"That remains to be seen," he said, in a voice that was surprisingly level.

I let go of his wrist. "Okay. Elliot, start moving. We need to get inside."

"We did it for Faerie," Elliot protested, as he began to walk again.

"Will that make it easier for you to sleep at night?" asked Tybalt.

I couldn't blame him for his anger. I shared it. "What happened after the problems were brought to light?"

"We were going to rebuild the physical interface," Elliot said, in a small voice. I could finally see a door on the wall ahead; it took everything I had to stay calm and keep walking.

"Was Gordan still going to be in charge of the project?"

"There was going to be a review."

"Did she know?" He nodded. "Was that when the deaths began?" He nodded again. "Did the recording device always connect at the wrists and throat?" So help me, if he said yes, I was going to throttle him.

"No." He opened the door. The familiar hall past the cafeteria was waiting on the other side. Quietly, he added, "The wounds are new."

"You know it was Gordan, don't you?" I asked, as we walked slowly down the hall.

"Yes. I do." He sighed. "I just don't want to believe it."

"Did you know all along? Did you suspect?" I wasn't shouting; I was too angry. My voice was quiet, calm, and level as I asked, "Did you even *care*?"

"Look at Yui's body, or Jan's, and ask me if I cared," said Elliot, wearily. "We screwed up. We made mistakes. But we were here of our own free will, and we made those mistakes on our own. Everyone I love is dead. Is that enough? Or should I grovel?"

"It is enough," said Tybalt, as gravely as a judge passing sentence. He was a King of Cats. The people of Tamed Lightning wronged his people. In a way, he really was passing judgment on what Elliot had done.

Elliot met his eyes, and nodded, accepting the sentence. "We're almost there."

"Good. I—" My foot hit something damp and I slipped, nearly falling before I caught myself against Tybalt. I looked down, and went cold.

"Are you all right?" asked Elliot.

"No," said Tybalt. "She isn't."

The blood I'd slipped in was still fresh enough to be wet and red. There wasn't much of it, and I hadn't been expecting it; that explained why I hadn't caught the smell of it before. Now that I was "looking," it was everywhere, almost overwhelming me.

Pulling away from Tybalt, I sprinted down the hall toward the futon room with an energy I hadn't realized I still had. Dizziness and panic fought a brief war for control of my actions, and panic won, spurring me to run even faster. I'd told myself Connor and Quentin would be safe where they were . . . and we had a killer who killed her best friend, working with an accomplice who could walk through walls. I'm an idiot. All I could do was hope that I wasn't already too late.

Sometimes hope is the cruelest joke of all.

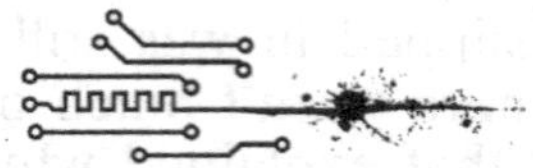

THIRTY-ONE

THE FUTON ROOM DOOR WAS OPEN. I skidded to a stop as I turned the final corner, staring, before beginning to walk slowly forward. It felt like I was moving in a dream.

That only lasted as long as it took for me to realize just how much blood had been spilled, and that there was a dark, torpedolike shape lying motionless in the middle of the floor. There was no sign of Quentin. "Connor!" I exclaimed, almost falling over myself as I dropped to my knees next to the seal. "Don't be dead, don't be dead, come on, baby, don't be dead . . ." My hands fumbled across his blood-tacky fur, looking for a pulse. "How the *fuck* do you find a harbor seal's pulse?"

"He's not dead." Tybalt was standing in the doorway, studying the blood splattered on the walls and floor as casually as a man studying the menu at his local diner.

"How do you know?"

"He doesn't smell dead."

That would have to be good enough. I stood, wiping my hands against my jeans as I looked around the room. I hadn't wanted to believe that they could be in danger.

I'd wanted to believe I was just panicking, paranoid as always, and everything would be fine. You can't always get what you want.

"He went to seal form when he was injured," I said, my voice sounding distant to my own ears. "It must have been a shock. That's usually what triggers an involuntary shift in Selkies."

"You mean like this?" Tybalt stooped to pick something up, holding it up to show me.

A stun gun. "That'd do it," I agreed. I walked over to the futon, running my fingers along the mattress. The blood matted on its surface was sticky and still warm. Once again, we'd almost made it in time.

Quentin wasn't Gean-Cannah; there was nothing special about his blood, nothing I could use to save him. He was going to die, just like all the others. Just like Dare. I was going to have to bury another one. I was . . .

I stuck my fingers in my mouth, trying to break that train of thought before it reached its inevitable destination. I was rewarded with a brief, unfocused flash of blackness and silence as the blood-memory flickered and broke. Oh, thank Maeve. He was asleep when he bled. Not dead, not yet. Just sleeping.

"Toby?" Elliot was standing in the doorway, face gone whey-white. "What happened here? Where's Quentin?"

"Gordan took him." I was starting to see the blood trail on the floor, marking out the way in blotches and streaks. Only half of it was real blood. The rest was potential blood, ghost-blood, made visible by the magic I inherited from my mother. I could track him. As long as he was bleeding, I could track him. "She messed Connor up, too. Pretty badly."

"What can we do?"

"We go." I looked squarely at Elliot. "We go now, because there's no time to wait. Tybalt, can you—"

"I'll guard him. I should be able to coax him back to human form."

"Good." I started to follow Elliot back into the hall. Tybalt caught my hand, stopping me, and I turned to stare at him. "What—?"

"Be careful," he said, voice pitched low. His eyes searched my face until finally, with a sigh, he let go of my hand. "I'll keep the seal-boy safe. Go. Find your charge."

I nodded, and turned, following the blood trail into the hall. I followed the blood; Elliot followed me. We made our way through the knowe and out onto the lawn, my eyes never leaving the floor.

All the cats in Tamed Lightning seemed to have gathered while we were inside, waiting for us on that lawn. Tabby faces peered out of corners and calico bodies covered picnic tables; all of them fell into step behind us as we passed. I ignored them. They were there because they'd been betrayed by one of their too-rare Queens, and they'd lost her as a consequence. They wanted revenge. More importantly, they wanted to know that justice had been done.

There was a slight wind blowing, but it wasn't enough to distract me from the scent of blood. I paused to taste the air, making sure the wind hadn't somehow shifted the trail, then grabbed Elliot's arm. "This way. Come on."

"The cats—"

"Let them come," I said, opening the door to the entry building. "They have as much right to see this end as we do." And if we failed, they'd tell Tybalt what had happened. He'd avenge me. I hoped.

The lights were off in the cubicle maze, but I didn't need them; the blood trail was all the guide I needed, and even in the dark, it was bright and clear as day. I put a hand on Elliot's shoulder, motioning for him to be quiet. Gordan was somewhere nearby, and the Coblynau have some of the best night vision in Faerie. I, on the other hand, was practically blind while my eyes adjusted. That put us at a dangerous disadvantage.

"Where's the light switch?" I whispered. If we could make a bright light, we might be able to turn Gordan's night vision against her.

"Other side of the room," Elliot whispered back.

So much for that idea. "Stay down. We're taking this slow," I said, and stepped away from the door. Elliot followed me, his footsteps echoing. I winced. I'm not as stealthy as, say, Tybalt, but at least I've had a little training. It was clear that Elliot hadn't had any.

"Elliot, be *quiet,*" I hissed.

"I—"

There was a flash of light as the gun went off ahead of us. I shoved Elliot backward, diving for the floor. There was no new pain; she missed. That didn't mean she'd miss again.

"Cover your mouth!" Elliot shouted.

The smell of lye rose in the air, hot and insistent. I covered my mouth and nose, closing my eyes just before a tidal wave of hot, soapy water washed over me. The cats yowled, caught in the flood. This was no simple steam cleaning; I felt myself lifted off the floor as the water rose. I shuddered and squeezed my eyes more tightly shut, trying to pretend I wasn't floating. Repressing the panic attack was taking my full attention. I don't like water. I don't even like baths; just showers where the water never comes up past my ankles and there's no chance of going under. But now I was submerged by a magical wave I couldn't escape or control. I just had to hope Elliot knew what he was doing, and wasn't going to drown us both.

The water swelled and then receded as the wave broke, leaving me as soaked as the rest of the room. Elliot's magic hadn't extended to drying this time. I raised my head, gasping, and turned toward him.

He was staring into the distance, hands still raised. "Elliot . . . ?"

"Did I get her?" he asked. There was a dark stain spreading across his formerly pristine shirt. Gordan didn't miss after all.

"Yeah, you did," I said.

"Ah, good," he said, and smiled, before pitching forward onto the floor. I started to move toward him, but stopped as I heard the sound of footsteps on the catwalks above. Gordan was still on the loose.

Elliot was bleeding out; he needed medical attention. But he was inside the knowe, and I couldn't get him outside for the ambulance to find, even if I could explain where he'd gotten the gunshot wound. He'd flooded the room to drive Gordan back, and there was a chance the water had made it into the chamber of her gun, clogging the firing mechanism. It was a stupid chance to take: I knew that. It was the only chance I had.

The cats were clustered on filing cabinets and desks, wailing. Using the cacophony as cover, I ran to the ladder on the far wall and began to climb. Half the cats fell silent, watching me. They couldn't follow, but they would watch. I found that oddly comforting; whatever happened next, it wouldn't happen unseen or in secret. The cats would see, and they'd tell Tybalt.

Being soaked didn't make the climb any easier. The ladder ended just as I started to feel like my knees were going to give out, and I stepped onto the catwalk, my wet shoes making a marshy slapping sound. There were footsteps ahead of me, just around the corner. I leaped forward in a wild dash. "Stop right where you—"

April was standing over Quentin's body, looking back over her shoulder. Her eyes were wide and sad.

"—are," I finished, sliding to a stop.

"I'm sorry," she whispered, and disappeared.

Something pressed against the small of my back. Behind me, Gordan said cheerfully, "Maybe the gun works, maybe it doesn't. Now put your hands where I can see them. I'd say this wasn't going to hurt, but we both know I'd be lying."

Oh, *great.*

THIRTY-TWO

"YOU SHOULDN'T HAVE FOLLOWED. I'd have taken good care of him," she said. "Walk until you hit the wall, then turn and put your shoulders against it. Keep your hands away from that knife. It wouldn't do you any good, anyway."

"Why are you doing this?" I asked, walking forward. I couldn't count on the gun being waterlogged, and if it wasn't, there was no way I'd get Quentin clear before she shot one of us. For the moment, I needed to go along with her and hope for a chance to turn the tables.

"I need to be able to reach your wrists, and I can't trust you to hold still without incentive. Hence your pretty boy." She sighed. "Honestly, I haven't been able to trust you to do *anything*. You don't follow directions."

I reached the wall and turned, stealing a glance at Quentin. He was breathing. I covered my relief, looking back at Gordan. She was smiling and relaxed; the tension of the past few days had melted out of her like it had never existed. I'd have been relaxed, too, if I was the one with the gun.

"That's better," she said. "I'm glad you're being so

agreeable. It hurts the data if you're damaged before we begin."

"Haven't we already invalidated your data, if you need us undamaged?"

"I'm a little worried, yeah—are you always this fond of trying to get yourself killed?" She shook her head. "I was starting to wonder if you'd last until I got around to you."

"You were the one that kept trying to kill us," I snapped.

"Details. That was just an impulse." She waved a hand, keeping the gun trained on my chest. "I didn't want you calling your master and his hounds, not after I'd gone to so much trouble to keep him from knowing what was going on. April does a surprisingly good imitation of your liege, don't you think?"

"You little . . ."

Gordan smiled, seemingly unperturbed. "I'll admit, it was sort of hard to talk her into it. Little idiot didn't understand how it supported our project. Still, it had the desired effect; you don't listen, but you're still predictable. And don't worry about my work—I figure I can use you, injuries and all. It'll be interesting to see what happens when I start with damaged goods."

"What are you going to do now?" My options were limited by our surroundings: there was nothing for me to throw or hide behind, and if I went for the knife, we'd find out fast whether or not her gun worked. I was sure she'd planned it that way. A waist-high railing ran along the catwalk's edge, broken only by the ladder access gaps. Even if the gun didn't work and I managed to outrun her, I'd never get Quentin down.

"That's easy." There was a deep, wide madness in her eyes. It was there all along; I'd somehow mistaken it for grief. Stupid me. "April's gone for the equipment. You should be grateful. You're going to have a grand adventure!"

"Our last one," I said. Elliot was bleeding to death on the floor below, Tybalt was taking care of Connor, and Terrie was out for Oberon-only-knew how long; no one was going to find us until it was too late. She could kill us both and walk away unscathed. She was going to win.

"The odds that you'll survive aren't good, but it's not impossible. We've made great strides! Every failure is another step toward success!"

"You're talking about *killing* us!"

"Isn't it sad? But this is important! We're making sacrifices for the greater good!"

"Sacrifices like Barbara?"

Her manic cheer slipped for a moment, showing the anger behind it. "That was an accident," she hissed, finger tightening on the trigger.

I have a few basic rules for dealing with guns. First, don't let anyone else have one. Second, if you must let someone else go armed, try not to tease them. I put my hands up, saying soothingly, "I'm sure it was."

"I didn't know it would kill her! I thought I'd fixed the problems, and she was so upset about the cats. She was going to demand we abandon the whole project, and . . . and . . ."

"And you thought you'd show her just how well it could really work."

"Yes," she said, desperately. That's the nice thing about insanity: evil people kill you, but crazy ones try to make you understand. "I could do it one last time—do it *right*—and she'd see. We'd be finished. We could go public, and everything would be . . . better."

"But something went wrong." She was silent. I frowned. "You still don't know what went wrong, do you?"

"I'll find it!"

"I'm sure you will."

Gordan shook her head as if to clear it, and then

smiled. "I will, thanks to you and your courtly boy. Every bit of data helps. If you survive, it'll tell me everything, and if you die, you've helped save Faerie. Be proud. You'll be remembered as pioneers of our brave new world."

"Sacrifices are always remembered that way."

"If it bothers you to think of yourselves as sacrifices, don't. Think of yourselves as . . . explorers running the risk of sailing off the edge of the world. It'll only hurt for a second. Once the current starts up, you won't feel anything at all. You won't even be able to move."

That explained why none of their victims struggled. Use April to get the machine on them, flip a switch, and they were frozen while they died. April didn't help to kill Jan, and so she wasn't caught the right way. "Let Quentin go, Gordan," I said. "He doesn't have anything to do with this."

"Maybe if you'd sent him away when I told you to, I could have, but it's too late now." She glanced over her shoulder. "April should be back soon. It's nice, having an assistant who doesn't understand that space is supposed to be linear. She's so *efficient*."

I began inching away from the wall. She turned immediately, a small, chiding smile on her face. "Uh-uh. No funny business."

"You're using her," I said, slumping back against the wall.

"Who, April? I didn't use her. She came willingly."

"Did she understand what she was doing?"

"What *we* were doing, you mean? Of course she did. She understood we were helping others be like her. Of course, she didn't know they wouldn't come back after they were shut down, but that doesn't matter. She still agreed."

"It matters to me."

"It doesn't. No one's coming to save you. I'll kill you, and the boy, and then we'll take out your stray cat and the seal. Don't worry. I'll tell your liege you died heroically. So sad. April and I will be the only survivors, and we'll be heartbroken . . . but we'll continue our work." She glanced around. "Where *is* she? April!" The echo of her shout bounced off the walls. "Stupid girl."

I knew the cavalry wasn't coming; all I could do now was stall for time. "The only thing I don't understand is how you killed Peter. The generators . . ."

"Panic buttons can have multiple purposes." Gordan's smile grew. "April hooked him up, I pressed a button, and the power died. No way April could have done it. Instant alibi. And he'd never have gone off like that with *me*."

"And Jan? She didn't know what you were doing."

"She would've figured it out. Or you would've. She was going to tell you."

"So you killed her to protect yourself. Why did you kill her differently? None of the others were cut up like that. Didn't that hurt your data?"

Gordan narrowed her eyes. "Are you trying to keep me talking? It's not going to do you any good. It's over. You two are part of the project, whether or not you want to be."

"You're right; it's over. They're all gone. You killed them." She'd killed them chasing a dream they'd shared and would have helped her pursue, if she'd just been patient. None of them needed to die—no one ever needs to die—but I somehow doubted her madness would let her see that. She'd gone too far.

Gordan shook her head, snarling, "You don't understand! We were trying to save them! I was going to save them all!"

"You knew the process killed people. After Barbara, you had to know."

She glared at me, madness flooding back into her eyes. "You're nothing to them, do you realize that? Nothing—hell, less than nothing. Humans have iron and fire, but changelings? We have no iron, no fire . . . no power. We're tools to them. You have the nerve to wonder why I had to kill them? I'd expect that from him," she indicated Quentin with the hand that held the gun, and for a sickening moment, I was afraid she was going to shoot, "but not from you."

"I don't understand." I was lying, but I didn't think she could tell; I'm pretty good at hiding that sort of thing. She was standing on the edge of sanity, and I was afraid that if she lost her balance, she'd take Quentin with her. I couldn't let that happen. I needed her distracted.

"We'd all have been the same inside the crystal! There would've been no more borders and no more differences! We could all have been what we were meant to be!"

"Static. Dead. Unchanging." I shook my head, not caring how stupid my words were. She had the gun and Quentin was unconscious; I had to defend us both, and for the moment, words were my only weapon. "That's not life. That's just programming."

"It's the best chance we have for Faerie—for *us*. Have the purebloods gotten their lies so close to your bones that you can't see them anymore? Have you forgotten what they call you?" Her voice rose, taking on a sharp, mocking tone. Remembered pain and stolen mockery. "Half-blood. Mongrel. Mutt. Have you forgotten the way they hurt and hurt and never care?" Tears were gleaming in her eyes; she was too busy ranting to hide them.

"I'll never forget what I am," I said, softly. "But I know how to forgive."

"They own you! You're one of their dogs! When the purebloods order you, you go. You even baby-sit their kids while you're marching off to die!" She laughed. "We found everything we needed to know when we were trying to find out how we could stop you from destroying everything. Sylvester points and you go. Dog. Stupid, mongrel *dog*." Her words were meant to wound, but it's hard to hurt me with words. I've heard them before.

"I'm his and he's mine. Everyone owns their family, for good or bad. It's why we don't kill each other." There were only a few feet between us. If she kept distracting herself, I might be able to make it. "If I'm their dog, it's because they're family, and I want to be."

"Then why didn't they stay for *me*?!" Her grip on the gun was loosening. Hysteria was breaking her focus. That didn't mean she wasn't dangerous; it might actually mean we were in more danger. Insanity is unpredictable. "If family works that way, why didn't *mine* stay?!"

"I don't know, Gordan. I'd tell you if I did," I said.

"They wouldn't listen!" She was lost in her own private pain: my world and hers weren't meeting anymore. "They would never listen! Not my mother, not Barbara, not anyone! I wasn't pureblooded and they were, so I wasn't good enough to listen to! Idiots!"

"Why wouldn't they listen?" I asked, inching forward. I was almost close enough.

She didn't notice. "They thought being pureblooded meant they knew better than I did," she said bitterly. "No matter what we do, no matter how much we improve Faerie, it's never going to make them accept us. You should know that. It's not my fault Daddy left. It's not my fault I was born the way I am. So why do they blame me?"

The gun was dangling forgotten in her hands. I wasn't going to get a better chance. If I moved now, I might be able to shove her over the edge before she could hurt Quentin, even if she shot me in the process. It was my fault that he was in this mess in the first place. I had to do whatever it took to get him out of it alive. Lunging forward, I grabbed the gun out of her hand, spinning both of us around in the process. Now she was the one with her back toward the wall, and one little push would be enough to send me to down to Elliot.

Gordan screamed, landing an openhanded slap across my cheek. "Bitch! Don't you see? They're doing it to you, too!" Her fury was almost visible, and the air was swimming with the burning oil signature of her magic. No wonder I hadn't been able to trace the spell that blew up my car. The smell blended into the flames. "They'll never let you be anything but a pet! You're their dog, their stupid changeling dog!"

"I don't care," I said. "I like being what I am." I was baiting her to keep her distracted, and it looked like it was working. She wasn't looking at Quentin at all.

She lunged. I scrambled backward. My left shoulder slammed against the railing, and a bolt of pain shot through my arm. I cried out. "They'll kill you when they're done with you, just like they kill everything else!" I wasn't prepared to dodge this time, and her lunge ended with her hands closed around my throat. She squeezed, shouting, "They kill everything they touch! *Everything!*"

I beat my fists against her, suddenly aware of how useless the gun in my hand really was. I had no way to aim or brace myself, and I didn't know whether the chamber was blocked; if I tried to shoot her, I might blow my own head off. I couldn't even get the aim needed to hit her in the back of the head with her own weapon, satisfying though the idea was. I brought up one knee instead, planting it in her stomach. Unfortunately, it didn't have the desired effect: her grip on my throat tightened.

"Didn't it bother you?" she asked, with restored calm. She knew she was winning. "Knowing you were less than they were, knowing they wouldn't care if you died? There's always another changeling. You're nothing special."

Black spots were clouding my vision, and my fists were beating more and more weakly against her sides. Suffocation feels a lot like drowning. I don't recommend either. Gathering the last of my strength, I whispered, "Says . . . you."

That just made her angrier. She removed a hand from my throat, delivering another slap. I didn't care. I was too busy struggling to fill my aching lungs with air.

"Do you know the real reason I killed her that way?" she demanded. "I didn't back her up, that's why—even if the others come back, she won't. She's gone, and nothing your masters do will bring her back. How's that for the dogs, huh? How's that? We took down one of the kennel keepers!"

"But only one . . ." I whispered.

"It doesn't matter. I'll kill as many as it takes." She slapped me again, snapping my head to the side. "Why you and not me? Why did they want you? My blood's more pure than yours! Why are you their lapdog while they keep me in the kennels? Why?"

"I don't know," I said. Her hands closed around my throat again, and the black spots surged back.

"I hate you!" Gordan screamed. I closed my eyes, going limp, and waited to die.

The sound of splintering wood made me open my eyes. Gordan's hands loosened, losing their grip as she spun toward the source of the sound. April was standing behind her, holding the remains of a folding chair in both hands. I'd never seen the Dryad look so solid, and for once the look on her face was something more than a pale mimic of the people around her. It was bone-deep and weary, and very real.

"Let her go, Gordan," she said.

"Go back to your computer, April," said Gordan. "This isn't your concern."

"You hurt Mommy," April said, sounding puzzled. "You said she'd come back like the others. But now you say she won't, and I think you're telling the truth. Why did you lie to me?"

"Go *home,* April!"

"You killed my mother!" April brought the chair down again, hard enough that it shattered against Gordan's back. Gordan released me, swinging at her instead. I pulled away, moving along the catwalk, stopping to catch my breath once I was out of reach. I still had the gun—a fact that Gordan seemed to have forgotten.

"April, you don't want to start with me," Gordan said, ripping the remains of the chair out of the Dryad's hands and grabbing her by the hair, using it as a lever to sling her away. April yelped and slammed into the wall next to Quentin, going down in a crumpled heap. I couldn't see her breathing, but that didn't worry me: the impact hadn't been that hard, and I'd never seen her actually breathe.

Gordan had turned while I was watching April fall. I didn't see her move until she was on top of me, trying to grab the gun away. I shoved her as hard as I could before I had a chance to think. She stumbled away, falling toward the gap in the catwalk rail.

"Gordan, look out!" I shouted.

The warning seemed to startle her. She stumbled back another six inches, heels leaving the catwalk. She teetered on the edge, glancing over her shoulder and going white as she realized how far she had to fall. I dropped the gun and rushed forward, holding out my hands. "Gordan, quick! Grab hold of me!"

There was a choice there. It was a brief one, and a hard one, but it was still a choice. Faerie justice isn't kind—there's very little mercy in the immortal—and we both knew they'd never kill her. Death is too much of a stranger to the Fair Folk; they never kill if they can help it. If I saved her, she'd stand before a fae Court and be judged by immortal standards . . . forever.

Gordan looked at the differences between her possible fates, weighing an eternity of punishment against a moment of pain, and she chose the mortal option. In the end, her humanity won. Her arms stopped pinwheeling and dropped to her sides. I saw the moment of decision and lunged, still reaching for her hand, and for an instant she was almost, barely in reach. I grabbed for her . . .

. . . and caught nothing but air. She fell in silence, eyes open all the way down. I looked away just before she hit the concrete. It didn't change a thing. Maybe I didn't see her hit the bottom, but I could still hear it. She never made a sound; gravity did it for her, and the silence that followed told me that she hadn't survived the impact.

Wearily, I moved to kneel beside Quentin, reaching for his wrist. His pulse was weak but steady; he probably hadn't even realized he wasn't in the futon room anymore. I lifted my head, calling, "Elliot? Can you hear me?"

There was no reply from below. I winced, offering my hand to April, and said, "It's done now. You can get up."

She lifted her head. "Will everything be better now?"

"No. It won't. I'm sorry."

"Will Quentin remain on the network?"

"I think so, yeah. Elliot, too." It was over now. If Elliot was alive, Sylvester's healers would wipe away the damage like it had never existed. He and Quentin would be fine. I wondered if they'd keep the scars, or if the scars they carried inside would be all that was left to remind them.

She stood slowly, asking, "Will my mother come back on-line now?"

There were no words to answer that. I gathered Quentin into my arms and rose, waiting for her to understand.

"Oh," she said finally, and looked down. Something in her had changed, something more than her new depth of emotion. She looked, for lack of a better term, real. "Where is she now?"

How do you explain the concept of the soul to someone whose immortality is kept in electrons and wire? You can't. So I told her the truth: "I don't know."

"She won't come back? Not ever?"

"No, April, she won't. Not ever."

"Oh." She vanished, the air rushing into the space she'd occupied, and then appeared again. "Gordan has left the network. Elliot has not." Almost timidly, she added, "I secured his wounds to stop the bleeding, when Gordan was waiting for me. Was this right?"

"It was perfect," I said. I needed the confirmation about Gordan, but I hadn't wanted it. No death is pretty, or fair; Faerie wasn't born to die, and neither were her children.

"Good," she said, and looked up at me, eyes wide. "Who will take care of me now?"

"You're going to have to take care of yourself."

"Can I?"

"I don't think you have a choice."

"Oh," she said. Then, quietly, she asked, "For right now, until they come and take Gordan's hardware . . . can we pretend that you'll take care of me?"

"We can," I said, and smiled sadly, shifting Quentin onto my left arm so that I could offer her my hand. She laced her fingers through mine, flesh cool and slightly unreal—not that it mattered. Reality is what you make it.

We needed to get Quentin down; we needed to get Elliot someplace safe. But for just a moment we stood together in the dark, looking out across the darkened room, and the sound of our heartbeats mingled with the hushed whispering of the night-haunts' wings.

THIRTY-THREE

IN THE END, THIS is what happened:

April turned to me as the sound of wings faded, pulling her hand out of mine. "How do we get him down?" she asked timidly, indicating Quentin. "Elliot must be retrieved."

"That's true," I said, studying her. She was small, but she looked sturdy. "Can you carry live people when you disappear?"

"Only if I can lift them."

"Try." I stood, hoisting Quentin and passing him to her. She was able to support him, barely, by looping his unwounded arm around her neck and wrapping her own arms around his middle. A haze of static rose around them, and they were gone.

I raced to the edge of the catwalk and looked down, keeping my eyes away from the place where Gordan fell. Elliot was a dark shape on the floor, and in its own way, looking at him was almost as bad as looking at her would have been. I glanced to the side and saw April appear near the door, looking almost comical with Quentin hanging unevenly from her shoulders. When she saw me looking, she waved. Blinking back tears I hadn't realized were there, I waved back.

It took almost ten minutes to descend the ladder: my left hand was only grasping weakly, and it was harder to go down exhausted than it had been to go up panicked. But in the end, there was solid ground under my feet, and I was standing on my own. I nodded to April, leaving her to support Quentin as I went to kneel by Elliot's side.

His shirt was drenched with blood, and his pulse was shallow, but he was breathing. If we got him to a healer soon, he'd live. I slid my arms under him and lifted, straining until I got back to my feet. Elliot was smaller than I was: I could carry him, if I took it slow. Nodding to April, I turned, and we carried our respective burdens out into the afternoon sunlight.

Things ended quickly after that. April left me halfway across the lawn, teleporting herself and Quentin to the futon room before her strength gave out. I walked through the knowe with Elliot in my arms, accompanied by a cascade of cats. Justice had been done. They'd scatter soon, but for the moment, they still belonged at ALH. I don't know whether it was April or the cats who told Tybalt it was over, but he met me in the hall, scooping Elliot out of my arms without a word. That was good. I wasn't certain I could talk without starting to cry.

Riordan's men could only hold Sylvester for so long. He arrived at ALH almost an hour after Gordan fell, finding us clustered on the lawn in the midst of a sea of cats. Connor was awake and feeling well enough to snipe at Tybalt. Elliot's wounds had been tended as best we could, and Quentin . . . he wasn't any worse. That would have to be enough to tide me over until Jin could look at him. We were leaving ALH.

For good or ill, January's strange dream died with Gordan. The worst part is that I still don't know whether it would have worked. If she'd had the time, maybe Jan really could have done what she set out to do—but the clock ran out, and we'll never know.

I never saw Sylvester and Jan together, but the family resemblance between him and April was too strong to deny. He hugged her. He told her he was sorry about her mother, and that he'd send her people back as soon as he could. And then his men carried the wounded to the van, myself included, and he took us away. There would be no invasion. Not even Riordan could interpret a man coming to his lost niece's fiefdom as an act of war. I fell asleep in the back of the van with my head on Connor's shoulder, and I didn't dream.

Tybalt stayed behind, saying it was to take care of the cats who had been Barbara's subjects . . . but he didn't look at me. That strange new expression that had come to his face when he saw me wake Alex was still there, lurking. I wasn't sure how to feel about that. Mostly, I just felt tired.

The healers were waiting at Shadowed Hills, and I started breathing again as Jin, the oldest and best-known of his healers, came to take my hands. The others took Connor, Elliot, and Terrie away, but Jin treated me and Quentin together. She took care of me first, despite my protests; conditions hadn't been ideal for any of us, but the infection in my hand was farther along than the infection in Quentin's arm. Gordan really seemed to have done her best with the medical care—something that made a sick sort of sense, since she wanted us intact when she killed us. She did her best. It just wasn't quite good enough.

I started crying when Quentin opened his eyes. I couldn't help it. Part of me was certain we'd lost him until that moment; that the infection was too much, and he'd die without giving me the chance to say I was sorry.

"Jeez, Toby," he said, squinting at me. "You look awful."

I smiled through my tears. "You, too, kid. You, too."

The physical wounds were the easy part. There'd be a scar on his arm and he'd have to wear a brace for a few months—not even magical healing can completely repair damaged muscles, and there was a chance he'd hurt himself if he wasn't forced to take it easy—but that was all. My scars were worse. Blood magic leaves marks. Still, they were nothing I couldn't live with. The emotional wounds would take longer to heal. For all of us.

I stayed as long as I could, listening as the reports on the others came in. Connor's transformation into his seal shape had probably saved his life. Gordan shot him twice. As a seal, his blood circulated more slowly; Tybalt was able to patch him up after coaxing him back to human form. Elliot lost a lot of blood before April got to him, but they were able to save him. The healers said he'd be up and walking in a matter of days. Not bad for someone who'd been at death's door a few hours before.

Terrie was another matter. The sun went down and there was no change. Jin knew the situation by then, and told the rest of the healers to wait until morning before they passed a final judgment. I was pretty sure they'd get a surprise when the sun came up. When I perform a resurrection, I do it for keeps.

And then Sylvester called, and I had to go. I entered the throne room, got down on one knee, and explained everything. He and Luna listened in silence as I explained January's last days and the things leading up to them, the broken dreams and betrayals, the impossible hopes for salvation. It didn't take long enough. That sort of thing never does. When I finished, Sylvester said I was free to go, and I walked out without another word. I didn't say good-bye to Quentin. He'd be better off without me. I took a bus to the BART station and caught the next train home, where I fed the cats, coaxed Spike out from under the sink, called Stacy to offer vague reassurances, and went to bed. There'd be time to think about things later; there's always a later.

But later came and went, and somehow, there was always something else for me to worry about. There were bills to pay and laundry to do; there were cases that needed to be taken and solved. They were small, human things—missing children and wayward husbands—nothing supernatural or strange. Once again, I reacted to pain by turning my back on Faerie, and for a while, it worked. There were no deaths and no mysterious screams in the night, and I started thinking I might be able to sleep again.

The Luidaeg didn't come to kill me, and after a week had passed, I decided to stop waiting. I showed up on her doorstep with bagels and told her she could kill me if she wanted to. She laughed and called me an idiot, and we played chess for six hours. I still think she'll kill me someday. It's just not going to be anytime soon. Somewhere along the line, loneliness turned into friendship—maybe for both of us.

Sylvester called a month after I walked out. I hadn't seen or heard from anyone at Shadowed Hills during that time; not even Quentin. Not until the day I came home from following a cheating wife and found the message on my answering machine. "The funeral will be held at our estate in the Summerlands on the new moon. Please come." That was all he needed to say—I ran away from him once, but now, I always come when he calls. Gordan was right about that much. When you get right down to it, I'm Sylvester's dog.

Quentin called the next day, asking nervously if he could escort me to the funeral. I said yes. What choice did I have? If he needed to see me half as much as I suddenly needed to see him, refusing would have been cruel. We agreed to meet at the Japanese Tea Gardens and walk from Lily's knowe to the edges of the Torquill estate. I wasn't ready to go back inside the knowe at Shadowed Hills. Not yet.

Maybe not ever.

The day of the funeral dawned bright and clear. I met Quentin in the Tea Gardens five minutes after I'd said I'd be there. His arm was in a sling, and he was wearing a black doublet and hose that made him look like Hamlet's forgotten younger brother. A don't-look-here spell shielded him from tourists, eliminating the need for a mortal disguise; anyone watching saw me smile and link arms with nothing, then climb the garden's tallest suspension bridge. If they watched closely enough, they may have even seen me disappear. I don't think anyone saw. People almost never look that closely.

We walked through Lily's knowe, stepping out the back gate into the Summerlands. All the glory of the endless Faerie summer was on display, and I stopped, catching my breath. I've been living in the mortal world too long, and it takes time for me to adjust. Summerlands air is too clean for lungs accustomed to modern pollution, and the constantly changing twilit sky disorients me. I still love those lands, but they're not home anymore, if they ever really were.

The sky was the color of burnished amber, and the hills were bright with flowers. I picked a blue daisy, and smiled as it dissolved into a dozen tiny butterflies. The Summerlands are like that. Logic is just a convenience there; change is the only constant, and even that's false, because the Summerlands are founded on the concept that life—our life, the life of Faerie—can last forever. They're wild and strange and slowly dying. They weren't the first home of my people. They'll almost certainly be the last.

I was a child in the Summerlands. I won't say I grew up there, but I was a child there, and they'll always be a part of me. They have a lot in common with stories of

Never-Never Land—no one there grows up, just older. Faerie is a world filled with eternal children, forever looking for the next game and never quite learning what adult life is like. That's what we learn from the mortal world.

Quentin watched me, frowning at this odd frivolity. He was as serious as he'd been when we met; he'd lost a lot of the ground he'd worked so hard to gain. I could understand why: part of his innocence was gone forever, and while I hated the way he'd lost it, I couldn't say I was sorry it was lost. We all have to learn that leaving the Summerlands means leaving the nursery; he'd grow up or he'd die. Maybe that's cruel . . . but that's the world.

I straightened, wiping the pollen off my fingers. "Come on. We need to get moving."

"Of course," he said, and followed me across the fields toward a spiraling rose-colored tower. It was like something from a fairy tale, all spun sugar and elegance, and we reached it faster than perspective indicated we should.

The gardens around the tower were a maze of greenery and untended roses. I led Quentin through them, stopping at a tiny door almost concealed behind a wishing well. He looked at it, frowning.

"You know your way around pretty well," he said.

"I should." I pressed my hand against the door. It swung open and I smiled sadly. At least the house still knew me. "I used to live here."

"Will your . . ."

"Don't worry, Quentin. My mother's out." She's been out for a long time now. No one knows exactly when Amandine went crazy; she collapsed a few years after I vanished, moving into an internal world far stranger than the Summerlands. She doesn't spend much time in the tower anymore. Most reports place her wandering endlessly through forests and standing, motionless, at crossroads.

I wish I knew what she was looking for.

"I'm sorry," he said, subdued. "I didn't think."

"It's not your fault." I stepped inside, motioning for him to follow.

Amandine's tower has no mortal aspect: you can only get there via the Summerlands. I led Quentin through the gallery and up the stairs to my suite. My door was still closed, sealed with the wards I set on my last visit. Amandine was the only one who could open that door without breaking my wards, and she never would; my rooms would stay the same until the end of time unless I chose to change them. There was something reassuring and deeply sad in that thought. We stopped in what had been my living room; it was almost as large as my entire mortal apartment. Quentin looked around wide-eyed, air of sophistication fading as he took in the high windows and tapestry-draped walls.

"This is really nice," he said, sounding surprised.

"I suppose. Can you wait here? I need to change." We were only visiting the tower so I could raid my own wardrobe. I had nothing suitable in the mortal realm, and I didn't trust my magic to obey me well enough to keep me properly dressed for the entire funeral.

"Sure. But . . . why don't you live here anymore?"

"Quentin? If you don't already know the answer, there's no way I can explain." I walked through the door into the bedroom and closed it behind me, leaving him alone.

My old bedroom isn't large, but it's the only room in the tower that looks like it's been lived in. The bed grew to match me as I aged, and the shelves lining the walls are still piled with small, interesting items collected from the forests and fields nearby. I never cared much for toys after I came to live in the Summerlands, but I always loved running and finding things out. Everything I loved went into that room, right up until the day I left it.

The wardrobe doors came open at the touch of my

hand, spreading to show a rainbow of gowns. Most of them were designed for a young girl I don't remember being and may never have been at all. They were made of things both wild and strange: butterfly wings and cobweb silk, peacock feathers and dragon's scales. Faerie clothing is a bit like Japanese cooking—we use what we have. Amandine always chose the wildest dresses she could for me, putting me in colors that brought out the mortal tints of my skin and hair. It was a long time before I realized that was what she was doing. I'm still not sure why she did it.

The dress I was looking for was hidden in the back of the wardrobe, buried under the brighter gowns. It was made of dark gray velvet trimmed with slightly paler silk roses; I wore it to a ball in the Coblynau caverns when I was eleven years old. Amandine brought me with her, a small, half-mortal accessory for a haunted evening. I remember that they lit the darkest corners of their halls with jack-o'-lanterns and sparks of gleaming mist, and that the Candela came with their globes of dancing flame, and that when I danced with the master of the mine, his smile was kind. I remember.

The dress fit like it had been sized for me the day before. Faerie tailoring fits forever, no matter how much you change. I looked down at myself, swishing my skirt back and forth, and looked away. I'll always be Amandine's daughter. No matter how far I run, Faerie catches up with me in the end.

Quentin was staring up at one of the tapestries when I stepped out of the room, closing the door behind myself. I cleared my throat. He jumped.

"Come on," I said. "It's time."

Amandine's estate borders Shadowed Hills on the far southern side. Distances are smaller in the Summerlands: it took less than twenty minutes for us to walk to a place that I knew was more than an hour's drive from where we'd started. The grove where the funeral was to be held was at the heart of the family forest. It took another twenty minutes to navigate the paths through the forest. Long dresses weren't designed for walking in the woods. My mother could've made the walk without stumbling; she fits into the world that well, even insane. That's what it means to be a pureblood. I stumble and fall, and I always get up and keep going. That's what it means to be a changeling.

The grove was filling when we arrived. They were coming from all directions, meeting and falling silent: no one knew what they were supposed to say or feel. Pureblood wakes are things of deep, bitter mourning, but they exist for the living. Human funerals are sadder, holding a mixture of sorrow, relief, and terror, and they're held for the dead. Jan was a pureblood, but her funeral would be the first of its kind in living memory. That made it a changeling affair, mixing two worlds that didn't understand each other, and didn't want to. I think she would've liked that.

A pyre of oak, ash, and rowan boughs stood at the center of the clearing, piled in imitation of a phoenix nest and covered with a white silk sheet. Jan was at the center, hands folded over her midriff. They'd dressed her in a long red-and-gold gown that brought out the highlights in her hair and concealed her wounds. I winced when I saw her. All the obvious signs of who she'd been were gone, leaving only what she *was*. Pureblood. Daoine Sidhe. Fallen. That wasn't even half of her, but it was all she had left, and all she could take with her to the grave.

Quentin stopped beside me. "She looks like she's sleeping."

"I know." Fae flesh doesn't rot. She looked like she should wake up and demand to know where her glasses were. She wasn't going to. Even if the process was eventually reversed and the other casualties of ALH brought back to life, Jan was gone forever. Thanks to Gordan, she wouldn't even have the dubious immortality of the night-haunts. For the first time in centuries, a child of Faerie was genuinely lost.

Sylvester and Luna stood by the pyre, hands locked together. Luna nodded to me as we entered, one ear flattening in silent greeting. I curtsied deeply in reply, and then walked to the opposite side of the grove, standing in the shadow of the trees. Quentin followed. After a moment, Luna patted Sylvester on the arm and murmured something in his ear before walking over to join us.

"My Lady," I said. Quentin bowed.

"Toby—Quentin," she said, and offered a small, sad smile. "You're well?"

"As well as can be expected," I said.

"Good. We were worried."

"I'm sorry. I'll come visit soon." She probably knew I was lying. I didn't care.

"Good. And Toby . . . he's not angry. You did the best you could. Both of you." She smiled again and turned, walking back to her husband.

I suppressed a bitter smile as I watched her go. If ALH was us doing our best, I never wanted to see our worst. Quentin's expression looked as conflicted as mine felt, and I was willing to bet that his thoughts were running along the same lines as my own.

Letting my eyes drift across the crowd, I froze, my stomach dropping as I saw a flash of silver-blonde hair attached to a willowy woman in a tattered green-and-brown dress. "Mom . . . ?"

"Toby, what—"

"Wait here," I said, and started across the grove, yanking my dress up around my knees to keep myself from stumbling. Several people shot startled glances in my direction at my lack of decorum, but no one stopped me. It didn't matter.

By the time I reached the place where I thought I'd seen my mother, she was gone.

Quentin came running up behind me, wide-eyed and bewildered as he said, "Why did you run off like that?"

"I thought I saw someone," I said, closing my eyes and sighing. "Somebody I knew. Guess I was wrong."

"Oh," said Quentin, and quieted.

We were still standing there, silent, when a voice spoke behind me. "Please do not jump or scream or make any other exclamations of surprise. I am very tired."

The voice was almost familiar: female and slightly flat, like it had been run through a synthesizer. But it was an adult voice, not a child's. I turned. "Hello, April."

"Hello." April had changed in the last month, going from a teenager to someone that could have been Jan's twin, if you ignored the blonde hair and too-perfect skin. When she grew up, she grew up fast. She was wearing a black dress made of some glittering material that I suspected was actually solid light. "I'm glad you're here."

Quentin was gaping. I understood the impulse.

"We couldn't miss it," I said. "I didn't think we'd see you here."

"Elliot has used my mother's notes to establish a portable server unit. It only works for short periods, but it expands my range of motion considerably."

"That's good," I said.

"April?" Quentin asked, wide-eyed.

"Yes," she said, and smiled sadly. I looked at her expression, and realized she'd had a crush on him at ALH. Had; past tense. However strong it might have been, it was over now.

She'd outgrown him.

"It's good to see you," he said.

Elliot walked up behind her, leaning on his cane. He looked battered, but at least he was moving. "Toby," he said.

"You made it," I said.

"I had to." We embraced. It was a short, awkward thing; I was being careful not to hurt him, and he didn't seem to know how to balance his cane. Still, I think we both felt better by the time I pulled away. "It's good to see you again."

"It's good to see you, too, Elliot."

He looked toward Quentin, asking, "How are the Hippocampi doing?"

Quentin blushed as I looked at him, brows raised. "You took the Hippocampi?" I asked.

"They were a gift," he mumbled.

"Cool." I turned back to Elliot and April. "Is Alex . . . ?"

"He didn't want to leave our lands," April said. I was right about Terrie: when dawn came again, she'd turned back into Alex, and awoke. Every sunset brought on the same collapse. Somehow, I wasn't surprised that he wasn't feeling up to going out.

"I'm sorry," Quentin said.

"We're going to have to wait and see whether he recovers. Still, we thank you for all your help. None of us would be here without you." April offered her hand, and I took it, squeezing. Her fingers felt faintly unreal. I knew better.

"Not a problem," I said. April is too young and strange to share the standard prejudices about certain things—like saying thank you. Watching her grow into herself was going to be a lot of fun.

The arguments over succession in Tamed Lightning were venomous, but in the end, tradition won. April was Jan's daughter and the knowe recognized her as such, and so—in the absence of another legal heir—the County was hers. There would be no dissolution and no war; just a bit more healthy chaos. Duchess Riordan would have to wait.

In a way, April's assumption of her mother's throne

was the final, most bitter irony of all. She'd been a killer when she was too young and alien to understand what she did, and Faerie forgave her for her ignorance; Gordan led her astray, and for the justice of Faerie, that was enough. If she'd stayed ignorant, we might have called her a monster and killed her anyway, for our own protection . . . but she didn't. Her mother's death forced her to become a real person, and now that she understood her own crimes, she was fighting to undo them. By understanding her own guilt, she became innocent again.

Elliot started to say something, but stopped as Sylvester stepped to the center of the grove, clearing his throat. The murmur of the crowd faded, replaced by an expectant hush. Sylvester looked at us and faltered. Luna stepped forward, ready to catch him if he fell. He took her hand and cleared his throat again, steadier now. Sylvester never falls; he just teeters on the edge. I've never seen him refuse a helping hand. He's one of the bravest men I know. He survives.

"In the beginning, we were given a promise," he said. His voice was almost too soft to hear, and still loud enough to carry to every corner of the grove. I don't know where he found the funeral rites; there have been no funerals in Faerie since the night-haunts were born. But part of me recognized his words—they were the right ones. He found the right words.

"We were told we would live forever," he continued, looking straight at me. "That promise has been betrayed, and now Countess January ap Learianth, who lived among the mortals as January O'Leary, lies slain. She has crossed the line from which there is no coming back, and the promise we were given did not protect her."

He turned and leaned over the pyre, kissing her forehead before looking over the crowd once more. "She was my sister's daughter. She was my niece and the mother to my grandniece, and a thousand things to a thousand people, and she is gone. Mortality can strike even the immortal. Remember that, and keep the ones you love around you, and live each day as well as you can." He glanced toward the edge of the crowd. I followed his gaze and saw Raysel standing there, arms folded, looking bored. Oh, Sylvester. It's always the good ones that die.

"But there is hope." He took a deep breath, and repeated, "There is hope. In a world where one promise can be broken, perhaps others can be kept. She may yet find peace . . . but she will find it without us." He waved his hand and the pyre burst into flames. He straightened and stepped away. "Good-bye, my dear one," he said, even more quietly.

Jan remained visible through the smoke for a brief moment; then it closed around her, and she was gone. She didn't save Faerie—she didn't even save herself. She lived and died and left us mourning for her, and for all the lost souls of ALH, both the living and the dead. None of us got out the way we went in.

Not one.

Watching the smoke curling against the amber sky, it was hard to believe anything could last forever. Maybe Jan was right; maybe Faerie was dying, and this was the last gasp of a world that was already on the way out . . . but there was still time. April would rule Tamed Lightning in Jan's place. If there was a way to bring back the others—Barbara and Yui, Peter and Colin, even Terrie—she'd find it. Elliot and Alex would have time to rebuild their lives; Quentin would have time to heal; I'd have time to remember that not everything ends badly. We all had time, and a second chance to survive.

I would find my mother, and find out what was wrong with her. Why she'd broken; why, when she saw me crossing the grove, she'd chosen to run.

I put my arm around Quentin's shoulders, keeping my eyes on the sky. Maybe Faerie *is* dying, and maybe nothing lasts forever, but I'm going to believe Sylvester. Something endures, no matter what happens.

Something lasts.

The third Toby Daye novel from

SEANAN MCGUIRE

AN ARTIFICIAL NIGHT

Read on for a sneak preview.

LILY GRABBED MY WRISTS, and yanked me forward. There was time to yelp and catch my breath: then I was falling through a curtain of water, with Tybalt shouting in the distance. After that, I was just falling.

I hit the ground hip-first, rolling to a stop before I sat up. I was dry despite my fall through the water, and my hands didn't hurt anymore. I looked at them and laughed as I saw that the skin was whole and smooth again. Well, I guess that's one way to heal someone, assuming you go in for slapstick. "Lily, that wasn't—" I stopped, blinking. "—funny?"

The knowe stretched out around me in an array of ponds and flatlands, all connected by narrow bridges. Lily, Tybalt, and Karen were gone. "Tybalt?" No one answered. I stood, automatically reaching up to shove my hair back, and stopped as my fingers encountered a tight interweave of knots and hairpins. I pulled one of the hairpins free and glared at it before shoving it back into place. Jade and dragonflies. Cute.

My frown deepened as I looked down at myself and took in the whole picture. Lily apparently extended her services to healing my fashion sense as well as my hands:

my T-shirt and jeans were gone, replaced by a steel-gray gown cut in a vaguely traditional Japanese style and embroidered with black and silver dragonflies. A black velvet obi was tied around my waist, with my knife concealed underneath a fold of fabric. It wouldn't be easy to draw, but at least she hadn't left me unarmed. Pulling up the hem of the gown exposed one battered brown sneaker—she'd left my shoes alone.

"Not funny," I muttered, and started down the nearest path. We were going to have words if she'd vaporized my clothes.

Finding your way out of Lily's knowe is easy, as long as you don't mind walking. The boundaries of her lands are flexible—sometimes there are miles between landmarks, while other times it's only a few feet—but all paths eventually lead to the moon bridge. I'd gone about a quarter of a mile, grumbling all the way, when a throat was discreetly cleared behind me.

"Yes?" I said, turning.

A silver-skinned man was standing on the water, the gills at the bottom of his jaw fluttering with barely concealed anxiety. He was wearing Lily's livery, with slits cut down the sleeves and in the legs of his pants to allow the fins running down his calves and forearms the freedom to move. "My lady has . . . sent me?" he said, uncertainly.

"I can see that. What did she send you to say?"

"She wishes me to tell you she is . . . waiting in the pavilion? With . . . the King of Cats and . . . your niece?"

"Good to know," I said, bobbing my head. "Which way to the pavilion?"

"Go as you are and turn . . . left . . . at the . . . sundial?"

That seemed to be the end of his instructions. I was turning when he spoke again, asking, "Lady?"

I glanced back over my shoulder. "Yes?"

"Can I . . . go?"

"Yes, you can," I said. He smiled and dissolved into

mist, drifting away across the water. I shook my head and resumed walking. Naiads. If there's a way to make them smarter than your average rock, nobody's found it yet.

The rest of the walk was uneventful. A flock of pixies crossed my path at one point, laughing as they tried to knock each other out of the air. I stopped to let them pass. Pixies are small, but they can be vicious when provoked. Several flocks inhabit the Park and are currently at war with the flock in the Safeway where I used to work. I've been known to supply the store pixies with weaponry—usually in the form of toothpicks or broken pencils—and I didn't need a flock of Park pixies descending on me seeking retribution. I started again after they passed, crossing several more small islands and mossy outcroppings before I reached a sundial in the middle of an otherwise featureless patch of ground. It cast no shadow. I rolled my eyes, wondering why Lily bothered, and turned left.

There was no pavilion before I turned. As soon as I finished turning, it was there: a huge white silk pavilion decorated with a dozen coats of arms I didn't recognize, anchored to a raised hardwood platform by golden ropes. Its banners and pennants drifted in a wind I couldn't feel. Apparently, "turn left" didn't mean "keep walking."

Lily was kneeling on a cushion, pouring tea into rose-colored china cups that rested on a table so low to the ground that kneeling was the only option—not that she'd provided chairs. Lily can be a bit of a traditionalist when she wants to be, and that's most of the time. Tybalt sat across from her on a similar cushion, looking entirely at ease with his surroundings. That's another infuriating thing about him. He's so damned self-confident that he could probably have dinner with Oberon himself and not feel like he was outclassed.

Karen was asleep against the pavilion wall, pillowed

on a pile of cushions with Spike curled up on her stomach. It looked like she'd taken her own trip through the amazing Undine car wash and healing salon. She was wearing a white robe embroidered with cherry blossoms and her hair was combed into a corona around her head. She was just as pale as she'd been before Lily pulled her little stunt and, somehow, I didn't think she'd woken up. Her original clothes were folded on the floor next to her, along with mine.

"I see you've found us," said Lily. She waved a hand toward the other side of the table, indicating the place next to Tybalt. "Please. Sit."

"You could have warned me, you know," I said, walking over to settle as directed. My knees complained when I tried to kneel, and so I sat instead, sticking my legs straight out in front of me. Tybalt appeared to be kneeling as comfortably as Lily. I shot him a dirty look. Show-off. "Was there a reason you needed to shunt me halfway across the damn knowe?"

"Yes," she said, continuing to pour. That was really no surprise. I rarely get out of the Tea Gardens without stopping for a cup of tea with Lily, no matter how urgent my business seems to be. Still . . .

"I'm not sure we have time for this, Lily," I said. "We should be looking for the kids."

"There's always time for tea," chided Lily, placing a cup in front of me. "I 'shunted you,' as you so charming put it, because you needed to be healed. The damage was magically done, which made it fixable, if I was willing to be firm with it. As for why I didn't warn you, your dislike of water is difficult to miss. I thought you might resist if you knew what was intended." A small smile creased her lips. "A certain resistance to getting wet is a trait you share with our royal friend here."

Tybalt made a face. "I don't consider avoiding pneumonia to be a bad thing."

"If you can contract pneumonia in the waters of my

land, you have more troubles than a touch of moistness," said Lily. Sobering, she looked toward me. "I am sorry, October, but I can't wake the child. I tried. I can keep body and spirit together for the time being, but I fear that may be the extent of my capabilities."

"But what's *wrong* with her?"

Lily raised her teacup, using the habitual gesture to try to conceal the worry flickering in her eyes. "I don't know."

"Should I take her to Jin?" Jin was the Court healer at Shadowed Hills. She wasn't in Lily's league—almost no one who isn't an Undine even comes close—but she was good, and her skills were somewhat different. The Ellyllon aren't environmental healers, like the Undine; they work with charms and potions, and that can make them try harder. They aren't limited by what the water can do.

"I don't think so," said Lily. "Moving her before we know the source of her condition may do more harm than good. You did well to bring her here. I can watch over her until more is known."

"So we don't know why Karen won't wake up, we don't know what happened to the missing kids—I don't even know where I should start with this one."

"Ask the moon," said Lily.

"You keep saying that," Tybalt said, with a frown. "Perhaps you'd like to translate it."

"I can't," said Lily, calmly meeting his eyes. "If you wish to find your answers, you'll need to begin thinking, not merely reacting."

"Thinking," I said, and turned toward him. "Tybalt, when you went looking for the missing kids, did you notice anything unusual about the places where they normally slept?"

"Beyond their absence?" His frown deepened. "The air was sour. It smelled wrong, like things that shouldn't have been there."

"Things like what?" I asked, a grim certainty growing inside me.

"Blood and ash. And candle wax."

There was a crash from the other side of the table. We turned to find Lily picking up the pieces of her teacup with shaking hands. I stared. I'd never seen Lily drop anything before.

"I'm so very sorry," she stammered, rising. "Please move away from the table . . . I'll clean the mess directly . . . I am so sorry . . ."

I started to scoot back, but froze, staring at the tea leaves smeared across the table. There were shapes in the mess, almost clear enough to understand. Three loops, like arched gateways; a wilted rose; a tall, slim column tipped with a triangular smear. A candle . . . ?

Lily's hand reached across the table and grasped my chin, turning me to face her. Her eyes seemed darker, less like eyes and more like pools of water. "It's time to go," she said. "I'm sorry, but the leaves have spoken. He's too close for the safety of me or mine."

"Lily, what—" Tybalt began. Lily shot him a sharp look and he quieted.

"You have business to conduct, both of you, although the weight of it stands on Amandine's daughter," she said. "You must speak to the moon, October. Leave the girl in my keeping. Perhaps I can wake her, perhaps not, but she'll be safer with me than she could be on the road with you."

"But—"

This time the sharp look was for me. "You know there are things I can't discuss. I'm sorry they touch on your affairs. I can tell you this much only: you must ask the moon, for you'll find no answers here, and you must leave the girl behind."

"I can't just leave her!" I protested. "Her parents trusted me with her."

"Have you had an unexpected visitor?" she asked.

I froze. She continued, "One who belongs to your line even as mistletoe belongs to the oak? You can't lie to me. I know you."

"How . . . ?" I whispered. Tybalt was frowning, but I didn't care. If Lily knew about my Fetch, what else did she know?

Her smile was sad. "There are always ripples on the water. Some of us just watch them more closely. Leave the child and go. You have miles yet to travel on this road."

"Lily, I—"

"There's nothing else to say. You will go on your errand, and Tybalt's, and all the others who haven't time to reach you. You will go, because you must. Go *now*, October." She looked at the mess on the table. "You have little enough time to find your way. Go."